MOTHER'S MILK

Enjoy the pleasure is immediate and grand.

Your thoughts? Try to understand... more later

Best Wishes,
Louskip

[signature]

10/18/13

Mother's Milk

Based on a true story

by

Dwight G. Stackhouse

Rev. date: 07/17/2013

To order additional copies of this book, contact:
Xlibris LLC
1-888-795-4274
www.Xlibris.com
Orders@Xlibris.com
121650

CONTENTS

DEDICATION

With love, I dedicate this book to my parents. My gratitude cannot be overstated. You gave me a lifetime of memories and lessons I will never forget. I give to you all of my love. I miss you both.

Also, to my sons, and the many family members and wonderful friends who have supported me through the writing of this novel. Without your continued encouragement, devotion, love and trust, the telling of this story would not have been possible. I thank you sincerely, from the bottom of my heart.

INTRODUCTION

Breast feeding, which is a natural occurrence in mammals, provides a means to nourish their offspring during the early stages of development. *But perhaps something more occurs;* something that creates a bond between mother and child that is much deeper than anyone thought. A child is in danger, its mother senses that moment hundreds of miles away and begins to cry and sweat profusely while gasping for her next breath. This profound link between mother and child is well documented, and this bond has now become the subject of recent scientific studies.

During gestation the mother is everything for the fetus, supplying nutrients, warmth and sustenance, while her heartbeat provides a soothing constant rhythm. As remarkable as this may be, the field of genetic science has discovered something called microchimerism, the study of which has produced stunning results showing that male cells containing the "y" chromosome were actually found in the brains and circulating in the blood of women (mothers) and had been living there, in some cases, for several decades.

We are accustomed to thinking of ourselves as singular autonomous individuals, and these foreign cells seem to belie that notion, living and functioning as they do in the complex structure of our own bodies. Such cells were found in more than 60 percent of the subjects and in multiple areas. Understanding the data of this research is complex and varied. Results from the studies suggest everything from increased hormonal activity in the brain, tissue repair, genetic structuring, immune disorders and responses to a heightened spiritual and metaphysical connection (psychic activity) that may result from the exchange of cells across the placenta during pregnancy. Amazingly, this phenomenon occurs long before birth while the child is still in the womb.

New studies would also suggest the possibility that cells from an older sibling residing in the mother may find their way back across the placenta to a younger sibling during the latter's gestation. While finally, there is also evidence that suggest cells may be transferred from mother to infant, incredibly, through nursing. [1]

There was a story of a young chimpanzee that lived and died years ago somewhere in the tropical jungles of central Africa. That is not much of a story; a chimp died in Africa. It became a story, a sensational one, because of why the otherwise healthy chimpanzee died. It died, it seems, of a broken heart on the edge of a stream where its mother lie dead from causes unknown.

The young chimp found her there with half of her body lying in a cold stream; timeless water rolling gently over her flaccid body, and he could find no way within himself to leave her there.

The story goes that he did not eat and found no sleep except that which would come in the bosom of eternity. He could do nothing but grieve when he found his mother cold, lifeless, and taken from

---

[1]   Chan WF, Gurnot C, Montine TJ, Sonnen JA, Guthrie KA, Nelson JL.SourceClinical Research Division, Fred Hutchinson Cancer Research Center, Seattle, Washington, USA. fchan@ualberta.ca

him. He stayed, unable to go on in any other way; he stayed by her side until his life ended, and the crippling pain lifted, taking him presumably to that place where the stuff of life goes when it is finished here. The great ape took leave of his life senses, pressed by forces as great as death itself—insurmountable sorrow, preferring death to life without its mother. It is not known, there is no way to know, whether or not the animal intended to die, but it is clear that he could not find sufficient reason to live without its mother. Nor is it known whether or not the young ape had siblings, but only he died this way.

Perhaps the actual cause of the mother's death was later discovered, perhaps the record shows, and perhaps it even had some bearing on the chimp's behavior. Life is very creative in the ways of death, and death is not the real story here . . . grief, inconsolable grief is. It is a process of accepting the loss and adjusting to the changed situation. For some, it is more difficult. It may take longer than the initial development of the bond. The grieving period varies.

All of these studies, their findings and the reasons for this phenomenon are still being examined and certainly, as of this writing remain unclear, particularly for Jesse Brightmeyer. Jesse would have little patience for scientific explanation and studies. They do not explain why she is not here with him, or why she was taken. He knows something about grief and pain and why the young chimp died. He knows the agony—the destructive power—of an aching heart. In the same year one theory would be formulated, Jesse was actually living with the inexplicable pain caused by the loss of his beloved mother.

The narrator describes the emotional torment that befalls Jesse while at her bedside, holding her hand, as she takes her dreaded final breath.

> *"For even to say that no sound of life, or touch of flesh, vision or hope, thought of God or heaven, wife or child, could soothe in even a small way so visceral a dejection as this, does not begin to address the pain."*

With her passing, a part of him was lost forever. As she lay before him motionless and growing cold, something tangible and all that was sentient died within him. He would now live the rest of his days with something missing, or worse, decaying inside of him. He simply could not process her death. At twenty-nine years of age, he may as well have been a nine year old boy; he may as well have been that forlorn chimp. He had embraced the comforting words found in the great book of deeds, and had been able to provide comfort for many, who as it turns out, were braver than he in the face of death.

This is the story of Jesse Brightmeyer; a man who will spend the rest of his life trying to deal with the loss of a loved one, his mother. He had been relentlessly happy, admired, even adored in some circles. However, during the first fifteen years following her passing his behavior was without question unexpected; it was in fact unacceptable. He fell into a culture of corruption growing wildly out of control to a level that nearly killed him. He was broken. It stayed that way until the forces of that unrestrained bond between mother and child came to console him once more.

The tales of Jesse's attachment to his mother that were so amusingly told throughout the family, speak to a link not unlike that of the chimpanzee's attachment to its mother. Jesse himself remembers, as a young boy feeling the need to run in from play-time to search for her. Just to see her and to know that she was alright was enough. With the worrisome urge satisfied, he could go back to playing. As an infant, it is said that he would begin to wail the moment she got off the bus, some two blocks away, and would continue to do so until she walked safely through the door of their home. These and other stories would suggest an unusual (and now even cellular) bond that the scientific community is only now beginning to understand.

Anyone who has ever lost a loved one and could find no way to cope will most likely find this book a "must read." When death comes unexpectedly the ensuing trauma can be a torture worse than the death itself. It came to Jesse. He fell from grace and from his senses, and stayed lost for nearly two decades. During that period he suffered through some of the most baffling circumstances, and behaviors that could ever befall a "good" son. While in the process, he came precariously close to ruining everything and every life that mattered to him. During the entranced odyssey his mother's admonition "Jesse be nice," was repeatedly overwhelmed by bad judgment born of a grief he could not bear. The terrible sadness and the insurmountable feeling of helplessness; of being powerless against it . . . the finality of death, will ring familiar to all persons who have grieved. But the behavior; the behavior and response to her loss by this 'prodigal son' will likely surprise, disappoint, enrage, and bewilder the reader.

There are titillating moments with celebrities and famous people including James Baldwin, Jackie Onassis, Bill Cosby and others, but they were incidental. The young man at the center of the book allowed himself to be ruled by rage and madness. Jesse screams throughout the book, "I was in trouble," "I meant no harm," but he caused so much injury, the statements carry no weight at all. The understanding, or more accurately: remembering that there is a better way was too long in coming. Forgiveness—of himself more than anyone else—never came and his recklessness made absolution all the more improbable. While attempting to take out his grief, his anger, on the most inaccessible adversary, he found himself powerless against it. This folly and others led to a downward spiral that could not be halted by anything less than the power of "Mother's Milk"—her lessons and love supporting him from the unknowable beyond.

It is a story told through the happy and sad memories of the protagonist. Weaving in and out of past and present moments the narrator's overview is enhanced by revelatory dialog, and the reader is taken on a spectacular and most unpredictable journey. We hear the mother's voice, we see the family from whence Jesse came allowing the reader to understand the incredible depths of his descent into ruin.

Could there ever be redemption for Jesse? A most unlikely redeemer finds a way to him.

Every page promises to take you to places you've not imagined-places of quiet childhood reflections, love, anticipation, horror, disbelief, shock, anger and disgust. There are moments of calm, triumph, and elation; loving moments of family. You will find for yourself—in yourself—a reason to cling to the goodness in life, to endure, to trust in the love shared, the lessons learned, the unforgettable memories and the redemptive powers of love through a "Mother's Milk."

*Ever has it been
that love knows not
its own depth
until the hour of separation*

—Kahlil Gibran

CHAPTER 1

The Pain

He was holding her hand, touching her, as if doing so would keep her safe, keep her here, knowing that in a moment he would have to release her—forever—and wondering if he could. He had little or no awareness of the room, a sterile and colorless space where his mother lay dying. Time has its rank, and on this dreaded evening, time pulled it and left him and, he thought, the world in its wake. In 1976, a year belonging to our Lord, death—the last enemy—and time—the first one—conspired against him, against the whole of him, to this moment. Broken, he could not move for what seemed a very long time and was stilled, perhaps in defiance of these two accomplices (if only he could hold out just a little longer). He needed to talk to them, he needed understanding. "Why do this to me?" "What happened to our agreement, our relationship?" They had forsaken him; he had lost—everything. This caprice, this stroke so vicious, so undeserved, would be fought against, alas, if for only one moment longer. But the defeat was inevitable, upon him, staggering, absolute; there was no solace to be had.

Jesse Brightmeyer was to be alone for the first time in his twenty-nine years, a devastating aloneness that only her loss could bring. It was a dynamic loneliness that must be measured against the immeasurable joy of his life to be understood. For even to say that no sound of life or touch of flesh, vision or hope, thought of God or heaven, wife or child, could soothe in even a small way so visceral a dejection as this, does not begin to address the pain. Something terrible was ending, yes, but something even more frightening was beginning: a life without her. A loathsome wind was sweeping him up, abysmal, reckless, and unstoppable. A plummet as certain as evil—as certain as the one to which He had subjected her.

Jesse's life, his love was to be taken. He was to be hurt deeply, deliberately, for he had begged for a lesser sacrifice, himself perhaps, or some less-loved creature. His plea had been scoffed at; he had been humiliated and was now enraged. Jesse would strike back somehow. Somehow He would pay. From this murky pit, this indescribable place into which Jesse was sinking, and with nothing to lose, he would launch an attack. He would terrorize this Monster. He had done His bidding, had asked for nothing—only given thanks—and this was his reward. At every opportunity, He, the lone culprit in this sacrilege, would feel the wrath of this enervated and broken son. This murder must be avenged; and all who support Him would pay as well. You see, Jesse thought His loyalists would support Him, of this he was sure. He had been devoted to Him. He had made selfless sacrifices in His name, more than the rest, more than anyone. That others could not see or comprehend this betrayal meant they would suffer too. She was gone, and so too was Jesse, lost and adrift, with his mind, and his heart, broken.

How to punish Him, this god of good, this charlatan of justice, was well known to Jesse. He quakes in the face of wickedness, sin. He is weak there. Jesse knew how to hurt Him. He would empty a cannon of sin upon this theocratic imposter. He had been pushed from His grace, and now Jesse would push Him from his. My saddened friend knew sin well, having read His book so many times. He had studied this manual—so full of do's and don'ts. What a formidable arsenal from which to work. So many pellets of pain: lying, stealing, the very potent blasphemy, adultery, apostasy, and, of course, His sin, murder. Yes, he would devise a scheme and aim for His celestial heart.

His plan, however, lacked one vital element. Before any venom could be injected, he had to find a way to simply stand erect. He needed somehow to stop the cataclysm of tears, for he could not see or think or breathe. He was limp and helpless and beyond his own ability to wade through the torrent fed by the thunderous activity in his head. As she lay there, in that antiseptic place, he could only see her face, her remarkably youthful face. A face that had introduced him to the concept of beauty was now distorted by a malicious demon or a legion of them. These savages, His agents, had housed themselves in her body and were shoveling hot coals from a raging intestinal fire up into her mouth, her face, and her brain, and something stirred inside of Jesse Brightmeyer that he had never felt before. Something for which he had no antidote—a dread, a hatred so deep and wide that he had no way of reckoning these foreign sensations beginning to overwhelm him—taking full control of his senses. A bottomless, chaffing hatred so sudden, so deep, that his fall into it was too precipitous to stop.

Her face contorted in a manner not within Jesse's ability to describe, and he knew he would never forget this effrontery, this attack, this hatred. The sounds emitting from her mouth, her nose, howling from within—grotesque, unearthly sounds, would never be forgotten either. They cloaked his body like sweat. It was now inescapable, and it would feed his anger for the rest of his days.

Jesse had no thoughts about the room, but he was somewhat aware of other people in it. He wondered how different they would be when the unimaginable moment arrived. They were siblings after all, sharing one of the sad honors of kinship: to be alone at the last with a dying loved one. He knew them well. *They would become vengeful allies*, he thought. She was everything to him. She must be everything to them, and they were losing her too, the glue in their lives. Now they could only fly apart like leaves off a tree in a storm. Their mother was their anchor, their link to decency. Surely he would see the same chasm of anger in their eyes. Certainly they would join him in retribution. How could they not? *We must come together to defeat this monster*, he thought.

The moment came—her last breath. A gasp and a word . . . she uttered the Monster's name, and Jesse's rage bubbled to the surface like lava. He wanted, at that very second, to kill something, someone, anyone. That she was gone meant everyone could go—by his own hand, now and forever. Hatred swept across his being like a wave of filth, and nothing would ever be the same for him. A life of enviable joy was gone, never to return. Two lives . . . if He wanted to kill His own son, that was His business, but Jesse could find no way to understand or forgive this assault.

He could not release her hand. That would mean forsaking her. When they pried him away, his spirit, his life, his hopes went dead with her. They fell off him like molting skin, and they would be buried with her, underground and irretrievable.

In the corridor, the hospital staff carried on with their now-insulting endeavors. Gurneys and IVs going here and there, behaving as if nothing had happened here. The audacity of this behavior further enraged Jesse, and he determined to kill them. He needed only opportunity. He would hurt these people. They had better avoid him. They had offended him nearly as much as He had, but they were accessible—within his reach. But there was no recognition on their faces of his clear intentions. Could they not see the danger in his eyes? Perhaps, instead, they saw his feeble efforts to simply stand as the tears came flooding unstoppably through his pores. He fell, involuntarily, to his knees. There was no longer any purpose, direction, or strength in his movements. The pain was unbearable and unprecedented; they ignored this as well.

He was carried (by someone, as I remember it) to some transport and to her house, his mother's house, once his home, a place of memories—no longer a home at all, a place of pain, now only pain. Everything in it, all of the trinkets, the accoutrements, even the smells making their way room to room, were like poison darts, all firing at him in bitter allegiance.

The phone began to ring and condolences began to fly. Nonsense. They do not understand and couldn't. They did not know her touch, her smell, her motherly poise, the depth of her love, and her inimitable ability to please and calm. They could not possibly know his loss, and he wanted to curse anyone who said they did. The doorbell rang endlessly with people bringing altar like offerings of food, liquor, and flowers. They kept telling him it was going to be all right. They said he should draw closer now to her murderer, this

Jehovah. This was the fuel; the fire, wild and out of control, would come much later. They too will pay for their insolence. Everyone, all of them, were going to suffer. How could they remember the sweetness of her words or the purity of her intentions . . .

"Jesse, are you ready? Did you finish writing your talk?" Her voice lilting, cooling like morning mist, this being as demanding a tone as she ever used.

"Ah, Mom, I don't want to."

She would insist. She had written an introduction to a five-minute verse of scripture he was to read before a church audience, not something a seven-year-old relishes. Once a month or so, she would march him or one of her five children up on the podium to "praise Jehovah." This was her god of choice. The business of serving the Lord was of special importance to her, and she brought new meaning to the word zealot, spending hours going door to door, evangelizing, telling the world about her god and His promises. She could be heard most days, while going about her daily chores, singing aloud, what her religion called "kingdom songs." She wanted, more than anything, for her sons to be ministers. There was no chance of this with Franklin, the firstborn, or Ashton, her youngest. But in Jesse she saw something. Something more than his devotion to her. There was a softness about him, an innate kindness that she was certain could be directed to the work of the Lord.

"Come here, Jesse," she said, and the music of her voice came tumbling gently down around him. He went happily to her arms. She held him, as she always did, while planting her warm lips on his forehead.

"You be a good boy, and practice your reading. You'll be glad one day. Now go and make your mother proud," she said, slapping him affectionately on his bottom.

He practiced then and throughout his youth. It pleased her very much. He did everything to please her, for nothing pleased him more than seeing her smile or hearing the sweet rhythms of her voice.

She had a basket of laundry, and out she went to expose the clean, wet clothes to the sun. The sun, on the other hand, it seemed to Jesse, came out only to see her. She seemed to dress for it, in any case—today a pair of stunning green shorts, out of which flowed lovely appendages spun from sable or some such finery, defining those splendid legs. Her toes and fingers where long and perfect. She always stood erect and had a gravitas that defied her birth and humble beginnings. All the creatures in the modest yard would come to rest, I swear it, when she went dancing with the laundry (her movements were always dancelike, so smooth and precise) or any other occasion giving them a chance glimpse of her. When the laundry ballet was done, she would touch (sometimes deliberately and sometimes in passing) the flowers, the vegetables, and the earth; and they would respond to her like everyone else. They would do what she asked, little Jesse saw it that way: pretty, fragrant things would spring up and provide a backdrop for her splendor. The squirrels and mice, the birds and insects would come munching irritatingly on her produce. "They have to eat too, Jesse," she said, as if this was an important learning. He would take this and every lesson with glee and thoughtfulness. It was a way of making things better, making her happy by providing for all living things. Her every action was a lesson of some kind as knowledge, the business of learning was honored by her. She and her husband made this clearly known to their children. And in her voice, there was a well-seated joy in saying his name. Jesse heard it that way. He noticed this when she spoke the names of all of her children. Even in discipline, hearing her say his name was like hearing a song.

"Come Jesse, help me weed this garden. Can you smell them? They all have their own special aroma," she said, touching the leaves of the tomato plant, dearly respecting the life within it. "On this side of the yard we have our vegetables—tomatoes, squash, onions, beets, and carrots. Over here, we are planting flowers. We have our chrysanthemums, roses, four o'clocks' . . ."

"Why do they call them that?" he asked. This sounded like a particularly odd name for a flower. "And what was the other one, crisantenims?"

"Well, they blossom every day at about four o'clock, and that's chrysanthemums. Let me hear you say it."

Jesse tried a few times until he got it right, and he spent some time smelling each plant and memorizing their scents.

"That's my boy, my pretty boy."

How could they know? They have never felt her warm hand on their faces. They had not seen nor tasted what this capable woman could do with the most meager supplies or how beautifully she could prepare a table, a house, or a child. She was lovely in ways the world around her was not prepared for. "Pretty twice," her mother would say. She left him and others with little choice but to adore her. How could they know that she was his everything?

She did, however, according to Jesse anyway, find a way to marry beneath herself. What she found compelling in his father was a mystery to Jesse. Here was a potbellied man with ash on his skin and ice in his veins. A man of obnoxious behavior with a talent for meanness; he was a proper-talking fellow with a penchant for hard lessons and peculiar habits and so dramatic, frightfully dramatic, when angered or disappointed. He was brutal in his demands for excellence and unforgiving of those—his children—when they fell short of his high expectations. He seemed to consider himself and his progeny better than other people, while insisting that no one was better than anyone else (he was full of contradictions). He created for Jesse an environment of unease and tension. Simply being his child meant you were expected to excel. At the same time, because of him, life was entertaining and educational in the most unpredictable, even enjoyable ways.

He was what others called "brilliant," but this was difficult for Jesse to see. There was too much . . . bombast, too much cruelty in his style. But Jesse was alone in this view. Jesse was, in fact, the only person who ever thought his father anything but wonderful. For Jesse, however, everyone was diminished when compared to his mother, and everyone was compared to her. But even she found this rascal "wonderful." "He wrote such beautiful love letters," he heard her say to someone. It is fair to say that she loved him. Jesse was to discover much later how correct his mother and the others were, and how utterly wrong he had been about his father.

There was about him a kind of cerebral tomfoolery, a way of appearing to be the clown while providing sapient commentary on nearly every subject. He was sought after by many, who would bring their problems. They would come and go to "sit at his feet" and listen to his stories and wisdom. For his children, he would sometimes deliver his colorful stories from the toilet (a practice likely borne of a relationship with his own mother, in the fields and outhouses of South Carolina), expecting them to be attentive even under these circumstances. She found a way to tolerate this conduct.

"Oh, Brightmeyer, my, what you teach the children," she would say.

She always called him by his last name; perhaps because he seemed so proud of it. It was a kind of tribute to his self-esteem or perhaps to his father.

He, as life would have it, was somewhere in the same hospital, dying himself (while not knowing it) and weeping as she expired.

CHAPTER 2

The Neighborhood, the Family

The neighborhood in Detroit where the Brightmeyers raised their family was, for Jesse, a place of charm. In the early fifties, the City of Detroit was a destination spot. Jobs were plentiful, and people from around the globe came to enjoy the bounty, in the place known then as "the Paris of the Midwest." A grand boulevard, that circled the inner city, lent itself to this reputation. The boulevard was indeed grand, with its many fine brick homes as it snaked its way "horseshoe" fashion to and from the river, making a serpentine loop around the less grand but comfortable housing. The area it encircled was populated by a diverse group of humanity consisting of Slavic Europeans, Lebanese, Mexicans, Chinese, poor whites, and blacks up from the South. They all lived within this loop. There was no racial tension in this particular enclave, at least none that could be felt. Most of the adults stayed to themselves, honoring their own closed traditions. But the children played as children do, without the madness that plagued the adult world around them. Sounds of laughter could be heard everywhere, in and between the small houses, as the children of many colors found ways to embrace each other.

The streets were lined with modest houses that the underemployed occupants did their best to maintain. Lawns and yards were neatly cared for, and, in the spring and fall, the indigenous trees would do their ancient dance of color. The apple and cherry blossoms matched steps on their way to full verdancy. Chestnuts, sycamores and cotton woods stood proudly erect, and each of them arched as if they owned or protected a particular house. Twice a year they would carpet the quaint neighborhood in hues appropriate for the season. These colors came with equally lively scents and were enhanced by the mixing of aromas wafting from the various kitchens throughout the neighborhood. A sensorial cocktail, the sensations of which Jesse had no way of knowing, would stay with him for all of his days and make this place, this tiny neighborhood, a small village inside Detroit, the most precious place to ever make its way into his heart or his memory.

There was an innocence here that rather perfectly matched young Jesse's sensibilities. He learned every inch of it, climbing all of its trees, happily meeting and spending time with all of its people. The area was somewhat self-contained with every conceivable product or service being readily available just a few minutes' walk from home.

Brightmeyer came home as he always did at about four-thirty, seeing the neighborhood quite differently from his son, laden with the emotional dust of others, having ridden the bus with the masses, and spent the day, as he would bellow, "surrounded by stupidity." He came home to dust he could handle. They, his family, were what Middle America called poor. This was known to the parents, but not the children. They wanted for nothing, at least not for anything that mattered. They were filled with learning, sustenance, and love overflowing. These parents, this couple, had a way of making every necessary thing seem abundant in the house, and they shared as if that was the case. There seemed to always be someone, a friend or relative, sharing the small space with the family. The house had three small bedrooms and was fully furnished with fine things: Italian marble, French provincial furnishings and trimmings, though much of it "throwaways" from the rich white people for whom they worked. A fine oriental rug embraced the hardwood floor, and there were bookcases filled with all of the European classics and a very tattered set of Britannica, all in well-read but good condition. In the kitchen were found professional cooking utensils: KitchenAid, Chicago Cutlery, along with spices and seasonings in stunning variety. Both of Jesse's parents were chefs of the very highest order.

He had arrived as he always did with a newspaper under his arm. He sat in "his chair," lit his Pall Mall, and positioned himself for a few minutes of relaxation before going to his next job. He did whatever was necessary to take care of his family; he seemed to work endlessly and without complaint. He was able, and this confounded Jesse, to sleep nearly not at all, or for the briefest of moments, and be refreshed. Here was a man of hardened ways, the strictest sense of discipline who, during these brief respites, became, it seemed, utterly vulnerable. He was absolutely that to his youngest daughter, Allison; she, being as she was, the pretty and smart one. This combination has probably always been irresistible to loving parents.

He was a round man, un-sculpted, but with a physical strength not suggested by his form. Sometimes, terrifyingly, this strength would be on vivid display with a frightening fatherly discipline (that paled when compared to his rage when he suspected someone had wronged his family) stemming from some deeply rooted fear that he never directly addressed. It was likely a fear based on an absolute necessity that his children "be somebody."

During these moments of the day, he wanted quiet, peace. A difficult thing to achieve, given the bevy of active children he fathered, who, while adoring him, had a certain difficulty with quiet and stillness. They feared him too, respectfully. Only one of his five children had that dreaded, unhealthy fear that could not be overwhelmed by affection, and that was Jesse. The story is that this child could not stomach his father even as an infant. The child came into the world screaming at the sight of him, while clinging to his mother. While this fact was amusingly discussed among family and friends, there was no apparent reason for it, except what would have to be termed an instinctive, unexplainable attachment to his mother.

Anyway, Allison, his youngest daughter, came bounding into the room and fell heavily yet softly onto his lap.

"Oh, Princess, you're going to kill your father," he said, loving and hating it at the same time.

She would rub his bald head and kiss his face. She was the only one of his children who was demonstrative toward him in this way, and for it he had no defense. She would have her way, which was, as it turns out, his way. They had consumption and good taste in common, and as epicures both were insatiable. In this, he would forego his own desires for the sake of his children, but especially Allison. Of his children, she, it seemed, was most like him; and both reveled in this sameness. They were gifted with very active brains and the joy of using them. She would shower him with her impressions of the classics he had insisted she read. He insisted that all his children read them, and they did, but not like Allison. She consumed the *Iliad* (and any other reading material) in a single night, and remembered it as if she had lived it. She captured and perfected English at an early age, and spoke it gaily and colorfully. He glistened with pride as she talked. The rest of the children would stare at these exchanges without envy, only the indescribable pleasure of being in the presence of this kind of familial affection. They were all touched sublimely by these moments, and there were many of them throughout their childhood.

For Jesse, the joy, such as it was, had to do with the distance these occasions would allow him to keep from his father without obviously doing so. He turned to see where his mother was. It did not matter where she was or what she was doing; he needed only to see her. Something about the way she moved or the fragrance that accompanied her, something . . . he adored her clinically, and whatever was her pleasure was certain to be his too. She was busy doing something in the kitchen, pots and tableware ringing out.

Her name was Madelyn. It struck little Jesse as odd that she should have a name. She was Momma. That was her name, and no name is more precious to a seven-year-old. Her friends and sisters had names, but she was Momma. They were part of a bevy of women who seemed always to be around: sisters and best friends. They would say her name occasionally, but mostly they called her sister, again a point of confusion for Jesse.

They sat and talked, usually in the kitchen, where they were always busy, doing what was a mystery to Jesse, as their activity mattered far less than their presence. Yes, the pots would rattle, the aromas of food would swell in the air, and Jesse would notice this. But they brought with them pretty colors and aromas all about them—like hers, but different. They wore dresses, shoes, and carried bags that were irresistible to Jesse. These trinkets reminded him of the flower garden in the backyard. He would stare or gaze upon them excitedly. He loved watching them move: from one chair to another, a wave of the hand, and occasionally he would see them put on makeup and perfume. There was something bothersome about the perfume. For Jesse it distorted or exaggerated something—the indescribable thing he found so compelling about them. Being near them and seeing their apparent joy at being with each other pleased him in a way Jesse could not explain. He even had trouble understanding their need to consume. It seemed to him that they were complete as they were.

The talk on these occasions was banal. "Sista, where did you get these beans?"

"Lu, whatcha gonna do about Wilson? Girl, the way he treats you!"

"Madelyn, there's that boy again. He just loves being around his mother."

But no matter, they could have been sharing the wisdom of the ages; all Jesse heard was their harmony, and the only words that resonated were those spoken by his mother. She would speak primarily when the conversation turned to God. For Jesse, and this would always be true: there was no sound so endearing, none so meaningful, and none, absolutely none, more worth listening to. His mother had no way of knowing that the voice or the word of God, could never supplant hers in the ears of her young Oedipus. Her talk of God, her devotion to Him, and her endless encouragement to Jesse to "be good" and remember the Lord caused Jesse's young mind to look for Him. Everywhere. He never found this god, but he found a way to worship him, through her. He would say throughout his youth that he wanted to be a minister, but all he ever meant was that he wanted to see her happy.

There, on the table, was one of the great treats of his childhood. An opened bottle of Pepsi, his mother's favorite cool drink, set irresistibly on the table. Jesse, in fact all of the children, relished the chance to steal a sip from her bottle of Pepsi. A bottle of your own did not taste nearly as good. Madelyn would use these moments to point out the importance of sharing as if the cola was a prop, intended for this purpose.

Chapter 3

Fall from Grace

By the time the calling stopped, Jesse was drunk—drunk for the first time in his life. There was too much laughter here, and Jesse wanted out. The booze, he quickly discovered, allowed him to disappear. It was not enough. It did not stop the pain or the tears. He had never had strong drink before, but the stupor it induced fit rather neatly into his plans in that it made him feel as if he was slapping the perpetrator of his grief in the face. This face slapping would last for almost twenty years and led to many baleful maneuvers within Jesse's overall intentions to punish Him.

The idolaters and sycophants showed up, and said all of the usual well-meaning but insulting things. They will suffer. An old girlfriend was among them, several old girlfriends, in fact. They tried to comfort the family by speaking of Madelyn's gentle ways and wide-ranging influence, reaching as they might for happy memories. This only deepened Jesse's despair. His wife was somewhere in this mix, but she had no way of understanding what was unraveling before her. She had watched her husband morph into something, someone she could no longer recognize. She was not gifted in language, so she said nothing. Instead she did what she always did: perform her duty. She made preparations. She listened to her in-laws, looking for something she could do to avoid having to gaze upon her broken and crumbling husband. There was some hissing among the girlfriends and the wife, but Jesse was oblivious to it. His plummet continued, precipitously, relentlessly. He was slipping right before their eyes, but their eyes saw only the ritual, duty, and though he could not imagine it, pain of their own.

Among the calls, there was one particularly recognizable voice, the voice of Mamie Lacy. This is the woman who Jesse, at the age of eighteen, had decided to marry. They had known each other as children. They each had parents who devoted themselves to Jehovah at about the same time. Twice a week they would see each other at Christian meetings and exchange adolescent smiles. They did not talk or play much as children. Unlike the Brightmeyers, many hyper-religious families did not encourage fun for their children. They were all about study and taking seriously their devotion to the Lord. Mamie and Jesse had not been friends, but something was brewing between them even then. Her father, John Lacy, like Madelyn, was among the first black Detroiters to embrace this "new religion" and, by every measure that could be made from a distance, was as devout a Christian as Jesse's mother. Both the Brightmeyers and the Lacys were like so many black families up from the South: completely unaccustomed to being treated fairly, as equals, by white people. This religion, known as Jehovah's Witnesses, was in those days thought to be a sect, but it had the illusion of racial equality and, as a result, many blacks found themselves seduced and enrolled.

It was peopled by real students of the Bible, and they had quite a different take on the fundamental Christian tenants. John and Madelyn were not alone in this devotion to the "new" god. As in all religions, there is a core of zealots who support it—no exception here. Perhaps their most significant departure from conventional Christianity, and evidence of their dedication, was their tireless evangelism. These people were deeply committed to spreading the word. No matter that the word they spread did not resemble the teachings of traditional Christianity, the institution they called "Christendom." The word Christendom was uttered as if it was a plague on the land. Jehovah's Witnesses were different, to be sure, and compelling. There is the promise of everlasting life on earth, total peace among humans and animals, on and on it goes—a marvelous fantasy equal to any other in the strange world of religion. In any case, they attracted some of the brightest, most well-spoken people Jesse was ever to meet. Madelyn made certain that her children were exposed to these people, and among them were John Lacy, his astonishingly beautiful wife, and their children. Thus Mamie's beauty could not be helped, but it was like everyone else's, measured against the beauty of Jesse's mother. She came close enough for Jesse to be moved. After passing through puberty and teen hood, Jesse found the courage to ask Mamie out on a date. Her yes pleased him very much, and after a titillating courtship, Jesse asked her to marry him. She said yes, and Jesse was afloat with pleasure and expectation. He had barely told anyone when she called, now fully ten years ago, to announce that she could not marry him. This was crushing news to Jesse, and he wept while pleading for her to change her mind or at least to explain. She had moved to Wisconsin and was going to stay there. She hung up the phone repeatedly in Jesse's ear before finally providing an answer that left him befuddled and free.

"It's just that you are too dark. I'm afraid of what our children would look like."

Well, this insanity set him free of her. But here it was, ten years later, and she was calling with condolences. For an instant, Jesse remembered the excitement of having kissed her years ago, the way she smelled, and the pleasure of imagining a life with her. They talked as they never had and arranged to see each other. Jesse would take his first step down the road to sin. A decade ago, their Christian sensibilities did not allow them to even consider sex before marriage, to say nothing of extramarital coupling. But now he would take her. He would fu . . . he couldn't yet say the foul word. The business of sin would take some practice for Jesse. He arranged to meet her at a bar. A kind of place he had never been in. He had never been in any bar; he had never wanted to be. The darkness, the smoke, the smell of the place, and even the people, made Jesse feel as if the good god was watching and agonizing. It satisfied him. He was out of place, out of his comfort zone, and it invigorated him. They sat in a secluded corner of the room, but it seemed to Jesse that every spot here was secluded. He placed himself next to her. He could smell her, and their thighs were touching.

"So tell me everything," he said. "Where have you been? What have you been doing?"

She wore a bright green dress that was iridescent against her vivid black skin and the furtive dim light in the room. She had, and he remembered it now, a rogue scar on an otherwise lovely face.

"I'm married now, and I have a daughter."

"Really, what's her name? How old is she?"

"Sherrill, her name is Sherrill. She's seven. How about you?"

"I have two boys, Chad and Zachery . . ." Then, without warning, he kissed her.

He felt nothing, but he persisted. It was an act, a performance. He imagined his big brother bringing a romantic scene to life in the living room of their childhood home. He imitated him as much as he could, remembering his lines and moves, and soon found himself in his brother's apartment making love, having sex, slapping the foul Lord against His unrepentant face.

This was unsatisfying, but over the next few months, Jesse repeated this scene with every ex-girlfriend that showed up that night.

CHAPTER 4

The Marriage Dies

Several days raced by as Jesse sought ways to cope with his deepening grief. Soon, and the moment was not clear to him, it was time to return home. He and his wife, Beverly, hardly spoke during the drive. Their two little boys were eerily silent, as if intuiting the despair of their parents. Jesse wept openly the whole trip. Beverly did not know what to do, and she was shocked that her husband, the minister who had been called to so many deathbeds to provide comfort, was now incapable of finding any relief for himself. She began to think of him as weak, even hypocritical.

She had problems of her own that were not completely known by Jesse, and not yet fully defined in her own mind. She sulked incessantly and was short tempered with Jesse and the boys. "Why don't you divorce me?" rang like a mantra in Jesse's ears. She would utter this exclamation whenever she was upset or thought she had displeased her husband. Jesse thought it was simply a cry for attention. Now, it seems, she had developed a relationship with one of the young brothers at the church or "congregation," as Jehovah's

Witnesses referred to themselves. Perhaps the phrase was now rooted in a latent desire.

The young man, who had garnered her attention, was inordinately formal given his youth, but it all seemed affected to Jesse. His name was Thomas and he would not answer to Tom or Tommy. He was bright and well mannered, but Jesse thought him odd, which may very well have explained his compatibility with Beverly. The family from which he came was as narrowly focused as Beverly's. At seventeen, he was in that very age frame Beverly had missed out on as a result of her family's narrow view of life. She had missed many rites of childhood: the prom, the girly chit-chat, dating boys, and the other ordinary teenage passages. They spoke, as they say, the same language. It is certain that outside of the routine theocratic jargon of their esoteric religion, and the banalities of rearing children, she and Jesse were at a loss for things to say to each other. Tommy came over often when Jesse was home, and he welcomed his visits. Beverly was comfortable, even cheerful, with him, and he with her. At some point, he began showing up in Jesse's absence, and eventually, the relationship passed the ways of innocence. In his heart, Jesse had hoped that "something more" was going on, and he didn't care to know the details. What he did not anticipate was the illusion of love. This feeling descended upon them, and they fell for its seductive titillations. They spoke daily on the phone and arranged to meet when they could.

Jesse's guilt, or his wish to get to the end of what was now a hopeless marriage, led him to confess to Beverly about his assignations with at least two of his former girlfriends. The result was predictably horrible and terrifyingly dramatic. Beverly went temporarily insane, throwing dishes and threatening to kill herself.

She took an eight-inch knife by the blade and thrust it into her stomach, cutting only her hands. Jesse took the knife and returned it to the safety of the kitchen. They both wept, knowing that the end was upon them (weeping was now a constant for Jesse). Between, during, and after the weeping, ugly, hurtful things were said as they fought to defend themselves.

"You cheated on me," she bellowed. "I'm your wife. How could you do this to me?"

"You were cheating on me too," Jesse bellowed back, trying to protect his infidelities.

"I never had sex with him."

"You expect me to believe that? All I hear about is how sad he is. He's crying. What does he have to cry about? You spend more time with him than you do with me."

"You lost your mother, and he lost me." she screamed. "It's the same thing."

Here Jesse lost control. He grabbed her much harder than he knew and began shaking her violently.

"What? What did you say? You're going to compare that to the loss of my mother. Are you? Are you? That punk and some puppy love! You get the hell away from me. Get out of my life. I hate you. You had better never say that again."

"It's the same thing!" She yelled, scowling at full capacity.

Jesse slammed her to the floor and raised his fist to hit her. He could not do it. But he tried repeatedly, his fist stopping mechanically, involuntarily, in midair as if tethered to some irresistible force. She began to scream in terror, for there was a look in Jesse's now-crimson eyes that approached evil, with fluids flying off his face, like blood spewing from an open wound, and she did not know that he would not strike her. The children came running down the stairs and jumped on Jesse's back. At this he relented and rolled, trembling to the floor in what was a near-fetal position. There he stayed, sweating profusely as tears exploded through his eyes, while his children and his wife lay near him, all crying uncontrollably.

How long they stayed prone and prostrate is not certain, but when Jesse finally got up, he knew his family was a wreck. There were things to do around the house, he knew it but he had no idea where to begin. He went up and down the stairs as if he was looking for something. These were false movements as he tried, desperately, to find a way to busy himself. Just days ago he would have been on some project, something to fix, to do, or read. There was a need to feed the children, laundry awaited, and Jesse had to go to work. Work, how? A couple of years prior, Jesse had partnered with a friend, another young minister, and together they had built a small business that provided for their families and allowed them to perform their ministerial duties. The situation was ideal in that it gave them flexibility; they could cover for each other during heavy workloads. There were only a few employees, but that was the plan. They never intended to become a large company, only enough to provide "sustenance and covering," as the holy book admonished.

Things were different now: large or small, Jesse was unable to hold up his end. It did not need to be said; it was obvious that Jesse was dragging, nearly useless, and his partner could not understand this. Things within the business were falling apart, and while there may have been some sympathy for him, Jesse could not feel it. It felt to him as if nobody cared, no one understood, and he sank into self-pity, and brooded endlessly. He finally announced to his partner that he had to leave the business and that he could buy Jesse's share. Things had been going poorly between them for some time. His partner was not strong of character and had begun to distance himself from Jesse, even though he knew he could not carry on without Jesse or someone. They sold the business, and after all of the bills were paid, there was only enough money left to survive for about a month. This, like everything in Jesse's life, was ending.

He had to leave his house, and while how was not clear to him, he had to find some way to support himself and a wife he was leaving. He could not stay with a woman who had offended him so deeply, any more than he could stay with a god who had done so. He had no place to go, nor did he have the energy to face this fact. For a time he simply, almost blindly, came and went, meandering through his bitter days. He drank every day and always to the point of drunkenness. He found his way into a life were marijuana was commonly used, and immersed himself in its illusions.

Eventually he found a job, winding golf balls at a local factory. He worked nights, which was just as well in that he no longer slept, and when he did, his dreams were only a gray mass. His daydreaming was littered with thoughts of loss and pain. It was as if he felt he had no right to feel any other way. Doing so would diminish her life. This distress was his to wallow in and he could not, did not want to extricate himself from it. His mother was gone, and with her went any inkling of happiness.

On a particular night, standing before the relentless ball-winding machine, he found himself on his knees, having fallen there, as the memories of his life with his mother and family came over him as a tearful song. Strangely, a complete song about his mother and childhood came to him. When he got home, he tried to share it, the song, with his wife, but he could not get through it without the eruption of tears. She scoffed at this, saying, "It's been almost a year, when are you going to get over it?" Jesse wanted to strike her, but violence was not something he had yet learned.

CHAPTER 5

Back to the Stage

The ministry is a stage, and Jesse had been on it most of his life. In his current despair, his mind was a whirl. That he had slipped away from sanity was clear to no one. His mind was only gray matter, and as he tried to conjure his sensibilities, only those hazy gray visions would show in his mind's eye. More often than not, the only thing he could see clearly was her face. Now, a year since her passing, he did have occasional moments of clarity. During one such episode, he thought he would again take to the stage. Not the pulpit, but the stage of the local repertory theater.

In his youth, his parents had encouraged all manner of artistic activity for their children. They all took music lessons (only the girls excelled). They spent Saturdays in the library, searching out various crafts, reading, and drawing, something at which Jesse excelled; and of course, there was Jesse's private tutor in the dramatic arts, Frankie. As a child, Jesse had been in school plays. He showed a particular aplomb, a real comfort with remembering lines and the subtleties of character. Everyone said so, even when he was a boy.

He had seen a flyer announcing tryouts for a play with a group known as the "Ira Aldridge Players." They were housed in a small theater that, ironically, had formerly been a chapel, holding a hundred seats or so. The auditions, however, were held at a home belonging to a colleague of the director, a man named Cedric Ward. "That's Cedric, with two c's," he would say during the introduction. He was a large fellow with a compellingly interesting face. Each feature on it taken separately was odd, but together this oddness worked in a mesmerizing sort of way. He was graceful in his rotundity and spoke eloquently while hurling, what was to Jesse, foul language that somehow seemed perfectly appropriate. His voice carried a melodious rasp, and everything he said seemed rehearsed, or as if he had said it many times before. He was certainly directorial, and people in the room seemed intimidated by him. He had delicate hands in which his endless cigarette seemed magical, a wand, dismissing or inviting the aspirants. His large eyes never rested, but just beneath an ever-present glaze one could see gentleness; well, Jesse could, the others were quaking in anticipation of his judgment. All except two—Jesse and a fascinating woman named Jan O'Reilly.

Jan had a very similar style to Cedric's; she was self-assured and dismissive. Her entrance into the room suggested that it was hers, as if she was familiar with the place without being so. She introduced herself as if to say, "The lead is mine, why are you here?"

"Hi," she said, sprightly, "I'm Jan."

She didn't wait to hear their names, and she certainly did not ask. She moved very much like a woman, but not any woman Jesse had ever met. Her red pantsuit fit her just as she wanted it to, and her blond hair was precisely clipped. Finally she found some place to sit as Cedric began his declaration.

"Hello everyone, somebody lock the damn door. I am Cedric Ward, and I will be directing the play. This is Greg." He might as well have been talking to Jesse alone, as everyone else already knew him.

He threw the most casual gesture in the direction of a man who seemed at total peace with himself. He was the big fish in the small pond that was theater in Grand Rapids, Michigan. He was an actor, a stagehand, and a director in his own right, all the things one needed to be to carry the weight of a small repertory theater company.

"What the play is about should not concern you at this time. We are a repertory theater looking for people with talent. I don't give a damn what you have heard about how talented you are. I will be telling you if you have talent. From this point on, you are talented only if I say you are. I don't give a fuck about how cute you are—that's your momma's opinion not mine. I don't need cute, I need commitment. If you don't have that you can get the hell out now."

A knock came urgently on the door. Everyone noticed; nobody moved. Cedric kept talking as if no sound had been heard, as if there was no knocking. Someone got up to answer the door.

"Where are you going?" said Cedric.

"To get the door."

"Why?"

"Well, there's someone at the door. I was going to let them in."

"We started at seven. Anyone not here at seven is not welcome. If you open the door, leave us. This is not romper room. We are looking for commitment. If you don't value being on time, you don't understand commitment. If you don't understand commitment, you are not welcome here. He'll come back, or he won't. He knows the rules."

The person sat down, and that was that.

Cedric passed out scripts to the ten or twelve people who were on time. No one had ever heard of the play called *The Shadow Box*. He had them read lines without knowing how the lines fit into the story, looking for voices, intonation, and comfort with reading in the presence of strangers. He then paired them off and had them "read off" each other. During this phase, he made no comments except to make assignments. Greg was taking notes. Finally he told the nervous assembly what the story was about. It was a trilogy of death and dying, how families dealt with caring for the terminally ill. Eventually Jan and Jesse were placed opposite each other. They read as if they knew each other, almost as if they had been rehearsing for some time. Cedric, seeing what he wanted, acted as if he had not. He appeared to be completely unmoved by the performance, but Jan and Jesse and every one there knew that these two would be given leading roles. The two of them flashed subtle but knowing smiles at one another. This was to be the start of a strange but enduring relationship.

After about three hours, Cedric announced that he had seen enough. Everyone was given a basic form on which they were to place their names and numbers. Then they began to nervously file out. Jesse had locked his attention on Jan from the moment she entered the room. As they left he said, "So what do I have to do to see you again?"

Her smile was one of vast experience, well beyond what Jesse was prepared for. He called on his memory of Frankie, as she said, "Get cast, I guess."

"I'll wait until then if I have to, but what are you doing now? Do you have time for a drink?"

The look on her face suggested that she knew just what she wanted to say, but she was processing the choice not to. With a warm visage but less than a smile, she said, "I think I like you. I'd like for you to meet someone."

He did not know what to make of that but was willing to follow.

"I'm on my way to a party off Twenty-Eighth Street. Why don't you follow me?"

On the way there, Jesse allowed himself thoughts of his new circumstance. There were several attractive women at the audition—none so beautiful as his wife, but none who had hurt him. It was so unlike him to be anywhere but home that he had to find his feet, as they say. He wanted a drink. He needed one before thoughts of his loss came to overwhelm him.

The party was held in a modest, eclectically furnished apartment. There were artful pictures on the walls, photographs and paintings, of women of various colors and stages of nudity, along with interesting African and Native American artifacts, or rather, facsimiles of such on both the walls and tables. The owner of this place had her tastes on vivid display. It was a youthful space, and every piece in it seemed quite specifically chosen. There was a small balcony overlooking a courtyard that was rife with cheerful conversation. Jan had clearly been missed, as she was greeted in that style reserved for the anchor of the party.

"Did you get the part?"

"Of course she did."

"Cedric is an asshole, isn't he? I told you he was an ass."

"Was Charlotte there . . . ?

Jan, he thought, was the leader of this pack, as it suddenly occurred to him that there were only women in the apartment, and all of them were white. That is, until Jan introduced him to Beth. Liz Beth actually, and everyone called her that but herself. This was a remarkably handsome woman. But her most conspicuous feature was not a feature at all. It wasn't even her. It was something about her. All around her, even in the air, there was a calmness that surpassed anything in Jesse's memory. Her skin was certainly remarkable, glowing as it did in a hue for which there is no word. Her voice was mellow, as she spoke in nearly a whisper, but could somehow be heard above the background noise. Her hair was a marvelous flock of wool flecked attractively with gray, with a single dreadlock bouncing independently on her patrician cheek. She was older and younger than Jesse at once. She was ancient and childlike at once. But it was her peacefulness that Jesse found so endearing. He had never seen a person so attractive in these ways. Jesse thought, well, if this is whom she wanted him to meet, it was fine with him.

Jan, with an understandable level of pride and kissing that glowing skin, said, "This is my Liz Beth, isn't she beautiful?" Again she did not wait for an answer.

"Liz Beth, where is Lena? I brought her a present. Oh, there she is. Marlena, you get over here right now."

It was a very playful demand that Marlena playfully obeyed.

"This is Jesse. He was at the audition. I thought he was cute, so I brought him home."

"He is cute. Jesse. That's a cute name too. What's your last name?"

"Brightmeyer. Jesse Brightmeyer."

"Jesse Brightmeyer, that's some name. What are you doing with it?"

"My dad gave it to me."

"No, I mean with a name like that, you . . ."

"I'm just kidding. I know what you mean. I'm in sales."

She was pretty and charming, but the question was unsettling. Jesse was no longer anything, and he knew it. So recently he was a husband, a father, and a minister. Now he was a piece of a man who did not want to be uncovered, at least not now. Luckily she did not persist in this line of questioning.

Marlena was, or so it appeared, in her prime. Her prettiness was enhanced by an indefatigable cheerfulness. She was a skilled flirt and equally comfortable with men or women. There was a twinkle in her silvery eyes that must have been irresistible as they danced within her flawless skin. Her body and her attitude seemed unscathed by the rigors of time. She was certainly not a member of a pack, all of her movements being so purposeful, and with a directness that plainly announced her full womanhood.

The party was winding down, or more accurately, Liz Beth was ready to go. The average age of the women in the room was considerably younger than the cool clique of Jan, Liz Beth, and Lena. She was ready for some adult entertainment. As she passed Jesse, she said in her quiet way and into his private breathing space, "We play cards."

"I play cards," said Jesse, nearly duplicating her tone.

"Just follow us." She had the most perfect grasp of the spoken word, and she never used one unnecessarily.

They went to Marlena's house, back into the city and painfully close to his own. Earth tones were everywhere, dotted with purples and blues, and tastefully done. She did many things herself, and she was completely nonchalant about all of her fine domestic achievements. Nearly everything in the house had her personal mark on it: she had refinished or painted, hemmed or altered everything in it. Jan bragged about her good friend. The house was fresh. It smelled very much like the outdoors. On a fine antique table, Lena placed wine, beer, and a pearled case that was a bit smaller than a cigar box.

"Let's smoke a joint," she said. Then a near ritual unfolded that was so pleasant that it did not seem to fit into Jesse's sinful plans. Liz Beth opened the box and began shifting through the marijuana; it was not unlike watching a meal being lovingly prepared. The action and the result were pretty. Lena poured wine for Jan and beer for the rest of them. They talked ever so comfortably in that "getting to know you" kind of way. But it did not feel that way. It felt much more like old friends reuniting. There was an honesty and straightforwardness that had to do with who each other was, not what they did for a living nor what their achievements were. These women had the thing that Jesse had sacrificed to do the work of the Lord: they were free. He was completely seduced by this . . . this family. They talked, laughed, and played cards well into the night. Jan and Liz Beth left at about two in the morning happy and satisfied, and Jesse awoke in Lena's bed the next morning with the great weight of his shattered life only thinly disguised.

CHAPTER 6

The Play

The rehearsals for the play were like going to meet the mule. Cedric Ward was a taskmaster. He was completely committed to his craft, which was getting every morsel of talent out of anyone who dared to call themselves an actor. Most of the time, the rehearsals went well into the night. Cedric was more teacher than director, and he was a fine director. He had at his disposal, as all community theaters do, a mixed cast of performers. Some of them truly had no right to be on any stage. Cedric knew the limits of each of his students, and he pushed them to it during every session. The upstarts asked questions, to which Cedric would always respond with a question. He did not believe in acting. He wanted each thespian to "become" the character they played. To do that, you must "know" the character, and Cedric insisted that his players must know the role better than he, the director. He angered people, he made them cry, he would not let up. He and Jan, predictably, had arguments that disturbed the cast, especially those, like Jesse, who had not witnessed this kind of passion about something that was not even real life. To Cedric, it was real life. Some could not endure the surprising brutality of his approach and left the field. He was teaching them, as he put it, "how to live on stage."

"You must take the audience with you. They must be made to believe that they are seeing into your private lives. This is not song and dance. We are not entertaining them. The audience is a mob. If they are entertained, it is as voyeurs. They are gazing through the window of your bedroom, into your bathroom. These are sick fucks, and you do not know they are there. Are you laughing because the audience wants you to? Are you crying to win their sympathy? Hell no! You are laughing or crying because that is who you are. That is who your character is or what he or she would do. The world does not need another fucking actor. I don't give a damn about the audience until it is over, and they return to their reality." Cedric said this as if he were Dad or preacher, sans the foul language.

Jesse was taken by this point of view. This whole acting thing was what he thought he was there to do. Act like somebody else. Becoming somebody else, the thought of that, opened his eyes but left him wondering exactly how to do this. Cedric seemed to see this in Jesse's eyes.

"Now, Jesse, get up there, and let's do the scene again. What is your character feeling? Don't answer that question. Show me the answer."

Jesse went to the stage and did the scene opposite a young actor who played his child.

"Again," said Cedric, casually without any direction. "Again," he said.

He made them do the scene four times before telling Jesse, "Now give me some tears."

"Tears? When, how, where? I don't think I can do that," said Jesse incredulously.

"Do it," he said, as if he fully expected Jesse to achieve this directive.

Jesse made an effort that did not quite show. No tears came.

"All right, forget about it for now. Charlotte, let's work on your entrance." As she took the stage, Jesse thought he would have to work on producing tears on demand. He thought that only happened in the movies, with artificial tears being dispensed from a dropper. He decided he would practice on his own, without all of these eyes on him.

Cedric ignored the setup activities of Charlotte's scene. Instead he stood up and called to Jesse, saying, "You been moping around here crying like a baby cause yo' momma died, but you can't find a way to give me some tears for this important scene."

Jesse's eyes welled up at the mention of her, but he did not want to kill him. Cedric's statement did not appear to Jesse to be an attack or even disrespectful, but it certainly brought her face into view, along with his ever-present sorrow about her absence. In just few minutes, Jesse was crying profusely. Cedric had someone bring tissue and handed it to Jesse. He told Jesse, ever so tenderly now, to compose himself, and then try the scene again. Jesse, reluctantly, returned to the practice stage. This time, when Cedric called for tears, within the context of the script, they flowed from Jesse's eyes at such a rate that Cedric asked him again to compose himself.

The result of all of this was that Cedric produced a show with local actors that rivaled, was in fact superior, to the television production starring Paul Newman and Joanne Woodward. The local papers said as much, and described Jesse Brightmeyer's performance as being "more than that of a skilled actor, but that of a pure artist." Cedric knew what he had in this young apprentice, and while he was already known as a stalwart in the artistic community of his city, his reputation was again enhanced by this production and the fine work of this unknown actor, Jesse Brightmeyer.

It was after this and meeting with a member of the press that Jesse began thinking of himself as an actor. It didn't mean much because Jesse was no longer anything else. He was not the thing he had intended to be. Being an actor, or saying he was, gave him a way of answering the now annoying question, "What do you do?" But it was also something at which he was skilled, and people in this community knew it. To the few who really knew, Jesse was, as in everything else he did, just acting, now even acting as if he was an actor. For some years he managed to parlay this skill into a modest annual income. It was never enough to support him or even to send to his family. If the truth be told, after the loss of his mother, Jesse lived on his wits, acting his way from one episode to another. It was not his only skill, but it was his best one, the one he relied on.

CHAPTER 7

Pleased to Meet You, Mr. Baldwin

Hers was a water bed that sloshed with every move. The sloshing sound and the waves mimicked the activity in Jesse's brain. He made every effort to be honest with Lena about his pain; he wasn't clear, and he didn't know how to be. Her home was only a half mile from his own, where his wife, children, and all of that despair lay smoldering. True, his wife had offended him deeply, but she was suffering too, and he was about to bring her more pain. Jesse knew she would be relieved if he left but that she would not likely be honest about it, and she would be shredded as well, the whole "till death do us part" thing. He had meant those words, and now he could find no words.

Jesse was encouraged by Lena to get comfortable in her house. She wanted him to stay, and he had no will of his own with which to resist. There was so much to explain: his former ministry, a wife and kids just down the street, and the devastating loss of his mother. He was incomplete, and the conflict between his principles and his pain was unmanageable. It seemed he would have to learn to be cruel. But was it cruelty? Beverly wanted to be free of him, he was certain of this, but living with another woman would be unforgivable. *She deserved this*, he thought. How could she compare that boy's loss of her to his loss of his mother? This too was unforgivable—as it should be.

Marlena was supportive, but for her, and nearly everyone else on the planet, moving on after tragedy was simply a part of life. She could not find a way to understand what was happening to Jesse. She considered his grief, the dimensions of it, ridiculous, but she could not deny its real presence. She was certainly fond of him and could see a future with the man he seemed to be, during his moments of clarity, under the crusty pain. But his gloominess was a constant, and Jesse could see that he was having a deflating effect on this otherwise upbeat and positive woman. He busied himself fixing things; he painted her house. But after a few months, he found himself collecting his few belongings and saying goodbye. Marlena was predictably perturbed and conflictive in her relief.

Jesse called his sister to ask if she could house him for a while. If he could have, he would have moved back to the familiar confines of the old neighborhood—the old house, but it was now gone, the victim of a wayward vehicle steered by a drunken driver. He needed the comfort of a time now gone. Allison and her husband Steven said yes to Jesse's request to live with them for a time. They, by every outward appearance had a solid relationship, but having your brother-in-law or any additional family member in your house changes things and is necessarily interruptive. Jesse had nothing to offer. No job and no self, but Allison was Madelyn's child too, and she could not say no to her brother. It did not occur to Steven to say no either, as it would have had he perceived the great disturbance in Jesse's mind, and besides, they were genuinely fond of each other.

This is to suggest that he did not know the depth of his trouble. Jesse seemed all right to him. Anyway his tenancy was temporary, and it would give them many opportunities to talk and catch up. Steven was what people called "a nice man." He had a softness about him that was not unlike Jesse's. He was a schoolteacher and good at it, with an understated intelligence and a real wish to make a difference. He and Jesse shared an interest in sports, and he was a good uncle to Jesse's boys. However, he was not prepared for what had happened to Jesse. He had changed. Jesse had become a kind of nuisance. He was needy and aimless. He began borrowing money and asking for the car keys.

Some years ago, Jesse had brought a puppy home to his sons. The animal was a Great Dane and grew to be too large for the boys to handle. Allison and Steven (somewhat reluctantly) had agreed to give the dog a home. So now they had the dog, whose contribution was at least to match the furniture, and Jesse who brought nothing. Soon it became clear that both were more trouble than they had ever envisioned. But Steven and Allison (who seemed even less aware of Jesse's debilitations than her husband) were patient. Jesse did at least find a way to be helpful around the house, running errands and doing chores. He and the oversized dog would disappear at night. They would simply go out into the night, and neither Steven nor Allison would know where they were. He would return, at some absurd and disturbing hour, drunk, high, and in need of . . . something. They endured this behavior as long as they could.

Allison had many girl friends who would visit from time to time. One of them was as clinically depressed as Jesse. Allison had by now seen enough, and for all of the right reasons, warned her friends about her brother. He was sufficiently attractive and cogent often enough, that they would fall for his needy games with predictably painful and, often, embarrassing results.

Allison had also developed the habit, if it can be called this, of fixing broken wings. One of her friends, Shelly, was a terribly broken emotional heap, so much so that Allison warned Jesse about her. But this woman needed what Jesse had—a hopeless despair to share. They wallowed together in self-pity while smoking and drinking themselves into a kind of functional unconsciousness. Shelly Siegel used sex as a drug, and there was nothing sexual that she wouldn't try, and Jesse was up for anything that allowed him to flout his upbringing (slap the Perpetrator), or mitigate his pain. She and Jesse would have sex anywhere, everywhere.

Parties or social gatherings were among Allison's favorite things to do. She had decided, for reasons of her own, not to use her prodigious mind and talent in art, medicine, or business, as her father had wanted. Instead she took a moderately prestigious job and supported others and pushed them to excel. She would often invite people to her home for an evening of entertainment, which were primarily exercises in intellectual play. The issues of the day would be discussed, but to no real purpose except to prove that they were all educated and informed. Her friends included the elite from varying social stratum, people accomplished in one of the arts and sciences, or who seemed to be on their way to some notable achievement.

These people had rendezvoused at her house on a fine fall evening and Allison had, against her better judgment, invited Shelly. Her thinking was if she exposed this poor creature to people of means, people who had learned to cope with the vicissitudes of life, she might see a way for herself. Jesse had other plans. He lured her into a half bath just outside of the kitchen, where they created the unmistakable and very noticeable sounds of sex. Allison found a way to forgive this, even to explain it to her shocked, and, if the truth be told, entertained guests. Her brother, she said, was an artist, and her friend was, well, what she was. Steven was less tolerant, and without ever asking, asked Jesse to leave. The dog, it seems, got a pass.

As it happens, Marlena had moved to Detroit around this time, and Jesse, now in a somewhat desperate moving pattern, sought her out and rekindled the old flame. She was, as Jesse observed, one of the bravest women he had ever met. This was part of what made her so attractive. She had been teaching school for fifteen years in the quiet confines of Grand Rapids and decided, quite capriciously, to change careers. She sold her house, packed up her daughter and their things, and headed for the hostilities of Detroit. This meant a loss of half of her income and the distancing of herself from her friends; yet she went about it as if she were simply going to work—business as usual. She moved comfortably into an all-black neighborhood, took her daily walks, and enrolled her child in the public school system. Free indeed. All of this was topped by the rescue of Jesse, or rather, of Allison and Steven from Jesse.

She had considerably less to share now, given her new status, but she treated Jesse as if he was hers and she was his. They lived very much like husband and wife. Jesse found meaningless low-paying work, which, after sending money to Beverly, left almost nothing to contribute to the household. Marlena tolerated this without much complaining. She did encourage Jesse to seek counseling. His sulking was the one thing that disturbed her. She was not indifferent, but she was tired of not knowing how to help. There was no nagging, as it was not her nature, but Jesse went, at her behest, to be treated by a psychiatrist; but he went with no wish or willingness to conform to any therapy. At these sessions, Jesse's madness would be on full display. He would harangue against God, white men, and the culture at large. It was evident to the many therapists he visited over the years that this client wanted no help. He needed and thrived on the pain. Jesse eventually stopped going.

As much to give Marlena some breathing space as anything else, Jesse decided to audition for a play, to get out of the house. The play was written by the great essayist, James Baldwin. Jesse had read much of his work but did not know he had written a play. The director was very different from Cedric Ward. He was a man of subtle maneuvers, cultured and well-traveled. Not that Cedric lacked those qualities, but this man had clearly left behind the ways of the inner city. One wondered why he was in Detroit, as opposed to New York or Hollywood. His name was Walter, Walter Mason, and he had worked for or with some of the most famous people the world of entertainment has to offer, and one of them was Mr. Baldwin himself. At the audition, it was made plain that the lead was already cast; he was now looking to cast secondary roles.

When Walter heard Jesse read, he asked if he had any work memorized that he would like to do. Jesse thought for a second. He had a very short résumé and went immediately into the dream scene from *The Shadow Box*. When he finished, the director's assistant waved Jesse to the side and asked if he could stay until the audition was over. After nearly everyone had left, Walter approached Jesse, who was sitting quietly next to the diligent assistant, and said to her, "Will you excuse us for a moment?" She departed dutifully without saying a word.

"So where have you been performing? Why have I not seen you before? Obviously you have a well-practiced talent, and I'm just surprised that I haven't met you before now. You know the lead is cast. It's too late for me to change that. I could move you into the lead, but it would create a level of discord that neither of us would want to deal with. I hope you are okay with a secondary role."

"I'm from here, but I have been in Grand Rapids for about ten years, and yes, I am okay with any role you put me in," Jesse said while trying to figure out where this discussion was going.

"That would explain it. That's about how long I've been away. I decided to come back home to build a badly needed repertory theater here, in Detroit, which is my home too."

He was at ease, and he spoke as if Jesse was a colleague.

"Do you have the time to join us?"

This offer excited and unnerved Jesse. Could this man not see the madness in his eyes? How was it that his trouble, filling him up inside like a cesspool, did not show on the surface?

"I like the idea. Let's arrange a time to discuss your model." Jesse thought this answer concealed his misery.

Rehearsals began the next day. When Jesse arrived, he met a very large ensemble of men and women all eager to begin. The leading role had been given to a proud actor of marginal but adequate talent. He played opposite a fine-looking woman who had more beauty than skill. The rest of the group was an uneven assortment of hopefuls, all dreaming of becoming stars.

The assistant that had called Jesse aside the day before was a very attractive woman who was in constant attendance but somehow did not fit in. She had the style and presentation of someone other than a struggling actor. She dressed and spoke like a businesswoman. There was a shyness about her, the effect of which was to make her seem coquettish. They were seeing each other differently today.

There was something in her eyes that was not there yesterday. They were seeing something they liked in each other, and now Jesse was indeed comfortable with women and immediately went for every woman he desired.

"Hi. So what do you do here? For the company, I mean."

"Oh, hi, you're Jesse Brightmeyer. I'm Virginia. I just help out with the business. I'm not an actor."

Clearly. She was tall and cultured and carried fine bags with fine things in them. She obviously had more money than any small-time actor Jesse had ever met. Most actors had no real jobs—acting was their career path. They were committed to the craft, at least for a time, but most were not holding down real jobs. It often took years for some of them to realize that for every Sidney Poitier, there were thousands of wannabes. She was not one of them. She may have been a dilettante, but she was a devout one, with no illusions about her future in the arts.

"Well, do you paint or dance or something?"

Jesse said this playfully. There was a constant girlish smile on her face, and there was something, perhaps her long fingers, but something that reminded Jesse of his mother.

"I'm a dancer. I take lessons anyway. I'm trying, you know."

Jesse paused reflectively. "Dance, that's something my mother always wanted to do. She had two fantasies: to drive an eighteen wheeler and be a ballerina."

"Well it's never too late," She had not heard the past tense.

"It is for her. She passed away a few years ago."

Those words, any words about his mother being gone, always caused some quaking inside of Jesse. He hoped it didn't show.

"What kind of dance do you do?"

"Modern jazz, it's something like ballet. I don't perform though. For me, it is about the exercise and, as you say, the fantasy."

"Gather around." Walter had an easy way about him. He seemed more professorial than directorial. His manner and way of talking suggested high levels of education. He wore expensive but bedraggled clothes that fit him indifferently.

"We have a good cast," he said as if he believed it, "but we have a lot of work to do. We plan to travel with this production, so understudies will be needed. Some of you will have to accept that role. Some of you will not be able to travel, and we understand that. With such a large cast, I will be asking some of you to learn two or more roles. The good news is that the playwright is coming to see the show."

This possibility excited everyone, including Jesse. It was not his way to stargaze, but this man was one of two people Jesse had ever wanted to meet. Unlike the others, Jesse heard this promise with some doubt. He had been in productions before when there was the promised arrival of a so-called star. They never showed. But still, Jesse allowed himself to believe that James Baldwin would come, and he would finally meet him.

The night before the play was to open and in the middle of the dress rehearsal, Mr. Baldwin walked through the door with an ever-present male assistant. He was diminutive and effeminate, with large glistening eyes. He wore a kufi with a paisley scarf draped daintily around his neck. Relatively high-heeled boots made little difference in terms of making him look taller, but at least they fit—nothing else did. Jesse wondered who dressed the great thinker. Everything stopped when Walter clapped his hands to get the group's attention. He placed a chair in the middle of the stage and introduced the playwright in nearly worshipful terms. Mr. Baldwin seemed genuinely embarrassed by this gushing, as his large mouth and teeth went involuntarily innocent. He sat down without unbuttoning his coat or removing his hat and quietly said, "Hello, I am happy to be here, and I am impressed by all of these bright eyes before me. It pleases me to see you working on my play which I wrote so many years ago. It may interest you to know that there is a kind of revival happening with this play all across the country. Walter has told me that you all are one of the best casts he has ever been associated with, so I am truly looking forward to seeing it . . . again."

He laughed warmly, boyishly. With this, he tossed his scarf nervously into the air, as if he did not know what else to say.

"Are there any questions?"

Some of the cast had never heard of him—that is to say, many had not read any of his work and did not know his significance as a voice for the people. They had no idea that a literary icon was sitting before them. Others were disturbed by his conspicuous femininity. Still others were stunned to silence by the starriness of his reputation. In any case, no one said anything. The group, for the most part, had positioned themselves an unfriendly distance from where he was sitting. Not true of Jesse. He sat on the floor close enough for a private conversation. He had many questions, but this was not the forum he would have chosen for the exchange. But he wanted to be remembered so that when and if the opportunity presented itself, a useful familiarity would be in place.

"Mr. Baldwin, my name is Jesse Brightmeyer. Thank you very much for coming. This is a great moment for me because you are someone I have always wanted to meet. I have read much of your work, and I want to thank you for your enormous contributions to the race and the country. But to my question . . ."

"Thank you," he said, interrupting purposefully, "and call me Jimmy. Now to your question." He smiled broadly.

"Can you tell us something about what I think you called 'a nationwide revival' of this play? Are these troupes in contact with each other?"

Jimmy answered the question thoughtfully, and the result was that the cast got a glimpse of his gentleness, his intelligence, and it opened them up.

After about a thirty-minute "conversation" with the cast, Walter announced that Jimmy had to leave, and they had to get back to work. Jimmy and his handsome young assistant left to a palpable buzz, as all of the actors now felt, somehow, more important. While the rehearsal was under way, Walter had his assistant pass a note to Jesse that said Jimmy had requested his presence at a gathering that very evening directly following the rehearsal. Jesse was pleased, but he did not want the sexual confusion he sensed in the way the message was delivered. When the rehearsal was over, he went quickly to Walter and said, "Walter, you did tell him who I am, didn't you? He knows I'm into women, right?"

"Yes, I told him, but he wants you to come anyway."

The gathering was a party for gay men. Well, only gay men were there, except for Walter and Jesse, and no one else from the cast. Clifford Fears hosted the party. He was the local dance authority, having danced with Katherine Dunham, Alvin Ailey, and other luminaries in his difficult craft. This bevy included the local black gay intelligentsia, none of whom Jesse had ever met before. There were no caricatures, no obnoxiously effeminate men. These were well-dressed men, all shiny and spotless. Most were degreed from prestigious institutions, and they felt comfortable, even entitled to be in the presence of the famous James Baldwin, who was himself not formally educated. It was as if his presence made them feel more accomplished. Jimmy, however, it seemed anyway, was only waiting for Jesse to arrive. Jesse was wearing a gray cashmere sweater, gray jeans, and his ever-present baseball cap. When he and Walter walked into the room, the music was annoyingly loud, and while people appeared to be talking to one another, it was unlikely that they could hear each other. Perhaps it was Walter's stately presence, but whatever the motivation, the music was lowered to a more conversational level when he and Jesse walked into the room.

As the introductions unfolded, Jesse experienced something he had never felt before. The eyes on him were hungry, piercing eyes, and the murmuring in the room was salacious and had the effect of making Jesse feel he was being treated like a woman. A desirable woman, yes, but there was no mistaking the nature or intentions of the chatter. He was, in their eyes, "a piece of meat." He did not know what to make of this, and so he behaved as if it was not happening.

"Boy, where did you get that sweater? I want that sweater." Clifford was in control of his territory.

"Maybe on another day," said Jesse, somewhat surprised at the audacious familiarity.

"So this is the fine young thang we've been hearing about." He was circling Jesse like he was an auction piece.

"Well, Jimmy, he sho' is fine. Look like somethin' good to eat, and black as coal." He enjoyed lapsing into the entertaining ghettoese.

"I'll get back to you on that," said Jimmy, all aglow that this piece of meat was here to see him.

Jesse, of course, did not know what to make of any of this. When the splash of his entry was over, the evening became an interesting spectacle of amazingly diverse points of view and lively debate. After a time, certain men insisted on reading their poetry or essays to Jimmy. He listened politely and, at their behest, gave some mildly constructive criticism.

During this phase of the night, which lasted much too long, Jimmy had found his way to where Jesse was sitting on the floor. He sat close enough to touch him occasionally and seductively. His touches were like that of a woman, and for the moment, Jesse did not resist them. The other men in the room noticed this, and the envy in the room was thick. The stares of these men became hot in a very different way, and hissing gossip began. They suggested Jesse was a gold digger and an opportunist. Their envy was a kind of harmless hatred, but Jesse did not notice this. He was instead genuinely interested in talking to the man whose writing had touched him so deeply.

They talked well into the morning about many things, but mostly themselves. It was very much like the early conversations of courtship. They discovered that both of them had been young Christian ministers, they had disliked their fathers (Jimmy thought it ironic that Jesse disliked the man who was responsible for introducing him to his work), and both of them were holding rage at bay just behind polite demeanors. They were "mamma's boys," and this alone felt like grounds for a relationship. Jesse talked at length about his boys, how much he missed them, and that his absence from them was not part of the plan and was, after the death of his mother, the most painful part of his life. Jesse wanted to go home, back to his family but did not know how.

Jimmy, of course, while famous, had considerable pain of his own. Jesse, on the other hand, was trying to find his way and was currently lost. Jimmy knew that most people were lost. Jesse's despair was ordinary, and though this had been pointed out many times, for the first time, Jesse heard it put in other terms, in a context that did not hurt him. Jimmy's mastery of the language allowed him to say things in such a way that it provoked new thought and introspection within the deepest part of Jesse. It did not stay his pain or lift him from his emotional morass, but it gave him another helpful point of view.

At some point, people began to leave, and small private conversations erupted, like little geysers in the room. Eventually they were alone in the room, and Jimmy's touching continued. He rubbed Jesse hands and feet, touched his face. He told Jesse he was beautiful and sexy. Jesse did not bolt. He said simply and plainly, "Jimmy, I am not gay. I do not sleep with men. This has been a fine night, and I certainly enjoyed spending time with you, but you need to know that I am as hopelessly heterosexual as you are homosexual."

Jesse had been anticipating this sentence since the night began. Having gotten it out, he felt better. He had been honest about who he was; it had been a good night, and now he was ready to go home.

"Nothing could be more obvious," Jimmy said with a laugh, undeterred. "But even so, perhaps you would like to join me on the road. I have many stops to make around the world, and my agent thinks I need handling. He, and my dearest friends, believe me to have control problems."

The laughter was either genuine or well-practiced.

"I'm being sardonic of course, but I really could use some help."

Jesse's first thought was that he would be so far from his sons. He had begun calling himself an actor, and he considered the possibility that this move could make a difference in his theatrical career. Jimmy had been very complimentary of Jesse's skill as an actor, comparing him to a young Ossie Davis. He led Jesse to believe that there would be many opportunities to perform and "hasten his walk into the limelight." Jesse did not get caught up in the half-promises, as Jimmy's actual motives were not lost on him. Jesse was no stargazer and had very little interest in fame or money, but he was running from something, so he considered getting on this train.

"Let me think about it. How do I reach you?"

Numbers were exchanged. Jesse had only Allison's number to share, while Jimmy released the names and numbers of his agent, his brother, and his houses in New York and France. As Jesse prepared to leave, it dawned on him that he would be leaving Marlena again, and he began to muse about all of the people, who, even in his treachery, he cared about and did not want to hurt. But the thread he clung to was greased, and his grip on it was tenuous. He was indeed falling, and apathy engulfed him like the succubus; some force beyond his will was at work.

"So we'll be in touch. Thank you for a nice evening."

Jesse extended his hand to engage the male "goodbye" ritual.

"You could at least give me a hug, my fangs are in the suit case," he said, his wizened face brightly shining.

Jesse smiled and opened his arms. Jimmy held him tightly and kissed his cheek. The hug was uncomfortably long for Jesse. He released Jimmy, grabbed his shoulders, and gently pushed him away. This was a familiar gesture for Jesse, but never with a man in his arms.

CHAPTER 8

The Lord Makes a Way

Jesse's mother had been in and out of the hospital for nearly a year. This meant that Jesse had made many trips without his wife to see about his mother. Even before these protracted absences, his duties as a shepherd took him away from home for awkwardly long periods. Beverly, as a young wife and mother, needed him as much as the congregation, and Jesse was not as aware of this as he should have been. In this faith, one had to serve the Lord without financial compensation. The need to feed the family mattered, but nothing came before serving the Lord. The real devotees, of which Jesse was one, had no free time. There were constant mid-evening to late night visitations to brothers and sisters, sheep who needed tending. The sick, both physically and spiritually, had to be served. Jesse was diligent in this at the sacrifice of his young wife.

He thought that he had struck a balance between Jehovah's work and family life, but sadly, he had not. A discomfort, a tension crept in between Beverly and Jesse, and soon the quiet and mild woman became bitter and vituperative, slinging accusations and unpleasantries at Jesse. He tried to use his gentleness, and well-honed ministerial logic, the same as he used when talking to other troubled couples in the church. It did not have the same effect, or perhaps it did, and now, for the first time, he was seeing how ineffectual this shtick was, having to live with it himself. Beverly did not love him. Even she had not fully grasped this fact. She was reasonably fond of him, and it helped that she no longer lived with an overbearing mother. She had "won the prize" and enjoyed the acclaim and envy of the sisters, but they did not have to live with a man who seemed more devoted to them and the Lord than to his own wife. Where was the "forsaking all others?" Jesse saw the arrangement as unfolding just as the theocratic prenuptials had suggested. Together they would do the work of the Lord.

Beverly had come from a family whose culture, outside of Christian devotion, was completely antithetical to Jesse's. There had been little, or no, affection in her house. There was no emphasis on reading anything accept the *Watchtower*—the dominant monthly periodical that shaped the thinking of all Jehovah's Witnesses. The examination of cultural matters, the hearty debates, the joy of nature, the recognition of all the little things in life, and the study of them, were missing within her family. There was something about Jesse that unsettled her. Perhaps he was too popular, too smart, more attractive to others than he was to her; he was certainly not as attentive as her needs required. Whatever it was lessened his attractiveness to her. In any case, the fact that she no longer had to cope with a demanding, narrow-minded mother and the limited possibilities of her upbringing began, slowly, to free up her thinking. She now, for what must have been the first time in her life, had thoughts of her own. They were not clearly defined thoughts, but they were burgeoning on the edge of her mind, and she was trying to ferret through her new possibilities. Arguments erupted daily, and they seemed to come from nowhere. But indeed they came from a store well that was now ready to be opened.

On one of the occasions when Jesse felt the need to visit his mother, he announced a few days prior that he would be going. She did not want to go with him. His absence provided opportunities to further investigate a future with Tommy, an exciting opportunity for a woman who had completely missed the rites of teen hood-that and the fact that she was typically ignored by Jesse's family who now saw her as only a pretty, hypersensitive woman without much to contribute, gave her good reason to stay home. It was a Friday.

"I'll be back tomorrow at about six o'clock. Do you need anything before I go?" This was more perfunctory than sincere. Beverly knew it.

"No."

He hugged and kissed his sons, who were three and five years old. "You guys take good care of your mother. Daddy will be back tomorrow." Before leaving, they wrestled, and he gave them their exciting elephant ride. Jesse would put them on his back and sway left and right while making fairly convincing sounds of the great beast. The boys would howl with delight. "That's enough for now. We'll have some fun when I get back." Whenever Jesse touched his boys, which was all of the time, he would remember his mother's touch, and his joy was compounded.

When he got there, Frankie and all of the children were present. Madelyn was lying comfortably on her bed, and her children had gathered around it. Since Jesse's move to Grand Rapids, he did not see his siblings very often, so these visits gave Jesse badly needed contact with his past. They were all adults now, and Madelyn, gazing happily on her offspring, could fully assess her handiwork. Ashton had grown to be nearly as beautiful as Franklin, but he had no apparent interest in his appearance. He did not wear suits or shine his shoes. He was, or rather, he had become a family man. This was a somewhat astonishing development. As the last born, he had missed much of the educational nurturing under which the others had thrived. He got as much motherly attention as any of the children, but Brightmeyer was—it is fair to say it this way—distracted by the time Ashton came along. Ashton had received the most brutal corporal punishment, none of which impacted him in a way anyone could see. He took Brightmeyer's violent lashings as if nothing was occurring.

Instead he found his lessons in the streets. He did, it could be argued, what his father had demanded, "I don't care what you choose to do, just be the best at it." Ashton ruled the streets. He led a pack of hoodlums. Jesse had told his mother on several occasions to prepare for his funeral.

"Momma, he will never see twenty-one."

Such had been the level of his violent aggression. The family was, in the early days, before simply accepting it, surprised by this. There was a festering wonder about Ashton. He was brutally violent and absolutely fearless. He had a legend of his own born out of havoc and intimidation. One day he and his thuggish followers assaulted a boy at their high school, and this fellow was a prideful gangster in his own right. This boy gathered his troops and marched to the Brightmeyer home armed with sticks, chains, and knives. They called him out with blatant threats, but he was asleep. Madelyn, on the other hand, saw and heard this commotion, and was more incredulous than alarmed. Out to the porch she went, armed with the power of the Lord and the strength of righteousness, literally with Bible in hand. The mob, some ten to fifteen strong, hurled insults at her and dared Ashton to come out. The storm and chain rattling became loud enough to awaken him. Ashton came calmly, but aggressively, down the stairs and, with utter fearlessness, grabbed a chain from his arsenal (hidden somewhere in the house), swung the door open with malicious intent, and said, "Which one of you mothafuckas want to be first? Shit, all ya'll come on up here. It's gon' to take a whole lot more than what you got to fuck with me."

Madelyn was, of course, shocked, but she said with equal confidence in her voice, almost as if her son had not just shamed her, "The Bible encourages us to be peaceful and to love one another. Why don't you young men sit with me and talk about what's bothering you?"

"Talk, my ass," said Ashton, heading into the midst of them, "Ah'mo put some foot in these punks."

She grabbed his arm and, with a mother's touch, held him there.

I have no way of knowing which of them actually quelled the madness, but the mob backed sheepishly away. She brought Ashton into the house and gave him the sermon the thwarted gang had no time to hear.

But now Ashton was married and had children of his own, and while he lacked the overtly affectionate mien of the rest of his family, he was all business and ready to do whatever his beloved mother needed.

As they made themselves comfortable in the room, sitting on the bed or in the two upholstered armchairs, they talked primarily for their mother's benefit about what they were doing with their lives.

How Madelyn's grandchildren were doing, trips they had taken, how Allison's marriage was going, and so on.

Eventually the conversation turned to their mother's condition and the pressing matter of getting her to a hospital in New York for some special treatment. Who would accompany her? What about accommodations? And underneath these logistics, there was the unstated but palpable resignation that their mother was in great trouble. She needed a kidney transplant. Healthy, matching organs were difficult to find, but that was not the problem.

Madelyn's devotion to her Jehovah dictated that this procedure would offend Him, so she never even considered it. She would seek alternatives, but her love for Him and her faith in His promise—"You will be changed in the twinkling of an eye"—would not let her submit to "cannibalism." Her love of life was renowned but "What is death to a Christian?" she said. Jesse understood this. He had read the *Watchtower* too. At this moment, he was not disturbed. He knew, with certainty, that her god—his god, would not take her from him. He prayed in earnest, as he always did.

The plans were made. They would all drive her to New York. Rosalind and Allison would stay with her, and the boys would return home to perform the local necessities in their absence. The girls who were predictably wonderful cooks, prepared a meal, and there was more of the typical Brightmeyer family exchanges at the dining room table, happy talk about the past, the future, and the work of the Lord. Soon, it was five o'clock on Saturday afternoon. Jesse got confidently on the road, anticipating a peaceful drive home. It was his nature to sing aloud when he was alone. He would write songs as he went, usually committing them to memory. The drive was without incident, but when he opened the door to his house, Beverly attacked.

"You said you were going to be home at six, and it's seven-thirty." She was livid. Jesse could not believe she was as angry as she was.

"Are you happy to see me?" he said, reaching for a hug he knew he was no longer entitled to.

"That's not the point," she bellowed. "Where have you been?"

"You know where I have been. Why are you so angry? I was with my family 150 miles away. I'm an hour and half late, what is the big deal?"

The false fight was on. Well, it was not much of a fight, in that it was not Jesse's way to do so, but it gave him much to consider. These fights were becoming more frequent. To Jesse they seemed to be about the unsaid. Beverly was trying to say something that she could not find words for. She would blurt out, "Well, why don't you divorce me?" as if that was a solution of some kind. This had never occurred to Jesse, and it did not resonate the first dozen or so times she said it. He thought at first that it was a young wife's way of getting reassurance, but nothing he said reassured her.

CHAPTER 9

That's My Kind of Crazy!

She came sashaying across the room as if she expected everyone to notice her. Jesse did. The blue dress, clinging and agreeing with her every move, called his name as she went. He said to Jeno, "Would you look at that!?"

"What?" He said, expectantly, for they were always on the prowl.

"The blue dress coming this way."

"Oh lord," he said, with no joy in his tone. Clearly he knew something, and he was perfectly willing to tell it.

"That woman is crazy. She's been trying to talk to Jimmy for months."

"Well, she may be crazy, but that dress ain't." Jesse was drooling.

She made a beeline, as much as one could be made in this crowded auditorium, to where they were riveted—Jimmy being as he was, held captive by admirers. She went directly to Jeno, and he seemed to hemorrhage at the prospect.

Jimmy Baldwin was one of the world's great thinkers. He had published many books, plays, and essays. He was revered as, if not the conscience of the black community, its clearest voice on issues of race and culture. He had seen Jesse perform in one of his plays and thought he would seduce the young hopeful. He was a star of sorts and was accustomed to reeling young men into his stable. Jeno was one of these boys. He and his agent had "hired" Jesse to accompany him to do his bidding, during a six-month-long speaking tour. They traveled the country going from university to university, disturbing people with provocative dissertations. He was sold out everywhere they went.

"Hi," she said, with great expectations. "You remember me."

"Yeah, I remember you," said Jeno, dripping regret at the memory while doing a poor job of trying not to show it.

"Well, you know I have been calling for an appointment for weeks. You, for good reasons, I'm sure, have not gotten around to returning my calls." Her words were crisp and matter of fact.

Jeno was happy to point in Jesse's direction.

"You've got to go through him," he said, with relief and treachery in his voice. "He handles Jimmy's affairs now."

Her face lit up as she saw Jesse for the first time.

"Hmm, I think I would like to talk to him," she said, her emphasis on "him" being the first of many flirtations.

"I guess the gods favor me today," said Jesse, engaging the game. As he said this, he exposed his stunning teeth, using the tool the world of women had told him so much about. She added to the chorus.

"Wow, what a beautiful smile," she said, "shining under all of that pretty black skin."

She seemed surprised. Jesse thought perhaps she was just "selling" to have her way with Jimmy while fully enjoying the sparks between them. "Listen," she said, as if he was not going to, "my name is Ramona. People call me Mona, and I host a radio show called *New Directions*, and I have been trying to get Mr. Baldwin on my show for some time now, and your friend has been ignoring my calls."

She was talking fast, but it was her style; she was not nervous. There was that clear ring of intelligence in her voice, and she knew it. She flaunted it. This woman had, at least on the surface, much to be desired. The scent of rose came rising off her, and she gestured like one who knows how and was accustomed to getting what she wanted. Jeno walked indifferently away. Jesse's response, on the other hand, was to decide, immediately, to have this woman, to have her in every way he could. It appeared to be quite a mutual decision.

"So what can *you* do for me?"

"What is your wish, my queen?"

My queen? He had even surprised himself.

"Well," she said, "this is promising. You recognize my royal presence."

"I am well raised, my dear."

"A glass of fine merlot, a lobster dinner, a light dessert, and an evening of stimulating conversation, would do nicely. And oh, you can come too if you like."

Jesse flashed those teeth again, a warm smile at her play, and said without hesitating, "Only if it pleases you."

This was all a welcome change from the usual "roady" sexual pursuits to which Jesse and Jeno were accustomed. They were always only that—an opportunity on a stairwell or some dark little room for id sake.

"I am not certain it will please me, but it would please me greatly to find out."

"I'll see what I can do. We all have to eat." And he turned to rescue Jimmy from the adoring masses. Jimmy was clearly ready to go, and it was high on Jesse's list of duties to save Jimmy when he needed to be saved. Jimmy was not very comfortable extricating himself. He really believed that these people, his fans, wanted answers, and that he could show them the way.

"Excuse me, ladies and gentlemen. I have got to get Mr. Baldwin to his next adventure. I know this is abrupt, but it always is, you understand . . ."

No one actually heard him, but they certainly saw him take Jimmy's arm, gather his things, and begin pressing toward the door, which appeared to be one hundred yards away and littered with worshipers. Cards and slips of paper with phone numbers and barely legible scribble came flying at Jesse from every direction. Everyone wanted more time, their own private time with the great thinker. In this auditorium, only Ramona would get it.

Jimmy was a small man in his mid-fifties who appeared frail. He was, in fact by now, after years of abusing himself with liquor, cigarettes, reckless boys, and sleepless nights. Now approaching sixty, he was truly in need of assistance, many kinds of assistance if he was to keep the demanding speaking schedule. He tired easily unless he was in front of an audience. There was no longer much strength left in his arms or legs for carrying luggage, books, or anything of weight. Such burdens would wear him down quickly, having used his brain and not his appendages to make his way through life. What is more he was a good man with a deeply rooted wish to please what he called "his people," the forsaken, those clamoring for another view of themselves. There was an enormous amount of pain in him, and these people with their hungry minds and faces, so longing for his wisdom, somehow released it. Jesse loved and admired him and was sensitive to his peculiarities. Most of the time, if Jesse did not save him, he would get no rest or food.

Ramona, when her time came, grabbed Jimmy and held him like a long-lost brother. She kissed him, without fawning, ever so sweetly on his mouth. He was moved by this behavior, and it certainly made it easy for Jesse to get this woman to the dinner table.

Dinner was a hit. All, even Jeno to some extent, had a good time. At some point he forgave her for not falling for his clumsy wiles, which is all he meant when he called her a "crazy woman." It was a charmed evening with intellectual banter and discussion around classical literature, theater, and, of course, the state of the race. "Call me Jimmy," he said with a huge boyish grin, and that set the tone. They drank and talked into the night. They laughed and for once and for whatever reason, Jimmy did not seem to mind the conspicuous attention being shown to Jesse by a woman. This had been a point of contention since Jesse and Jimmy met. Jimmy was entirely open about his homosexuality, and Jesse was equally blatant about his devotion to women. He had been very clear about this with Jimmy when the invitation to join him on the road had been offered. In all of the letters and phone calls between them, Jesse had felt the need to be emphatic about this gulf between them. Jimmy had assured him that there were no deals. He was not asking Jesse for sex or romance. "I enjoy your recalcitrant mind," he would say. This was believable to Jesse as he liked his mind too. But that all changed on the road. Jimmy would make many efforts to embrace Jesse in ways he could not countenance. This created a tension that would, in the end, be the undoing of the relationship. But tonight

Ramona's charm or the wine, the scotch—something made all things right on this happy evening.

"Well, what a lovely evening this has been," she said, sounding the bell. "Now it's time for you beautiful black men to take me home." They were all ready and not ready at once. They had a long drive before them to get home, some ninety miles to Amherst. The winning chatter continued all the way to her apartment. She kissed Jesse and Jimmy but shook Jeno's hand playfully. Even this was a sparkling moment.

"Jimmy, you have so many, can I keep this one?" she said, grabbing Jesse's hand.

"I don't have that one," Jimmy admitted with no apparent bitterness.

Jesse walked her to her door, three flights up. Jesse could not imagine anyone living like this, having to walk three flights to your front door every day with whatever one had to carry. But this did not seem to faze Ramona or the thousands of people in this area who had this trek to make every day. She opened her door and asked him to come in. It was all he could do to not send Jeno and Jimmy home without him, but he knew that would be going too far. He kissed her, wet, deliberate, and crippling. They looked at each other as if they knew something that did not need to be said. There were no numbers to share. That had been done at dinner. Jesse promised to call and did so that night when he got home. They talked for hours, and something was born from them. Two weeks later, she found her way to Amherst, and they spent the next five years together. They were stormy and reckless years, for they had been swept away from their senses by an evening to be remembered and choices they could not forget.

CHAPTER 10

Frankie and the Kids

Jesse did not remember meeting him or seeing him for the first time. As it should be, I suppose. A brother, certainly an older one, is simply there, always there. Franklin was the first born and benefited from the honors historically assigned to this lucky progeny. He was treated like a prince, and it could be said that he earned it, in that he was truly special in the way an older brother should be. Protective and warm, he played with his younger brothers and sisters happily and willingly, at least until the girls discovered him. He did not resemble his mother, but he was beautiful in the way she was. To Jesse he did not resemble anything, or anyone—he was like a growing thing in the garden. It seemed to Jesse that he was unlike other living things. He seemed larger than other people and made differently. He was sculpted or created like art, and in spite of his foreboding size, he was gentle and graceful, he was pleasant and harmless but very protective of his family. These attributes were bothersome to other males, who saw him as a kind of challenge. They needed to climb this mountain, to surmount him, defeat him in some way. He appeared to have no anger in him. If that reflex was there, it was more often than not overcome by his love of play, a zest for life, and a genuine affection for others that was exceedingly attractive. The bullies, who unceasingly challenged him, always to lose, would invariably become his friends, or more accurately, his minions. He was so capable of physical harm that Madelyn feared he would commit some, so she insisted that he not fight, that he "be nice." And he was. Somehow a legend grew around him. He demonstrated an "otherworldly" ability in athletics. He had a natural skill with knives, balls, bats, and all things sports. He was not at all like Allison, his baby sister, whose contribution to the young prince was to do his homework. There were no sharp intellectual leanings or desires in him. His pleasures were primarily physical, and at an early age this was discovered by women—not only girls, but women. Not to say that the girls were not moved, only to say they did not know what they were feeling.

This prowess did not impress Brightmeyer. He was proud of Franklin in the way one is proud to own a grand stallion, but his real joy was in the formidable intelligence of his daughters. For Madelyn, Franklin was, if not her favorite child, the one she treasured. He was in so many ways what his father was not. He was compellingly beautiful in an Ibo African kind of way: black of skin with ridiculously perfect proportions. A considerable part of his legend was based solely on his appearance. Often, people—neighbors, children, males and females—could be found staring at him as if they were seeing something, a new species, for the first time. Madelyn was told repeatedly by friends and family, "Sister, that boy is going to be a lady-killer." It was said seductively, with a promise of excitement. Jesse would hear this warning often, so much that for years the word "killer" had a pleasant association in his mind.

Madelyn found a way to use him and teach him at the same time, as she did with all of her children. He was her pack mule, her confidant, her constant companion, and she taught him gentleness, kindness, and generosity. And she tried by example to show him that women needed to be honored and respected. She also spoiled him horribly. So much so, that she and her children served him as if he were royalty. They ran his bathwater and cleaned the tub after him. Brightmeyer, Madelyn, and all of the children, quite happily it seemed, made certain that whatever there was to eat, wear, or do, he got the best of it. Shining his shoes and ironing his clothes was, for a time, recreation for his siblings. They were justly rewarded for this devotion. Franklin had learned his lessons well (all of this family did) and treated his family to all manner of goods as his resources would allow. At an early age, he became employed, and he would bring gifts to his mother and trinkets for his younger siblings. He made nearly every day a holiday—with storytelling and gift giving. As the oldest, he got to attend movies long before the rest of the children. After each visit to a movie, he would come home and repeat it, actually perform it, for his brothers and sisters in such a way that it took many visits to the theater before they understood that moviemaking was anything more than fodder for their big brother. No movie star could bring a character to life like Franklin. He was adored by his siblings and by Jesse most of all. Franklin and his mother, by virtue of their very existence, gave Jesse his first conscious view of pretty, and every other beautiful thing, animate or inanimate, would be measured against them.

Like all healthy children, these were actively curious youngsters. It was not possible for so large a family to subsist on a single income.

Actually what was earned by Brightmeyer on either of his jobs could scarcely be called income. It took three sources of income for this family to approach a life style that Brightmeyer had envisioned for his offspring. Madelyn worked cleaning houses for other families. This meant that the children were sometimes home alone. Franklin was the oldest, but he was not given the responsibilities of the surrogate parent. That assignment went to Rosalind, who had a natural inclination toward leadership but brought with it a tyrannical edge. She was the firstborn girl, as stately as her parents but lacked the cuteness; the prettiness that Allison had. She was equally bright and more dutiful than any of the children, and the adults considered it nearly unlucky that she had not been the firstborn. She took to the role of "mother" with a verve that unnerved Allison, who was less than two years her junior, her intellectual equal, and every bit as independent and self-motivated. What discord there was in this family was centered here. Rosalind took her assignment seriously—aiming to please her parents. But alas, power corrupts, and those without power have a built-in resentment to those with it. With Allison, this resentment bubbled forth daily, or so it seemed.

This was not the case with the boys. Frankie, as the kids called him, was above the rules, given his princely status, Jesse was a relentlessly happy child who found fun in practically every assignment given, and Ashton was only recently relieved of his diapers. But when either parent returned from the rigors of the day, they would have to hear about the clashes, always involving the two girls.

CHAPTER 11

Can I Get a Witness?

All religions have their peculiarities. The one to which Jesse's family had linked itself was chosen for them by his mother—Jehovah's Witnesses. She found something about this faith that satisfied her in a way that the Baptist religion of her parents did not. There were many rewarding moments growing up with them. They were a dedicated and basically kind people who took worship very seriously, but Bible study even more so. They excluded others, however, as many sects do, and there was extreme punishment for breaking the rules: public humiliations with lofty-sounding designations. You could be put on probation, "disfellowshipped", and all of this before a shamed, devoted congregation. These and other disciplines would be exacted when one was found guilty of "conduct unbecoming a Christian." There was a strong emphasis placed on being good, being righteous. The reward for this behavior and devotion to the rules was to be everlasting life in an earthly paradise. This was attractive, even to a seven-year-old, perhaps especially to a seven-year-old. Jesse was raised within the narrow confines of this culture. Good behavior came easily to Jesse, as he had no bad inclinations. He was, as his mother had recognized, an intrinsically good boy.

Over the years, he had taken his theocratic lessons seriously enough to have risen through the ranks and was, by the age of twenty, a highly respected member of the "society." His rise, locally in any case, was likely enhanced by his appearance. He was, according to his mother, a pretty boy, but it turned out others thought so too. She had been putting him in business suits since he was seven or eight years old, and now his clothes fit him deliberately; he liked wearing them, and he had inherited good taste. He had been speaking in public before adult audiences since he was a boy and was now a very accomplished orator. He was sought after for speaking engagements at weddings, funerals, and didactic ecclesiastical deliveries. Jesse had become a minister.

His instinctive kindness had become well known, and his mother was consistently being congratulated for having raised so thoughtful a son. He cared for the sick and the aging, doing so willingly and cheerfully. There were many occasions when he would go sit with the elderly, simply giving them someone to talk to, bringing them food and other comforts without being asked to do so. This he would do even for some of their older neighbors who did not share his faith. After having shoveled the snow for an elderly "sister," in what was for him an ordinary act of kindness, his mother was approached by one of the church elders.

"There's more than one way to give a witness," the older gentleman said, "and your son is a gift to the Lord's work. He is a true blessing."

For Madelyn and Jesse, he was simply doing what he ought to do as a shepherd of the flock. He remembered and embraced, as if it was his life's mission, the self-deprecating words of the Messiah, "You are a good-for-nothing slave. What you have done is what you ought to have done." But in reality, it was genuinely who he was.

When requested to speak at weddings and funerals, he would bring comfort and unprecedented insights to both, talking about love, forgiveness, patience, and long-suffering in ways that suggested a man given wisdom beyond his twenty-five years. He was, it seemed, an authority on all things loving, as children and animals were drawn to his gentleness and a spirit of loving-kindness.

It was as if there was only goodness in him, a child born with a natural selflessness that, while his mother was aware of it, even she did not know what to make of it. She was simply proud as she watched her tree-climbing little boy become a man, a pastor who simply shepherded the many sheep placed in his care.

During this time, the happiest of his life, he was an exemplary student of the Bible and a servant of his god and His people, an evangelist spreading the gospel to all who would listen. It was a time of contentment supported by the sublime pleasure of innocence, familial encouragement, and the unwavering knowledge that he was doing the will of God while giving his mother further evidence of the wisdom of her devotion. He was the good husband, the good father, and the good son. He had become all he ever wanted to be.

The congregations or churches of this religion were typically small—one to two hundred members. Any more than that and they would divide like a primal organism. In this way, they would measure their growth. My, how they grew, fanning out across the city, the state, and the country, preaching the word as they went. They were old and young, black, white, Hispanic, and they bragged about having representatives in fifty-three, seventy-eight, 103 . . .

lands around the globe. They would stage large assemblies, where zealots and members would come from all across the globe in a show of spiritual strength.

In 1975, such an event was staged in Chicago at Comiskey Park. Jesse was invited to speak at this convention before an audience of fifty thousand or so. There were not very many people his age who were given such high responsibility, and almost no blacks. Madelyn was as proud as she could possibly be, seeing her Jesse so respected and so committed to the Lord, enough to be invited to speak before so large a family of true believers. The forty-minute "talk," as these sermons were called, gave the attendees, especially the black ones, a feeling of comfort and deepened their faith in Jehovah. Madelyn, being the mother of this young servant, was received throughout the four-day affair with the honor reserved for the mother of the prince.

A young minister in any community holds a high rank. But in a poor black community, he is very much like royalty. He was considered smart, handsome, respected, and this young prince was single. What is more, he was well liked, bright, and devoted to Jehovah. By now, even Jesse considered himself a servant of the Lord. He was sought after for prayer and study groups. He took the lead in door-to-door evangelizing. He exorcised demons and preached the word to all who would listen. He was considered a supreme catch, and the young "sisters" knew it. They were conspicuous in their pursuit of him and, given his upbringing and his genuine devotion to Jehovah, he didn't even know it. His sisters did, and they were virtually "hounded" by the young women who could get to them.

"Tell me about your brother."

"Does he have a girlfriend?"

"When is his next talk?"

"May I have your phone number?"

Rosalind and especially Allison took a good deal of pride in having such an admired and pursued brother. His humility, or rather his ignorance, about his worthiness made it all the easier for them to orchestrate dates and virtually conduct interviews. Jesse was not yet a ladies' man.

On a particular Sunday, he was assigned to give what his religion called a talk, a Sunday sermon. The subject, not that it mattered, was the importance of love and long-suffering. This was something about which Jesse considered himself an authority. He knew and understood love because he had been showered with it all of his life. He had suffered nothing, so tolerating others was simple enough, and he had, obviously, excerpts from the great book to support his position. There is nothing like preaching to the choir. As long as one stayed within the finely honed teachings of the "organization," one is considered to have done well. But Jesse, given the influence of his very dramatic family, and having grown up watching Frankie's incredible performances, brought something else to the podium. His sisters had made certain that he spoke English professorially. They, well, Allison, coordinated his tie, handkerchief, and socks, and his mother was a constant encouragement.

When Jesse took the stage, after a suitable introduction by one of the older brothers, he was silent a moment longer than is recommended, and it provided great dramatic effect. He panned the audience and saw the unusual number of lovely young women. These suitors had come from afar to see and meet this young star. He saw his mother beaming, and the light from her eyes made it impossible for him to do anything but shine. He delivered a riveting conversational discussion that warmed the hall and achieved his primary goal, which was to see his mother smile.

How his sisters decided which of the young ladies would be invited to their home to meet him was not known to Jesse. To be sure, there were enough to pick from. They wore their best outfits and were appropriately attentive, taking notes and nodding in a timely fashion. When it was over, there was the requisite discussion of the high points of the talk. These people were dedicated students after all, not simply worshipers. Given their intellectual nature, perhaps this was the litmus test used by his sisters.

The woman who showed up, with her own sister in tow, was remarkably pretty. She was quiet in the extreme, but when she talked, she said all of the things a young Christian girl was supposed to say. To Jesse, she epitomized the "quiet and mild spirit" a young servant of the Lord should be looking for. It did not occur to Jesse to consider other girls. This is the one that his sisters had delivered, and she would do. After all, a wife is chosen to assist you in doing the work of the Lord. They courted for about a year, finding true love in the sinews of their common faith and were married to the promise of everlasting life.

This is the spirituality he brought to his marriage. He had found in Beverly the love he had become accustomed to, gentle and calm. In her he found a love so deep and joy so overwhelming, and such was his devotion to Jehovah that he "forsook all things" for the sake of the Lord. His misgivings about much of the esoteric doctrine were set aside as he immersed himself completely in the mercies and promises of "the truth," as he and all of the followers referred to their religion.

He found himself adoring his god, and his time among the fellow believers. He was unceasingly happy, even to the point of incredulity. He was an innocent with no bad in him. As attractive and obvious as this was when he was a boy, it flourished irresistibly as he became a young man.

There was a messianic edge to his joy, believing as he did that he was bringing the word of the Lord to the wayward masses, and he would receive his reward in an earthly paradise where his gladness would be extended throughout all eternity. So complete was his faithfulness that he would pray, thankfully, to his god for providing him with a lovely wife with whom he could intimately couple to experience the unsurpassed joy of sex. This he would do with the regularity and conviction seen normally when Christians pray over food at mealtime.

CHAPTER 12

Sentenced

The sixties were times of great unrest. Civil and racial discontent cracked and erupted all across the country. Rioting in major cities was common, and around the world, the planet virtually heaved under the pressure of revolution. "Saviors" appeared in every social stratum as the American quilt began to unravel. The war raged in Vietnam as the Western block of nations sent troops to do its devilish work. Young people were being conscripted to die to the beat of generals while mothers all across the land did what they could to keep their babies home. Everywhere there was violent discontent and resistance took many forms. Everywhere except among the self-proclaimed "servants of Jehovah." These people were above or beneath the fray. It is not as if they were oblivious. No, the unrest meant to them that the end of the world was upon us, and soon a new order of things would be ushered in. The Son of their good god was coming, on a cloud, to bring salvation to his loyal subjects, which of course, excluded everyone but them.

Amid these wonderful expectations, Jesse was called, like thousands of others, to go fight for the country of his birth. Even in the absence of his commitment to the Lord, Jesse would never have considered going to war, but given his adopted beliefs, he could stand righteously against it. He was a minister opposed to violence; he was opposed to war, not just this one, but all war. War was the purview of his god, "Jehovah of armies," and he fights them in his own time.

Jesse's conscientious objections carried a price. He was to be incarcerated, but the prisons were full. The state, however has "many mansions" of its own, and Jesse was assigned to work in a hospital for twenty-four months, at minimum wage, in the city of Grand Rapids, Michigan. There he would move with his new wife to carry on the Lord's work amid this very satisfying Christian sacrifice. To be punished by the "world" was almost certain proof that one was favored by God, so Jesse, and all in the faith who knew him, considered this martyrdom further evidence of his unalterable devotion to Jehovah.

Grand Rapids was a small city when compared to Detroit. Its ethnicity was decidedly Dutch, and it had the distinction of having more churches and venereal disease per capita than any other city in Michigan or the country, I cannot recall, but you get the point. It was also known as one of the finest places to raise a family, and these were about the only things Jesse knew about the place before moving there. He made his arrival known to the local body of Jehovah's Witnesses, where he was welcomed like a brother. After all of the rounds and introductions, Jesse found a place to stay.

The good brothers there were amazed and embarrassed to discover the level of racism in their town, or at least they acted that way. Jesse had never lived in a "white" neighborhood, but the local brethren as much as insisted that he stay among them, and this, again, given his upbringing, was fine with him.

He nestled in and made friends with the local Christian leadership. Soon he was recognized as one of the leaders among them, and life settled into a fairly familiar Christian routine. His wife had stayed behind while he found accommodations and got situated in the new town. He returned to Detroit to pick her up, with the understanding that they would return home after the twenty-four months of "sacrifice" had been served. Another point of interest about the city of Grand Rapids is that people who moved there temporarily tended to stay. This is what happened with Beverly and Jesse; their two boys were born and raised in this community.

This is where the happy life of Jesse Brightmeyer was to continue, and for several years that is the way it was. Jesse did his time at the hospital with integrity and without complaint. It was, as it unfolded, the last of his happy years. The birth of his sons provided him with a happiness, a satisfaction, that was beyond measuring. He called his mother on their birthdays, and those days became, for him, holidays. His children, as with all children born into a loving family, were the highlight of his life. He talked to them while they were fetuses, which of course allowed for the greatest intimacies with his wife with whom Jesse, like the good servant he was, had had no premarital sex. When they entered the world, he read to them even when they were too young to understand. He played and frolicked with them at such a level that Beverly felt she had three boys. Jesse was happy. He was doing just what his mother had wished him to, and it all seemed good.

Then, one evening while he was at their place of worship, greeting the members and preparing the place for that evening's lessons, a phone call came in for him. This was not only unusual, it had never happened before. The call was from Rosalind, announcing that his mother was desperately ill and that he should come home as soon as he could. This news startled Jesse and unsettled him in the most visible way. He began breathing deeply as if gasping for air, and the coldest of sweats showed all over him—his face looked as if someone had thrown a bucket of water on it. He began to weep uncontrollably. This had the effect of upsetting everyone who saw him, but especially Beverly. She did not weep, but she very nervously, on the edge of panic, began to gather the children and prepare to leave. Jesse finally calmed down, and he, along with his young family, set out for Detroit immediately.

They arrived too late. Madelyn had been hospitalized and could not be visited at ten o'clock in the evening, which was their time of arrival. Rosalind, Allison, and Frankie were at their mother's house, talking plainly and solemnly about their mother's condition. (Ashton now lived in Cleveland and had not yet arrived). She had been sick for some time, and the disease had progressed rapidly, and without immediate intervention, she might die. In the presence of the family, Jesse was able to stay his tears, but it felt as if the blood in his body was running in sheets through his frame, having broken free of his veins. To Jesse, his family seemed unreasonably calm, but they were there during the emergency, and perhaps the telling of it made it sound worse than it was.

The next day they all went to the hospital to see her. She was sitting up in the bed when they arrived, and she smiled upon seeing them. They all gathered close to her, kissing her and rubbing her hands.

"Momma, what happened? What is going on?"

"Oh, nothing really, I just had some pain."

"Pain? Where? Where does it hurt?"

"Now listen, children. This is nothing. The next time you see me, I'll be doing the boogaloo. Now stop worrying. Go get the nurse, and help me get home."

"But, Mom, they wouldn't put you in the hospital for nothing."

"No, really, I'm fine. The pain is gone, and I just want to go home."

One of them went to get a nurse.

The nurse said as she walked into the room with her eyes glued to a clipboard, "The doctor has not authorized her release yet. We have to run some more tests."

Rosalind took the lead.

"What kinds of tests? What is the problem, I mean, as you would describe it?"

The nurse was uncomfortable answering these questions and deferred to the doctor.

"Dr. Bledsoe will be here shortly, and he will answer all of your questions."

The doctor did not show up for another twenty minutes, which felt very much like an hour, but he was polite, and patient, with good bedside manners.

"Hello, everyone, you all must be the family I have been hearing so much about. I'm Dr. Bledsoe."

He went directly to Madelyn, lifted her hand, and said, "So, Mrs. Brightmeyer, how are you feeling today?"

"Like I could dance a jig," she said cheerfully.

According to Jesse, she certainly looked fine. His fears dissipated, and he felt relieved.

"Well," the doctor began tentatively, "may I speak freely here?"

"By all means," said Rosalind, with her siblings nodding in approval.

"In lay terms, your mother is suffering massive kidney failure. Her diaphragm is collapsing around the urethra, and toxins are backing up into her body. This is not good. She has made it clear to us that she will not submit to a transplant, which in any case would be difficult to accomplish in the time we have remaining."

"Time remaining, what do you mean?" Jesse piped in.

"It takes time, and often a lot of it to find a proper donor. There is a waiting list for healthy kidneys." The doctor deftly dodged his point.

"Now, taking her position on this matter into consideration, this is not an acceptable solution anyway. What I am recommending is a visit to a specialist in New York who is doing some very promising things with this disease."

The brief but horrible silence that followed restored the tension for Jesse. What was happening here? Disease! This was an immutable word. It carried dread; it was a word with which Jesse had no affiliation. He could not find a place for it in his mind. Foreboding, yes, but foreign as well. Disease in this splendid body, this incongruity placed Jesse on tenterhooks, and he fought against its entry into his consciousness.

Jesse had had some experience with hospitals. His stint at Butterworth Hospital, as an orderly, exposed him to the horrors of disease. This was difficult enough: watching people die and families deal with it, but what exacerbated it was the nature of people assigned to treat and comfort the sick. Serving others is what the ministry is about, and in service, Jesse imagined a sameness among all caregivers. He expected, naively, to find people like himself, who were gentle and caring. Few of them were.

He had a twenty-four-month commitment, or sentence, as the brethren liked to call it. His time was not served without incident. Jesse was assigned to the radiological department. There were six radiologists and about twenty technicians on the day shift. The chief radiologist was an irascible fellow named Dr. Wahlid. He was brown, in an all-white enclave. He was as brown as many so-called blacks. This struck Jesse as a bit strange, in so racist an environment, and Jesse took an empirical interest in watching this man negotiate the delicate terrain that his color imposed. His particular ethnicity was not known to Jesse, but it was believed that he was Pakistani.

There was considerable hum behind his back. This made him wary of others and caused him to develop an unapproachable persona that, to some extent, at least in his mind, protected him from the hurtful abuses of subtle racism. He was initially unsettled by Jesse's appearance on the floor; even as an orderly, Jesse's "skin," being more like his than the others, could somehow (this is one of the peculiarities of racism) reflect poorly on him. Jesse's demeanor, work ethic, and his ability to communicate allowed Dr. Wahlid to feel some modicum of pride (this too is one of the peculiarities of racism), as Jesse seemed to win over the professional staff and most of the technicians. Jesse was relentlessly happy, and it showed. Dr. Wahlid was respected as a successful radiologist, but he was not liked.

The chief technician was a fellow who had arrived at the position by tenure alone. He often bragged about having been there for thirty years. Henry Bristol had been an X-ray technician back when all of the equipment was housed in wooden boxes. He was as white as Dr. Wahlid was brown. He was not smart or charming. He was not communicative and had no visible leadership qualities. The one thing he had, and this made him invaluable, was nothing else to do: no wife or family, so he seemed committed. He was religiously punctual and was in constant attendance, even when he was too ill to be there. This was about the only thing he demanded from his staff of young "techs" and interns. His interns were an assortment of young white males and females for whom this work of taking X-ray pictures was simply a job. He had little or no control over them, as all of them knew—it couldn't be hidden—of his grievous limitations, made all the more conspicuous by a generally known dependency on alcohol. A few of them were very dedicated, but most were there for reasons of ego and income. The males consisted of frustrated athletes, former football and baseball players. Some were skiers, and one of them bragged about being a former lieutenant in the United States Army. With whatever else they may have had in common, the thing that welded them was a visceral dislike for black people, which none of them could explain. These youngsters, to a person, had never been in the presence of black people. Their response to the presence of Jesse ranged from indifference to intrusive curiosity to blatant hostility. It did not help that Jesse was a minister or that he was "puppy dog" friendly.

First of all, they didn't consider Jehovah's Witnesses to even be Christian in this town so steeped in Calvinism, and his friendliness put "their women" in his orbit. On more than one occasion, Jesse found himself trapped—in one or another of the small treatment or filing rooms—having his life threatened or having one of the young or the older females exposing herself and nearly demanding sex. These moments intrigued Jesse more than they frightened him.

Like his mother, Jesse often sang as he worked. He didn't just sing, he worked on songs he was writing. His anniversary was approaching, and Jesse was working on a song to sing to his young wife. The opening line was a melodious, "I think you're beautiful," and several of the women decided he was singing to them, and they made secret plans to confirm it. At some point during every day on the job, there was nothing to do, and this would annoy many of the technicians. The orderlies, of whom Jesse was one of three, were at the beck and call of every one of the technicians. Of the three, only Jesse did not have a master's degree, and he was a practicing minister. This meant that, the doctors notwithstanding, the orderlies were more educated than anyone giving them orders, yet another point of irritation for the ragtag group of techs.

One day, stemming from no episode that Jesse was aware of, the young men began testing Jesse. It wasn't so much testing as it was feeling him out. They began, one after another, as they passed him, to squeeze his biceps, his shoulders, and his stomach. Five or six of these young men did this, and some would offer comments like, "You're tight" or "So you lift, huh" or "You're pretty fit." The other orderlies, who were not built like Jesse, saw all of this with a wry curiosity. Matt, the most senior of the orderlies, said, "What's that all about? It looks like they are sizing you up for something. It doesn't look good. You might want to talk to someone about it. I have been hearing things, but I did not think they were serious."

"Yeah, I know what you mean, but I have no idea where this is coming from."

Jesse was indeed nonplussed by these goings-on. He had been on enough athletic fields and courts to know that the testosterone levels had risen, but he had experienced no overtly bad moments with these people, so the direction or purpose of these aggressions was not clear to him. Later that day, the most athletic of the crew, in the presence of the other orderlies challenged Jesse to an arm-wrestling contest, something Jesse had done a lot of in his teens. There was some relief in this, because Jesse and Matt had thought something much more sinister was coming. The challenge certainly appeared to be a friendly offer, and Jesse, of course, liked games.

They gathered in one of the exam rooms during a slow period of the day. The other orderlies chose not to participate, given that they had no interest in physical contests of any kind. When Jesse got to the room, the six most athletic men were there. They had one-dollar bills clutched in their hands like you might see at a cockfight or like the older boys back in the neighborhood shooting craps. Even this did not disturb Jesse. Jesse had lots of experience in this game and was quite good at it. He had never beaten his brothers, either Ashton or Frankie, in an arm-wrestling match, but he had never lost to anyone else. His thin build disguised his well-structured arms, and he had very strong hands. The young men lined up to do battle while the leader put his right elbow on the table, spreading his legs to get positioned.

"Hey, guys, this isn't fair. I'm left-handed," protested Jesse.

"That's too damn bad," the lieutenant said, apparently the orchestrator of the whole scene. Jesse could not tell if his tone was bravado or hostility.

"Look," Jesse said, "if I go right-handed, then it's only fair that you guys go left-handed."

They all seemed very agitated, perhaps because Jesse did not dismiss the contest entirely. They were all in line to wrestle one guy who didn't seem the least bit bothered by the prospect. As the contest unfolded, there was no contest at all. All comers were easily defeated, with the left or right hand.

When the word got out within the department, even the women begin to "feel" on Jesse as they passed and with comments of their own. Whatever talk there was among the women, it had the effect of infuriating the men.

The stockiest of them, and the youngest, eventually stormed into the holding area, where the orderlies would wait until called to work. The young man stormed into the room, shouting at Jesse.

"You think you're so tough. You think you're so damn smart. You're gonna get yours, and it's gonna happen today."

"What are you talking about? Get my what?" Jesse was completely surprised.

He grabbed Jesse's shirt at his chest with such force that his watch exploded off his wrist. Jesse, stunned by this, made the poor choice to say, "Well, that's what happens when you shop at Kmart."

"Well, at least I didn't buy it from some nigger on the street." He was on the verge of tears in his anger, his face went quickly scarlet, and his blond hair turned dark with perspiration. "Tonight, you bastard," he said and hurried from the room.

The three orderlies were silent in disbelief. Before they could find any words to say, the lieutenant slinked into the room. He sat down, calmly, across the floor on stacked cardboard boxes holding paper supplies. He took out a switchblade and began throwing it open, making a snapping noise each time. He looked menacingly at Jesse, who was sitting on boxes too, about eight feet away. He then took the knife and threw it skillfully into the box just inches from Jesse's face. Jesse did not flinch. The lieutenant stood up, casually pulled his knife from the box, walked to the door, where he turned and said, "Tonight, I'm going to cut you up."

Jason, the other orderly, rose and said, "I'm going to get Dr. Immelman." This was the radiologist on the floor closest to their age and the most affable of the professional staff.

"No," Jesse said, and he followed the knife thrower out of the room. Jesse watched him walk into the largest exam room, where he and the others had gathered to plot their night's entertainment.

Now it was their turn to be surprised. Jesse walked in and closed the door behind him. They were pounding their fists into their palms, the lieutenant was popping his knife open and closed again, and there was a palpable ferocity in the air. Jesse stood there for a second and took a deep exasperated breath before saying, "Guys, can we talk? I came into this room to tell you that I really have no idea what's going on here. Have I done something to you fellas? I guess I have, but you need to know that whatever it was or whenever it was, I'm sorry for it. And you also need to know that I do not know what I did to offend you. I will say this, if you said or did something to me that bothered me, that insulted me, or even made me angry, I would come to you to talk about it, just as grown men should. If you are willing to talk, even now, I am willing to listen."

There was the briefest of pauses as the mob began to crumble.

"Listen, Jesse, I'm sorry too. I shouldn't have said what I said, calling you names. Can we just forget about it?" This from the fellow who had broken his watch; he was still red, but this was the color of embarrassment.

"Look, man, we got you wrong, okay? We didn't mean nothing by it. You're a good guy. I just got a little excited. All square, right?"

All of the men extended apologies, and it felt to Jesse that they were genuine.

"Do we need to talk? Maybe we just need to know each other a little better."

Just then, Dr. Marshall walked into the room with Jason. "What's going on in here?" he demanded.

"Nothing at all," offered the lieutenant, "just guys talking."

"Jesse, is everything all right?" He had been told that an explosive situation was unfolding.

"Yeah, Doc, everything is fine."

After this there was, for the rest of the day, a kind of awareness, clinging in the air. People talked slyly about the incident and the way the young orderlies had handled a potentially fiery situation. A new respect was assigned to them, but no one ever spoke of it again.

Jesse thought of his mother and the way she had handled the volatile situation involving Ashton, all those years ago. He never told her about this episode.

CHAPTER 13

The Help

In the early 1900s, James Alexander's father invented something: the paper clip, cotter pins, collar stays, or something. Whatever it was made him rich. He had fathered two children, a daughter who was mentally disabled, and his namesake, who had inherited his wealth and was now fifty-five years old. Jim, as he wife called him, was a very educated man. That, essentially, was all he was. He was, in fact, a lifelong student. He did not need a particular skill, and he had none, unless one includes dutiful socializing in clubs and guilds-too many to mention. He had studied nothing with a career in mind. What he studied, was nearly everything, with a conspicuous leaning toward the arts and social studies. He, with his wife and three children, traveled often and had visited every continent. These were primarily encyclopedic sojourns for him and vacation for his family.

He was not rich in the way that the Carnegies or Rockefellers were, but without working, he and his family lived enviably in Gross Pointe, the fine suburban community just east of Detroit. In keeping with the culture of his community, the Alexanders did not clean their own house and rarely cooked their own meals. Beginning in May of 1956, these duties went to Madelyn Brightmeyer.

The Alexanders had had more than a few housekeepers in the past. They were adequate, and beyond the occasional late start or an unpleasant quip, their tenures were essentially unremarkable. For some reason, however, there had been many of them, and that reason was the indelicate style of Beatrice Alexander, the wife of James. As often as not, they would be hired and fired without James ever even knowing they had been there.

One Monday morning, after preparing himself to visit one of his many clubs, he descended the winding staircase of his home for his usual breakfast of toast, a grapefruit half, and a cup of coffee. He noticed, as he was coming down the stairs unusual sounds, and the most satisfying aromas emanating from his kitchen. His teenage children were chatting happily in the dining room, and his wife was strangely cheerful. When he entered the kitchen, his toast was ready to be dropped, his grapefruit was sliced, and in the smell of coffee, there was a hint of cinnamon. But there was more: a veritable buffet was present. It was not overdone—there was no excess, where food would be wasted, and except for the aromas, there was no evidence in the kitchen that any cooking had been done. The smell of breakfast is a fairly ordinary event in a house, but this was different. For a moment, James felt as if he was in the wrong house.

"Good morning, Beatrice. Did you sleep well?" They were a formal family.

"Yes, my dear, I did. Are you leaving so early?"

"Well, I was, but I think I'll sit for a moment and enjoy this fine breakfast. What got into Eunice? She's outdone herself this morning."

"Oh, James, I'm sorry. I forgot to tell you. I hired a new housekeeper. I was uncomfortable with Eunice."

It was Beatrice's responsibility to hire housekeepers, but she was always a bit nervous when she did it. She was the docile sort around her husband and always sought his approval, but in his absence, and certainly with the hired help, she had quite a different persona. She was a college grad herself, but it was only a credential. She had met her husband when they were children, and a career as anything but a housewife was never in the plans.

"Madelyn," she called, "would you come here for a minute? I'd like for you to meet my husband. It's only right—he does pay the bills."

When Madelyn walked into the room, whatever image James had in his head, based on years of nannies and housekeepers coming and going, did not prepare him for this visual. She wore a predominately soft pink sundress, trimmed in green with tiny red flowers about the tasteful neckline. There was nothing about her dress that suggested a uniform; it was much more like the warm and pleasant dress of a housewife, with a matching apron being the only hint of servitude. He was captivated by her height, which was not all that different from his wife's, or perhaps, it was the way she carried it. She was certainly younger than he or his wife, but her stature and shoulders, were not that of . . . well, he expected something else. She seemed, and he did not know how to put it or think it, unused. Normally he took introductions to new hirelings as mere courtesies, having no significance whatsoever, except to be respectful. Here now, standing before him, was a woman, indeed a woman, whose splendor unsettled him in ways he could not quite understand. He held out his hand, and she extended hers.

"How do you do, Mr. Alexander? It is a pleasure to meet you. I do hope you enjoy your breakfast this morning." She had her gaze politely on him, not looking away.

The gesture of shaking hands was not lost on Beatrice—she had never known him to do that with a housekeeper.

"Oh, I'm sure I will," he said, leaving his eyes on her longer than he knew.

James Alexander had been many places in his life. It puzzled him that he had seen no woman like this in his time. Or had he?; and simply not looked up, not bothered to notice. There had been many nannies in and out of his house down through the years. He began searching his memory for their faces. He thought about his time in Northern Africa, in Mexico, and other parts of the world where he might have seen this brand of beauty. It made no sense to him that he should now, suddenly, be seeing this complexion, this stature and grace for the first time and in his house.

"I have many things to do today. I'll be upstairs if you need me. It was good to make your acquaintance," said Madelyn as she left the room.

"Yes . . . thank you, it was good to meet you as well."

He was incredulous. In his life, he had known many well-placed people, from bankers and secretaries to corporate executives and political leaders, but he had rarely seen, he could not remember ever having seen, such dignity in a human being. That so poised a creature was serving his food and cleaning his house somehow made him feel small and undignified. These feelings haunted him.

"So, Beatrice, where did you find this woman?"

"The Willinghams. She cleans for the Willinghams on Wednesdays, and they spoke highly of her. She seems different from the others, doesn't she? She's cheerful and calm."

She could sense that her husband was pleased with her acquisition.

"She seems different from everyone, don't you think?" he said, still pondering the mystery cleaning his house. Cheerful and calm did not quite capture it.

"What do you mean? She seems to be a good housekeeper. I don't know what you mean when you say different from everyone." Beatrice had not noticed this, or, if she had, it had not yet registered. Her query had the slightest edge.

"Her deportment, it is unlike any maid or nanny or housekeeper I have ever met. You don't agree? You haven't noticed?" He was now speaking very casually, guarded, so as not to reveal just how impressed he was.

This matter of not being noticed by white people was not new to Madelyn, or any black person. Some years earlier, in the early forties, Madelyn was rendering maid service at an elegant hotel in Richmond, Virginia. She and others in her family had moved there from a smaller Virginia town. She and the other descendants of slaves, cleaned, cooked, served, and generally maintained the hotel. They, like the wait staff of any facility, were little noticed, if at all, by the administrative staff or the public. This usually meant they were doing their jobs. Franklin Arthur Brightmeyer, her husband, and father of their young children, worked in the kitchen of the same hotel. Here was a man who was as educated as a black man could be in the American South of the 1940s, which meant he had more formal training than most white men he encountered and for whom he worked. The custom, though, dictated that he could aspire to nothing more than a cook or a porter. But Brightmeyer was more than educated—he was talented, hardworking, and cunning, which resulted in his becoming the de facto head chef in a kitchen that employed thirty people, most of whom were white.

This was news that embarrassed and displeased the management, and they were fixed on doing something about it. They met in the conference room, a collection of twelve administrators, and one agenda item was to decide what to do about the "uppity niggra in the kitchen." The assignment to serve these people went to Franklin Brightmeyer's young wife, Madelyn. Her presence in the room was completely unnoticed by the racist attendees, as they determined that they would fire this talented but wrongly colored man. Madelyn, of course, shared what she heard with her husband, and within six months the Brightmeyers were in Detroit, facing the same dog with only a few less fleas.

That Beatrice did not notice Madelyn, or her extraordinary demeanor, was no surprise at all. The shocker was that James Alexander did. His recognition of her, at so high a level, certainly stunned his wife, who, like the management in the Southern hotel, albeit for different reasons, decided to let Madelyn go, after weeks of noticing and tolerating her husband's curious distraction. Jim had done nothing improper, and would not, it was not within him to do so, but Beatrice found him staring at Madelyn once too often. It took her some time to effect the dismissal.

In the interim, as was their way, Jim and Beatrice gathered from their abundance contributions to the less fortunate, which were typically dispersed by their many charities. Jim, however, began making things available that his wife did not consider part of the donative cache, things that to her were not excess: marble statues, fine woolen rugs, cashmere blazers and sweaters, even some nice dresses, given that Beatrice and Madelyn were nearly the same size; and he bypassed his charities.

Brightmeyer himself was taken aback by the stream of generosity, but he enjoyed receiving and talking about the fine acquisitions, especially as he could call them his own. The business that Madelyn was in was transient, so it came as no surprise to him when his wife had to find other work. For her part, Madelyn was never aware of James Alexander's fascination with her.

He looked over the spread of food in his dining room. There, amid the grapefruit, was delicately and artistically sliced cantaloupe, and peaches with cream. There was thickly sliced bacon and a bowl of chopped onions, tomatoes, and peppers, next to an assortment of breads. The display was almost too pretty to eat, but eat he did.

CHAPTER 14

Goodbye, Mr. Brightmeyer

Jesse conferred with friends and family about the wisdom of going on the road. Cedric felt he should go and took some credit for Jesse's apparent success. Walter Mason had introduced the two, and his vote was to go without question. Jesse's family, that is, his siblings, wanted him to go, thinking it would advance his career as an actor. It had an exciting ring to his boys as well. The predictable comments and speculations about sexual preferences were endlessly joked about. Some even quite seriously began to suggest that Jesse had latent tendencies that were about to sprout. Underneath it all was the hope, and the good wish, that Jesse might very well be on the edge of stardom. Everyone wished him well and encouraged him to "go for it."

Jimmy returned to France and, true to his word, called Jesse soon after he arrived. They talked many times, and Jimmy was convincing with his seductive flattery about Jesse's mind, talent, and "incredible" good looks. He sent Jesse autographed copies of all of his books and a ticket to fly to New York, where he was to meet Jimmy's agent. This provided several weeks of excellent and silly speculation among

Jesse's friends and family. The when, how, where, how much, pink socks, and more. Jesse was, in a manner, simply going along. This opportunity meant more to others than it did to him.

It cannot be said that Jesse was an experienced traveler, but he had been to New York many times. The Brightmeyers had family ties there, but he had only been on an airplane a few times and took no pleasure in it. He gathered a few necessities and was ushered to the airport by Steven. During the brief flight, Jesse's mind went hopelessly to the past. He thought about his father, now dead, who had introduced him to Jimmy Baldwin as a writer and thinker. He knew that his father, not his beloved mother, would finally be proud of him. At least he would be pleased about this new relationship. Mr. Baldwin had been interviewed on television many times, and on those occasions, Brightmeyer would insist on quiet—everyone must stop what they were doing, come and sit quietly to see what your people were capable of. He did this with all of the famous "negro" stars who made their way in front of a television camera. In this way, Jesse "met" Mahalia Jackson, Paul Robeson, Sammie Davis, and others. But with James Baldwin, the emphasis from Brightmeyer was on listening, not to simply see and be proud, but to listen. There was never, as Jesse recalled, any mention of Jimmy's private sexual preferences. It was rumored that Brightmeyer himself had similar leanings, which of course meant nothing to Jesse, as his dislike for his father had to do with other nonsensical things.

Life was different now; Jesse thought fondly of his father. In the end, Brightmeyer had gotten very ill. He was a double amputee and had shriveled to half his weight from the ravages of diabetes. During this time, it was often necessary for Jesse to touch his father—for the first time in his life—lifting and placing him in the car, wheelchair, or on the toilet. This touching was meaningful. It connected Jesse to his father in ways that surprised and pleased him. Before he died, Jesse made a planned visit to the hospital to talk, to apologize to him. Some years ago Jesse had a belligerent confrontation with his father in a very improbable scene, given Jesse's fear of him.

Jesse awoke to the definite sounds of Brightmeyer threatening his mother. Jesse ran down the stairs grabbing a broomstick and plunged it into his father's chest, protecting his mother. But that was not the point of the apology. Jesse wanted him to know that he finally understood. He understood the maniacal discipline, the insistence on excellence, all of the lessons Jesse pretended not to hear in his youth. But Brightmeyer stopped him. When Jesse said, "Daddy, I need to talk to you," Brightmeyer said, "No, you don't."

Jesse tried to insist, but his father was prepared. It was almost as if he knew this moment was coming.

"I know son, I know."

Jesse packed his things for his second flight to New York: dress suits and shoes, socks, ties, and underwear. He loaded books, paper and pencils, toiletries, and everything he could imagine needing during his time on the road with James Baldwin. He was not certain how long he would be gone. He was to fly to New York for some final details with Jimmy's agent, Justin Nedling, but more importantly, to meet Jimmy's family. He had spoken of his beloved brother, and his sister Gloria, who, to some extent, handled his business. Jimmy had also spoken of his mother. His affection and attachment to her was not unlike Jesse's devotion to his mother; this too bonded them in a way they both made much of. The fact was, if they did not approve of Jesse, it would be a short trip. There was little chance of that, given how Jesse compared to the relatively long list of predecessors.

The itinerary was to be presented at this meeting. Justin had booked Jimmy at several venues for a six-month-long speaking tour. A fairly wide-ranging group of audiences were on the list. Several historically black colleges, elitist preparatory schools, Ivy League schools, and some artist's coalitions had found the money to invite the renowned writer to one facility or another. Jesse was to see to Jimmy's needs on the road, everything from toiletries to dealing with whomever the contact person was at the various engagements.

It had been a few months since Jesse's last trip to New York, and in that time Jesse had gotten fairly comfortable with the idea of being on the road, starting what appeared to be a new life.

When the plane landed, Jimmy's agent was there to pick him up. They had swapped descriptions so that it would be easy for them to find each other. People who looked like Jesse were not in abundance at LaGuardia, and Justin Nedling's appearance was even more distinctive than he had admitted. He was tall and white just as he had said. But he was "whiter" than anyone Jesse had ever met. He was only a few years older than Jesse but had a full head of absolutely white hair, and his skin, equally pink, seemed too thin to stay there. He had the thinnest lips, and the narrowness of his aquiline nose had Jesse wondering how he could breathe through it. His movements were those of a much older man. His posture suggested a failing frame, but a vibrant, youthful way of talking redeemed his actual age. He was warm in his greeting, in that formal sense of the term. Jimmy remained in France, but he called later that day to discuss how things went and to say he would be in town tomorrow. Justin was impressed by Jesse, but this is a relative statement. Relative to the parade of young men (Jeno was one of them) Jimmy had presented in years past for Justin's approval. Yes, he was handsome, like all of the others, but he brought something more: a swagger in attractive concert with intelligence and what appeared to be humility. Justin was actually relieved, not recognizing that what he was really seeing was a polite indifference supported by a cultivated confidence sharply honed by Jesse's parents and visions of Frankie's performances.

The next day when Jimmy arrived, he was met at the airport by both Jesse and Justin. They went directly to Justin's office, where papers were signed and hands were shook. They then went to an early dinner where Jimmy beamed, as his new acquisition not only impressed his agent, but sat quietly, as the suggestion that they were lovers went unchallenged. It was to be this way throughout their time together, as Jesse simply did not care what anyone else thought. That he was heterosexual did not seem to be anyone's business any more than Jimmy's homosexuality, and neither preference seemed important. But alone with Jimmy, in the dark of the night, things were quite different. Living a lie, any kind of lie, was difficult for Jimmy, and it would not be long before this deception would begin to chaff at his core.

CHAPTER 15

Getting the Boys and Settling In

Ramona's apartment was quite cluttered with things of art and years of living in a place too small for her life. She and her teenage daughter were making the most of the space, evidenced by overflow in every direction. She and Jesse had decided to be together, but this apartment was not to be the point of beginning. The three flights of stairs were enough to deter Jesse, but the small space, along with the endless and indescribable collection of stuff belonging to a woman who did not know how those three flights impacted her daily decisions, was a bit more than Jesse wanted to deal with, certainly not on a daily basis. In addition, he had visions of getting his boys to come from Michigan to live with them. A bigger place was a must, and Jesse had to find a job. Jesse was comfortable with his ability to make money, in spite of the fact that he had so little interest in it. He had no formal education, but so much about him suggested that he did. He was a learned communicator, and while he was better with his hands, his charm and eloquence always seemed to land him in sales of some kind. It was just as well because the only tools he needed were always with him; he could "travel light," as they say.

He and Ramona, more Ramona than he, combed the papers, talked to friends, and walked the cobblestones and brick pavers of Cambridge and Boston looking for a suitable and affordable place to stay. Coming from Michigan, the rental fees in this community astonished Jesse. What one paid for rent here would afford a four-bedroom house in Michigan, with a garage and two bathrooms. But eventually they found, that is, Ramona found, an acceptable three-bedroom flat, with only one flight of stairs, in Cambridge.

This was to be home, a troubling word—home. Somewhere in his mind, in his heart, that word was reserved, like mother, for another time, a different place. He liked the look of the place and the idea; it was, after all, a match with his youthful intentions, to settle down and raise a family. But a vortex of conflict spun in his head, and it all seemed contrived. Ramona had done a fine job putting the house together. Her daughter was happy to have a space of her own, and Cambridge, according to Ramona, was quite the place to be—the home of no less a citadel than the consecrated Harvard University. Cambridge was, of course, the little sister of the historically significant city of Boston. This city was an area of ghettos, tribes, if you will, of Irish, Italian, Africans, Portuguese, and the product of their miscegenation, the strangely beautiful Cape Verdeans. In this new cultural landscape, so foreign to him, Jesse had to find a job. Jobs—Jesse had had so many that he had become an expert at getting them, which is not much to say, given the kinds of jobs they usually were. He, and this explains it, was not very good at keeping them. He would flash his smile, play unfairly with words, and always get any job he wanted. He actually never wanted any of them. He was as lousy an employee as he had been a student. He was good at learning, having been raised to do so, and he was a very hard worker, but he learned primarily by living, and he lived moment to moment, and now had little interest in consequences. The only consequence that mattered had already occurred, and nothing else could impact his consciousness as meaningful. He paid an enormous price for this frailty.

Jesse called home, that is to say he called his estranged wife. Beverly had gone, if not happily, bravely on with her life. Jesse's financial contributions to his young family had not been enough—it was not what it should have been. He had been sending money home, but Jesse, who had now been away from home for five years, had only consistently sent money during his three-year stint with James Baldwin, and even one week with no money was hard to bear for a mother with two boys to feed and clothe. It was true that he sent her every nickel beyond sustenance, but even that says little, as his needs were so simple. Jesse thought that now, given his new "marriage" and family, he could bring his boys to Boston, actually raise them there, and start again a life of normalcy. He put this idea to Beverly, and while she had some immediate apprehensions, she thought it was Jesse's turn with the kids, and she needed a break. Chad and Zachery, Jesse's young sons, were excited about the prospect and pushed their mother to cooperate.

Beverly's nervous concerns extended to putting her sons alone on an airplane, but more deeply, she worried that Jesse would make a mess of things. She had a mother's wit about her, a radar that she trusted explicitly. Even when, as was often the case, she could not clearly articulate her trepidations, she remained certain of her feelings and trusted them. But she relented, and soon, just in time to enroll them into the local school system, the boys arrived at Boston International Airport.

Jesse beamed as he saw them, and inside he wept with a consummate and, as always, conflicted joy, as he saw in their faces the "happy sad" that he had foisted upon them; and he determined that he would now begin making it up to his precious boys. His sons were excited, curious, and anxiously looking forward to this "new life." Zachery, the younger, was, like Jesse, quite the "momma's boy," and almost immediately began to worry about her. Chad, given his budding intellect, found a way to immerse himself in the very different culture and took his younger brother with him. The boys now had a sister in Patience, Ramona's daughter, and that difference alone was enough to create an interesting level of excitement. Their new sister was strikingly pretty and as bright as she was lovely. Having been an only child, one might have thought jealousy would rear its head, but the gender difference offered too much anticipation, and for the moment it overwhelmed any possible sibling rivalries. She would be taking them to school and conducting the tour of the new lay of the land. Both factions were happy to have a new sibling to introduce, brothers to protect, and a sister to be proud of.

Very near to his new family's residence, there was an automobile dealership. Jesse had sold many things in his life, but never cars. He had wanted to, but American life had not allowed it or made such a thing difficult for people who looked like him. There had even been a fearful reluctance to pursue this line of work because in America, racist traditions put many jobs out of reach for black people. But now many things had changed in the dappled culture, and Jesse feared nothing. It was clear to him that the worst thing that could happen already had.

The job hunt had to begin somewhere, so he placed a call to the dealership and asked to speak to personnel. Someone named Jerome Fulilove, who was said to be the general manager, came to the phone. He spoke with a decided lisp as he put Jesse through the perfunctory interrogation before inviting him in for an interview. The following week Jesse made the three-block walk to the dealership to meet the general manager. Jesse was taken by the ordinariness of the place. It was ancient and not nearly as clean as Jesse had expected it to be. It appeared to belong to a bygone era. Only the windows and cars resembled familiar things. In fact, except for the presence of vehicles, there was nothing here that he would have expected. The people working there were bored and disinterested. They wore ill-fitting suits and large weather-ready boots, appropriate for the time of year but, with their pant cuffs tucked into them, so incongruent with a business suit. There were no black people working here, which was not a surprise, and the only person there who was not white did not seem to know he wasn't. He was an overly educated Eurasian fellow working his way through graduate school at Harvard. There was the potbellied vest-wearing, pipe-smoking patriarch who had been there since the doors first opened decades ago. There was the tall young Jewish family man who was learning the business and seemed perpetually nervous, and an old mysterious fellow, who only did commercial sales. In the offices worked "the womenfolk," as Jerome would condescendingly refer to them, doing the necessary paper shuffle.

The general manager himself was a peculiar fellow with a name that did not suit him at all. Something about his name sounded black, if you will, and the only thing he was full of was indifference to others, supported by a bottomless greed. His greed was such that it lent him a skillful demeanor and the appearance of being a tireless and committed servant to his client base. He was a pudgy white male, and everything about him was suspicious, even the way he dressed—all in inordinately clean and pressed polyester and wing-tipped, perfectly shined shoes. In repose he resembled a mannequin fitted for the plump, oversized man. His eyes darted about on his chubby scarlet face, like a predator's, as if searching for some advantage. Jerome Fulilove was as dishonest a man as one would ever meet, cloaked in a proper job. He was innately nasty, with a sharply cultivated, syrupy cover or, if it was learned, he was quite accomplished, and all about him there was a toxic miasma that infected and unnerved those around him. Anyway, when it comes to indifference, he met his match in Jesse. Jesse's apathy, however, was supported by grief, and it is worth pointing out that despite everything, he was well raised, and even in his madness and insuperable emotional conflict, he had deeply rooted principles that carried him in business, if not in his private life. On the other hand, Jerome Fulilove simply did not care about anything but money. Nothing supported his behavior but this.

The interview was a play at the old game. A suit and tie, shined shoes, eye contact, firm handshake, and now Jesse's fairly interesting life traveling the globe with a relatively famous writer, who, surprisingly enough, was known to this wrongly educated and unpleasant man (this made Jesse think he was gay, as opposed to literate). It was obvious that Jerome was surprised by Jesse's appearance, not just his color, but he seemed to recognize how well Jesse was dressed. He certainly was not prepared for Jesse's skill with the language. Jerome was not certain that Jesse could sell cars, but he liked the new look his presence on the floor would bring to his otherwise sterile dealership. Jesse was hired. This did not mean much to his bank account, as the job paid only a commission, something to which Jesse was accustomed.

Jesse started work the following Monday. The custom, the rule actually, was to arrive thirty minutes before the doors opened to hear the day's strategy and, on this day, for Jesse to meet the "guys." They had, as is typical in retail, what is called an "up system." This meant that the salespeople would simply take customers in a predetermined order. You only approached a buyer when you were "up." Jesse did not enjoy selling, but he was good at it. The business of talking people into things seemed . . . unfair to Jesse. Here, at least, the people came voluntarily to purchase, what was for many of them, a luxury item.

The staff gave Jesse advice and told him not to expect much. In a good month the store would sell thirty cars, but usually fifteen to twenty or so was all that could be expected. Each of them would be happy if they sold four or five cars a month. On his first day Jesse sold four; he sold twelve in his first week on the floor. This was unprecedented and created an electrifying buzz in every department. At this rate, Jesse would out sell the whole dealership by himself, and so he did. His co-workers were amazed enough, but Fulilove was beside himself. He and his credit manager called Jesse into his office to discuss what he was doing. Jesse was casual about his success as, indeed, he had simply done what he always did. Jesse knew that the other salespeople simply had low or no expectations, but he did not say it; he had no magic to share with them. Jesse's approach was contagious, and everyone had a better month of sales than they had ever had. The newfound success of the dealership was not owed entirely to Jesse's productivity. Jerome Fulilove had increased his advertising budget, he cleaned the place up a bit, and he started "sales training." Jesse had participated in dozens of these trainings in his career and could teach them himself if asked, but he had no interest in such things, and, of course, he was not asked.

But the manager had big plans. He hired two new salespeople and ordered more vehicles from the factory than the dealership ever had. The new hires included an enormous black male, who introduced himself as Big Nate. However big he was, he would certainly not have been hired in the absence of Jesse's performance. The other new salesman was a handsome street-wise white male named Chuck Landis. He was the spoiled son of a well-known Boston businessman, but had found his way, defiantly, into the streets. These were two very competitive fellows. Fulilove knew this, so when he introduced them, he made Jesse the target. "And this is Jesse Brightmeyer, our number-one producer. So pay attention to how he works. You might learn something."

Chuck, a proud, good-natured white boy about Jesse's age, was all about the fun and the challenge. He looked at Jerome, smiled confidently, and said, "He'll be number two by the end of the week," while flashing a competitive wink at Jesse. Fulilove was ecstatic, enjoying what he had set in motion. Big Nate, as confident as Chuck or Jesse, said, looking at Chuck, "So you'll be happy with number three?" At this everyone laughed, and Jerome Fulilove swaggered away with a look of satisfaction on his face so broad that it annoyed Jesse.

What Jerome Fulilove did not see was that he now had three street boys working his floor. Perhaps any one of them alone would have been manageable, but together, well, the stodginess of the dealership disappeared immediately. There was laughter and slapping hands as deals were closed. The credit manager needed to work twelve-hour days just to keep up, and the women handling the business upstairs made frequent trips down to the showroom, primarily to meet and watch this Jesse Brightmeyer and the "new guys" ply their trade. These three brought colorful language and dress to the showroom. They brought fun and a new atmosphere, which spread to everyone. The dealership was having a revival of sorts, and no one appeared bored anymore. Everyone sold more cars than they ever had before. Even the mechanics in the service department could not believe what was happening, as they too were making money at last. Ramona was happy too. Jesse, having very little interest in money and even less ability to handle it, simply brought it home and, minus some pocket money, gave it to her. She also enjoyed having a new car to drive; Jesse had won the rights to it as a reward for his achievements.

Fun and salesmanship were not the only things Big Nate and Chuck brought with them. They also brought cocaine and the foul intentions forged by it. People behave differently when they have money in their pockets, and young men all the more so. This whole triune consisted of married men. Only Chuck was childless, but the responsibility of returning home after a workday belonged to husbands and fathers. The days were long, and the time of the year meant they were always leaving the workplace after dark. One night, with full pockets, pumped up by the successes of the day, they all decided to have a drink before going home. There were many neighborhood bars, but Jesse had not been in any of them. Chuck made the suggestion.

"Man what a day. I made fourteen hundred dollars today." If that was true, he made more than Big Nate or Jesse, both of whom had had good days. Big Nate said, "The white boy's buying."

"Damn right, I'm buying. I'm going to take you guys to my spot. It's right down the street, so let's take my van, and I'll drop you guys off after a few pops."

"All right, let me call home and let my people know I'm going to be late," said Jesse, trying to do the right thing.

"What, you gotta get permission?" Chuck was making the classic "I dare ya" challenge. He and Big Nate laughed loudly and began to tease Jesse. Jesse took it well and called home, but nobody answered the phone.

When they got into Chuck's van, they all lit cigarettes. Big Nate had a flannel bag in his briefcase that once held a fine liqueur, one of those in a regal color, and had a pull string through the mouth of it. He lifted out of it what looked like a woman's makeup compact, from which he produced a packet of the devilish white powder, a razor blade, and a plastic straw with a spoon-like shape on one end. As the three of them discussed what would have to be called nothing of importance, he cut lines, snorted one, and passed the plate to Chuck, who took a line in each nostril. When the mirror was passed to Jesse, who in his life had never had cocaine, he snorted without hesitating and handed that plate back to Nate.

"Good shit," he said, playing a new role. "Where did you get it?"

"Ahhh, that's my secret. I got my sources. Drop a C-note, and I'll get you a gram." Big Nate was doing business, but Jesse was learning a new game.

"It's all right," said Chuck, "but if you really want some good shit, check out what I bring in tomorrow."

Chuck started the engine, and they headed for a bar that they could just as easily have walked to, someplace called "Around the Bend," a strange name since it was right on the main drive. There were people here who seemed as if they had been here all of their lives, all leaning hopelessly over bottles of beer. They all knew Chuck, calling him by name, even "Chuckie," and "Snaps" (whatever that meant), and many seemed to expect something from him. This collection of humanity did not seem to be the kind of people, given what little Jesse and Big Nate knew about him, Chuck would hang out with, but he clearly liked the adulation. They were mainly older, and those who were not were dazed or lost were certainly, already well into the "bottle." Some of them seemed homeless. The bar was a small place, and only eight or ten people were present. Chuck said to the bartender, loud enough for everyone to hear, "Let's get a round for everybody, whatever they want." Chuck enjoyed being the big fella. Nobody ordered a beer except for Jesse and Big Nate, and Chuck insisted on buying them a shot "kicker." They began talking, as they had not heretofore, about their adventures and conquests.

Chuck was a ladies' man. His claim was that he could get any woman. Since this was Jesse's forte and he lacked any real competitive drive, he told a story or two, choosing to let it be. But Chuck heard something else. He heard a challenge. He needed to prove he was the man. Jesse didn't bite. "I'm a married man," he said.

Big Nate's thing was drugs. He only took a job to get some heat off himself. He could get any and all of the drugs you wanted. Chuck revealed himself as a man with a clinical need for approval. This need energized him even more than competition. The reality is that he was not all that competitive—he sought approval, especially from men. There was a competitive trace in his behavior, but it was quite secondary. Jesse could see this.

When Jesse first moved from Detroit to Grand Rapids, Michigan, in 1970, he found himself in a predominantly white community. He, as was pointed out earlier, was an accomplished public speaker, but it was only known to the small culture of Jehovah's Witnesses. In Detroit, he had become a star, in demand for special speaking assignments. He was the "heir apparent," if you will. Religious denominations are like clubs, and each church or congregation were like chapters of the club. The Grand Rapids community had its own clubs and chapters. They all had their young stars, and they were all young white males. One of them was the "Chuck Landis" of his peer group. He was handsome, well spoken, and completely full of himself. William Oosterhuis was his name and, like Chuck, he did everything to be seen and to impress others, especially men, the elders within the congregation. There was nothing genuine about him. His style of dress was neat polyester that he would accessorize with brand-named jewelry, shoes, and the ubiquitous attaché. Unlike Jesse, he did not have the complete look. He did not understand fit, cuff exposure, mixing fabrics, patterns, and colors. In short, he did not have Allison. But he did recognize that Jesse's wardrobe was finer than his, and his clothes somehow fit him more precisely. He was Jesse's age and nearly exactly his size. When they met, Will, as he was known by his friends, sized Jesse up as if they were to be combatants, but it was neatly masked as a "getting to know you" brotherly love ritual. He noticed the wool and silk that Jesse wore, the prettiness of his wife, and his fine grasp of the language. All of this took him by annoying surprise. You see, the blacks in the Grand Rapids club were, for the most part, subservient, well received, well treated, but they were not considered the equals of the whites. They were not as educated, not as respected; they were present without being, shall we say, necessary.

They were the result of well-meaning missionary activity. Will knew immediately that Jesse was more like him than he was like the people he resembled. Will had an eye for good-looking things. It crossed every line. He understood, even if it was only a superficial understanding, that pretty could be found everywhere, and, to his credit, he, unlike so many white people Jesse had met, could even see it in black people. Jesse's good looks unsettled him.

It got worse when he first heard Jesse speak in public. William Oosterhuis had been the local prince of princes within the local family of Jehovah's Witnesses, and now, in Jesse, he found not simply a fine orator, but his superior, and he was being told as much. This development grated on his nerves, but Jesse's humility gave him no place to take his angst. His efforts to bait Jesse into a rivalry simply did not work. Jesse was only doing what he had been taught to do, his best, and with the same humbleness his mother had infused into him. Jesse had this attitude about all competitions, not that this was one, but Jesse never managed to care who won or who was impressed. For Will, and now Chuck, winning and impressing was everything.

"You ain't trying to say you're in my league," said Chuck, longing for some kind of action. Chuck had no interest in real games or athletics. His games centered around drugs, women, and social interaction. He could talk shit around the clock. Like Jesse, although undoubtedly for different reasons, Chuck seemed to care very little about money. His earning it and spending it had to do with showing off, impressing others.

"Oh, I've got some skills now, if that's what you're saying. But you know, like I said, I'm a married man." Jesse thought of this as just talk, playing around.

"Man, what are you guys talking about? It's easier to get pussy than it is to get drugs. Anybody can get some pussy. Hell, the hos want it bad as you do. What I got is better than pussy." Big Nate was certain of this; he made his comment as if he were teaching Jesse and Chuck.

"Shit, man you must be crazy. There ain't nothing better than some good wet pussy," said Chuck, speaking from his gonads, with lessons of his own. "I like drugs as much as the next guy, but not as much as I like getting my dick sucked by a hot young piece. How about you, Jesse? Pussy or some goddamned cocaine?" Chuck laughed, as if recognizing the absurdity of the question.

This was a conversation for which Jesse was not prepared. Frankie's lessons had never gone into this arena. Jesse was on his own, and it was important to him to fit in. The business of slapping God around was now simply the way he lived, especially when compared to his former life as husband, father, and child of God. He was wayward now, and while he had no daily conscious thoughts of it, he was distancing himself from the decadent god. This was his psychotic goal. The distance between him and his family, his former life, and his premarital plans of fulfillment had not yet been calculated. It had not yet entered his mind. Pussy, cocaine, something about the question, however playfully it was meant, bothered Jesse. Not so much the question, but that here he was, feeling compelled to respond to so inane a question as this one. This boy talk, and all of its braggadocio, went against his grain.

"I like them both, and I get plenty of both," he said dismissively. He had become a liar of some skill, but he thought of himself as an actor, on the great stage, sharpening his skill. But still he felt like a coward.

They continued in this way for a few hours. Soon it was after midnight, and Jesse felt the discomfort in his stomach that comes from knowing you have disappointed a loved one. Ramona had no way of knowing where he was; he had forgotten to call home a second time. At this hour his sons would be in bed, and he had missed saying good night to them. Big Nate and Chuck had wives to get home to as well, all of them had to be at work in the morning, but there was no indication that either of them was ready to go home. The bar was the kind of place where doing lines of cocaine right on the table was permitted, and they had done several throughout the evening. Jesse still drank and smoked marijuana almost every day, but rarely anymore to drunkenness. The cocaine did not appear to affect him at all, that is, until he got home.

Ramona was justifiably worried and disappointed. She rightly expected Jesse to be home at the family hour, but she admitted that she had not been home at the time Jesse claimed to have called her. In Jesse's mind, the fact that he had called, walked home, and left his accomplices in the bar meant he, in the end, had done the right thing. Ramona complained that she did not want to have a drunken husband, and she was not about to take care of his children alone. "I am not a hired nanny," she said. Her complaints were fair, but her style was not. She went on and on about Jesse's disregard for his family, that he had to be more responsible. She was behaving as if she was the moral standard that Jesse should emulate; she brought up past lovers and their failings. Jesse, an hour into her dissertation, had had enough. "All right, you've said your piece. Now just stop, let it go. I need to go to bed."

Jesse undressed and got into the bed. He wanted to sleep, but Ramona kept talking. That she would not stop annoyed Jesse, but what was even more disturbing was the fact that he could not sleep. He was discovering one of the side effects of this white powder. He fought with the sleep gremlins that apparently lived within the white stuff. Ramona's yammering did not help, but Jesse determined that he did not like this drug. Anything that disturbed his sleep was a thing to be avoided. Sleep had always been one of Jesse's great pleasures. More than food or even sex, sleep gave Jesse a kind of comfort he could find nowhere else. Even as a boy, there was never a need to force him into naptime. The parents would have to find, and threaten, the other children; but Jesse could always be found, curled up in bed, in a peaceful slumber.

CHAPTER 16

The Presidential Rebellion

A few weeks went by without incident. The children were enjoying their new relationships, and the surroundings in "Beantown" were sufficiently different from Michigan to keep the boys excited. A family was blossoming, and all of the participants were engaged in making it work. Things on the job were going along very well, but Jesse's first impression of Fulilove could not have been more accurate. Jesse thoroughly disliked him. He disliked his style, his maneuvers, and most of all, the way he treated people. He was dismissive of others, however compelling they may be, and completely indifferent to fundamental human needs and feelings.

Jerome Fulilove had a marketing brainstorm. He decided that all of his salesmen should dress in nineteenth-century costumes in honor of Presidents' Day. Banners would be strung, balloons, and the whole red, white, and blue celebration. The outfits consisted of wigs, hats, and stockings, a fairly accurate representation of presidential regalia of the early 1800s. This was to be fun for everyone; it was, except for Jesse. He had railed against the evils of white men, especially slave owners for as long as anyone could remember, and now he was expected to wear clothes that in his mind would honor racist slave owners. He simply could not do it. The founding of the country was a despicable time for Jesse's ancestors, to say nothing of the indigenous inhabitants, and, to him, dressing like their tormenters would dishonor them, and himself, in a way he could not countenance. He went to Jerome Fulilove privately to make his point.

"I cannot do this. It's insulting to me and my ancestors. I am willing to do something else, almost anything else, but I cannot wear this outfit," Jesse said staunchly, riveted in his position.

Fulilove had already bought the costumes and, being the boss, had not discussed this idea with his sales staff. This game did not seem to perturb anyone else, not even Big Nate, and the general manager seized this to make his point.

"I don't get it. This is just marketing. It's just business. Have some fun with it. We're going to make a lot of money. What's the big deal? It doesn't bother Nate, and he's black." With that, he really thought that he had said enough.

"Well Big Nate's sensibilities are his own to live with. I, like you, have to live with mine, and this is something I cannot do. I will do this: how about me wearing the rags of a slave? You know, to help authenticate the period."

Jesse said this with all seriousness, looking the fiend unswervingly in the eyes. Fulilove chuckled, but he had run out of what little patience he had and said, "You'll wear the costume or find another place to work. The promotion is a week from today. I need to know by tomorrow in case I have to replace you."

Jesse was ready to tell him to go fuck himself, but he thought he could foment a revolt on the floor with the others. He was, of course, completely wrong. These people were making money for the first time in years; they were not about to risk their newfound riches.

"Come on, Jesse, it's only a couple of days. Let's just have some fun," said, Brian, the young Jewish father.

"If he asked you to dress up like Hitler, would you do it? These sons of bitches are the Hitlers of my people. He can kiss my ass. I will not honor them in any way."

To this, Brian had no response. He simply skulked away. Jesse's boys, Chuck and Nate, were not with Jesse; they were not uncomfortable with the demand, but they thought Jesse should do whatever he had to. Lewis Wong, the Eurasian intellectual, pondered and dissected this history and the principles that disturbed Jesse and decided that Jesse's moral stand was . . . noble. The others had no comment. They even seemed stymied by the thought of this discussion, having never been in such close proximity to any black people, and this one defied everything they thought they knew about blacks—he had principles. Roger Hubble, the round older gentleman who always wore a vest and smoked a pipe, found the whole episode compelling enough to begin to befriend Jesse, asking him questions, hoping to have some private discussion of the matter. He went as far as to invite Jesse to his home, where Jesse was to meet his wife. He had discussed this matter with her, and she was eager to talk to the person she called "the brave young man." Roger and Jesse found moments throughout each day and talked for many hours about things ranging from society, politics, religion, and sports; they shared story after story about growing up in days and times gone by. They became friends; well, they could have become friends had Roger not introduced Jesse to his wife.

CHAPTER 17

Goodfellas, Bad Boys

Chuck and Big Nate were late for work. Chuck looked as though he had been up all night, because he had. Like Jesse, Chuck lived for the moment, but unlike Jesse, he could function without sleep. Apart from a bit of a rasp, Chuck sounded okay, but he certainly looked like he needed a bar of soap and a toothbrush. It had been a night of drinking, drugs, and shit talking with his boys. His boys, Jesse was to find out, were a bunch of "*Goodfella*" imitators. In their world, however small, they were the high rollers. Chuck was not big on keeping promises, but when it came to showing off, which is what bringing the drugs was about, you could count on him. Chuck, however, did one better: he had one of his boys show up with the white gold. At about three o'clock, when Chuck had finally found his legs, in came what appeared to be a gangster, drenched in black. He had a patch over his right eye, and one of his hands was mangled by a knife or a bat from one of his many fights. He wore a wide-brimmed hat and a long, tattered double-breasted cashmere coat that seemed too large, as he walked with a slight limp into the showroom. He had, on his face, a look of absolute confidence, as if he had won the battles that so disfigured him.

"What's up, Beast? Hey, Jesse, I want you to meet my main man. This here is Harry "the Beast" O'Connell." Chuck was very proud of his friend. He and Harry were of Irish descent, but they had perfected the whole Italian street-corner persona.

"Hey-y-y, my brotha," the Beast said to Jesse and then looked sharply away, as if casing the place.

"I hear you used to be the man down here," he said, looking in passing at Jesse but deferring to his friend Chuck, who postured like the boss of this man.

"Yeah," said Chuck, "he used to be the man before I showed up. I'm the man now, huh, Jesse?" He was laughing and waiting for the high five.

Jesse happily gave it to him, knowing he was done here, saying, "Nobody's on top forever."

Chuck essentially ignored the comment, as none of it meant anything to him—it was all bravado. He turned to Harry and said, "Show him the beast, Harry."

Harry instantly let out an almost comedic ghoulish laugh. It was perfectly sinister, and everyone laughed. Together, they reminded Jesse of so many hoods he had seen in the inner city, going for tough and ready for almost anything.

In Jesse's childhood, in the neighborhood where he was raised, there were many unsavory characters who made their way around the periphery of the otherwise idyllic community. One of them was a white male who had been raised, due to his mother's choices, in a seedy black section of town. He grew up to be one of the few white pimps in a black bastion of crime. Jesse never got to know this fellow, but he was somewhat famous, in the world of pimps, hustlers, and street-corner thugs. He was called "Black Patty." He was a white man, certainly in his twenties at the time, who had decided to be Black, in the way Chuck and Harry had chosen to be Italian. This man was blond, with blue eyes, but he wore processed hair, what the locals used to call a "do," and often wore the "do rag" exactly as the Black thugs did. This of course, made no sense. The point of a "do" was to have straightened wavy hair, which he had by birth. Well, he did not have waves, thus the process. This look and what was called a pimp walk, along with other dandy accessories, which took some practice to perfect, were the hallmarks of the mean streets and the pimps that lorded over them. Black Patty drove the famed "deuce and a quarter," the Buick flagship of the time. It was a triple-white convertible, which caused him to be envied, opposed, and, alas, it gave him a place to die young.

These men, somehow, together, brought Black Patty into Jesse's mind, and he knew that they were able to launch him into "the all manner of sin" that he was no longer certain he wanted. Jesse had ceased with the daily crying, but the tears still came all too often, and Ramona, like Marlena before her, had been encouraging Jesse to seek some professional help. He was aware of his ongoing madness, but his anger had not subsided, and he did not have the will to halt the inexorable descent into a life of indulgence. As the lost among us seem always to do, Jesse unwittingly took his grief out on himself, running directly into any situation that spelled trouble. There was inside of him a separate self, barely recognizable, and resolute in his belief that he could do enough harm to make God, an increasingly vague figure, regret the destruction of his mother.

The ranting continued, but primarily in private settings. In public, in the presence of people he believed would never know him or couldn't help him, he found a way to behave as he had been raised, to act on the lessons of his parents. But something would switch on, or off, when he was with those he thought would help him antagonize this . . . this god, this god who had deprived him of his precious mother's milk.

"Yo, Snaps, did you tell the brotha about the plan?" Jesse made a mental note to ask about this Snaps thing, remembering that is what the forsaken people at the bar had called Chuck.

"Naw, man, not yet. I figure we'll talk about it over a couple of shots tonight. How about it, Jesse, you got some time after work? Big Nate, let's do this." Jesse assumed they wanted to demonstrate the superiority of their product.

"Let's take them to my place. I'll meet you guys at the Barrel, up in the square, about nine. I'll have the girl with me." Harry was referring to cocaine, and "girl" was one of its many nicknames.

The day passed slowly for Chuck, who found places and moments throughout the afternoon to sleep off the previous night's indiscretions. It was one of those days wherein not much happened, so he was able to get away with it. The dealership closed at nine o'clock, and Harry's bar, the Barrel, was not far from the shop.

Chapter 18

Roger's Wife

Roger's house was a large, finely decorated three-story Italiana. The window trimmings alone had to be worth many thousands of dollars, to say nothing of the exquisite Persian rugs that were in all of the first-floor rooms. Jesse wondered why Roger worked at the dealership; he certainly was not making enough money there to support this style of life. He apparently did not need to work at all, least of all at so forsaken a place as the dealership. As it turned out, and no one was to know it, Roger was the previous owner of the place, which in some small way explained this house. There was a luxurious Steinway grand piano set at the end of the enormous living room, some distance from an ornate floor-to-ceiling fireplace. The stone-and-hardwood-paneled structure was even grander than the piano. His wife had a grandeur of her own and was pretty enough for people to wonder what she was doing with Roger, who was at least twenty years her senior and would not be considered attractive, physically, by anyone even in his youth.

JoAnne introduced herself to Jesse. She was warm and friendly in doing so, almost as if they were on neutral ground, at a social event. She was at total ease, and it was apparent that she, unlike her husband, had had some contact with black people or had a deeper understanding of the makeup of humanity. She was more than comfortable with having Jesse in her private space; she held Jesse's hand, in both of hers, as she greeted him. She was, from every appearance, a housewife, bringing wine, cheese and crackers, cloth napkins with the family name embroidered on them. She then sat down to entertain and be entertained by her husband's new friend.

"So you are the young man who has turned the dealership around," she said smiling, with a purposeful exaggeration of Jesse's role.

"Well, I wouldn't put it that way," said Jesse. He smiled back, graciously accepting the compliment.

"You know, Roger has been there forever, and we have never seen anything like this. You should be very proud of yourself."

"I am," Jesse said, "but it has nothing to do with selling cars." She wanted to pursue this answer, but Roger spoke first.

Roger said, "I was telling JoAnne about your stand around the Presidents' Day promotion. She was interested in talking to you about it. I didn't want to speak for you. One thing I know for sure is that Fulilove doesn't get it. He is probably going to fire you."

"If it comes to that, it will be all right. I am not dependent on him or selling cars. I am able to sell many things," he said.

"I get the impression you are able to do many things," JoAnne suggested.

There was flattery in her comment and a perceptible twinkle in her eyes. Jesse was deliberate in not letting on that he noticed it. He wondered if Roger had taken the same position.

JoAnne was obviously educated and bright enough to have pursued any career, and housewife was her choice. She was interested in Jesse's education and why he had settled for "selling things." There was, within her way of talking, a quiet, unspoken request for more than could be had in this room, under the casual and unsuspecting gaze of her husband. Jesse had seen this subtle behavior many times before and had always taken advantage of it. In truth, he was always the one taken advantage of. Here it was again, and now Jesse would wait to see just how aggressive this "wife" would be in her efforts to seduce him.

Since the loss of his mother, Jesse had found himself in the beds of countless "other people's wives." It could even be said that he was comfortable there, which is somewhat surprising, given the number of bedroom closets he had been trapped in or the number of balconies he had leapt over. It was some time before Jesse understood that this endless pursuit of him had more to do with his mind, his way of being, than it had to do with his sexuality. Frankly, he was only barely conscious of either point of value.

"It's just that my interests are more artistic and intellectual than they are capitalistic," he said, getting back to her question. "I have never had any particular fondness for money. I have always found myself resisting its influence in my life, seeing so clearly how it makes the average human being behave. That is probably my biggest problem with Jerome. It, that is money, appears to be his only motivation." JoAnne was watching Jesse closely and listening with pleasure on her face.

JoAnne was a non-practicing Jew, who had essentially become a non-practicing Catholic, deciding early on that the folly of religion produced more despair than anything. Her husband was, on the other hand, devoted in his beliefs, which meant, simply, he went every Sunday to church. Like most people in his life, sans JoAnne, and now Jesse, he did whatever his parents did, without much thought about what it meant or even what he actually believed. His wife was accepting of this, considering that it was, in fact, the position of everyone she knew. In Jesse she was seeing, she thought, someone like herself. Someone courageous enough to flout the nonsense that underpinned so many traditions and to think independently, and she found this, and what she was to call his "exotically beautiful face," irresistible.

Jesse stayed with the Hubbles for about two hours, during which JoAnne, who was an avid reader and on the fringe of the various social movements of the sixties, was enthralled with Jesse's stories. She was taken by his love for his mother, which led to some discussion about the joys of childhood. That he was an actor and that he had spent time with James Baldwin, (a person for whom she had enormous respect) had her feeling that, in Jesse, she had found a person with whom she could finally talk. In marrying Roger, she had lost most of her friends, and her orthodox family had long ago forsaken her. There was a prevailing loneliness to her otherwise comfortable life. Her exchanges with her husband had become routine, and never in their time together had Roger really listened to her, not in the way, she thought, that Jesse seemed to. She wanted more and knew she could not get it in this setting.

Jesse prepared to leave, and Roger, who had said very little during the visit, left the room to get his coat. JoAnne seized this moment, seeming to know exactly how many seconds she had. She walked up to him, kissed his cheek, and kept hers on his face while whispering, "I love your pretty face and the softness of your mind. Call me tomorrow, at three, at this number." She put a piece of paper in his jacket pocket. The closeness that moment demanded gave Jesse a chance to smell this woman, something that, since he was a boy, being around his mother, aunts, and their friends, to say nothing of the garden, was a large part of the way Jesse determined if he would be near to or far from a person or a thing. While never being able to tell what aromas moved him or how to describe them, he was always certain of this touchstone. JoAnne carried a seductive fragrance that was not reminiscent of any Jesse had encountered. He would see her again.

CHAPTER 19

Higher Ground

Driving through the Boston-Cambridge area had Jesse missing his home. The little neighborhood in Detroit that presented itself so plainly in his mind was by now only a memory. It lived clearly in his heart, but it was gone in every other way. The house he was raised in had been run into by a truck, and as it was built on piers with no foundation walls, it toppled like the house of sticks that it was. Jesse lived elsewhere at the time, and it was months before he learned of its fate. All of the old families were gone too, having moved, like the Brightmeyers, to higher ground, and the small houses with their manicured lawns were now just dirt, with well-worn footpaths through the foliage where the houses used to be. The recollections though of its brighter days were so vivid in his mind that he compared everything he saw in Boston, and anywhere else for that matter, to that tiny forgotten community. The friendliness and simplicity of the life he knew there could not be found in this place, which seemed so cold to Jesse. But more than anything, he missed his mother—her touch, her face, and the beauty she had managed to create within her family.

His attempt to replicate that wonder with his own family had failed. Whatever the particular skill was, he had not inherited it, and now he was in a place he had not intended to come to. This new emotional terrain was so unfamiliar and so void of pleasantness or intrigue that he could not anchor himself in it. It was as if he was being carried by forces unknown to him, to places that did not, could not matter to him. Like a dandelion seed, taken by the wind, riding it to destinations unknown.

He remembered his formative years among the Jehovah's Witnesses, going door to door all over this community. He had been on the porches of nearly every house in his neighborhood and in the living rooms of most, peddling God's dogma. Actually, the time he recalled was when he was simply an observer, a child, chaperoned from house to house, learning the business of evangelism. But he remembered the clean porches and the friendly people, not that everyone was friendly or that every place was clean, but within his reflections that is how it was, and he could not imagine being a child here, in this treeless place. There was too much concrete and not enough grass. He could smell no bread baking, and there were no pies cooling on the windowsills. It did not enter his mind that he had grown up and, like himself, others had grown up and were facing their own trials, and the laughter of children was missed by them as well. He was falling forward and backward at the same time, teetering in two places at once.

Ramona and others regularly pointed out to him that he was living in the past, that he should let it go and live in the now. The now, however, had become an unwieldy place. The conversation with Roger and his wife touched off delicate memories, and when Jesse went to those conjured images, it would take time or something, an interruption, to pull him out of it. He would go tumbling back to happier times, reaching desperately for his mother's milk . . .

"Rosalind, help me with the sandwiches. Allison, don't forget the ice and sugar for the Kool-Aid. Now, Jesse, you find enough copies of *Watchtower* for all of us, and remember to bring the Bible."

It was seven o'clock on a Sunday morning, and Madelyn was gathering fruit, sandwiches, blankets, and the accessories for a picnic. It was not to be a daylong affair. At noon they would be at the "Kingdom Hall," which is what Jehovah's Witnesses called their place of worship. Edison was with them now. Eddie, as the kids called him, was her nephew, the son of one of her younger sisters who had made a bad choice for a husband, and now she needed help in raising her only child. Eddie was a fine young boy, just a year younger than Jesse. Soon Jesse and Eddie were nearly inseparable, as Ashton was, at three years younger than Jesse, somewhat in the way. That is to say, he demanded Madelyn's attention, and while Jesse was not conscious of it, Ashton's need for his mother unsettled little Jesse enough that he unwittingly distanced himself from his baby brother. He even had some vague awareness of seeing his mother suckle the little one. It completely bewildered him. What was this boy doing in his mother's arms? Jesse, as a child, assigned Ashton to the place his father occupied—a necessary nuisance. But he needed someone to play with, and Eddie had never sucked his mother's breasts.

"Eddie, are you ready?"

Eddie was always ready; Madelyn liked that about him. He had a certain adult quality about him. Like Rosalind, he was dutiful, and "cute as a button," the adults would say. While he played as little boys do, Eddie was a student, with a natural inclination to reading and memorizing and repeating what he read. He had a head full of soft curly hair, and even as a six-year-old, half of it was gray, giving him the aura of a grown-up. He endeared himself to Brightmeyer, with his affection, curiosity, and the very warm nickname he had for Brightmeyer, calling him ever so comfortably, "Big Daddy." He became an integral part of the family.

Brightmeyer himself was never a part of these affairs. He found some value in the "religious thing" in that it gave him time to himself, and he was able to see how, practiced the way the Jehovah's Witnesses did it, a sharpening of the minds and confidence of his children was under way. He had some religious illusions that mattered to him, but nothing that he held dear, having opted for the pragmatism of surviving in the here and now.

Madelyn wanted everlasting life for her children, the great promise of her loving god, and the ambience of the morning sun, in a park called Belle Isle, enhanced the prospects of them embracing this dream as their own. There was the study of the *Watchtower* and the reading of the Bible. Each child would be assigned a paragraph to read aloud. The bottom of each page had written on it the simplest of questions, the answers to which could be found by glancing up the page. During the actual formal discussion at the place of worship, members would raise their hands, and the "Watchtower Servant," who led the discussion, would call them by their theocratic names, Brother or Sister So-and-So, and they would essentially read the answer, which was going to be read anyway by a very favored brother at the microphone. In this manner, the lessons and brainwashing proceeded. The more devoted among them were much more committed to the learning and prepared with the kind of pre-meeting research such as Madelyn was initiating. They would embellish the text, adding subtle understanding to the discussion.

"Now, Rosalind, find Isaiah 25:10, and let's see what it offers to the discussion. The *Watchtower* is only a guide, you know—it's the Bible where the actual word of God can be found." Rosalind found the verse expertly and read it like a scholar.

"And what do you think that scripture offers to the discussion? How does it help you answer the question?" Madelyn said, and all of the children raised their hands, practicing for their moment to answer a question before the congregation. Jesse, of course, was immediately distracted by the squirrels, birds, and the occasional deer. These sweet memories, and hundreds like them, filled Jesse's brain, and it was as if those memories were his to protect, only his, and they could not have been made anywhere else.

CHAPTER 20

The Witch and the Scoundrel

Jesse heard from his sister announcing that she and Steven were coming to Boston. That they were coming pleased Jesse very much. They had not met Ramona, Jesse had not seen them in years, and they had never been to Boston. The plan was to take them out to one of the local clubs on their first night in town. The boys too were giddy about their coming, as Allison was their favorite aunt, and they always had fun with Uncle Steve. This was about six months into the family affair that was Ramona, Jesse, and their children. They all went grocery shopping, buying goodies to satisfy the tastes of both the adults and the young ones.

Ramona had some excitement that was all her own. An old friend and sister in the arts had moved back to Cambridge, after having spent the last ten years in Germany. There, Greta and her two children had become fluent in the language of that land and were quite a curiosity—little black-skinned children speaking fluent German. They had moved, somehow unbeknown to Ramona, into the flat below. The discovery of this happy coincidence threw them into each other's arms in a very animated reunion. Ramona's friend was strangely beautiful, having traces of many races clearly emblazoned on her face. Had her skin been just a shade or two lighter, she could have been Greek, Indian, Mexican, or nearly any race known to man. These features notwithstanding, she had a cold, somewhat bothersome appearance. There was something "witchy" about her, thought Jesse; he also thought her name suited her. She wore her rather straight hair pulled tightly back, with a matronly bun sitting haughtily at the back of her head. Her gait suggested a struggle to lift each foot, as if the ground gave reluctant permission for each stride; still it managed to be proud. Her style of dress matched the universality of her face, a mix of all of the aforementioned ethnicities and somewhat indescribable. A steady voice trickled from her thin lips, and, while lacking cheer, her intelligence, like Ramona's, was on display with each syllable.

In any case, Ramona introduced the two of them. During the chit-chat, wherein Ramona seemed completely overjoyed to see her, the phone began ringing upstairs, and she hurried up to answer it. In her absence Jesse, seeing how pleased Ramona was, decided to invite her to join them, along with Allison and Steven at the club for a night of fun. Greta was reluctant for reasons of her own and said she would get back to Ramona. Jesse went back upstairs, and when Ramona got off the phone, he told her about the invitation. She reacted as if Jesse had broken a bond of trust. She was adamant, without equivocating, that she did not want this woman to go out with them. She was fuming in her objection but gave no actual reason for it, acting as if Jesse had made the most grievous of blunders. This created a tension that Jesse did not know what to do with. Luckily, he thought, the woman did not seem particularly interested, and perhaps the two of them knew why. He relaxed with this reflection.

This was the same day his family was to arrive from Michigan. Jesse picked up Allison and Steve from the airport, leaving Ramona home with the boys as a minor surprise for them. What a surprise it was. The boys were beside themselves. Auntie was here and, as always, bearing gifts, but more than that, she listened to them with real interest and showed almost equal interest in Patience. The introduction to Ramona had the effect of dissipating the angst Jesse's invitation had created, at least for a moment.

After the surprise of Allison's arrival, the boys and Patience went to their rooms while the adults settled into getting to know one another. It was not long before Greta knocked on the door to announce that she had decided to stay home to finish unpacking or some such thing. But before she could leave, there was another round of introductions, whereupon Steven and Allison found her too interesting to let her go. Drinks were poured, and good conversation lit up the room. They inquired about her travels, the excitement of a new language, especially as it related to the children, and they were very impressed with her interests and achievements in the world of art, in Europe no less. They insisted that she join them for the evening. When she relented and agreed to go, Jesse glanced at Ramona and noticed that she was holding her anguish in check.

"You go without me. I have lost all interest in going," said Ramona, pouting, sneering, but not explaining a behavior that did not seem to fit the moment. They had gone into their bedroom, ostensibly to get ready for the night out. Jesse rolled a joint, lit it, took few hits, and handed it to her. "I don't want to get high," she protested. "That's your answer to everything. Just get high."

"Could you give me your answer? I'd like to know what's going on here. You were so happy to see her. She seems affable enough. Look, I'm sorry about my slipup, but even you have to admit there was no way for me to know that this would upset you."

"I just don't want her imposing on a night when I'm getting to know your family. It feels intrusive."

"Well, my family seems to be enjoying her, and you have the rest of the week to get to know them," said Jesse, snorting a line of cocaine.

She was certainly agitated, but she picked up the smoldering joint and took a hit. She even angrily snorted a line of coke. Jesse wondered why Ramona ever did drugs or took a drink, as none of these things ever had a visible effect on her.

They found a way to all cram themselves into the small vehicle that Jesse drove and headed for the club, which was in a newly renovated hotel. There was not yet a real club in the place. An excellent jazz band was staged in a fairly accommodating section of the lobby. Even in the dim light, one could see that the owners had spent a great deal of money on the rehab, with marble columns and floors, beautiful moldings, and artwork hanging tastefully about.

The staging area was somewhat tight and very near the front windows, which were floor-to-ceiling assemblies, looking out on an expansive circular driveway. Seating was awkwardly close to the band, so close that when the band started to play, conversation was forced to end. While waiting for the entertainment to begin, which was not very long, the satisfying conversation continued. Allison especially enjoyed talking to artists, and Steven's innate curiosity was insatiable. Allison sat on Greta's left, Jesse to her right, and Ramona on Jesse's right, with Steve bringing up the end. The two women of the arts had captive audiences in Allison and Steve. Jesse sat contentedly in the middle, gathering bits of detail from both conversations. Ramona was the center of some attention, and it seemed to soften her mood.

Then the band, a quartet, started to play, and the lights dimmed to what initially appeared to be total darkness. The volume and the proximity to where they were seated made talking pointless, but it seemed to play into Greta's plans. She turned from Allison and began giving Jesse her attention. She made an effort to say something to him, but it was futile, with the music reverberating at such high levels. Through the loud rhythms, he could hear nothing she said. She pressed in, closer, to say something more, and to do so, it was necessary for her to literally put her lips on Jesse's left ear. Even so, he could only make out a word or two. She began squeezing his bicep and licking his face. Here under the weight of the music and the darkness, Greta was making an overt sexual advance. Jesse understood the foulness of what was happening, but he thought more about the improbability of it. The audacity of her stealth impressed and titillated him, but he considered it a moment in the night that would be over the moment the lights came up. She began rubbing his thighs, kissing his neck, and she seemed fascinated by his arms, which she clung to like a needy spouse. To Jesse's right sat Ramona, completely unaware of these goings-on.

After about forty-five minutes, the band took a break, and the darkness faded into a more manageable light. The chatter began again, starting with the quality and the volume of the band. Everyone one was a little dazed; at some point, music simply became noise. They decided to have another drink and leave before the next set. While they talked, Jesse announced that he was going to the restroom. The room had to be found, as it was far from the entertainment site. While Jesse wound his way through the corridors, the events in the darkness dissipated like the darkness itself. It was over and, he thought, now he understood Ramona's apprehensions but dismissed the whole episode.

It was not over. Jesse found and entered the large spotless lavatory, going casually to the urinal to do his business. As he finished, he felt someone's whole body pressed against his back and his penis being handled by a stranger. He braced himself for what he thought was certain to be a confrontation with a gay man.

Before he could gather himself, the words "Give it to me," echoed in the marble room, in an all-too-recognizable voice. Jesse turned, and there before him was Greta, a woman in the men's room. He was, for just second, stunned by this development alone. The look on her face was not salacious—there was no lust in her eyes, but a steely determination, something wicked foaming just behind them.

She whirled Jesse around, kissing him almost violently, while backing herself up to the urinal and sitting on it. She then took Jesse into her mouth, stoking him with her tongue, lips, and hands. Jesse and his body responded predictably to this stimulation, and he did not resist her. They were in full view of anyone who bothered to open the door.

"Let's get in a stall," Jesse said, now committed to the base game. He turned her around in the stall and entered her from behind, thrusting with a violence that matched her kiss. Suddenly it was sex, as she moaned and howled with a primal, beastly pleasure.

And then, a voice, soft, motherly, detached, said, "I see you in there. Stop that. You stop that right now." Ramona had come into the men's room. Yes, two women, on the same night, found their way into the men's room. She clearly was in shock, utter disbelief. Then came salient clarity and an outburst, roaring, deafening, and completely violent: it was the violence of rightful indignation. She came rampaging to the stall, taking the swinging door into her hands, and repeatedly pounding the door into Greta's head. Greta fell back into Jesse, who was by now trying to figure out how to get out of the stall with his life. Ramona screamed obscenities, and "screamed" understated the facts. The blast from her lungs brought security running into the room, and then the band, and finally Allison and Steve, who had, regrettably, witnessed this nonsense before. Steven's face dripped with disgust as Allison began plotting a resolution.

The guards, the band, and the other employees who caught the tail end of this rank human drama were disgusted. There was no blood, no damage, and no one to arrest. There was only disgust and the embarrassment of having seen such a public event. The management did ask Jesse to leave, but that was unnecessary. He did not want to be seen by anyone.

Ramona rescued herself from this morass, calling a cab, going for a ride, and trying to find her composure and some way to not commit a murder of passion amid this most deceitful scene. Greta called a cab as well, but it was certainly not to find a peaceful place to reflect. Jesse rode home, shamefully, with Allison and Steve. The ride was peppered with ridicule and disbelief.

Jesse had done it again: he had ruined a perfectly good night and undoubtedly sent his children tumbling into more heartache. They did not deserve this. Jesse thoughts turned to his mother. With what he had done, his life was a heaping pile of grief and degradation, he could hear his mother encouraging him to be nice. "Jesse, be nice.

Learn to put others before yourself, and life will reward you." He had shamed her again, and this did not feel at all like retribution against her disappointing and guilty god.

When they got home, they had, of course, to walk by Greta's front door. Allison and Steve went up to prepare the children for the coming storm, and Jesse sat on the front porch smoking a cigarette while pondering this new low in his life. This wreckage was more than even he wanted to face. There was no way Ramona was going to be in the same house with him tonight or perhaps ever again, and he could not blame her for that. He knew without thinking about it that he would never have forgiven her, had she done this awful thing to him. But his sons, what was to happen to them now? They had only been in town for six months. They had settled in, were enjoying themselves and the new surroundings, and now Jesse had crushed their lives again.

He rose to go up and face his boys. As he opened the door, there she was again. She grabbed his arm saying, "Come on in and finish it. You know you want to finish it." Jesse could see that he had been seduced by a devil or was she completely insane?

"Finish, are you out of your mind? Don't you understand what's happened here?" He was speaking much louder than he knew, and he did not hear Ramona coming down the stairs clutching a hammer with vengeful intentions. Before he could react, she had taken her first swing, just missing Greta, whose point of view allowed her to see it coming. She closed her door, almost casually, but just in time. Ramona began beating the door with a savage brutality that the door could not stand. As it began to collapse, Jesse caught her, wresting the hammer from her as she cried out in anguish such as Jesse had not intended for her but had hoped to foist only upon the murderer of his mother.

Chapter 21

The New Job

The day of Jesse's rebellion, his unwillingness to wear the costume, effectively marked the end of Jesse's run at the dealership. That very day, there came into the store a man looking to purchase a truck. He was a young man, appearing well fed and very self-assured. He had seen his choice on the lot, a fine-looking two-tone blue pickup with a short bed. The vehicle was more show than a simple utility. It was the kind of ride a young man would want as a showpiece; it was, as they say in the auto industry, loaded. Jesse showed him other vehicles, but he stayed with his first choice. The deal happened seamlessly. As it turned out, this young man owned his own business and was doing well enough to buy himself a toy. He and Jesse had a nice exchange, so much so that he asked Jesse to come see his facility and consider working for him. It didn't matter much what he had to offer, Jesse was done with selling cars. He would leave the dealership even if he had no place to go, but here was an interesting possibility that had arrived at just the right time. Jesse, of course, knew nothing about the business Eric Cowens was in, but he was, as always, supremely confident in his ability to sell anything.

His place of business was on a side street, in a small dingy storefront, where he was in the business of moving people and their furniture, through the difficult tributaries and elevations of the Boston-Cambridge area. The limited space on the streets, the age and smallness of the housing stock, made it nearly impossible for people to move themselves. Jesse was to discover that furniture movers were a culture all to themselves. It was a business of brawn and tenacity. In this city, with its limited elevators, narrow stairwells, it also required skill and practice, and these people had lifted it to the very highest level of excellence.

Oddly, it was also the place where the warring tribes came together to work. The employees here, and at most of the many moving companies in the vicinity, came from every ethnic group on the East Coast. Some of the companies were Irish, others Italian or Portuguese, but this company employed them all at once. There was even a black-owned operation, predictably employing only white people. They were like competitive sports franchises. This all made for fascinating and sometimes violent interactions, not unlike the gangs of New York in the nineteenth century, fighting over building fires.

Eric's business was the best-known small moving company in the city. It had been founded by an earthbound fellow, a kind of sage in the furniture moving business. He was a man who preferred life in the forest and lived there, finding his way into the woods as often as he could. Along the way he attracted several disciples, who sacrificed their bodies and private lives, while building a sterling reputation in this very competitive industry. They would place pianos on their backs and crawl up the many flights of stairs or hoist and rig them through windows. These young men performed like athletes, literally running boxes and furniture up and down the difficult housescapes (if you will), for which the area is known. One of these men was Eric Cowens, who at the age of twenty-six, had ruined his back and knees, but had won, through his commitment, ownership of the celebrated young company. He had a younger partner in this arrangement, who, while not having the history with the company that Eric had, was equally committed to keeping the legendary company alive and growing it. What is more, there was about this youngster, a single-mindedness that, in the long run, would save the company from the troubles to come. His name was Roland Johns.

They had a salesman already in place. Like so many salespeople Jesse had known, this man spent most of his time shuffling papers and trying to decide what to do next, which was a way of not doing the thing one was hired to do. He had been with the company for six months when Jesse arrived and had made very little difference in the bottom line of the enterprise. It was immediately apparent to Jesse that this man would never bring the kind of expansion the two new owners had envisioned for their company. He took Jesse through some procedures, which he was developing himself, but they amounted to nothing that would result in sales. Jesse was not about to ruffle papers—an office was not a place where Jesse could be effective, nor was he comfortable there. He needed to be out among the people.

Eric had hired the wrong fellow, a well-meaning but inept fellow, who simply did not know how to promote or sell anything, but he was very good in the office. Jesse spent a couple of days following him about before suggesting that they do a territorial split of the area. Jesse then took his leads that had come into the office and began making phone calls and appointments. He made arrangements with the owners to actually go into the field with the movers to see and experience firsthand what it was like to move a house full of furniture, pack a truck, and unload it. He discovered it to be the most grueling work he had ever done, and he discovered that furniture movers were drinkers. At the end of the day they went directly to the bar, where they would revisit the day's events, like chess players discussing a previous match.

Jesse had never noticed moving trucks before, but now he was seeing them everywhere. The company he was working for had made its reputation moving households, and they were the best, but Jesse observed during his travels large national moving companies, moving offices, whole businesses. In some cases, from floor to floor within the same building, and in other cases, massive weeklong moves involving dozens, and sometimes hundreds, of people. Neither Eric nor Roland had ever dreamed of such work, but Jesse could see possibilities. Their company only had three trucks, and they were small, making them unable to compete for the "big jobs." Jesse believed he could get the big jobs, but he had to have their support behind him. They had to believe it, they had to believe in him, in order to set up the company to accommodate the work as it came in. When Jesse approached Eric and Rollie, as he was called, their first reaction was to laugh. Jesse made them a deal.

"I don't think you guys know what you have. When I'm out there, people sell me on your company. Many of the households you have moved are owned by people who own businesses, and the way this city is growing, businesses move as often as families. I need you to trust me on this. I can bring you lots of commercial business, but we must be ready to handle it. I need you to school me on air-ride trucks, cubicle dismantling and assembly, storage, and the things a business is likely to need or ask for during a large commercial move."

They listened intently but had many doubts. "What makes you think you can bring in commercial business? Do you know how much business we would need to buy the trucks and equipment to handle commercial moving? And the competition—lots of the companies specialize in these moves. They've been doing it for years. I don't think we can compete with them." Rollie was very nervous, and was prepared to cast a "no" vote.

Eric, who had seen Jesse's flair firsthand, said, "Do you have any leads? How big a move are you talking about? When? When would we have to be ready?"

"You tell me," said Jesse, "when could we be ready and what size commercial moves we should start with. Most commercial moves are known several months in advance, so we will have some time to get ready. But yes, I do have some leads. I'm telling you, I can bring it in. You've got something pretty grand here. You just need to capitalize on it."

"Hell, we can rent trucks if we have to. If you get us a big move, the money could be a down payment on a new truck, hey, Rollie."

"The whole thing makes me a little nervous, but if you bring the eggs, we'll sure as hell fry 'em," said Rollie, now thinking about the money.

Jesse paused before saying, "Here's what I'd like for you to consider. I will work for a stipend, just enough to feed me and gas my car, and you keep all commissions. Use the commissions to equip the business for growth. In six months, we sit down and review what we have, how much growth there has been. What I want is

20 percent of the new work, but as a partner, not just a salesman. If I don't double the size of the company in that time, you owe me nothing. If I pull it off, then I would own 20 percent of all new business and whatever percentage that would be of the company."

It seems all Rollie heard was "double the size of the company, keep commissions." He saw no risks in this. Eric was comfortable as well, but he did not doubt that Jesse would make a difference—how much did not matter much to him. They were both comfortable with Jesse's request to own 20 percent of new business only. It was deemed a fair proposition in that they had nothing to lose.

They signed nothing. Jesse was from a place where a handshake was all that was needed. He did not know these men well enough to trust them, but it was his way; it was how he had been raised. They repeated the terms of the deal, discussed a few details, and shook hands. Jesse went to work. He spent one week in the office making phone calls, doing what he called "the dance." Then, for about a month, he was almost never there; he would check in from time to time, but he spent most of his time in the field. He would call in to ask questions about process and capability, but primarily he seduced clients with confidence, smooth talk, exquisite dress that was unusual in this business and proved to be useful conversation points.

The business started rolling in. The first few commercial jobs were relatively small, larger than most households, but small, given Jesse's ambitions. Jesse had been courting decision makers for some of the largest and most enviable jobs in the city. The day came when Jesse had sold but not signed some very big jobs. These moves would be large enough to demand pre-move production meetings with the contacts at the various companies. It was necessary, Jesse thought, to bring either Eric or Rollie to these meetings so matters of fine detail could be discussed. In addition, he wanted them to see his success firsthand. Jesse was learning the business, but there were things about the process itself that he was not comfortable discussing. He wanted Eric to join him, primarily because he was the older of the two and would make a more stable appearance. They spent the day together driving from deal to deal in the fine two-toned blue pickup that Jesse had sold Eric on the day they met. The day was beyond the expectations of Eric's dreams, even his dreams. They would be moving musical archives, the finest new furniture, and even a large medical facility.

By the day's end, Eric did not know what to say, and he was visibly nervous. Whether he was nervous because of the vastness of the scope of work and how the company would handle it, or, as he put it somewhat incredulously, "Jesse, you just made one hundred thousand dollars in one day."

Jesse casually responded, "No, the company just made that money. I get mine when I have doubled the size of the company."

Eric, still dazed, said, "If we get every job we saw today, it will double what we did all of last year." He seemed nearly depressed and then, as if he suddenly saw the real picture, he screamed, "Goddamn it. We need to hired more movers, buy some more trucks, we need more dollies, hell, we'll make twenty thousand just selling boxes. Damn, I've got to call Ben." Ben was the esoteric founder of the company. Jesse had sold more business than Eric knew what to do with. He wanted to confer with his mentor and his partner to start planning. He called Rollie first, and they went to a bar to celebrate and discuss how they would deliver these very profitable services. It had to be pointed out that, while this business was there to be had, it was not yet theirs; but they were convinced that if they got even half of it, the company would need to double its resources.

In about nine months, Jesse took the small but fabulous moving company from simple notoriety to stunning success. They went from a core group of six to ten movers to daily employing twenty-five to thirty people. A new office staff was hired, and three new trucks were purchased. They moved into a new facility that allowed storage, inventory, and a private yard for parking trucks, shining brightly in the newly paved lot.

CHAPTER 22

The Boys Go Home

On the plane ride home, Allison and Steve did what they could to settle and comfort the boys using the usual avuncular methods. It appeared to work, but sinking into their mien was the viral sadness that Jesse brought with him everywhere he went. Now having no dependable rudder, at least not the one they needed most, the boys, Chad, especially Chad, stared out into the vague and disparate sensations of his mind while sifting as best he could through the wreckage in his heart. The boys had wanted to be with their father. Their father had wanted to be with them, but his actions had sent them, his loved ones, fleeing, as it would turn out, for their lives. Jesse, unbeknown to himself, was headed into places of impenetrable darkness. Perhaps the gods were saving the children.

Jesse and his sons had been enviously close, romping and playing in that happy familial way. Jesse had imagined, and it could even be called an ambition, that he and Beverly would have many more children. His concession to macho was to have all boys—something about raising a baseball team. On those quiet nights while she lay pregnant, so full and beautiful, he would place his ear to her stomach and ask God (it felt more like a simple agreement with Him) to produce a particular kind of child. It never entered his mind that just a healthy child was enough. He imagined his firstborn to be beautiful like its mother, bright like its grandfather, and he hoped he would be happy like himself. He knew he could bring the happy for it was all he knew. When his sons were born, he made a complete nuisance of himself, stopping total strangers to proudly show his baby pictures. He soon learned that two kids were a handful and quite enough. He and Beverly would be content to raise their little family. *It would last forever—forever*—he thought. Zachery was, as Jesse himself had been, a momma's boy. He even had the look of his father, as Chad had inherited the look of his mother. Chad, on the other hand, was more like his father in other ways, given to reading and contemplation. But together they were all play and affection. They played ball, went for walks and to the movies. They played games as Jesse had with his brothers and sisters and laughed, how they laughed, almost constantly. There were trips to Detroit to see their beloved Auntie Allie and Hammy, which is what Chad's infantile grasp of English had dubbed his grandmother, Jesse's mother. The wonder of Jesse's childhood was being extended into the next generation, and Jesse could not have been happier. It was as if his dreams, all of them, however modest (and indeed they were modest) had come true. There was no additional thing he wanted. Jesse went nearly no place without them, and there was no place he would rather be than with them.

That life, looming in his memory like a fantasy, was gone now. Gone forever, like everything else that mattered. He could not retrieve it. Nor could he find anything or anybody on which to lean. Leaning may have been out, but wallowing in self-pity, spiced with drugs was in. He got drunk and high in his now endless pursuit of oblivion.

The boys, his sons, were crushed. Jesse was in the wind again, heaping pain on himself, and now, without calculating the effect, on his children. They had to gather their things, leave school, go home to Grand Rapids, Michigan, and the sadness Jesse had left there. Uprooted, they were suffering in ways neither of them, at their age, could describe or understand. They felt something, love, in fact, for their father, but it was laced with a disappointment so overwhelming that it altered them, weighed them down with a grief nearly equal to their father's. It became impossible for them to see their father in the same way. He had betrayed them. Once again, while flailing at the god-ship, he pounded himself and the ones he loved. He was to his children, and there was no way to refute this, as much the culprit, as the god he now despised was to him. There was no image of this grief in the billowing smoke of his pipe. The amber mirror at the bottom of the bottle adequately blurred his view of himself, just as it did with the grief. This level of companionship had become, had to be, a constant for him to go on.

This was not clear to Jesse. It was purposeful and relentless, but it was not clear. The drinking and doping had long ago ceased to make any difference. He was numb to anything but the memory of her, and always her image flowering in his mind would bring tears, pain, and a hunger for nothing at all except the past. While certainly not planned, this point of madness lent itself to his intended retribution. He had committed a foul act. He was now immersed in a life of foulness. It had become his way, and Jehovah must be suffering. But so were his sons.

Chad, upon arriving home, found himself increasingly covered in despair, building up on him like callus. As he went back to school, the old patterns, the bus route, were not happy reminders. He sat staring into the distance, feeling lost, neglected, and abused. It was a seminal moment that gave birth to sorrow, a sorrow that would last for decades. Chad had been the happiest of children, a bundle of joy, as they say. Now misery came to join him. It would be his companion in the way stupefaction was his father's.

Beverly was validated. She had told others how useless Jesse was, that the arrangement in Boston with his new wife would not work. Jesse was too immature, too selfish. Her satisfaction, however, was tempered by the reality of her loss of well-deserved freedom. Loving her children was not in question, but she had begun to build a life of her own, free of the daily pressures of having to make the constant motherly provisions. Now it felt as if Jesse was dumping the children on her. It was his turn, and he didn't have the maturity to handle it. The children he sent back to her were different. Chad brooded. Zachery lost interest in the basic things. They blamed him and her, and the loss of what was became intermittently unbearable. There were unpredictable eruptions based on no apparent thing. Once well behaved, the boys became unruly and occasionally disrespectful.

Far away, Jesse, removed from this wreckage, told the story of his wayward night, putting, without intending to, a manly spin on a despicable episode.

CHAPTER 23

The Cork 'n' Barrel

The Barrel was indeed Harry's place: it was his kind of place. With all he and Chuck had in common, they socialized very differently. While Chuck enjoyed women and drugs, just talking shit was his way of entertaining himself. He lived to talk shit. He could do it all night, as it was, after women and drugs, his favorite entertainment. A throng of sycophants in rapt attention was just another form of intoxication. The bar was his favorite stage, but he would take an audience where he found it. Harry, on the other hand was a gamer. He gambled on everything: dogs, horses, darts, and, of course, the four major national sports. The Barrel, or "Cork 'n' Barrel," as it was actually called, was his house. All of the gamers came to talk sports, play games, and place bets. There was something here for Chuck as well, as long as he bought drinks and shared lines of coke. This he would do until he or his listeners were too altered to pay attention.

The Barrel was not on a main street, but it was very near hallowed ground—a stone's throw from one of Harvard's halls. It sat on a side street claiming an entirely inadequate parking lot that didn't seem to belong to any one particular entity. At the door, and greeting everyone with a rather staged hostility, was a huge man named Sal Lippio. This bearded beer-bellied fellow was presumably the bouncer. He had very muscular arms beneath a layer of fat and wore a constant scowl that matched the variety of tasteless tattoos scarring his massive biceps and forearms. These hairy appendages fell out of a sleeveless leather vest that only in some small way covered a tattered T-shirt emblazoned with fading images of an equally grotesque rock band that protruded over a large buckled belt.

"Who's the spade?" he said as Harry, Chuck, and Jesse hit the door, his mustache fully covering his upper lip while moving in sync with it. "He's with us," said the Beast, causing him to drop his guard, but not his scowl, as he stroked his grizzly beard.

"Give him the respect." This Harry said while giving Sal the culturally approved handshake, but barely making eye contact. He swaggered in slapping hands while calling everyone who approached by a playful nickname: "What's up Toad," "Grog, my man," "Pea Brain, how's it hangin'?" This was a busy place at nine o'clock, but by eleven it was shoulder to shoulder. A much younger crowd was present than at Chuck's favorite haunt. It was like Drinking, Smoking, and Drugging 101, not at all like the seasoned inebriates at 'Around the Bend.' There was an obvious alliance with the bartender, an Irishman, like Harry himself, who actually ran the place. There was an assortment of ruffians, young toughs, who would happily do physical harm to anyone who violated the unwritten "house rules" or who may have wandered in unwittingly. It was a den primarily of the young Irish and Italian disenfranchised—even lost souls. The males outnumbered the females by only a small number. It was essentially an uneducated crowd, which struck Jesse as ironic, given its proximity to Harvard University. Jesse would fit right in except for one glaring fact. He was the only black person in the place. This required some delicate diplomacy. Blacks were not welcome here, or, for that matter, in any community outside of their own. The staring and whispering was immediate. But Jesse had come into the place with top dogs, his ticket in, and so was given "the respect."

The place was reasonably clean, but it had the smell of, how shall I say this . . . poverty. These were working-class people or not working at all. Despair of some kind pervaded the room, hung over it like a moldy mist. The conversation was simple repetitive gossip, dealing always with the banalities of the poor. The language, almost without exception, was profane and crude, rolling off the lips of a room full of people who had already learned all they ever would. Jesse did notice however, in passing, a woman reading a novel and looking, in doing so, nearly as out of place as himself. Primarily though, this was a hapless flock, easily controlled by the deceptively clever Harry "the Beast" O'Connell.

In this unaccoutered establishment, Harry had his own table. No matter how crowded, his table stayed unoccupied, unless he gave permission for someone to sit there. There was a very long bar on the left that greeted the patrons the moment they turned into the room. Across from it was a stand-alone bar-like structure running the length of the primary bar, but narrower, with stools only. Behind it sat a series of ordinary square tables adorned by nothing more than ashtrays and beer bottles, most of them rocking from years of abuse. A jukebox was housed here playing rock and country music, and all of it too loud. In this area, Harry's "office" was located. Apparently, in this place, Harry was boss. As he said to Chuck, "Take care of your boy while I handle some business." At that very moment a waitress with no identifying badge or uniform brought a tray of Dewar's shots and four bottles of Killian's and set them on the table.

Chuck, in his usual playful style, said, "Hey, Gina, I want you to meet a good friend of mine. This is Jesse "the Black Snake" Brightmeyer. We got some business to do, so keep 'em coming." Happily for Jesse, the "black snake" thing did not stick.

"You know I will, Snaps. You just better remember to take care of me this time." Gina was thin, worn, and overly made up but not unattractive.

"Don't be mean, Sugar. I thought you were my girl."

"Duckets, Chucky, I got mouths to feed," she said as she hurried away.

Chuck began pointing people out and telling Jesse about them. Who could be trusted, who could not be, who wanted in, and who were the lackeys. He pointed to the easy pussy and "the one or two bitches" nobody could have.

"So can we trust this guy or not?" Harry showed up and uttered this formality, knowing full well that Jesse had already passed muster.

"If we can trust him, does he have the balls? We can make some serious jack if he's got the stones and wants in. Did you tell him anything?"

"Look, Jesse, selling cars is for shit," Chuck began, as much as confessing that the whole dealership thing was just a game. "There's real money there, but it ain't in selling cars. It's in stealin' 'em. We got a little plan," he said, wearing what the locals called a "shit-eatin'" grin.

"You've got a plan. Let me hear about it. How do I fit in? I assume if you didn't need me, you wouldn't be telling me about it."

Jesse liked the sound of it, as boy talk, but he didn't think they were serious.

Harry took over. "You guys are the big fellas, am I right? You're the hot dogs selling most of the cars. That means you got the keys or you can get 'em. Perfect. I'll send five or six of my people, buyers, you know, all dressed to the nines. You guys take them on a test drive. I got Jake down at the hardware, ready to cut keys. Five minutes up to the square and back. You put the keys back in the cage, and we've got copies for a midnight run."

"So you got the keys, and you got the cars. Who's going to buy stolen cars? The dealership still has the paperwork." Jesse was now nibbling at the bait.

Harry interrupted, "Let's have a couple of drinks, snort a few lines. We'll talk later. I gotta kick some ass in darts. Jesse, you play?"

This was so abrupt that Jesse was not certain that his question had not upset him.

"I've never played, but I usually hit what I'm aiming at."

"Oh, a shit talkin' motherfucker. Well, come on, let's see what you got."

"Hey, man, I thought we were going to do some lines," said Chuck, having no interest whatsoever in throwing darts.

"We're going to the court. You got the shit? I gave you the shit at the dealership."

"Yeah. I got it. Let's do a G in one hit. Three-foot line. Jesse, you want in?"

"Let me get this straight. You're going to do a whole gram in one hit? I think I'll just watch."

"The man's a pussy. Let's show him how real men get high."

There was yet another bar-like structure surrounding the dart court. In an exercise of power, given the possible legal consequences, they cut a line of the seductive sugar right on top of the bar that stretched almost four feet. Chuck conspicuously and cleverly rolled a hundred-dollar bill, making a straw, while Harry took out of his wallet a brass straw that looked very much like gold. They then assumed positions at opposite ends of the linear mound. A crowd gathered, as this was not a common sight, and of course, bets were placed. Much of the commotion was envy and the possibility of getting some of the leavings, but it was great fun for this bevy. People asked them to wait for them to get their drinks, find their seat, or find a good place to stand for the event.

It was a ridiculous display that was fully enjoyed by all the locals. Chuck bought beers and shots for the most devout among them. Even a few were invited into the "back room" for some more snorting. The back room was actually the storeroom of the bar with heavy cardboard cases of full and empty beer bottles stacked high; some were used as seats and tables. If you were here, in this room, you belonged. You were in.

Harry took command. "Look, fellas, we've got to have a meeting tonight. Little job, we don't need everybody, but everybody here is a brother . . ."

"Fuck that. I don't know this motherfuckin' spook." The Bostonian patois, sounding almost like a foreign language, came bellowing out of the mouth of one of the big hairy fellows, who evidently had enough favor to be in the room.

Harry, who was not a big man, in fact he would be one of the smaller men no matter what room he was in, got directly in this muscled fellow's face, looking him up, down, and finally up, and said, "What's your problem?"

This fellow, who could very well have been Sal Lippio's twin, did not cower at this; but it was obvious that the Beast had "the respect."

"I just don't like niggers," he said with pride and embarrassment at once.

"You calling my brother a nig . . ." Jesse interrupted here, seeing Harry posturing and preparing for a fight.

"Harry," he said, only slightly raising his voice, "let me handle this. Sounds like me and—what's your name, partner?"

"Mario, my name is Mario, and I ain't your fuckin' partner."

"Yeah, well, it sounds like Mario and I have something in common."

The six or eight guys in the room hushed. Having never met Jesse, and fighting being their manner of settling disputes, they were eager to see one. Jesse continued without any street-wise affectations. He spoke from the heart, as if he were back in one of the private rooms at the Kingdom Hall providing ministerial counseling. He entered Mario's private space without touching him.

"You see, I don't like niggers either. Most niggers don't even like themselves. Most don't even know they are niggers. The difference between us, that is, me and you, is that I know one when I see one. Nigger is not a color, it's not a neighborhood, and it is not a people. It's a behavior stemming from ignorance. You know, people who act without thinking, people who don't understand respect, friendship, or caring about someone other than themselves. When we go back out into the bar, look around—you'll see lots of people like that. I've only known Chuck for a few months, and Harry for just a few days, but we were brothers in an instant because we understand this. There may be some niggers in the bar, you may even have some niggers in your family, but there are none in this room." That last statement being a concession to the present company.

Mario winced at this, as if he finally felt something, something he had never felt before. He was insulted by this speech, and under any other circumstances he would do battle. If Mario had been speaking for others in the room, this brief sermon silenced them as well. To the extent that a thug can beam, Chuck and Harry did so, as they were proud of their newfound brother, and they became, as they say, as thick as thieves.

"Can we get to the business? Everybody here's got something to do. Some more than others, but we need everybody to pull this off. When the bar closes, we talk some more, I'll give you the details. I don't want people wondering. Besides, I got to kick Jesse's ass."

Everyone laughed, but it was the laugh of the stunned, the confused, and the not so happy. They all did a couple of lines before going back out onto the floor to engage the various frivolities of the forsaken.

"Oh, that's it. The Beast finally found somebody he can beat, fresh meat," someone said.

Chapter 24

Final Moments, Final Thoughts

She had grown weary of the pain. It had made its way into all of her pain centers, both physical and emotional. The perfect alliance of spirit, flesh, and fluids had broken down. This whole dusty, chaotic place, from which we had all come and for which she had the greatest affection, had become more than she could bear. "I'm not giving up, children, my body is giving out," she said. There had been talk between them, Him and her, discussing her transition. Prayer was her way, after years of giving thanks and asking for nearly nothing, she would now seek His blessing and higher ground by giving herself and her pain over to her god, who would deal with it, in His way, within the "twinkling of an eye."

The crisp sheets on which she lay were making it more difficult for her to feel her own skin, and the glistening, blinking medical equipment blurred before her eyes. Movement, however slight, was arduous. Sensations waned as is the way, one guesses, with the slow coming of the final enemy. For her, he seemed to come in peace, for when he arrived, the howling demons departed and her face assumed the beauty of her youth.

Her thoughts in these final moments went to her children: all of them were here in the sacrificial room. They had on their brave faces an acceptance of the inevitable, all but Jesse, whose face was pulped with moisture, and there was no courage on it. Rosalind was secure in the knowledge that she would see her mother again, in the new world, the promised paradise. Allison was, or seemed to be, working out through the sadness, the final details. She remembered that her father was upstairs in the same hospital, a double amputee now. Frankie was in the room but not actually there. His mind had drifted to "yesterdays" when he was her everything. He thought about buying her small pretty things, such as his first job would allow, in the years before her success as an insurance saleswoman, in the days before she traveled the globe, enjoying the privilege of her achievements. So many times, with his marvelous physicality, he would swoop her up into his arms, kissing her playfully while spinning her dizzy. He remembered recognizing for the first time that she was beautiful and how this was first brought to his attention by his teenage friends, both male and female. His father, to whom Madelyn's prettiness mattered as much as her intelligence, insisted that Frankie accept his mother's beauty as his standard, and any female who did not meet the high standard of his mother with her stunning attributes would not even be allowed in the house. Frankie smiled as he drifted to what in the end was a laughable episode in his march to manhood.

He had brought home a young woman that he was proud to introduce to the family. She was pretty enough, petite with inky black skin. Those were her gifts, but she had managed to do nothing with them. Her teeth were discolored, misaligned, and some were missing. She smiled reticently, as she was fully aware of this. The

Final Moments, Final Thoughts

foliage on her head barely resembled hair—it was more a tangled mass of greasy wire. There was something cute about her manner of speaking, but it fell far short of the perfect English that Brightmeyer demanded of his own children. It was a clumsy mix of a deeply Southern accent and the unmistakable sounds of the undereducated. Jesse, being just a boy, found her and all of her differences amusing. Not so for Brightmeyer. He brought a forced politeness to the introduction. After a few minutes of courteous chit-chat, Brightmeyer announced that it was time for Frankie to walk the young lady home. When he returned at about nine o'clock in the evening, he found everything that could be called his own on the front porch, stuffed in a suitcase and brown paper bags. The door was locked. Brightmeyer let him knock on the door for some time before going out to meet him on the front porch.

"Boy," he said under the glare of the porch light, the smoke from his ever-present cigarette climbing through the glow, and closing the door behind him "Tell me about your mother."

Frankie was completely flummoxed. "What . . . ? I don't know what you mean."

"Do you believe I got you a pretty momma?"

"Yes, Daddy, I guess momma is pretty."

"Do you think your mother is a classy woman?"

"I guess so . . . I . . ."

"So I get you a beautiful classy woman for a mother, and you think you can bring this trash home to meet your family."

"But, Daddy, I was just . . ."

"Don't 'but' me! Now you are not welcome in my house until you understand who your mother is and the kind of woman you have

184

to have in your life. You take your things and find someplace to live until you understand this."

With that, Brightmeyer went back inside, closed the door behind him, and locked it. Frankie was beside himself, completely confused, but for a moment he felt free. He no longer had to respond to the overbearing nature of his father. He could have his way in the streets. It wasn't long, as he walked the dark streets, before he realized that this was not really his idea of freedom. Within the mounting grief, this memory somehow brought a smile to his face.

Ashton labored with the peculiarities of her religion and her decision to die. She had a choice. There was a possibility for a transplant. A risky chance but plump with hope. *Why would her god disapprove?* he wondered. The procedure was complicated only by the limits of medical science in the mid-seventies, *but the chance should be seized*, he thought. He had trouble understanding his mother's position. "What is death to a Christian?" she said, with all the confidence and satisfaction of a woman who had fully embraced the promise of eternal life. She was convinced that taking the organs of another human being, even to save her own life, was tantamount to cannibalism—an unforgiveable offense to her god.

Edison, sitting quietly, would rise occasionally to touch her hand or caress her brow. He was, in many ways, closer to her than he was to his own mother, Madelyn's sister. She and Brightmeyer made no distinction in how they raised their nephew versus their own children. He was every bit the good son, and he suffered, but he too thought of her as having fought the good fight and would await the Lord's redemption, at resurrection, which of course was coming soon. Eddie was not the most affectionate son, but he touched each of his cousins in his most loving way.

Madelyn began, almost casually, talking about her things, who should have what from her accumulations. There were three houses, all modest, but there was some value in that they were paid off. There were two cars and a house full of furniture, to say nothing of insurance and bank accounts.

There was also a new husband. Eight months earlier, Jesse, still a Christian minister, had officiated the wedding of his mother to an unremarkable fellow who had received mixed reviews from family and friends. It was not that he was white, although that immutable fact did seem to bother some in her circle. It was the belief that he brought nothing with him, nothing of his own. He certainly did not have Brightmeyer's intelligence or sophistication, but that was not expected. He was sufficiently good looking and affable enough. He served the same god, which of course was a requirement. Rather it was his lack of any trait that could be called interesting. Ted Harrison was boring. In a family like the Brightmeyers, there was probably no greater offense. What is more, as her husband, he had certain legal rights, and he was diligent in exercising them. He even seemed, according to the girls, to be plotting. This unnerved them and created a level of distrust that was unpleasant and distracting. It was decided not to share these concerns with their mother, choosing instead to take up this fight later when she was . . . gone.

For his part, Jesse simply could not understand. This moment could not be real. She could not be leaving. It just didn't make sense. What was the purpose of prayer? What was he supposed to do? Was he supposed to accept this nightmare as his? What was all of this talk about her things? His family must be mad. A tick, a click, and he was adrift again . . .

"Just a few more minutes, and we'll be home. Come on, Jesse, you can do this. Let's slow down a little, Frankie. Your brother has had enough excitement for one day." She had walked a half mile or so to the Western Farmers Market to buy fruit and vegetables for canning. She took Frankie along as usual for his muscle, his patience, and company. She could not keep Jesse away, as these were his favorite people in the world. She was a bit reluctant, given the great crowd at the market and Jesse's small size and young age, but relented as Jesse pleaded and promised to be good. It helped that Frankie was comfortable watching over his little brother.

Jesse loved the many smells and the colors of the open market. New aromas were all around: cut flowers, fruit and vegetables of an amazing variety, even the smell of rotting vegetation was a curious development for the nine-year-old boy. There were live and slaughtered chickens, ducks, and rabbits. For Jesse, it may as well have been an amusement park.

Frankie was just doing his mother's bidding, watching her thump the melons, feel and smell the leafy plants and herbs in order to make the best choices for her family. The process required them to take their eyes off Jesse for moments at a time. During one of those distracted moments, when they looked up again, Jesse was nowhere to be found. He had been absorbed by the crowd and was being ushered unwittingly away from them. The detachment was known to young Jesse long before it was clear to his family. With his eyes welling up, he began to call for his mommy. Within seconds, the loss of her from his view caused him to cry out loud with the deepest dread he had ever known in his short life. Even as a boy, he began to breathe heavily, tremble uncontrollably, and perspire. A well-meaning adult did what he could to comfort the boy, holding his hand, and staying with him until his mother responded to his cries.

"When we get home, I'm going to make you a nice blueberry cobbler. Would you like that, Jesse?" she said, knowing full well it was already on the menu but that it would also make him feel better to hear it this way.

"Yes," he whimpered.

They had to carry quite a load of produce, and little Jesse was trying to do his part, but he was more in the way than anything. It was necessary to stop several times for him to catch up and catch his breath. When they got home, all of the children pitched in to help cut the fresh fruit and vegetables and store the goods. Madelyn made fried chicken, hot homemade rolls, and prepared some of those fresh vegetables. She told the family about Jesse getting lost and what a brave little boy he must be and what a big help he was on the walk home. Frankie smiled and rubbed his little brother's head. After the food was put away and before Madelyn began cooking, little Jesse darted into the backyard and up a neighbor's mulberry tree, picking more fruit for his loving mother.

Now there would be no fruit to pick and no one to hold his hand. This time he would be lost in the crowd, and apparently never to be found.

Chapter 25

Dinner with JoAnne

She had a place in Quincy. No, not Quincy, that was where Jesse got entangled with two Irish sisters. It was two months of sexual abandon. There was the husband, a boyfriend, drugs, an arrest leading to a couple of nights in jail, but that story gets me off the point.

JoAnne Hubble, Roger's wife, had a place near, that is to say, overlooking the ocean. The phone number she had given to Jesse rang there, about a forty-five minute drive from the Boston-Cambridge area. It was about three-thirty when Jesse got around to dialing it. She answered the phone cautiously, needing to be certain it was Jesse before revealing her delight.

"May I speak with Mrs. Hubble," said Jesse, ever so formally and even slightly disguising his voice. He too was cautious, and she was not fooled. "Hello, Mr. Brightmeyer. I was hoping you would call."

"Of course, I could hardly wait. Your scent has been with me since we met. I am longing to see you again." He had not rehearsed this statement. It was true, but it was said for effect.

"Oh my," she said, "you have such lovely things to say, and I love the way you say them. It has been some time since I enjoyed a conversation such as we had at my house."

"Thank you, me too, I enjoyed our time together. You have a fascinating way of being. I am hoping for much more." He wanted to be sure the goal was shared. There was the briefest pause between every sentence.

"Do you suppose I could buy you dinner?" she said.

Jesse was now living in yet another suburb of Boston. The affair with Greta and Ramona left him homeless and spending a few nights at Chuck's place in South Dorchester until he could find an apartment of his own. It struck Jesse as strange that Chuck would let him stay in his home, alone with his wife, in that Chuck was so seldom home and he knew who Jesse was. Perhaps he knew better who his wife was. In any case, both Jesse and Chuck's wife were honorable during the brief stay.

What he found was not an apartment at all. It was a basement of a house in the community of Somerville. A clammy place with a cot and a half bath: a toilet and a sink. The house was owned by an imperialistic French dowager, who insisted on being formally addressed as Mademoiselle DeSusse. Her house was small, with a quaint and a once-beautiful garden as a backyard. It had arched trellises adorned with unruly climbing vines. The interior of the house was not dirty, but it was neglected, needing a good dusting. An assortment of curiosities were carelessly placed throughout, and the carpet was somewhat matted. One was tempted to think of the art on the walls as original, but closer examination made that conclusion too great a leap. Her accent was something other than French, being as it was, influenced by several other languages, picked up somewhat incidentally during her youth. There was no pretty sound in it, but it was interesting.

The ad in the paper said, "Apartment to let. Must be single, no pets." She was not looking for a tenant at all. What she really wanted was a servant, and a dark-skinned one matched her memory of a life long gone.

When Jesse arrived to see the place, he was pleased by the quiet cleanliness of the neighborhood. It, and the exterior of the house itself, completely disguised the accommodations. The basement was a dank, unkempt hovel. Jesse was even accosted by a rat, hurdling from a window well over his soup and sandwich. What was worse were her silly demands: he must be in by eleven, he would have to do chores, he could not have use of the kitchen, and she wanted him to accompany her—drive her car—as she made her errands. Jesse said yes to all of these conditions because it gave him someplace to be, and the rent was so manageable. He also decided, in spite of the fact that she was approaching seventy, to seduce her and lay down some rules of his own. It wasn't long before he was driving her car without her in it and coming home when he wanted to, albeit to some irritating barbs.

The invitation to dinner was exciting for at least two reasons. He really wanted to be with this woman, for however long, and he did not want to go home and deal with the insanity of Mademoiselle DeSusse.

"Why, yes, I think you can have me for dinner. Let's think of it that way: me for dinner, you for dessert." JoAnne laughed out loud, anticipating an evening of fun with her new wordsmith.

"Well," she said after the laughter, "I like the sound of that. I like that you make me laugh . . . you make me think too . . . and remember. I feel as if I have found something I had forgotten I was looking for." There was something strangely somber and reflective in her comments, coming so soon behind the laughter. Still, Jesse could tell that they both were sensing that a fine evening awaited them.

"So, my dear, where shall we dine?"

She was coming into town that night, and there was a fine isolated restaurant on Beacon Street in Boston where she felt comfortable. It was a French establishment, which of course brought Mademoiselle DeSusse to mind. Jesse dismissed the image immediately and agreed to meet her there at seven o'clock.

This section of Beacon Street was a commercialized strip of row houses. Decades prior it had been residential housing. It was now considered one of the more prestigious areas to shop, dine, or just be seen in. Bistros and bazaars lined the street, and the presence of all of that relaxed humanity enhanced an already irresistible evening. However isolated the restaurant, the street itself was so popular that Jesse thought JoAnne must be more comfortable being seen with him in public than he imagined a married woman would be. The people who came here were essentially the "well-to-do," and they would use this avenue to show off their wealth, wearing their finest clothing and accessories. As it happens, Jesse, while at work, was appropriately dressed for this fashionable society, wearing a pinstriped designer suit. He wished he had worn a different tie, and he needed to have a shoeshine.

Jesse arrived a few minutes before seven. He had some minor difficulty finding the place, as indeed it was isolated, on a street veritably cluttered with shops. The avenue was elegant to be sure, but the signage all along the way seemed garish and noisy. One descended to a lower level, between two small but exclusive clothing shops. Gated wrought-iron rails, shiny and black, greeted the clientele, but their configuration made it difficult to determine which way to go. While his race and his company made him conspicuous, he felt in every other way as if he belonged here. JoAnne had only just arrived herself and was standing before the maître d', looking absolutely ravishing. She wore a black sleeveless dress with a translucent black shawl that had many bright colors on it. Her nails and lips were painted exquisitely, and her toes glistened through stylish fabric-covered sandals that almost exactly matched her shawl.

When she saw Jesse, she lit up like a young bride and walked shamelessly into his arms, kissing him as she had wanted to since she met him. The kiss was too salacious for a public place, especially given the possible racial tensions, but it was witnessed by only a few, and those few seemed undisturbed by the overt display of interracial affection.

"Dessert first," said Jesse, at which the formally dressed maître d' smiled.

"I guess I missed you." She paused while the two of them eyed each other, deciding that they were pleased with the way each was dressed. Jesse was glad he had taken the time to get his shoes shined.

"You look wonderful," she said, beaming with a pride that suggested ownership.

"I could start my meal right here," he said, looking purposely at her thin but deliciously painted lips, and returning the compliment.

The tables were round, small, linen covered, and dappled with the daintiest floral arrangement, consisting of a single rose, baby's breath, and a green garnish Jesse could not recognize. Two and four-seat assemblies added up to less than thirty settings. The lighting was romantically dim, but cleverly placed pendants shed just enough light over each table. A huge renaissance-style painting hung like a mural on the only wall capable of accommodating it, with a soft revealing light of its own. The patrons had the appearance of so many sophisticates, with quiet chatter floating in the air.

JoAnne had made reservations, which of course was required. They were seated beneath that massive mural, and, given its light, it almost seemed as if they were on stage. A location about which JoAnne said, "This is interesting. I've eaten here many times but never at this table. I like this spot."

"It's very nice," said Jesse, "I feel like I have you all to myself and the whole world is watching."

She asked if she could order for him. There was a particular meal she wanted him to try, but she wanted him to choose the wine. She seemed overjoyed that he would allow it and that he was comfortable choosing the wine. Roger, she said, had the most uninteresting eating habits, that he wouldn't even eat here, preferring American fare—meat and potatoes.

The evening progressed comfortably with the anticipated rapport unfolding as hoped and sexual tension pulsating just beneath the conversation. They flirted only with their eyes, as it was in some ways a continuation of the conversation begun at her house, furtively, in the presence of her husband. The touching started after two glasses of wine. JoAnne reached across the small table and touched his hand as he fingered the stem of his glassware. The touch was a signal announcing that she had something more poignant to say. She wanted his attention in a way she had not demanded earlier in the evening. She looked down at the linen cloth, her damp fingers caressing his, and said, "I know that you are married . . . well, I am married . . . and . . . I should not be wanting this or saying this . . . but . . . I want you for my own. What I mean is . . . I have never been untrue to my husband. I never wanted to be despite the fact that our life together has settled into what many would call a boring routine. Roger is a sweet man, and I do love him. I am not excited by him, but I do love him."

Here Jesse tried to interrupt, but she moved the glass and seized both his hands, pressing them into the softness of her own. She wasn't finished, did not want to be interrupted, and this gesture was enough to make her point. It was just as well because Jesse had no clearly formulated thought to share.

"I have missed, I could even say, I have never had . . . anyone stimulate my mind in the way that you do. I want now to be selfish and have something for me. I want you for me, to hold you, to kiss you, to call you when I need you. I want to give myself to you. Will you have me? Please don't answer that, at least not yet." She seemed suddenly nervous, as if her speech was poorly rehearsed or completely impromptu. She continued with the promise of secrecy, gifts, and advantages.

The talk had the effect of making Jesse feel sorry for her. It wasn't a pitiful kind of sorrow, but Jesse understood something about longing. Her eyes steamed up, and a twitching showed at the corners of her mouth, which conversely had Jesse feeling the need to take her in his arms, in her bed, and make love to her. The advantage, such as it was, was his, and there was no wish to seize it, but there was a subtle learning: JoAnne had a profound sadness of her own. Jesse had unwittingly brought it to her attention. In all the world, he imagined only himself to be suffering; he was the only lonely one on the planet. Such was the nature of his madness. This woman's pain was unlike his, but he was able to feel it as if it was. His solution, to take her into his arms, somehow felt ministerial.

"I will be there for you, but you must be mindful of my limitations," was among his responses, but he wondered if she had been listening to him. Could she not see the oozing emotional chancre on his spirit? Or hear the thumping of his heart when he talked about his mother? He had so often been accused of flowery language; perhaps he had been too eloquent or poetic in his description of his own sorrow, his own condition, for her to see the depth of his despair. Somehow, in his crippled condition she found him to be a helpful ally. She wanted him. No one else did. Ramona and Beverly quite rightly did not.

For years Jesse had been a counselor of sorts as one of his ministerial roles. He had taken his Christian lessons seriously, and any sober conversation always came from that place. It wasn't so much that he composed a supportive pastoral talk, but rather he simply lapsed into it. It was his mother tongue, if you will, the jargon he knew best. He was so practiced at it that his words were always comforting in such a way that people would seek him out during their greatest trouble. Now he sat gazing upon this pretty woman whose trouble could only be called ordinary. He had shared his feelings about his catastrophic pain, he thought, in the way that broken hearts do, and she found in it a place for herself—not unlike a homeless person taking refuge under a cold and leaky viaduct.

CHAPTER 26

The Dart Culture . . . and Bernie

They played steel tip darts passionately. A group of young men, who seemed serious about nothing at all, except this game, would gather at the court to hustle and play. Various levels of skill existed among them, but to a person they treated it like something much more than a game.

Jesse observed that the bars in Boston were constantly full. It was apparent that no one wanted to go home. Home in the Boston area was an unwieldy affair, especially for the poor. Rents were high, quarters were tight, and people would share living space with anyone who was available and could afford to pay their share. Unavoidably these conditions led to some very unpleasant, even hostile, relationships. Sleeping arrangements were crude, including floors and tabletops. Some bedrooms here were the size of closets anywhere else. Most roommates were drunk when they came home, or if they came home at all, they would often end up in the wrong room or bed, which led to unplanned, unwanted, and unremembered sex, and, of course, fights and arguments. A basic cultural hostility grew from this and poured over into the crowded streets of concrete and brick. It was a hard place. The softness of trees, flowers, and birds was missing. There was even an arboretum where one could go to see trees as if they were relics from the past or an endangered species. Most of these people found their family, such as it was, and their peace at the bar. Jesse wondered if the rows of liquor bottles, so colorful and varied, provided the kind of comfort for them as the trees in his old neighborhood had done for him. Was this cacophony of loud music, bitter talk, and the clashing of bottles and glasses a sound they had grown accustomed to? Did it please them like the singing of birds and the laughter of children had done for him?

The dart crowd was also the drug crowd. Well, if the truth be told, everyone here did drugs. Most of them were addicted to drugs and alcohol. Darts was an addiction of its own, along with the gambling and competition. A few of the guys were exceptional, and they made up the six—to eight-man team. Yes, there was a league, a highly competitive league, that could lead all the way to a national title. No one here was good enough for that, but regional titles were within their reach.

There were six horsehair dartboards, and always there was line of people waiting to play. The boards were dominated by the eight or ten guys on the team because in order to stay at the board, you had to win. The minimum bet was a beer. So eventually, as each night wore on, the team would occupy the two most visible boards, and the upstarts, the rookies as they called them, would rotate on the remaining boards. Harry was the captain of the team, and he ruled it like he did everything else at the Barrel. He walked on the court saying, "I got next," putting his initials on the blackboard used for keeping score and writing Jesse's initials beneath his.

True to his boast, Jesse hit what he aimed at, and there was something in it that was reminiscent of his childhood, throwing rocks and balls at just about anything that he could reach . . .

"I'm not kidding you. You should see my little brother's arm. The boy can throw, hard and straight. Nothing but strikes, I'm telling you. He hits what he aims at."

Frankie was being recruited by pro baseball scouts even as a sixteen-year-old. He wasn't talking to the scouts though. Some of his friends were with him, and he had been bragging about his own prowess at hitting a baseball. He actually did excel at it, and while his best sports were football and boxing, his skills with the round stick had come to the attention of the pros. Now he was just horsing around with his boys, placing quarter bets about who could hit the most home runs and who could hit his little brother's pitching. They were not really home runs, but balls hit far enough to land on a rooftop some 250 feet away from the makeshift home plate. He walked into the narrow space between the houses, into the backyard, yelling, "Hey, Jesse, where are you?" looking eagerly for his young sensation. To Jesse, the sound of Frankie's voice was second only to his mother's, and if he was within an earshot, he would come running.

"Frankie," he said, beaming at just being called by his brother. "What cha doin'?"

Frankie rubbed his head and pushed a hard rubber ball into his chest. "Jesse, you want to play some catch?" He chose not to announce that he simply wanted to show him off.

This was not a typical occasion. Frankie was sufficiently older than Jesse so that they did not socialize when Frankie was with his friends. Frankie played with his siblings as big brothers do. He had, in fact, showed Jesse how to throw and catch, but here he was with his buddies, and Jesse loved the idea of playing with the big boys.

He had been in the crawl space under the house, having followed one of the many feral cats into the dirty space, the dust flying off him when his brother placed the ball in his torso.

"Check out my kid brother," he said, almost whispering, not wanting to put Jesse on the spot. Everybody had gloves except Jesse. That he was the only left hander in the neighborhood, and his father was not into sports, meant he never had a properly fitted glove. Frankie took a glove from one of his pals and tossed it to his little brother. Little Jesse took the off-handed glove and disfigured it oddly on his right hand. He was accustomed to doing this, as he did not yet have a glove of his own. Even as a ten-year-old, he could catch and throw as well as the much older boys. Every day Jesse would play some manner of baseball. Even if he was alone, he would throw the ball against a concrete wall or porch steps and catch the caroms. A strike box had been drawn on the back wall of a commercial building, and little Jesse practiced so much and had such natural ability that he could land the ball in the box nearly every time he threw it. In the alley there were many rocks, as it was paved in gravel, and Jesse would often spend his time throwing them at trees, rodents, and utility poles, striking them every time.

Jesse ran to the end of the yard and threw the ball to Frankie, who threw it to some else, who in turn threw the ball to yet another person. With all of his bragging about his brother, one of the guys hurled the ball harder than he should have to a ten-year-old. That's what he thought, but Jesse caught the ball with ease and fired it back even harder. "Man, that boy can play. Did you see that? He sure can throw, but I know that little punk can't strike me out."

They took a bat and walked down to the field where the strike box was drawn on the concrete block wall, the back of a retail store. This was Jesse's spot, given that he was there every day, practicing and leaving ball marks in every inch of the strike zone. Not that these older boys were great ball players, but Jesse didn't miss, and there were pop-ups and ground balls that dribbled all over the makeshift field, but nobody, not even Frankie, hit a home run. Jesse did not care if they hit the ball. All he wanted to do was place the ball in the box, which he did throughout the hour or so exercise. Frankie was all smiles as he collected his quarters.

Before they finished, a group of neighborhood kids gathered and a full-blown game of baseball erupted. The custom was for a so-called captain to pick his team from among whoever showed up. Jesse was always picked first, because he was equally good with the bat. What he lacked, and this was crucial to the world around him, was a competitive edge. He just never cared who won. For him, it was all about the game, doing his best and having fun. It seemed as if he was just as happy to see anyone else do well. This was something that Frankie could never understand about his brother, and it was not to be understood by his new friends in New England.

Harry was a good player, and he had style, posturing at the line almost as if he was in a photo shoot. He had a preparatory ritual of sharpening his tips, wetting his flights, and cleaning his shafts. It was more than just show; he won his game and began razing Jesse.

"Come on, rookie, let's see what you got."

Jesse cared even less now about winning and losing. Most of these players were better than he, hitting the mark more often, but it was clear to them, given that Jesse had never played darts before, that he would be a good fit on the team. Jesse lost, of course, and it took a moment for him to grasp the odd scoring system. So there he stood on the sidelines, waiting for his next opportunity to play when he was approached by the clear-eyed and well-spoken woman he had seen reading a novel as he entered the bar.

"Hi," she said, "my name is Bernice. Bernice Hollingsworth. You're Jesse, right?"

"Yes, I am," he said, not the least bit surprised at being approached by a strange woman.

She had the straightest hair descending along her narrow face, touching her shoulders and staying without a flutter as still as her perfectly erect posture. Her eyes set unswervingly on him as if there were no one else in the room, and her lips barely moved when she talked. "I heard about your sermon in the back room, and I thought, 'I want to meet this guy.'"

"Sermon, is that the way you would put it? The word travels fast in this place."

"Well, my boyfriend was there. He's the one with the . . ."

"Hey, man, that was some ballsy shit you said in there." He was the one with the thick glasses, Jesse assumed, as this was the only thing that set him apart from the others who had gathered in the back room.

"You made some friends and some enemies at the same damn time."

"Well, I hope Mario understood. I think he did."

"Hell, that stupid fuck don't know shit from Shinola. He's probably walking around now with a headache. Besides, who gives a shit? He's just a damn gumba. I'm Al, this is my girlfriend, Bernice. Everybody calls her Bernie."

Bernice was annoyed by the interruption and finally spoke to it. "You do know you're being rude, right? I had just started a conversation when you showed up and started blathering. Sheesh, some people. Don't mind him, Jesse, he's always a bit uncouth. So I guess it got a little ugly in there, hey?"

"Aw, just boys being boys, protecting their turf, you know. Most people are afraid of the unfamiliar. We either flee or behave badly." Jesse still had that ministerial edge to his conversation. "So it's nice to meet you both. Tell me something good."

"Something good, huh, you're in the wrong place for that. Or don't you know where you are?" She smiled broadly, and dimples creased behind her curtain of hair.

This question, uttered ever so casually, gave Jesse something to think about. It made him look around, much more than he did under Chuck's tutelage, or certainly in a different way. Within the pause and the review, Jesse looked at her and wondered why she was here. What was her story? She, it seemed, had coupled beneath her station and had chosen to socialize, even settle in a place that could not have been predicted based on what he imagined to be her past. A past not known to Jesse, but now, suddenly, he wanted to know.

"Well, let's just say I am among friends," Jesse said with more hope than fact, but Harry's defense of him had been convincing.

"Okay," she said, "but where are your . . . other . . . friends?" framing "other" in verbal quotation marks. "I mean, you didn't just fall out of the sky. Where are you from? You are obviously not from around here. Not many people come into the Barrel who can speak in complete sentences."

"And yet, here you stand," said Jesse. "I could ask you the same questions."

"Oh shit, here we go. In a minute they're going to be talking about books, politics, and shit." Al actually enjoyed listening to his girlfriend converse and seemed genuinely glad that finally there was someone in the bar with whom she could. She was so unlike the other women (for that matter the other people) in the bar.

"I'm actually not from around here either, but I have been here for over ten years. I'm from New York."

"New York, I've got people there on my dad's side of the family. I spent a lot of time there in my life, but it is not among my favorite places. I'm from Detroit."

This kind of introductory talk was burdensome or unsettling to many, but Jesse accepted it as a necessary route to getting to know people. He had become comfortable with it. It drew people to him in a way that led to a kind of dependency, which, while he should have, he didn't see coming. He was approachable and a good listener.

Bernie saw this and began talking. She had much to say about her past, her current situation, and her hopes and dreams. As she talked, she drank voraciously and yet, somehow, daintily.

"Hey, Jesse, you're up, or are you gonna talk all night? What is this guy, a fucking priest?" Harry had won again, actually four in a row and wanted to humble Jesse again.

"Shit, let 'em talk. I'll take his game," said Al.

There was a man rule about to be broken—talking to a woman instead of playing with boys would be a sacrilege in this place. So into the court he went to receive another lesson.

"I gotta go, Bernie. Nice talking with you. I've got to humble the big boys, you understand."

Bernie was suddenly hurried. "That's okay, I have to go to work, and I'm about to be late."

"Work? At this hour? What do you do?"

"I tend bar around the corner. I'll see you guys in . . . four hours," she said looking at her watch and carrying her narrow frame quickly toward the door. Al let Jesse borrow his darts, saying they would fly better than Harry's. Yes, there was competition even about equipment, you know, "my dog is faster than your dog."

Jesse liked games. All games. As a child he and his siblings had played cards, Monopoly, marbles, checkers, you name it, and Jesse enjoyed them all. The innocence of games and the camaraderie of it suited his spirit. Everyone laughed and a familial sense of safety accompanied it. Jesse saw games that way; it was never about exerting superiority. He never found a way to be bitter or even disappointed about losing a game.

But here, in the dart court at the Cork 'n' Barrel, a very different attitude prevailed. Winning was everything.

CHAPTER 27

The Storefronts

The success at the moving company placed extraordinary demands on the young leadership. There was such an increase in the workload, so much more money in the bank, and so many more things to do with it, that work days began to last eighteen to twenty hours. Someone had to be in the office at the end of each workday, and many times one or more of the staff literally spent the night there. The office was somewhat new to them. While it was certainly an upgrade from the former storefront, it was still, nonetheless a storefront. Much more accommodating though, with storage and more square footage for office stations. There was only one separate space that was large enough to be considered an office, and it was quite small. The building was the kind of place one would expect to find on an active thoroughfare in one of the oldest communities in the country and situated among the working poor. The front wall consisted of large glass windows, with a recessed door, allowing for full viewing into or out of the place. They were original to the building, circa 1880 or so, and delineated by rusting metal mullions. They were accompanied by a certain historical charm, but it would require days of effort to actually clean them, so an everlasting haze clung to the surface. Still they provided what curb appeal there was and fit aesthetically into the surrounding structures. Three such windows had been installed on the borders of which, along with small ancient cracks, there was a promotional remnant of an enterprise that may have occupied the space decades ago. The stuff was impervious to every solvent known to man. Even so, it wasn't unsightly, just dated. The "new" office sat on a corner of a main street, but much of the activity, indeed the primary point of entry for the movers, was on the residential side street. There were apartments above, and the once-fine finish of the interior was as dull as the ancient colors affixed to the large glass windows. There was nothing particularly attractive about the colors either, having been done in the now-fading green and yellow.

It was the habit of the movers to have a drink, or several, at the end of the day, at a bar of their own choosing. On one of these late nights, when there were still three trucks out, Jesse got the idea of having a few drinks for the guys when they returned to the office. He himself had been out well into the evening, networking and seeking more work, and had had a few drinks with some potential clients. Eric and Rollie, both of whom were exhausted and ready for a drink themselves, were more than agreeable; they thought it was a great idea. Jesse agreed to "fly" if they would "buy." There were nine movers still out in three trucks, and with their appetites, that meant a couple of cases of beer. Jesse took the liberty of buying some hard stuff, suspecting that not everyone was a beer drinker.

It struck Jesse as odd that all three teams showed up within ten minutes of each other, but he seemed to be alone in his surprise. When the trucks pulled in and were all inspected, Eric offered a beer to the crews. Among the movers was a recent hire whose claim to tough-guy fame was that he was a second cousin to one of the local crime families. He even had a last name that sounded like it belonged to this dubious society. His proof, which of course was needed, was his easy access to high-end and inexpensive cocaine and marijuana. As the revelry began, shit, as they say, began to fly, fish stories if you will. The many challenges faced during the day, sexual come-ons by single women, and so on.

Rollie was happier than he had been in years, so taken was he by money. He was known to be frugal, and buying beer was a major splurge for him, and for once, he was spending with a smile. As the night wore on, Eric, on the other hand, grew somewhat agitated; something was missing—he wanted more. Mere celebration, the beer and liquor were not getting him where he wanted to be. What he wanted, the new guy, whose name was Leo, had. Leo was all about showing off or, more accurately in this case, sucking-up. Whether or not he was connected to some Mafioso family, he certainly was able to deliver high-end drugs and do so in buckets. This was, given Leo's access to drugs, his willingness to provide it—and no one sensed it—the beginning of the end of the meteoric rise of the young company.

Eric pulled Jesse aside and said through the booze, "You got any cash on you?" Jesse did not know that Eric was an abuser of alcohol and drugs. No one had spoken to him about it, but it was apparent that Rollie and some of the other movers were aware of it.

"I've got a little. What do you need?"

"Twenty bucks, that's all, just twenty. I'll get it back to you tomorrow." Jesse reached into his pocket and produced the money.

"My truck is locked in. Can you give me a ride? Just down the street." In a sober state, Eric would never ask for even a small favor.

Jesse had gotten comfortable, drinking and talking. Well, doing more listening than talking, and he wasn't excited about going back out for anything. Eric was the boss, however, and it was obvious that he shouldn't be driving, so he made the errand without begrudging. The destination was as Eric had said, just down the street where Jesse, who sat in the car, waited only a few minutes for Eric to do his thing and return. When he got back in the car, Eric said, "Pull over, I want to get this hit before we go back. Rollie would be pissed. You want a hit?" That statement and the hit were seamless, as if they were the same activity.

"Hell yeah," said Jesse, wanting the behavior more than the drug.

Eric snorted half of the package and handed the rest to Jesse. Jesse took, as he always did, a light hit, and handed the folded paper back to Eric, who immediately took all that remained. Just as immediately, he said, "You got any more money?" In the dark of the vehicle, Jesse could see Eric's glazing eyes darting. He had seen this before and knew instinctively he was in the presence of an addict. But he didn't care. "I can do better than that. There's a shit load of this stuff right there in the office."

"In the office? What the hell are you talking about?" His eyes widened and a smile broke on his round face.

"Leo, the new guy. Leo always has drugs on him." Jesse said this unhesitatingly. Just two hours prior, he would not have, but it was clear that Eric was "on the hill," and now nothing would be more important to him than getting some more of the elixir. Besides, Jesse did not want to continue making drugs runs into the dark of the night.

The ambience in the office had become more like a bar than a place of work. Beer bottles, smoke, and cigarettes were everywhere. There was so much laughter and talk, that Jesse luring Leo into one of the back rooms was done without notice.

Eric was mildly reluctant, even in his altered state. He was not certain that he wanted his new workers to know about his disability, but the urge was on him, and it, as it nearly always does, won the battle.

"We need some of that girl," Jesse said, as if he had been doing business with Leo for some time. Leo was taken aback, but he relished the moment.

"I don't know what you're talking about," he said, flashing a huge knowing smile. "You ain't working with a bunch of choirboys," said Jesse. "What you got on you? Hook us up."

"So you guys like the white pussy. What kind of jack do you want to spend?"

"You got a gram on you?"

"You got a C-note?" Jesse was aware of Leo's merchandising style and approached him in a manner Leo could not resist.

"You trying to get me fired, Jesse? Providing drugs for the boss man? I got a connection you know, but I still need my job."

"Don't worry about it, man. We're going to put you in charge of the warehouse anyway. You're part of the leadership. We're going to keep this little transaction between us . . . only us." Jesse looked over at Eric for confirmation.

Leo's promotion had been discussed but not decided. Now with Eric being completely compromised, he nodded approvingly and would have agreed to almost anything to get more blow. Leo knew he had a good hand and played it as well as any street huckster would.

"Let's have a taste. See if you like it. I got this shit out of Florida. Dominicans don't fuck around."

He was laying out for Jesse and Eric his credentials as if it mattered to them. Leo longed for respect, and he launched into a dissertation that was more for him than them: where it was grown, how it was packaged, how close he was to the cartel. Eric simply wanted more, and Jesse was, again, just acting, acting as if he was in the life, the life of junkies, criminals, and miscreants. It dawned on him that he could use this contact to impress Chuck and Harry at the Barrel and get some credentials of his own. Jesse had no plan, but he liked the idea of playing with the boys on his own terms. He knew enough to know that Chuck and Harry diluted their cocaine to improve their profit margins. They could get away with it because their clientele was always inebriated when they bought the product. This is probably why they always arrived at the bar late in the evening. They also typically only brought enough with them to drink for free and maintain their reputations.

Leo produced the hardware: a small brown bottle with a cap that had an even smaller spoon attached to its underside and a mirror about the size of a credit card. He opened the bottle as if some special skill was required to do so, then delicately tapped the glistening powder onto the spotless glass. Eric was waiting impatiently, like a child anticipating a birthday present. Leo was no addict, but he had an enormous appetite. He was like many drug aficionados, taken by the ritual almost as much as the drug itself. For himself he dipped the tiny spoon back into the little brown bottle and politely snorted the caviar, savoring it like a food critic assessing a special dish in a high-end restaurant.

"Have at it, fellas," he said, apparently wondering why Jesse and Eric had not already sampled his product.

"You got a blade," said Jesse, looking longingly at the mound of flour.

"Oh, I'm sorry. I thought you guys had your own shit." Leo knew they didn't, and holding back was quite deliberate; it gave him a sense of power.

With that, he went again into his stash of paraphernalia, producing a bronze tool with an angled handle designed to receive a razor blade and two metallic four-inch straws, both with spoon-shaped ends, allowing one to scoop or snort.

Jesse was impressed by the display, thinking that there must be a whole industry supporting this criminal pastime, but Eric simply wanted to deepen his euphoria. He nearly snatched the surgical tool from Leo's hand and brutally hacked off a large line of coke and hoggishly snorted it.

"Damn, you got an appetite," said Leo, while Jesse took a smaller and less aggressive taste.

"This shit is pure. Not that shit you're used to. If you ain't careful, you'll get too fucked up to get home. So how much do you want?"

"A gram, but I only have eighty dollars on me. Can I owe you the sawbuck?" Jesse had picked up the term "sawbuck" somewhere along the way; it was not a word he had ever heard in Detroit, and here somehow it referred to a twenty-dollar bill.

"Hell yeah, you guys are the boss people. I know you're good for it."

Jesse gave up the last money he had on him, Eric agreed to make good on the 120 dollars he now owed and disappeared into another room, into oblivion. Jesse went to work on Leo.

"So you're right this is some pretty good stuff. How much of it can you get? Can you get me a quarter ounce?"

"A quarter ounce, what the hell do you want with a quarter ounce?" Leo was as eager as Jesse. Like a businessman, he was always looking for new clients.

"I've got a little plan," said Jesse.

"Well, I've got a little business going on here. I don't need any competition from the boss. You know what I'm sayin'?"

"Look, Leo, my little business has nothing to do with this place. I can't afford to be seen selling this shit in here, and you better be careful. Eric is high now, but what is he going to say tomorrow? And no way should Rollie know about this. I got my own little place, and they sell garbage in there. I'm going to start my own little enterprise. So can you get me a quarter or not?"

"All right, man, cool your jets. I can get any amount you need, but I only got high quality. You can cut it in half, and it'll be better than anything you buy on the street, but it ain't cheap . . . and no credit—this is business. You got five big ones?"

"I'll bring it in tomorrow. What about all that nice hardware you got? Can you hook me up? You know, scales and shit . . ."

"Damn, Jesse, you sound serious. Tell you what I'll do: you bring me a grand, and I'll drop a heavy quarter and bring you some stuff to get started with, is that cool?"

"Yeah, that's cool, but I may need another week to get you a thousand dollars. But I'll have the five tomorrow."

It was now nearly one-thirty in the morning, and while Jesse had thought, mindlessly, to call Ramona earlier to say he would be coming home late, there was no one to call. Home, there is that word again. That word had become a dyslexic jumble of letters and emotions in Jesse's head. So much was missing; there was no home to retreat to. She had put him out; so rightly, she had sent him away.

His need for family, touching, laughter was such that he consistently misread people's intentions. He was like that lonely hound dog wagging his tail to anyone who would allow him near enough. Love, the thing he thought he knew so well and had such an abundance of, was nowhere to be found, so he invented it, a delicate minuet of laced-together agape. He erected things to be loved. Here now, he would bring drugs, a devilish seed, into a devilish place and win favor. He was already addicted . . . to his past, his memories. He was in a world of addicts who, unpredictably, would be caught up in his affliction, so compelling was it: all of those happy times that had forged this soft creature and made him so attractive, so vulnerable, would become, through his storytelling and his ministering, a new addiction for a bewildered and lost collection of humanity. These new people in his life would be so drawn to him, and the way he brought something most of them had never experienced, someone who would listen, make them think, push them to share. Jesse did not know, could not see, that he was bringing something far more useful and more intoxicating than drugs. He brought stories and lessons from a lovely time, and they longed for it. It filled a vast empty space. So many would require what he had.

Jesse's view of himself and the life around him was twisted. He looked for, unconsciously, childlike remembrances of a warm idyllic life . . . these were not hard to find, as they were always there on the edge of his mind, like a garnish left on the plate after a fine meal.

Chapter 28

The Kiss

The East Coast was, or may as well have been, a foreign country. New York, to Jesse, resembled a massive graveyard with large headstones adorned with windows. He did not like the city. The smell of the place was offensive, rife, with dead and decaying things. The stifling indifference of its millions crowding and pushing on every corner and its narrow streets created unease within him. Its three dimensions were glass, steel, and stone, and all sterile. It was as if Mother Nature had been murdered here and the sun dethroned. The place seemed rickety to Jesse, with rust and corrosion on its many bridges and abutments aching for relief.

It also was the place where the "Vatican" of Jehovah's Witnesses, a place known as Bethel, was headquartered. It was the holy place, if you will, of his mother's religion, the place presumably blessed by the god who took her from him, a huge multiplex in the heart of Brooklyn. Jesse had been there as a child, and he remembered the reverence, the awe in which it was held by the obsequious devotees. This is the place where all of the dogmatic literature was printed, the missionaries were trained, where what was called the "governing body" was housed, and a place where Jesse, in his youth, to please his mother, aspired to go.

In passing it, Jesse felt the rage descend upon him. He could get to his tormenter there. He could crash the "holy gates" and have his vengeance. *Stop the cab!* he heard this . . . plainly in his head. It was deafening, and for a moment he wondered why the cab kept going. This ephemeral moment came and went, like so many others, bringing with them a shortness of breath, an instantaneous burst of perspiration, and a longing to kill. Soon he heard Jimmy's voice, catching the sound of his words in midsentence, allowing him to break free of his horror.

It may be another of the great mysteries: how memories are born and cherished because, for Jimmy, this was home, and he lit up driving through it in the same way that Jesse beamed when he was in his beloved Detroit.

Jimmy was uncomfortable with his fame, and particularly so when being formally honored for it. It was fairly early in the day, and that evening Jimmy and several other literary giants were being honored for being just that. Jimmy was nervous. His prodigious mind did not allow him an awareness of his worth. He was comfortable with his achievements, but not his celebrity, and tonight he had to don a tuxedo with the requisite black tie and be praised. Honorees included Bill Styron, Phillip Roth, Claire Bloom, and among the invitees were Bill Blass, Jackie Onassis, Bill Paley, the owner or major stockholder at that time of CBS Television, and others worthy of mention if the point here was to drop names. On this night, James Baldwin had to stand and be recognized by his peers and critics, and he was all aflutter. This list of dignitaries meant little to Jesse. For him they were just people, and, of course, he did not have to impress anyone and was not concerned that anyone would or would not be impressed by him. It did not enter his mind that he was to be perceived as Jimmy's date. It was his job to get him there and on time. Nothing in Jimmy's nature respected punctuality, and this made Jesse's assignment all the more difficult. Jesse had already taken him to be fitted for the formal attire, but it had to be picked up, several people had to be called, and there were many related details to handle.

"So maybe we can stop and have a drink?" Jimmy said, he said, almost as if he was seeking permission.

The taxi had picked them up at his mother's house, a four-story apartment building that would never be called a house where Jesse was from. They were going to run a few errands, then settle down for a few hours' rest before embarking on the unnerving evening's activities.

"We could stop and have one at my brother's bar before going back to his house."

They had spent the night, several in fact, at his brother's apartment. His brother did not own the bar, but he had worked there so long that even the owner sometimes called it "David's Bar." Jesse had placed a liquor-compromised Jimmy Baldwin in front of enough microphones to be worried about the wisdom of this decision. But he was not the boss of the man, so he relented, saying, "Yeah, I guess that's cool. I'll have one with you, then go pick everything up and come back to get you."

"Oui, d'accord," said Jimmy, lapsing as he often did into French.

It was about four o'clock in the afternoon, and they had to be at the stately New York Library, where the event was being held, at seven. Jesse calculated that he had just enough time to satisfy all of the details without any rushing. When they opened the door to the bar, the patrons turned, saw Jimmy, and the party was on. Jesse decided not to have a drink. Instead he endured the introductions and announced to Jimmy that he was going to the apartment to prepare.

The ride to the historical library was accomplished by a limousine. Even it was a bit bothersome to Jimmy, as it seemed "conspicuous, ostentatious," he would say. Jesse was thinking during the ride that this must have been what the young man who had accompanied Jimmy in Detroit, when they first met, must have been going through. A new groom would have been less nervous.

There was the red carpet, the regal doormen, and a train of limos and expensive automobiles. Upon entering the building, escorts showed them to the assembly hall, a baroque, spotless, and tastefully painted facility, the design of which seemed to have as its primary goal to diminish the stature of anyone who walked into it. Luckily, one of the first persons they encountered was Bill Styron. Jimmy knew all of the honorees at one level or another, but he was most comfortable with Styron, who as a white male had had the audacity to write the controversial book *The Confessions of Nate Turner*, and Jimmy had defended his right to do so. There was the polite, "How have you been" conversation which relaxed Jimmy. Within this ventilating exchange, a volunteer interrupted with a bag of trinkets or memorabilia for the celebrities. There were seating assignments apparently well thought out, and baubles of some kind were placed on the tables as well. Jesse thought these treats were silly and useless, but everyone smiled politely as they were handed out.

A buzz, excited murmuring, suddenly spread throughout the vestibule just outside of the hall; and everyone turned their heads to find the cause for it. Jackie Onassis and her date, Bill Blass, had entered the room. She was lovely, and Mr. Blass was predictably splendid. She wore a dark (Jesse could not tell whether it was black, gray, or blue) outfit and looked every bit the international sophisticate she was. Her equally dark hair was manicured to a strand, giving her a royal visage. Jesse thought of, was reminded of, his mother. Somehow it took everything, or nothing at all, to bring her to his mind. Every woman he would be drawn to had something that was reminiscent of her: fingers, posture, voice, something, and this woman's poise brought Madelyn into view. Bill Blass was wearing a gray suit, fitting him perfectly, and a foulard tie that both matched and contrasted the fine ensemble.

Jimmy beamed at the sight of her. During the civil rights movement, he had occasion to meet her, and he was sincerely moved by the fact that she remembered him and greeted him warmly. Jimmy had never met the famous designer at her side, so she introduced them. Jesse was mildly annoyed at Mr. Blass' apparent indifference to the introduction. This somehow emboldened him. When they shook hands, he said something that implied they were social equals, which had the effect of making Bill Blass look again at Jesse for some hint of familiarity. He eyed the fine suit Jesse was wearing, and one could see him assessing the perfect fit. Had he been one of his models? How, as he searched his memory did he know this fellow? Jesse let him ponder and turned to Ms. Onassis, as if he knew her as well, lifted both her hands, kissed them, and then her, full on the lips. A peck, if you will, from a boy from Twenty-Third and Butternut, on the lips of one of the most famous women in the world. For her part, she seemed rightly surprised, but not offended; and her eyes, like her escort's, wondered, however briefly, who was this shiny young man in the pinstriped suit who had found his way to her soft lips.

After the gratifying evening, the honorees decided to go for a snack and a drink. They selected the Waldorf Astoria as the place to convene and wind down—one famous establishment to another. Within the vast lobby, there was a seating area that was attended to by the wait staff. It was after eleven, and so full meals were no longer being offered, but one could choose from a fairly accommodating selection of hors d'oeuvres and appetizers. Before they could be seated, Bill Paley, a very rich man, not known to Jesse, politely, but imperialistically, approached Jesse and said, "Ms. Bloom would like some scrambled eggs." With that statement, Jesse began to roil inside. How could this man not see that he was with the group? At least for this evening, Jesse was in this company and certainly not a waiter. He was carrying, as others were, the gifted paraphernalia of the night. He was dressed as well as anyone in the group and was clearly engaging the fraternity in the light conversation the evening produced. Jesse remembered his father extolling, "There is no one better than you." He thought of his mother and how no one in the room was her superior in style and poise. He reached for Mr. Paley's arm. He could see Jimmy quivering, knowing that Jesse was insulted and hoping he was not about to make a scene. While holding his arm tighter than he should have, Jesse looked him in his eyes and said with equal imperialism, "Would she now? Well, perhaps if you behave yourself and are a good boy, the waiter will bring you some." This entire moment took place in the presence of everyone there, and all of them were watching with just the right measure of embarrassment and anticipation. It was clear on Jimmy's face that he wished Jesse had taken another approach, and he said so. Jesse bellowed, somehow just above a whisper, "Fuck him. The racist son of a bitch," while Jimmy did all he could to calm him down.

Jesse did not care about consequences. The worst thing that could happen to him already had. To his credit, Mr. Paley was contrite, and the evening proceeded without any further unpleasantness.

It was not the kiss, or perhaps it was, that sent Jesse adrift during the proceedings. He heard none of the program as he took leave into his delicate senses, his memories. Perhaps it was the celebration itself . . .

It was Madelyn's night, as he remembered it, when she was to be honored. It was a smaller world to be sure, but still . . . to be honored by one's peers. This mother of five, domestic worker, and evangelist, found her way into the field of life insurance, after years of cooking and cleaning for hers and theirs. Options were limited for black people in the sixties, and selling life insurance was a way to make money doing something that was, to some extent, considered prestigious. To date, all insurance agents in the village were white males. The business allowed its practitioners to dress well for their work, giving them some of the aura and accoutrements of professionalism. They might as well have been senators or schoolteachers, as those who excelled at it were considered leaders in the community and made as much money as some doctors.

Madelyn excelled immediately. She worked for a small black company, of which there were several in those days, all setting up shop in neatly decorated storefront offices. Some of these companies did well enough to build mid-sized office buildings with their names emblazoned on them, miniature replicas of the big boys. This meant that her clientele, her co-workers, and all of her in-house superiors were black people. This was an attractive position to be in, given that most minorities worked all of their lives for white people doing menial jobs or worked in the factory's promised lands, those greasy, sunless plantations. The liberating effect of no longer having to answer to them cannot be overstated. It also meant, if you were good at it, you could make more money than most blacks ever thought possible. You could be your own boss, set you own schedule. Madelyn was making more money in a day than she had in a month cleaning houses.

Anyway the day had come for her to be recognized. She was to be "crowned" queen for a night or a year, memory fails. All of her children, now young adults, put on their finery and arranged their affairs to be in attendance. Her co-workers put aside their envy or brought their admiration to the gala. A banquet was being served, and they even decorated an oversized chair to resemble a throne.

She wore a straight white satin dress with shoulder straps trimmed in silver sequins, with the rainbow of colors bouncing from these prisms to the very realistic-looking tiara. A long flowing train of matching fabric swept the floor as she walked, so elegantly, to the podium. There was the apparent indispensable cache of treats, and the guests brought gifts as well. She had colored her lovely hair in a kind of subtle reddish-gold and had pearls about her graceful neck. Her children seemed proud of her, proud to be there. Jesse though was mixed: pleased and agitated with all this gushing over his mother.

That's my mother, he thought.

He and Frankie had always been very playful with her, so he decided to sneak up behind her and plant a big wet kiss on her striking neckline. Her attention was so completely divided that this was easy to do. Even the onlookers who saw him coming played along. But just as he was about to plant his lips on her neck, she turned, mouth open to address someone, I suppose, and Jesse's open mouth landed precisely on hers. For one second, lip to lip with the most beautiful creature he had ever seen, who happened to be his mother. Everyone laughed, even Madelyn, saying, "Jesse, you are such a clown . . ." or something. Jesse laughed too, feigning embarrassment. But sensations ran through his body that defied the senses. There was no place to put this moment without the invention of a sixth sense. Her mouth was cool and wet, fresh and invigorating. He tumbled amid the laughter, softly into that unknowable, childlike place, which could not have been more heavenly than her lap, her apron, her pillow, her breasts . . . her milk. Yes, perhaps it was the kiss.

CHAPTER 29

The Cote D'Azur

Jesse thought it would be a good idea to learn to speak French. It was one of the four languages that his father had mastered as a young man, when he thought he would spend his adult life as a translator working for the United Nations. This dream was lost to the rigors of raising a family and a culture that almost certainly would have denied him anyway. He died at home while living with Franklin, only a year or so after Madelyn's death. His passing did not disturb Jesse in any way. He shed no tears, feeling and acting more like a distant relative during the whole affair. But things had changed. He and Jesse had finally made good their father-son relationship, and by now Jesse had begun to understand the exigencies that made his father what he was, but it was years of reflection that finally led to Jesse fully embrace, even adore, his long-dead father. He had forgiven him. His learning French would be a tribute to his forgiven and now-appreciated father.

Brightmeyer never saw in Jesse the kind of heritable intelligence that Allison and Rosalind had and that he so fully expected from his progeny. Jesse was indeed bright enough to satisfy his father's ambitions, but in the formative years, they paid almost no attention to each other, and, of course, Jesse was a momma's boy. That he never developed a sense of competition did not help matters, nor did the fact that Jesse preferred climbing trees and sports to reading classical literature. He was not able to imagine himself superior to others nor could he grasp a connection between the name Brightmeyer and intelligence. The oft-heard phrase uttered by his father, "You are a Brightmeyer, act like it," did not resonate with Jesse. He had met others with the Brightmeyer moniker who were not intellectually inspiring. But his father would drone on about "his seed," the beautiful mother he had provided, and that excellence was the only option.

Jimmy had convinced his agent that he needed a protracted respite before taking on a demanding speaking tour—all those airports and hotel rooms. He was going "home" to the south of France and wanted Jesse to accompany him. Why not learn the language while he was there? This was pure vacation time, but it meant Jesse had to face the one phobia he had, one that even the loss of his mother had not altered: water, deep water. Flying over an ocean created for Jesse a discomfort one would have to be truly phobic to understand. In his youth, just crossing the Ambassador Bridge, which connected America to Canada in Detroit, would create such anxiety that he would have to close his eyes, find his way up a tree or some other place of comfort in his imagination. This irrational fear troubled his mother, and she felt some responsibility for it. Early in her ninth month of pregnancy, she and the fetus that would eventually be Jesse had to endure a fall down a flight of some twenty stairs, bouncing around in the maternal pouch filled with life-sustaining amniotic fluid. She had determined that this traumatic episode had debilitated her son, something she shamefully confessed to him when he was in his early twenties. Somehow this made sense to Jesse, and from time to time he would imagine his mother falling and doing all she could to protect her cherished issue. It generated within him an even greater respect for his mother.

The hills of the Cote D'Azur were spectacular, providing alluring vistas at every turn. A commuter plane took them from the Charles de Gaulle International Airport to a landing strip nearer to the village of Saint-Paul-De-Vence, which made no impression, but driving through the medieval landscapes provided a sense of calm for Jesse. There was nothing about it that was reminiscent of Detroit, or Michigan, but unlike Boston or New York, one could still feel the planet, its vibrations, and not the mechanical hum of most large American cities. In New York, even the wind felt like a contrivance, and the cobblestones of Boston were no match for the naturally sculpted sandstone, the result of centuries of brushstrokes delivered by unfathomable hands. There was no street here designed with a vehicle in mind. They were narrow and circuitous. It seemed as if one could put their hand out the window and touch every house they drove by. The driver and Jimmy conversed casually in French, mostly though, they drove in silence. During one of the periods of silence, the driver said something in French, as if talking to himself, that Jesse asked to have translated. "It means, 'God is good,'" said Jimmy, who did not appear to be as pleased about his arrival here as one would have expected.

Jesse thought, but did not say, *What an ignorant buffoon. God may be creative, but He certainly was not good.* This was an apparently decent human being, but Jesse wanted to hurt him for defending the heavenly miscreant. *She is gone. Can you not feel it? How can you forgive Him?*

But the place was earthbound; the smells were earthlike. The obvious manmade accessories had not disturbed it, had created little or no disharmony. That lifeline, connecting all things, was palpable here, and Jesse felt a familiarity. This was all completely disrupted when the tourists arrived, from everywhere it seemed, arm to arm, shoulder to shoulder. It became quite suddenly a noisy place.

In any case, his father, more than his mother, would be proud of this move, as he was not the least bit impressed with Jesse's rise through the church. The prestige was too limited, but this relationship put Jesse close enough to "high society" to give Brightmeyer bragging rights. Jesse could hear, could see his father pridefully telling his associates about his son's achievements. Such a moment never occurred while he lived. He bragged about his daughters, even boasted about Frankie, though he placed no esteem on his athletic exploits—he knew others would. But Jesse had belonged to his wife—she celebrated his accomplishments. This one, however, would mean nothing to her. It would have been all his.

When they arrived at the villa that Jimmy called his second home, there was again the feeling for Jesse that he had been here. He knew this place. It was a walled, fortress-like structure, the gates of which were wrought iron, and ruggedly anchored between very thick sandstone walls. The stone itself was yellowish brown in color, crumbling at many spots along its two-hundred-foot length, as it was as old as the residence, which was older than America. The front yard, if it could be called that, was vast, and one had to walk past an outside dining pergola, somewhat crudely erected, before getting to the main entrance of the house, which was guarded by a massive antediluvian door. A small orchard with edible figs, peaches, and oranges was to the west of the house. On the east and south, the property dropped sharply, near cliff-like, a hundred feet or so with stands of trees as far down as one could see. Looking out at the horizon, beyond the hills and trees, the eye was met by the fabulous blue sea, the Mediterranean. Jesse was told that the "mistral," an impish northeasterly wind, would soon come and bring clouds enough to fully obscure the fabled body of water, and then it would, from this distance, perfectly resemble a desert.

The house was primarily stone with timbers in use around the doors and on some of the ceilings. It was approximately fifteen hundred square feet but appeared much larger from the outside. The small rooms seemed even smaller, given that each of them had to accommodate a fireplace. Jesse did not know whether Jimmy bought the place with the furniture in it, but that was his guess because all of the furnishings seemed centuries old. Interesting but tattered rugs were in place, while appearing to not have been walked on in decades. It seemed spotless, which the Spanish housekeeper and cook attributed to the abundant and tyrannical geckos clinging to the walls of every room. They were as welcome here as cats would be back home.

Introductions were in order. Herschel, a thin, tall, well-built man was Jimmy's man when he was away. He took care of the mail, the phone, the yard, and generally handled the business affairs of the house. He was particularly effeminate, and upon meeting Jesse, his deportment immediately registered jealousy. It was not readily clear who he was jealous of, Jimmy or Jesse. Talking endlessly and aimlessly with great flair, he was wearing all white: pants too tight and a shirt too large and open, displaying a hairless chest. Having lived here for twenty years, he was fluent in French but was born and raised in some small Midwestern American city. He doubtless said which one, but it was lost in the cacophony of his relentless dissertations.

Anna was the domestic worker, cleaning and preparing food. She would come in the morning at about ten and leave at about six o'clock every evening. Her English was useless, but she tried bravely to use it at every opportunity. It was said that her French was only marginally better. Jeno was here too, carrying a look of bewilderment with him, often getting lost in thin intellectual affectations, trying his best to appear as if he belonged in this erudite company. Jeno was lost between sexual poles as well. He was handsome but disproportionately assembled and seemed womanly soft and manfully hard at the same time. A previous lover of Jimmy's, he was utterly comfortable in these richly ancient environs.

The plan was to be here for about four months. Jimmy had to finish a book to satisfy a contract with his publisher. But everyone else, except the cook, was simply enjoying his largess. Anna prepared two full meals a day, but throughout the day she would provide a variety of fruit and delicacies, and always wine. They would consume on average a dozen bottles of wine per day, while smoking cigarettes and engaging in endlessly stimulating conversation (sans Herschel), made all the more so by a veritable train of visitors. Upon finding themselves in the south of France, anyone who thought of themselves as "somebody" would come to sit with the great thinker. Not so much for any real edification, but simply to say they had.

Jimmy kept very strange hours, sleeping primarily during the day while working all night. Rarely did he make an appearance before one or two o'clock in the afternoon, which is when Anna was expected the have the first meal of the day prepared. Often, hopefuls would come too early and miss the main attraction. Most, however, would visit with Herschel and Jeno, as indeed it was a vacation spot, and all but a few had nothing else to do.

Lines were inadvertently drawn between generations. Jimmy enjoyed the company of young people, but their generally limited points of view caused him to place polite barriers between himself and them. Jeno had been in France for some time, and many times, all of course on Jimmy's dime. He was a bit of a waif, very comfortable roaming the streets, asking for things as if he was not begging. His requests were so casual and his appearance so able that people were disarmed and, as often as not, said yes. He typically only wanted drugs or money with which to buy them, and he happily shared whatever he had. This he would do as if he had acquired the treats through some practiced and respectable industry, which, given his skill at winning favors, I suppose it can be said he had. Some were invited back to Jimmy's residence, so he developed a small following of his own, as the young crowd gravitated to him.

Herschel's age put him neatly in the middle. He was a rabid drug user, but very private. He would sit with Jeno's coterie just long enough to get high and then disappear. During the many weeks Jesse was there, he saw every room in the house except the one occupied by Herschel. It could be argued that he viewed the entire compound as his bedroom, strolling about most days barefoot and shirtless, in only his colorful bikini underwear.

When Jimmy showed up, he was always greeted by more than his housemates. Everyone would be kissed on both cheeks, and all of the initial greetings were in French. Jesse enjoyed these affectionate moments as it took him home, remembering the warm household of his youth, being hugged daily by sisters, his mother, and aunts. These tender displays among men did not disturb him. Rather, he thought that this is how all men should behave, as opposed to the often-painful and competitive manly handshake so expected in his home country.

Local and international celebrities were in regular attendance. When legendary artists from around the world arrived in the south of France, many would find their way to his table. Bobby Short, the cabaret singer would be there one night, Bill Cosby with his fetching wife on another. Nina Simone would arrive boisterously in the early hours of the morning and stay until some other star showed up. When she was present, she demanded his full attention, refusing to share him with anyone, not even his house mates. Jimmy loved this woman. But the woman who captured most of his attention and created the most intrigue, at least for Jesse, was the octogenarian French matriarch from whom he was buying the house. She was a feisty woman who would arrive once a week in a chauffeur-driven Bentley, to debate the issues of the day and yesterday. She adored him but apparently was not the least bit in awe of his mind—as others were. They fought like rivals, seemingly angry, ugly affairs, lasting well into the night. The adoration was mutual; Jimmy enjoyed these bouts as much as anything Jesse was ever to see him do. Their sparring would always end with hugs and kisses.

Herschel would unfailingly make his brief appearances and just as consistently behave as if his presence was somehow required and announcing his leave as if he would be missed. He had been a fairly accomplished dancer in his youth and acted as if he were still pirouetting in the limelight.

During those occasional moments when no guests were present, Herschel would come and share his drug of choice with Jesse and Jeno. He was a lonely man, or rather, he was a man who preferred being alone and would only entertain when he was sitting at the head of the table. He never took that seat unless he could justify being in it, and when high enough, his own glorious memories gave him the nerve to command that space. With nothing to offer but drugs and no one to impress but the needy Jeno and the indifferent Jesse, he could have the chair without challenge.

In the first week of Jesse's arrival, Herschel took from his billowing shirt pocket what appeared to be an ordinary cigarette, stocked with tobacco. It looked factory rolled, not twisted like a marijuana joint. It was tobacco, hand rolled and laced with hashish. There was no leafy marijuana here because Jeno, Jesse was to learn, was insatiable. He consumed everything as if he would never have it again: food, novels, drink, and all manner of intoxicants. Herschel smoked so much hashish, and had been doing it so long, that he rolled tobacco by hand to look like a machine had done it. He lit up, taking a deep drag, distorting his face, strangely prune-like while holding it in. While his face seemed frozen and grotesque, he handed the fire to Jeno, who had his own style of inhalation, who passed the hot stick to Jesse, who would be having it, and tobacco, for the first time. He took his hit and liked it. Herschel now had an audience and commenced the painfully disjointed prattle that was his way.

Amid all of this excitement, the new people, the new drugs, the learning of French for Jesse went the way a career in linguistics went for his father.

His father . . . Jesse remembered . . .

Brightmeyer had come to Grand Rapids Michigan for a visit. This happened only once, Brightmeyer showing up at his son's house for a visit. Jesse could not remember what led up to it or why he had come. He could not even recall if his father was alone. What he remembered, wispily, was Brightmeyer being in his home with his young family. Perhaps he had come to see his grandson. Chad was in diapers, and Zachery was only a thought at the time. The conversation with his father was predictably stilted, uncomfortable. Perhaps he had come for the same reason that Jesse approached him in the hospital all those years later. Maybe he wanted to talk and straighten things out, father to son, to uncover what underpinned the strange distance between them.

What he remembered clearly was the unwieldy moment wherein his father lit up a cigarette in his apartment. Jesse had rarely seen his father awake without a cigarette. He disliked his father, but what is more, he was afraid of him, and neither thing had to do with his smoking cigarettes. But this day Jesse found a way to tell his father he was not allowed to smoke in his house. This was no small thing. Making a demand of his father required more daring than he knew he had.

By now, of course, he was fond of his father and missed him. He thought of him often and warmly. Somehow the smoke allowed him to feel new kinship with his father – Daddy; now gone just as his mother was.

Jesse had hated cigarettes and could not understand why anyone would engage in so foolish a practice, and here he was smoking and enjoying it. It did not feel retributive. At thirty-five years of age, and, having hated this weed all of his life, he sat smoking under the same sky where he had railed against it for all those years. This seemed completely incongruous to him. There was no getting the good god. He did not even think of himself as smoking. He was simply getting high. The medium of tobacco was incidental, but it was worse than the hashish; it was worse than any other drug. He recalled what was only a few years prior, a time when he, as an elder in the church, had to discipline and dismiss from among the purity of the congregation a woman who had suffered from this addiction.

He began asking for cigarettes each morning, smoking three with a morning coffee and no more, but this could not last, and soon he was buying them. Buying them, he said, just to pay back what he owed. He would never allow his children to see him smoke, he thought. He could see his father inhaling a cigarette with what appeared to be exquisite pleasure, like a child enjoying a Popsicle.

He recalled the time when he woke to the sound of his bellicose father yelling a threat at his mother, something about throwing hot coffee in her face. Brightmeyer was a belligerent man, but he never would harm his wife, and his brutality when disciplining his children came from a rightful fatherly place, however cruel it seemed. But the thought of someone, anyone, harming his mother turned the normally docile Jesse into a dangerous animal. There was no threat he would not face to defend her.

Jesse leapt from his bed, grabbing the nearest weapon, which happened to be a broom, and ran down the stairs of their home and stuck it somewhat forcefully into his father's chest. Brightmeyer, for his part, was stunned into what appeared to be submission. This behavior would not have surprised him coming from Franklin or Ashton, given their bravado, but from Jesse it was too unexpected for a ready response. In truth, Brightmeyer was more pleased than not that this son, who he had considered too soft to make it in life, had found some courage.

Jesse was not a coward, but he often behaved like one, cowering in the face of any angry confrontation. He had so little anger in him, and that is what he thought it took to respond to angry conflict that it nearly never reached the surface.

Jesse screamed, "You will not harm my mother! Not today you won't!" Even Madelyn was amused as she too incredulously considered this improbable moment unfolding before her eyes.

Brightmeyer (and one imagines him snickering within himself) grabbed a knife from the drawer as this episode took place in the kitchen and bellowed back, "Boy, I'll cut your heart out and feed it to the dogs."

Somewhere inside of his parents, there was the absolute knowledge that neither of them would hurt the other. But Jesse had never understood his father's fits of rage, and he did not know that his father would not hurt his mother. So he stood his ground, *the higher ground*, he thought.

There he was in France but cocooned in a colony of artists who opted for English. The native tongue was spoken daily but not patiently or with any aim to teach. Jesse learned a few words and picked up some mannerisms, hardly a fatherly tribute.

Nevertheless, Jesse found no way to fit in. The sexuality of the compound being essentially antithetical to his own was not the problem. There were the occasional flirtations, but eventually the regulars got comfortable with the stranger in their midst, who was struggling constantly, unbeknown to his housemates, with maintaining mental stability. He spent much of his time drawing and writing letters home, primarily to his sons and Allison. He wrote poems, weak pitiful poems and songs, inspired by his unceasing grief.

All of this had him longing for home . . . There was no home. He was a wave on a black sea, tossed and immersed in the great unknown. Where was this place, this home he sought? It existed now only in his mind, and as such it was without address or order or rest or anything but a dream. Nonetheless he wanted to go home. This longing certainly fed the madness . . . wanting to go to a place that did not exist. He was a tangle of disparate emotions, having no thoughts about himself that made sense or brought peace. He would recall the joy of innocence among the obsequious religious followers and the bliss of that naiveté. *Perhaps*, he thought, *he should find a Kingdom Hall, prostrate himself, and plead before the god of his mother.* He could find a way to forgive the mean one and go on in blissful ignorance. He quivered at the thought, but he wept at it too.

At some point a friend of Jimmy's, a photographer, showed up at the enclave. He was a native Frenchman and, according to Jimmy, one of the most sought after photojournalists in France. His approach to photography was anthropological, and he found in Jesse's face something he called "an African visage unlike any African visage I have ever seen. I just want to kiss him," he said in that French accent Americans find so compelling.

"You want to kiss him?" said Jimmy in a tone so sardonic that it bubbled with sexual futility.

He would call on his mother tongue to talk Jimmy into convincing Jesse to do a photo shoot.

"You want me to model for photos? I've never done anything like that before, but I would like to get some head shots for my auditions.

What would I have to do? Would we do it here or someplace else?" Jesse put up no resistance, as in fact he liked the idea. It unnerved him a bit because he thought modeling implied beauty, a quality he never saw himself as having. In his life, only his mother had ever called him pretty. He was born in that place and time when one could not be beautiful and black too. This talk about his beauty, exotic or otherwise, took him by surprise. *What are they seeing?* he thought. It didn't matter much to him. He needed head shots to pursue his acting career, and this was as good a time as any to get started.

He had with him an assortment of clothing with which he could create a variety of looks: suits, shorts, jeans, and shirts, both casual and dressy.

The photographer, whose name was Bernard, wanted to schedule shooting in just five days. As far as Jesse was concerned, they could have started that afternoon, given how little there was to occupy his time. To the question of what he should wear, Bernard wanted to know if Jesse had a swimsuit, and he wanted to put Jesse in flowing white shirts. The rest was left to Jesse's own sense of style.

He thought about all of those shopping sprees with Allison and her insistence on fit and color. In a way, he had been modeling clothing for years under the critically watchful eyes of his sister. He remembered his father marching his daughters around with books on their heads to improve their posture and poise. *I can do this*, he thought, *I have done it for years.*

Bernard showed up on the assigned day, announcing that he wanted to take shots on Jimmy's property but that he also wanted to take Jesse to a friend's house to finish the session. They would have dinner and socialize afterward.

Apparently he had not heard or understood Jimmy's sarcasm following his "I want to kiss him" comment. He must have thought Jesse was, in fact, a gay man because he brought along his assistant who was a beautiful woman in her late twenties. She was a well-built creature, with the nerve to wear a fishnet dress in blazing red and nothing, or nearly nothing, under it. She was tanned, as was common in the south of France, but she managed to be darker than Jesse's children. Taken on skin color alone, this woman would have fit neatly in the middle of the pack among American Negroes. She was shaped, if you will, like a black woman, with curves and hips reminiscent of those luscious women who were in constant visitation at his home in Detroit when he was a boy. Her hair came naturally to her shoulders, and it appeared she had done nothing to it, and she had no need to. She saw in Jesse what he saw in her, something to have . . . for a time, for the taking.

As it turned out, Bernard's other venue for the shoot was a very modern house "in the hills," he said. It had a pool, one of those pools that was indoors, in a sunroom, where one could swim all day without going forward. There were jets built into it that allowed you to swim into a gentle current while going nowhere. Jesse had never heard of or seen anything like this, but it explained why the woman was dressed as she was. The "nearly nothing" was a bikini, or at least the bottom of one.

They took many photos on Jimmy's property, during which Bernard flirted endlessly with Jesse. The woman could see, even if Bernard could not, that he was wasting his time. Her behavior could not be called flirtatious. It was knowing, simply knowing, in the way that a woman of the world knows, that she would wrap her arms around this prize.

CHAPTER 30

The Long Road Home

He was in France, the lovely and renowned south of France, all of the summer, but it felt to him as if he had been in prison. This is what life had essentially become for him. He announced to Jimmy and his housemates that he had to go. Jimmy was not pleased about Jesse's defection; he said so and pouted relentlessly. Jesse promised to meet him in New York in three weeks to begin the speaking tour, but he had to return home. He could not be still, here or anywhere.

Jesse packed his bags as if he would never return. He did not intend to be here; this was not in his plans. He had no plans, but this place was too decadent, with all of the leisure, all of the fun, without his beloved mother to share it with.

The final sounds rising from her soon-to-be corpse stayed with him . . . always, denying him anything that resembled pleasure. He remembered having to attend the funeral of his uncle some years after his mother's. When walking through the cemetery to the grave site, his knees buckled, he began to sweat and tremble. He couldn't keep his feet on the ground, feeling with every step that he was walking on her grave, walking on her. He began to cry uncontrollably and had to be escorted from the sacred ground.

Where were his children? He would go back to his life, his wife. He would find the peace he once had; he would return to it.

A car was called to the villa. He would be making the trip to the airport alone. His limited use of French was cause for some trepidation, but the pull of home reduced this concern to a minor inconvenience. He had learned a few phrases, enough to get him into the air and over the ocean. The plane was to land at JFK International, which was only a relatively short drive to Richmond, Virginia, where his mother's siblings, his aunts, and his cousins, resided. This is where he was conceived, and while his mother had not lived there in thirty years, he felt as if this would place him, somehow, close to his mother or to her "things." He called and announced that he was coming. The fact that they were happy to see him gave him a sense of belonging. He wanted to place his eyes on things she had seen or perhaps things she had touched. He tried to get his aunt to talk about her sister, his mother, but it was not in her nature. Death to her, and everyone, was an accepted inevitability. Let the dead rest in peace. He stayed for two days before heading to Detroit.

Allison picked him up at the airport, and, as was her style, she had lots of questions. Had she been in France, it would certainly have been a vacation. Jesse described his time abroad to his sister in terms that she, a bon vivant, would appreciate. In truth, he often thought of how much she, above all others in his life, would have enjoyed being in the south of France. He described eating at the famed La Colombe d'Or. She would have loved this place with its utterly fine cuisine, history, and elite clientele. She enjoyed hearing his stories about his having talked to Marlon Brando and Elizabeth Taylor on the phone.

He told her about his trip to the historical village of Carpentras in the southern hills of France. She was amused by the story of the old French woman who came running up to Jesse and his entourage calling excitedly, "Alain, Alain, Ou avez-vous ete? Comment faites-vous?"

Jesse of course had no idea what she was saying.

"She thinks she knows you," said Jeno. "She thinks your name is Alain."

This happened on three separate occasions, people looking Jesse directly in his eyes and swearing he was someone else, but this was the only time it occurred in France. He was Raymond to someone in Atlanta and Bookie to a lady in Mississippi.

She asked about the wine, the daily menu, and all the local style.

"Well, when are you going back? What about your career as an actor? Are you getting any roles? This could be the start of something great! Do you think you could get Jimmy to come here . . . to Detroit? We could have a big party. I could invite . . ."

Jesse answered those questions, but she never asked how he was doing. Jesse saw no sorrow on her face, and in fairness, she did not seem to notice his. His being home was simply what brothers do. It is what family does—they come home. She could not (no one could it seemed) see or sense the depth of his sorrow, his need. He had expected to share the joy and the sorrow with his siblings, to reminisce and find some comfort in the arms of people who could feel his pain exactly the way he did. It did not happen, and it caused him to feel more desperately alone.

Steve seemed happy to see him and was willing to let Jesse use one of his cars to go to Grand Rapids to see his children, and he was gracious in doing so. Seeing his children was to be the highlight of his trip home. He would get to spend time with them, enjoying all of those simple pleasures he remembered so well and had expected to last always.

He surprised himself by stopping at a party store and buying a six-pack of Stroh's beer, cigarettes, and papers for rolling marijuana, smoking and drinking the whole way—two hours or so on the road. When he arrived, he found no one home. Beverly had been called; she knew he was coming, but there was no evidence that anyone was home. Jesse assumed they had not heard the doorbell. Maybe the boys where napping. He got into the car to go to a pay phone when he saw a curtain move and a glimpse of Chad, his older son. Jesse picked up some pebbles and tossed them lightly onto the window. There were his boys at the window, crying and waving. Beverly had decided that she did not want Jesse in the house and did not want him to take the boys. Beverly was quick to see the betrayal of the boys who had been told to stay away from the windows and act as if no one was home. She grabbed them and pulled them away from the window while the boys tearfully resisted her maneuvering. The joy he had anticipated began to ooze out of his heart, and he was soon overcome with sadness. He waved to his sons, who may or may not have seen it, and decided to go get a drink.

He thought to look up an old friend with whom he had sold shoes at a high-end salon, not knowing whether or not he still worked there. This was the place where Jesse first worked after leaving his federally imposed tenure at the hospital. David LaHore was his name. This fellow knew Jesse at the end of his ministerial career. He had watched as the brethren from the church hunted Jesse "like the CIA," he would say, when they decided that Jesse was no longer fit to be among them. He saw him go from "sugar to shit," as he would put it, in just a few months. This was the person with whom Jesse first smoked marijuana, and he seemed, for a time, the only person who understood the depth of Jesse's grief.

David's life was shit according to him. Half Native American and half European American, he found no way to reconcile his "savage" ancestry with the treasures of the white world he so desperately wanted. Indeed he could and did pass for white. He accumulated, as he thought he should, the accoutrements of his oppressor: boats, guns, wing-tipped shoes. He was handsome, given to boyish frivolity and grim reflections. When he drank, which he did daily and to great excess, bleak remembrances would hound him, and he would search out people, even strangers, to hear his horrors. Jesse, the young minister, had listened to him endlessly railing against white people and their arrogance. He would talk about being teased when his young friends met his mother and how he had to fight his way through school. Now it was his turn to listen to Jesse, who had realized, for the first time, that he had left his children.

The shoe store, or salon, as it was called, was in downtown Grand Rapids, and across the street there was a staid family-owned department store called Herpolsheimer's.

On one of its many floors, there was a once-elegant restaurant that had slipped into something less than elegant over the years and was now just ordinary and falling. But still the old guard came and went, as if not wanting to let go of its past glories. There were nests of these patrons scattered about in the now-too-large dining room. This is where David and Jesse decided to meet. David ordered, one at a time, of course, his usual six-pack of beer for lunch, and Jesse ordered a tuna melt but never got around to eating at all. It was in this place and in this company that Jesse suddenly understood the breadth of his loss. He never intended to leave his children; it just didn't occur to him. This realization sent him tumbling into a despair nearly equal to that which descended upon him when his mother took her last look at her stricken children, and he wept like a worshiper at the Wailing Wall. It was disruptive, visceral shrieking, such that the management approached and considered calling an ambulance. He bawled uncontrollably for many minutes, until some composure came to relieve him and his tear-soaked cloth napkin.

David did what he could to calm his friend, and, as is the way of man, found some comfort himself in knowing that his misery, so ancient and ignored, was somehow shared. He was not alone. One after another, in rapid succession, he drank his beers, and when Jesse dried up, he began to talk about his own travail—how the white people had betrayed him.

The lunch hour ended, and luckily they had only to walk across the street for David to return to work. He was not the only salesperson who drank too much. They all did, so the puff of alcohol that accompanied him offended none of them. It is certain that none of them had any respect for him. They saw him as a simpleton, who did his best to mimic the best salesman among them. They laughed at him and unkindly ridiculed him behind his back and sometimes in his presence. He had married a white woman, and she too found his behavior obsequious, demeaning, and embarrassing. At some point she lost all respect for him. This was well known to him, but he could not stop himself. His desire to please the fairer side of his clan, coupled with his envy and hatred, created a madness that hounded him like bees on a hive.

The effect of years of this internal conflict, all he had ever known, led him eventually to a liquor store, his gun rack, the woods, two hours of ranting self-degradation, and a bullet through the roof of his mouth. Jesse was to learn about this human drama, this predictable and yet improbable end, some years later. Jesse heard about it and did not weep. He set alone in that ever-present bar and thought warmly and sadly about his friend. He would feel for his friend for all of his life and wonder about how different it might have been had he not been so mired in his own forest of pain.

In any case, on this day it seemed Jesse would be denied the chance to see his sons. He could see his time in Michigan being squandered, and soon he would be back on the road without having seen them. He drove through the city where his children were born, where their memories were made. The thought of playing ball on the lawn and raking and playing in the leaves entered his mind, and his loss swelled within him like a boil. He pulled over, turned off the engine, and sat crying in a parking lot. Alone again behind the Kingdom Hall, he could hear the zealous laughter and see through the walls the devotees sitting in rapt attention, listening to the word. He remembered dressing up his son as he himself had been dressed and delivered to the stage of the Lord, to say his words and begin the indoctrination. He had not intended to come to this spot, this tiny piece of land that he had swept and shoveled in the name of the Lord. These memories and this land made him uncomfortable, and he quickly started the engine and headed back to his former residence where his angry wife and sad sons quarreled. Several hours had passed when he finally knocked on the door.

"What do you want?" she said angrily, as if he had not been there earlier.

""I have come for the boys," he said, assuming the coy role.

"They are not ready."

"How long will it be? How much time do you need?"

"Just wait, can't you just wait?"

"Sure, I can wait, but you knew I was coming. They were supposed to be ready hours ago."

"You don't run this house, and you don't tell me what to do. Not anymore you don't." She had tears, angry tears, in her eyes.

Jesse had never thought of himself as running the house. The phrase seemed out of order, as if she was talking to someone else. When he thought about their life together, he thought of something mutual and communal. Against the rocks now, dashed and crushed into too many pieces, he felt parts of himself floating away. He went and sat in Steve's car and waited, waited for her to relent.

Chapter 31

Fair Trade and a Little Patience

Leo and Jesse were true to their words. Jesse brought five hundred dollars, and Leo showed up with a gram scale, paper for creating packages, and even some inositol for cutting the cocaine and increasing profit margins. He even brought a grinding bowl and pestle for crushing and mixing the product into a fine powder, and, of course, a quarter ounce of the wonder drug.

"I hooked you up, my brotha," Leo said, beaming.

They met in a commercial high-rise where Jesse had sold an on-site furniture moving contract. It was an old eight-story building that was being refurbished to house an interior design center. Leo, as promised, had been given the job to manage this space. There were many empty rooms, actually whole floors were unoccupied, and Leo had taken the time to explore every inch of the place. He took Jesse to one of the more isolated corners of the building and began the tutelage.

"Did I set you up? Huh, you're ready to roll now. You do this right, and the five bills you spent should be fifteen hundred. Do the right thing with that, and you, my brotha, are in business."

"You sure as hell did. All right, I got the shit. Talk to me. How do I use this stuff?"

Leo set out on a nearly scientific dissertation on the do's and don'ts of selling, mixing, and packaging drugs, condescending with his new fledging nearly every step of the way. In his adult life, Leo had developed a fascination with the Jamaican culture and had spent at least a month there every year for the last ten. In doing so, he immersed himself in that style and spoke Jamaican patois perfectly. He would turn to it when doing or discussing drugs. Jesse enjoyed hearing it, the sound of it, but the pomposity came through despite the exotic rhythms.

Jesse did exactly what Leo said. He showed up at the Barrel with denominations of the product: grams, halves, and quarters. He also had a "bag" for sharing lines, to get the word out. "The house bag," Leo said, "should be a higher quality than what you are selling. Now, Jesse, this is important: don't sell any product until the regular dealers sell out. You don't want to come in trying to take over, making enemies and shit. Give your boys a hit first. This shit is going to blow them away."

On Jesse's first visit into the Cork n' Barrel all those weeks ago, he was wearing a suit and tie, the required uniform at the dealership. He was compelled to wear the same uniform at the moving company. This gave him, along with his skin, a rather distinct persona, and had the effect of making him look even more out of place. This professional look had the effect of drawing some patrons to him and repelling others. Sal Lippio began calling him "the Doctor" or "the Professor."

Sal did not understand racism. He behaved like a racist because that is how and where he was raised. He had to posture and impress his "boys," and he did this very skillfully. But something inside of him knew it was nonsense. In Jesse, he found a way to explore his misgivings, as he was one of the first to discover that Jesse knew how to listen. For what appeared to be the first time in his life, someone listened to him and responded intelligently to what he had to say. It pleased him so much that he began to tell others that Jesse was a good guy. "You ought to talk to him," he would say. Before the Beast showed up, Sal would almost forsake his job as bouncer and spend as much time as possible talking to Jesse. To some extent, this was Jesse's doing. When Jesse came into the bar alone, for the first time, with the elixir in his pocket, Sal was at the door and appeared crestfallen, to which Jesse said, "Hey, Sal, what's wrong? You look like you just lost your best friend." Sal looked at Jesse with surprise, as if to say, *"How the hell would he know that?"*

"Hey, Professor, what's up?"

He paused, trying to decide if he wanted to pursue a discussion about his trouble. Jesse could see in his eyes, Sal equivocating about whether or not to share his pain. He had already announced to some others in the bar that his best friend had been stabbed during a mindless assault, wherein he himself was the assailant and was now in prison. "Dumb fuck," or something like that, was the general response, "What is he, an amateur?" So many of the regulars had been in jail that it was no big deal to any of them. None of them could see behind his eyes, the sadness or the pain.

"You want to talk about it?" said Jesse.

"Hell no, I just want to get fucked up. Harry's s'posed to be here with some shit."

"Why don't we do both? We can talk and get fucked up too. Let me buy you a beer."

This surprised Sal, but he was very pleased. Bouncers, as it turned out, get perks on a daily basis, but this one was particularly timely, and Jesse was enhancing his welcome here.

"Let's do a quick line," said Jesse, as if this was an ordinary moment in his world.

"You got some meds? Cool, follow me."

Sal did not have the power or enough respect to get into the back room as Harry had, so they went into the women's restroom to do their business. Somehow it was thought that this was safer or more private than the men's room. There was a counter in the room for women to do their thing, but their thing, as it turned out was as much about getting high as it was about makeup and toiletries. It felt strangely inappropriate to Jesse to be in the "ladies" room during business hours, even in a place like this. But he was to learn that this habit did not disturb the locals in the least, nor did it stop them from doing anything they would do if they were alone in the room. It was fairly early in the evening, so they were only interrupted once. The woman who came in was someone Jesse had seen every time he was in the bar, but he had never met her. Jesse took out the house bag and expertly tapped out a larger mound than was normal when just giving it away. He had his kit with him, and he took out a credit card and cut lines expertly.

"Hey, Kim, you want a hit?" said Sal, knowing that this was the way. It gave him his own sense of power and spoke to his influence.

"Yeah, I'll take a hit. You going to introduce me to your friend?" she said.

"Oh, yeah, this is the Professor. His name is Jesse. Jesse, this is Kim. She's one of mine."

"Bullshit," she said, "Sal, you are so full of it." And they laughed a laugh that Jesse had never heard before. It was too much, ill-placed, and Jesse had heard nothing funny. He was getting a sense of this odd culture and its reliance on nonsense.

Jesse rolled a dollar bill to make a straw, not the C-note that Chuck was known for. He handed it to Kim. She took what would have to be called a polite hit, saying, "Damn, that's some good shit," at which point Sal said, "What do you think? I ain't the garbage man."

"That's what you usually have," she said, laughing as she left the room.

Sal had seized the moment to enhance his role, and, as it turned out, the bouncer was second in command in the bar, right behind the bartender, a fairly rowdy fellow named Bruce. If you were going to do business in this bar, you had to have both of them on your payroll; that is to say, free drugs and drinks.

He took his turn with the coke, snorting a line in each nostril. "This is the best shit that has ever been in this bar. Where the fuck did you get it? Fuck that, you got any more?"

Ramona had relented. She and Jesse were living together again. The circumstances of her softening and allowing Jesse back into her life were these: Jesse had gotten a frantic phone call from Ramona. While walking casually across the street, simply coming home from school, Patience her daughter, was struck by a vehicle, tossed high into the air, and landed headfirst onto the hood of the car that hit her. She had been rushed to the hospital, and her life was slipping away. A closed head injury was the result and meant that even if she lived she would likely be left in a nearly vegetative state. A closeness had developed between Jesse and the child, and he left Mademoiselle DeSusse's house, running the three miles to the hospital. When he got there, Ramona was in a predictable state. As you might imagine a mother with her only child hanging flimsily to life, and in this moment, the person closest to her was Jesse. Yes, he had befouled the relationship with unseemly behavior, but now the great need for someone to hold was upon her. Galean, the Swede whose arms she found and with whom she coupled in the aftermath of Jesse's shameful behavior, could not be immediately located, but he had been called as well. So had the biological father of the child, but he lived in Albany, and it would be hours before he arrived.

Jesse was as breathless upon entering the hospital from running as Ramona was from hyperventilation, and they fell into each other's arms. He held her lovingly, and she clung to him with a need greater than she had ever known. He kissed her tenderly on her forehead and used his cheeks and his sleeves as a kerchief. She wept as the moment dictated, and until she found her strength, wherein she looked at him and said, "I need you. What are we going to do?"

"Whatever you need, my dear, I will be here." Jesse meant that with all that he was. He would do anything now, anything that was needed. What she needed now was certainty: to know that he could be depended on, that he would come when she called.

Ramona was no needy woman, and she had essentially been without Jesse in her life for months. They would be at the hospital for a couple of days with only minimal coming and going. Jesse, within his meager means, would bring what was needed, do what was needed to comfort her. Eventually, the medical staff convinced her that there was nothing she could do—the child was unconscious, comatose, and she should go home. They promised to call the moment there was a change in her prognosis.

"Stay with me, please. Don't leave me."

Jesse took her home; well, he drove her home in her car. She found a way to cope. Somewhere deep inside of her, she found a guarded place for this pain. She did what Jesse could not do. He admired her for it but could not understand it. That night they slept, weary and stricken, in each other's arms, and Jesse could not believe that he was again in her bed.

The last time he was there, Galean was in her bed, and Jesse, drunk and homeless, came knocking on her door, begging for some place to sleep.

"I have company, Jesse. You can't just knock on my door whenever you want to. I can't help you. You should go back to wherever you have been sleeping."

Jesse was too drunk to get anywhere else, although he sobered a bit with the mention that his wife had company. She shut the door, and Jesse fell, slinked against the exterior wall beneath the porch light. He probably would have slept it off there had she not come back and helped him up the stairs and placed him in the empty room once occupied by her daughter. How she explained this to her friend, with whom she was finding support, is not known, but Jesse, now prone in his stepdaughter's bed, found no way to sleep. Instead he heard every sound in the night, and all of them said, "She is making love to someone else with me in the house." There was no jealous rage but just the turbulent knowledge that he deserved this improbable discomfort.

In the morning her friend was gone, and she, disgusted but not bitter, told Jesse he must never do that again. She explained that Galean was a good man and neither of them deserved to be intruded upon. After chastising Jesse, in an almost motherly fashion, she announced that she would like for the men in her life to meet. "You are both such gifted and wonderful men. You really should know each other. Why don't we have dinner together, and you guys will see what I'm talking about."

"Have you put this idea to him?" Jesse was willing while being incredulous.

"No, but I am sure he would be willing. I think he would like to meet the man who ruined our otherwise nice evening. We got no sleep at all after your intrusion."

She laughed when she said it, a hardy, unexpected laugh.

They did have dinner, and it was a nice evening. The boys where well behaved, as was their nature, and Ramona decided, after Galean playfully suggested she needed to choose between them, that she wanted them both, and both of them she had until Galean's life called him back to his homeland.

In the ensuing weeks and months, they had gotten close again, and there was no mention of Jesse's previous indiscretions. Now another sad, even horrific, chapter was about to begin, and it had everything to do with the sweet poison that Jesse brought with him into the Cork 'n' Barrel.

"Yeah, I got more but it's at home, just a few packages on me right now." That was true. Jesse had brought five hundred dollars' worth of assorted weight, nicely packaged and color coded. In minutes, after going back into the public space of the bar, listening for about a half hour to Sal's sad story and providing ministerial comfort, even hugging the burly fellow, Sal came up to Jesse and said, "You got a quarter to sell?"

"Yeah, sure, who wants it?"

"Never mind that, just give me the shit."

In less than an hour, Jesse was out of product and had five hundred dollars in his pocket. At just about that time, Harry entered the bar, making his rounds and slapping hands. He came to the court where Jesse and Sal were playing darts and said, as if expecting Sal to ask, "Motherfucker stood me up. I got no girl, damn it. All fucking night with no coke, shit."

"That's why I brought my own shit," said Jesse, "that and the fact that I owe you some hits."

"Goddamn right, you owe me some hits. You got some shit on you."

"Hell yeah, I'm going to let you be the bitch tonight. I got you, my brotha."

"Then set it out, what the hell you waiting for?"

Harry did not want Jesse to "hook him up" on the bar as he and Chuck had done because not only did he not want to share the power, he did not want attention drawn to the fact that someone else was making the provisions for which he was known.

The Beast headed directly to the back room, simply throwing a wink at Bruce the bartender, who was an addict as well, and he came running, getting there ahead of the wayward trio.

"My treat, fellas. You guys have been serving it up since I met you, so here's a little payback."

Bruce the bartender came in, taking control. Jesse tapped out a little cocaine on a wax-laden cardboard case filled with empty beer bottles. They were stacked high enough to be at shoulder height. Bruce seized the equipment from Jesse quickly, but not in a rude way. It was just that he had to get back to work and wanted his hit first and immediately. He filled each nostril and said, "Goddamn, where did this shit come from?"

"I told yeh," said Sal with a bit of a boast.

Harry was next saying something like, "Yeah, good stuff. Where did you get it?" There was a hint of envy in his comment.

"Damn, Harry, we all got sources. Just one of my contacts. It ain't always this good," said Jesse, preparing them for what was to come.

"That's cool. You got any more?"

"Not on me, just my private stash. I'd have to go home."

Sal spoke up. "We got to get some dope in here tonight. What about it, Beast? Your guy didn't come through—people are going to be on my ass all night."

"I don't give a shit. Jesse can bring his stuff in. There's enough business to go around. Have everybody still come through me or you. We'll come to you, Jesse, but keep you out of the mess, ya know. People don't know who you are. How long will it take you to get back?"

"At least an hour, it ain't like I got the shit all packaged."

"Well, let's do it. That's just about the time it gets busy in here."

Harry really did not seem to mind. If people where still coming through him or his team, his reputation would not take a hit. Jesse was the new guy on the team, and all he had to do was provide and lay low. There was no talk about splitting the money, commissions, and such.

"I'll be back on my feet tomorrow," Harry said.

Jesse went home. "You're home early." Ramona was doing her thing, watching a movie. This was one of her favorite pastimes. She could watch thirty or so movies a month and still get so much done that it often left Jesse thinking she manufactured hours.

"Not really, I have to go back." With that, he handed her five hundred dollars of crumpled and assorted bills. It looked like it was more than it was, as her eyes lit up at the sight of it.

"Where did this come from?" she asked, yet still sparkling as she began to count it.

"Well," Jesse said as if he had landed a new well-paying job, "It looks like I'm selling drugs."

"Selling drugs! You have got to be kidding me. Out of my house? No, you are not. This cannot happen. What the hell is wrong with you?" She threw the money on the bed as if it were laced with pepper spray.

"Look, baby, this is going to be all right. I don't really have to sell it, I just bring it in. I made that money in one hour, and I didn't have to do anything but show up with the stuff."

"I don't care how long . . . one hour, are you serious? You made five hundred dollars in one hour? How did . . ."

"I would have made a thousand if I had more of the stuff on me."

"A thousand dollars an hour?"

"I guess, I mean, I just ran out. Look, baby, just help me make a few packages. I got to get back there—people are actually waiting for me."

Jesse went into a closet and pulled out a case that Ramona had never seen. In it was all of the equipment he had gotten from Leo.

"My goodness, it looks like a pharmacy in a bag." She didn't know whether to be impressed or afraid.

He took some of the papers that Leo had provided and filled them all with the appropriate color-coded weights. He showed her how to mix the stuff, fold the papers; they had fun and laughed a lot while doing it. Ramona counted up how much money he should return with and playfully said, "Go to work and make that money."

When Jesse returned to the bar, Sal was at the door, and he virtually yelled, "The doctor is in the house," and unlike the black snake thing, this moniker and its cousin "the Professor," stuck. Jesse went to the dart court and commenced with the hand slapping, dart throwing, and general foolishness that passed for entertainment here. It wasn't long before Jesse was tapped on the shoulder to make a package available for sale. Sal and Harry, but primarily Sal, would come with the money for grams, halves, and quarters of the neatly packaged panacea. Jesse may not have been known to most patrons in the bar before this night, but the sly efforts by Harry and Sal failed to protect Jesse from the watching eyes of the collective. In addition to people quickly learning the source of the drug, the word had spread about Jesse's ability to listen and respond intelligently and helpfully to the various problems and stresses of this needy population. A veritable line of people began queuing up to talk to him with confessions of inner-family abuse, bad choices, unfair moments or interactions within the bar itself, and questions about what they should do about this or that. All the while, Sal and Harry would show up, and Jesse would, as stealthily as possible, reach into his left pocket for the miracle drug while filling his right one with ever-bulging wads of uncounted money.

The night progressed this way right up until the place closed. It was always a little surprising that people were still standing erect, given the great quantities of alcohol and drugs that had been consumed. Indeed many were not standing and had to be driven home or slept in cars wherever they were parked. As Jesse prepared to leave, Bruce the bartender approached him and said, whispering,

"Can you stick around after?" with unexpected friendliness. "We hang out awhile without all of the crazies, have a few pops on the house before we go home."

Apparently this ritual was known to many of the regulars, and some of them were jockeying for an invitation to stay. All but the predictable inner circle were dismissed.

With the place essentially empty, a new party began. It was pretty much the same entertainment but without the interruptions. Bruce provided the drinks, and Jesse, as expected, provided the drugs. This had been Harry's role, but he didn't seem the least bit annoyed having Jesse assume the role. There were ten guys remaining. They were comprised primarily of the same group that had been in the back room the night of Jesse's sermonizing. As it turned out, Bruce had a great deal on his mind, and, given what he had been hearing about Jesse, he wanted to have his turn with his listening ways. It was a macho confessional about the wife, the parents, his job, even his best friend, who, while not officially working there, was in constant attendance, as a kind of bouncer's assistant. His friend, Charlie, was the most manly fellow in the bar: athletic and muscled, with not a hint of concern for anyone but himself. This, remarkably, was largely what Bruce wanted to share with Jesse. They were both fighters. Sal was the bouncer of record, but if there was to be a skirmish, Charlie and Bruce were just as likely as Sal to throw the first punch. They found it peculiar, almost impossible to believe, that Jesse could be from the violent city of Detroit, built so athletically, be the street boy he appeared to be, and have no interest in violence. His resume gave him credibility, but his friendliness, his manner of speaking, as much as his ability to listen and respond, made him a mysterious and protected commodity. "Damn . . . ," said Bruce, after

Jesse opined, "He is not angry with you at all. He is disappointed with himself and doesn't know how or is afraid to face that mirror."

"I see why everybody wants to talk to you. You have a hell of a way of saying things."

It might have been his next trip, but certainly within a few weeks, Harry found it necessary to put time lines on access to Jesse. "We're trying to build a fucking team here. This ain't no goddamn church. Shit, Jesse, I ought to start charging people."

Soon Jesse knew more people by name than anyone else in the bar. This lifted his status even more. Most had no wish to share their innermost feelings with Jesse or anyone else, but that he remembered their names had them feeling he really cared when they exposed their hearts. They came to the Barrel to play games, get high, and perhaps find someone to go home with. Many, however, were looking for that big brother, a surrogate father, or just somebody who, for even a few minutes, would hear their troubles.

Among them was a young man, nearly twenty years Jesse's junior, who attached and endeared himself to Jesse. His name was Jingles, or at least that was what everyone called him. He was a nice enough fellow with a warm immediate smile. Like everyone else, he drank too much and was absolutely committed to drugs. He had an amazing crop of bushy black hair growing aggressively but neatly in every direction. It was obvious that he cared less than a little about his appearance, wearing always an ill-fitted, oddly colored arrangement that seemed, synesthetically, to yell obscenities. He was bright, bright enough to have done something other than drive a delivery truck for a living. His first love in life was baseball, and he kept detailed records of every inning of every game the Boston Red

Sox had played since he was ten years old. He carried with him a notebook chronicling the last three years of their performances and had in his head the stats for every starter, and all secondary player's stats were neatly canonized at home. He loved drugs too and did nothing without lighting a joint first. If he had no marijuana, which was rare, real panic would register on his face, and it would stay there until he was certain he had made contact with his dealer and the herb was on the way. But what he loved most, I should say who, was a very pretty eighteen-year-old who, even at that age, was as experienced as anyone in the bar about the use of every kind of street drug there was. Everyone knew she was underage, but more often than not, she was allowed into the bar. She carried on her face the sweetest look, childlike, as, in fact, she was. Her efforts at makeup and adult hairstyles did nothing to conceal her youth. But after several drinks and her drugs of choice, she often became nasty and obstreperous. She would violently attack any and everybody who, as she put it, "Gets on my fucking nerves." Russian born, she had a name that tattered the American tongue, so everyone called her Jackie. She was so small and so young that she was, for many, pure entertainment, a curiosity nearly as strange here as Jesse himself. The locals knew just where to find those "nerves," and they would prick them at every opportunity. This would cause her to lunge at people, flailing like a banshee, at which any male in the area, and they would be purposefully near, would wrap her up and haul her away while she screamed threats of the most disturbing kind. Everyone would laugh.

This is the person who taught Jingles how to cook cocaine, producing the infamous crack.

When Jesse got home, Ramona was asleep, but she woke up immediately. "Well, I sure hope it was worth it. It's almost three o'clock."

Jesse kissed her face, saying, "Well, let's see what you think," and began emptying his pockets. It took about twenty minutes just to separate the denominations and unwrinkle the bills. Not even counting the ones and fives, there was over fifteen hundred dollars. Ramona did not quite know how to respond. Sure there was cash on the bed, equal to a month's income, given the arrangement Jesse had made with the moving company, and, certainly, with all that was going on with Patience in the hospital and the thought of bringing the boys back, there was no shortage of things to do with these earnings.

In a few hours Jesse had to be up and on the job at the moving company. In his life, he had never had a job he enjoyed more than this one. It is sad irony that he himself was to be the best and worst thing to ever happen to the company. He did not bring drugs or alcohol to the company, but the style he brought with him sanctioned it. He was casual and informal, too much of both, blurring the line of acceptability. Drinking at the end of the day became common, even expected. They would play cards after hours, and after hours came earlier in the day each week. Jesse even bought a dartboard and the office became a kind of game room. Movers hurried through their assignments, often falling beneath the high standards that won them their fame. They would sometimes party so much that the crew began showing up late, hung-over, with the distinct smell of liquor on their breath and clothing. Insurance claims were going up. Complaints, something so rare in the history of the firm, were now common and increasing. Jesse, of course, did not see his culpability in this, but he did see that he no longer had a product that would sell itself. They began losing business. During a three-month period wherein he discussed this problem with the two owners, only Rollie brought up the matter of the new debilitating culture of decadence. Even he thought simply that it should be curbed, perhaps deferring to his older partner. They had a meeting with the core crew to discuss this, after which the beer was brought out, then the drugs. Rollie, to his credit, left the office, but Jesse and Eric stayed and participated in the revelry. Jesse, of course, had his other job to go to; the natives were waiting.

Jesse began spending more time at the bar. Ramona was bothered by this, but Jesse did bring the money home, and she spent it as recklessly as he did. For his part, Jesse still had nearly no interest in money. He essentially gave it all away. They did get the boys back for a time, and each of them received two hundred dollars a day for their pleasure. He bought clothes and gadgets for them having moved far away from the fatherly inclinations of learning and discipline. He was now behaving as if they were his associates, as if they were consenting partners. He had them preparing the drugs, packaging, and even at the ages of ten and twelve, he passed the marijuana joint to them, encouraging them to get high with him. This he did without compunction. He did it without thinking about the foul Lord or the wholesome dreams or anything. He had transformed his life into something that no one who knew him, in his previous life, would have believed or recognized. He rolled a joint gave it to his oldest child and watched as the youngster took a hit, a deep draw that caused him to cough and his eyes to curl back into his head. Jesse was not alarmed; it was more like watching his child wobble as a nine-month-old taking his first steps. He simply helped his firstborn into bed, saying he should lie down for a while and sleep it off. Zachery, seeing his brother falter, chose not to partake, at least not now, but soon both of his sons were smoking marijuana regularly, and their father was, as perpetrator, provider, and trainer, all right with this.

For nearly a year Jesse sold drugs in this bar, routinely bringing home five to ten thousand dollars a week. This was small money in the lucrative drug trade, but for Jesse it was more money than he had ever had and more than he knew what to do with. He was as popular in the bar as Harry was, but he did not compete with him for business , or anything else for that matter, falling comfortably in line behind the hierarchy.

After an event that must be called unrelated, Jesse decided to quit the moving company. In his heart he knew he was about to commit another disaster, the seeds of which were planted with his arrival. He had done some good, he was certain of that, but growing like mold spores in the delicate lining of his mind was a grief that had morphed into the worst of all emotions: indifference. He even left the deal on the table, potentially many thousands of dollars, simply walking away having decided to kill.

It was during the end of the rush hour on the overcrowded streets of Cambridge, Massachusetts. He and his family were unloading groceries. They had only a few bags, enough for each family member to carry one or two into the house. Ramona was driving, and she stopped the car in front of the house, but on the opposite side of the street, and they began unloading. At that point a patrol car pulled up alongside them, demanding that they move the car. Zachery was in the passenger's seat, and Jesse was in the rear seat on the driver's side. Opening that door would have created more congestion. Jesse told Zachery, his youngest son, who was sitting in the front seat, to get under the wheel and move the car forward and over a few feet, allowing cars to pass. Zachery, of course, being a young boy, was eager to get under the wheel, but as he did so, the angry police officer showed up on foot, demanding to see his license. That is when it got unpleasant.

Obviously Jesse had made a mistake, harmless as it turned out, but a mistake nonetheless. The officer, seeing this family, with the father in a business suit and carrying an attaché, the wife in all of her motherly fashion, and three children, decided to haul young Zachery to jail. Ramona and Jesse were in complete disbelief. "You cannot be serious," bellowed Ramona.

"This is not going to happen," Jesse said, fully believing that the officer was just trying to frighten the youngster.

"Just watch me," said the officer, and he put little Zachery into handcuffs and into the backseat of his car with the lights flashing. "He'll be at the police station in Central Square. If you want him, you know where to find him." He fled the scene to Ramona screaming obscenities and a steely Jesse nearly frozen in disbelief.

When they got to the station, only moments away, Ramona and Jesse where stunned to see, only a glimpse, but they saw Zachery in a cage, behind bars, and Jesse decided that this officer was going to die. The arresting officer strolled casually out to a waiting area where the family was, and Jesse grabbed his wrist, tightly, with hatred on his face. The officer attempted to pull away, but Jesse's grip was strengthened by rage. The officer said loudly, sounding an alarm, "You had better release my arm."

"You had better release my son," said Jesse, glaring hostilely at the now red-skinned officer. The officer struggled and glared right back. The other officers pulled their weapons as the captain appeared, wanting urgently to know what was going on. As Jesse let go, it seemed as though everyone began talking at once, but Ramona could be heard over them all. "I am a news reporter, and this whole episode will be brought to the attention of the community. You can bet there will be an investigation. Do you know how many witnesses there are to this outrage? I can promise you we will be here with cameras tomorrow, and this will be on the news."

The captain entered the area and earned his stripes, speaking with the calmest of voices. "Ma'am, if you will just give me a moment or two, I will get to the bottom of this. Clearly there has been a misunderstanding." Jesse and the arresting officer never broke eye contact. It was not readily apparent what was on the mind of the officer, but Jesse's face, to say nothing of his mind and heart, had determined that this man was going to die. Jesse thought of his boys at the bar and how much they would enjoy fucking up a police officer. But he decided he would do it himself.

It was, in fact, only a few minutes before the captain returned. Ramona, and Jesse, had he not been so overrun with anger, could hear, but not make out what the officers were discussing—only that it was heated. "Mr. and Mrs. Brightmeyer, I have been briefed on the details that led to this arrest, and I would like to apologize for my officer's poor judgment. You don't need to be told that under no circumstances should a twelve-year-old be allowed to sit at the steering wheel of a moving vehicle, but hey, no harm done. But let's try to not let something like this happen again. This is certainly an over-reaction, and I hope that we can end this here and now with the release of your young son."

This was enough for Ramona, who certainly had more to say, but the threatening attitude had subsided.

Not so with Jesse. This son-of-a-bitch had to die. As lost as he was, he went, if it can be believed, even more insane. The only place he knew to find the offender was at the police station, the place with all of the guns and people trained to use them. Jesse did not own a gun, had never fired one. In his madness, he found in the backyard of their residence an old delaminating oak table. He pulled one of the legs from it. Its weight felt lethal. *A blow to the head*, he thought. He took a few swings with it. But he gave no thought to how to do this, the logistics of it.

The police station was built early in the early twentieth century and had architectural features that would allow a person to hide in the shadows. It was squeezed between other buildings that had been constructed over the years in this very congested square.

Jesse waited for darkness to come and drove his car up to the square, less than a half mile from home. He parked a block away and wore the same trench coat he had on during the arrest, and he used this cover to hide his bludgeon. His victim's face was etched firmly in his mind. This face, this creature who had had the audacity to imprison his son, was the one to die. His retribution was specific, and he could see the man's face bashed and bleeding. "I'm going to hurt this motherfucker," he said aloud to himself. He placed himself in a shadowy cubbyhole and waited. He waited two hours, standing in the ever-cooling night air. During that time only three people came into his view, and to his great luck, none of them was the perpetrator.

Jesse, feeling cold now, and futile, decided to head to the bar and re-plot the death of his new enemy. When he got there, much later than usual, Sal yelled, "The doctor is in the house," and immediately began bringing orders for drugs. Not only had Jesse been at the police station with deadly intentions, he also had on his person two thousand dollars of packaged cocaine. "Where the hell have you been?" Harry said. "We are getting ready for our in house tournament. We need you on the court. Get back there and pick a card. Teams will be based on suits and face cards. Hurry the fuck up so we can get started. We got a four-hundred-dollar pot."

"You know me Beast; the ace of spades is mine."

"Yeah, right, I'll be there in a second."

The dart court was busier than usual. People had put up an entry fee for elimination rounds, and most knew from the beginning who the likely winners would be. The Beast showed up and began orchestrating the affair. "Everybody pick a card. The suit tells you what board you play on, and the number tells you what order; aces high."

People lined up to pick their card, and Jesse was about fifteenth in line. "The ace of spades is mine," he said, and when it was his turn, he reached into the middle of the spread of cards and turned over the ace of spades.

"Jesse, you are one lucky motherfucker," someone said.

Lucky indeed, that could not be denied. For his indiscretion, the officer Jesse wanted to kill had been sent home. For Jesse that was the luckiest moment of the day, perhaps of his life.

Chapter 32

Jesse's Great Luck

October brought with it the colorful arrangements for which it is known. In 1962, it also brought a day of unpleasantness for young Jesse Brightmeyer. It began ordinarily enough with his morning breakfast of oatmeal and toast. He and his siblings were scurrying about, getting ready for school, packing their paper-bag lunches, and gathering their homework. It was a cool morning and one of those days when everyone had to leave the house at about the same time, which produced a heightened level of chaos and laughter. The furnace of the small house was mounted under the floor in a crawl space with a central three-by-five floor vent, which, on cool mornings, everyone flocked to like butterflies warming their wings, Rosalind especially, given her hypersensitivity to the cold.

For Jesse and Allison, given that they attended the same school, there was to be a half day, some celebration or school business, I cannot actually recall. Anyway, some years prior to Jesse's enrollment at the junior high school, Frankie had made a name for himself that still hung in the air of the junior high school corridors five years later when Jesse arrived.

Bullies have been around since time began, and several of them had decided that Frankie was their next target. This had to do with Frankie's splendid physicality, its being noticed by all of the girls, and the fact that Frankie would not fight; he would not defend himself. He was, as all of the Brightmeyers were, dark of skin, and he had very large classically shaped lips. As was common in those days, these were not characteristics that one generally associated with good looks. These hooligans would pick on Frankie because of these attributes, calling him gorilla, jungle boy, and other inanities that where intended to hurt him. They did hurt, but he had familial adoration to buffer him against those comments. They began to push and punch him in an effort one guesses to see how far they could go with this big fellow, and soon they decided that Frankie was a pushover. To Frankie he was simply being the good son, doing what his mother had asked of him. His temperament was kind, friendly, but additionally he had been told repeatedly by Madelyn not to fight. Her fears stemmed from Frankie's formidable physique, her clear knowledge of what he was capable of, and, of course, the gentle nature she herself possessed. But the day came when Frankie was just tired of it.

Frankie always enjoyed dressing well, and his siblings were always happy to ready him in his finery, shining his shoes, pressing his shirts and slacks. So it came as no shock when he asked his father for the enormous sum of ten dollars to buy some new clothes. Brightmeyer nearly always said yes to his children, but especially Allison and Frankie. This amount of money approximated a third of his weekly salary, but he found a way to make it happen. The shock came in what Frankie purchased: a pair of jeans, which were not popular among the well dressed in those days, a wide black belt, and a pair of brogans. This ensemble was as close as Frankie could get to the look of his tough cowboy movie idols. It was also so completely different from his usual attire that it raised eyebrows, as they say, at home and when he got to school.

Frankie had decided to fight, and he felt he needed an outfit for the occasion. He waited for the lunch hour when the leader of the bullying pack and his gang would all be gathered in the school's cafeteria. He felt menacing and invincible in his getup. In his mind, he was about to stage a bar room brawl, such as he had seen so many times in westerns, his favorite movie genre.

He walked directly to where the gang leader was sitting and snatched his chair from under him. Frankie was surprised in that this stout fellow did not fall, but sat still as if the chair remained under him. Frankie had no time to think about this, so he grabbed him by his belt and the back of his collar and threw him facedown along the adjoining dining tables, scattering food and splashing drinks all the way, a scene and a sound that immediately got the attention of the unsuspecting crowd. The bully's cohorts sprang into action, trying to tackle Frankie, and they were on him, but not for long. Frankie whirled, landing a thundering fist to the face of one of them. He fell and did not get up. Another he lifted, almost as if he were weightless and tossed him across the room. He was fighting so deliberately, it was as if the whole affair had been rehearsed. He headed then to the leader, who was angrily getting up and so fully covered with food and drink that he resembled a walking mound of garbage. Frankie said nothing then or through the whole affair. He took this boy's breath away with a punch to his chest. He too was immobilized and began hacking and gasping for air. Frankie was not finished, as he turned to confront the two left standing, bringing pain and humiliation that had everyone in the cafeteria stunned as the seemingly orchestrated violence unfolded. By this time, the principal and several teachers had been alerted, and one of them made the mistake of trying to restrain Frankie from behind. Frankie, not seeing who it was, and thinking it was just another hoodlum, reached over his shoulder, snatching him up and hurled him violently to the floor. When he saw him, this victim being in a suit and tie, something told him there were no more comers, and he stood there, in the midst of destroyed tables and chairs, with fellow students standing about, gasping, panting, turning full circle as if to see who else would oppose him. It was in this semi-dazed state that he heard the principal's voice yelling for him to stop, calm down. "Look what you've done, Frankie, look what you've done."

When the news of this event got to Brightmeyer, he was not surprised. After talking to his son, he came, the very next day, dutifully to the school. He came not to hear about the mandatory discipline but to defend his son.

This was Brightmeyer's way. He had raised his children to never lie to him and would always believe them no matter what anyone else, even other adults, had to say. This was a fine thing about him, and his children, out of fear and respect, never lied to him.

It happened during Jesse's stay at the school as well, Brightmeyer having to make an appearance at school. Someone stole a purse, and since no one would confess, the teacher had everyone in the class write five hundred times: "I will not steal." Brightmeyer, who always made certain his children were taking their lessons seriously, noticed Jesse writing this and demanded that he stop. "Did you do it?" he asked.

"No, Daddy," said Jesse.

"Do not write another word."

For his part, this assignment meant very little to Jesse. He did not even feel accused but rather thought of it as a chance to practice his penmanship. In some small way, he even thought that it would have pleased his father to see him doing so.

The next day Brightmeyer showed up in his own menacing outfit. With his roundness, his large arms pressed firmly against a T-shirt that had his ever-present Pall Mall cigarettes rolled up in the short sleeve, underdressed, it must be said, for such a cool time of the year. There was nothing about the look of this man to prepare the school leadership for his savvy intellect. This look, which all of the children got to see from time to time during their years in school, was embarrassing to them. It did not match or fit the persona that Brightmeyer demanded of them. But Brightmeyer brought a practiced persuasion to all of these meetings and left, always, having his way and the vindication of his children.

Anyway, when Jesse and Allison enrolled in the school, the legend of Frankie Brightmeyer still pulsed. As Frankie and Rosalind were at the school at the same time, so were Allison and Jesse. Allison's cuteness and intelligence belied her feisty, combative nature. She, unlike Jesse, who would always opt for diplomacy over conflict, would stand her ground against anyone. It so happens that the younger brother of the lead bully was enrolled in the school along with them, and he had decided to avenge his older brother's beat down, or he had simply inherited the same domineering disposition. He found Jesse early in the day, and without any provocation that Jesse was aware of, announced that he was going to beat Jesse up. "I'm going to get you after school," he said. This fellow, whom everyone called "Red," had already established a reputation for beating people up, so Jesse took his threat seriously and almost immediately began to whimper. When the bell rang, announcing the end of class, Jesse ran out to find his sister.

"Allison," he began with panic and fear in every syllable, "Red said he was going to get me after school. I'm scared."

"Who is Red?" she said. "And don't be scared. Nobody's going to do anything to you. I'll meet you at the front door, and we'll walk home together."

Jesse felt all of his fear, every iota of anxiety, leave his body. He did not have the stuff, whatever that was, for fighting. It was not his way. But his family did, and all of them were utterly fearless.

When the final bell rang, Jesse hurried to the front door, and he saw his sister sauntering toward him with her friends, laughing and talking. Red was waiting for him just outside the door. Allison walked with her younger brother to where Red was standing with his intentions plainly written on his face. She handed her books to Jesse, said nothing, but placed on her face a look that was so frightening, so threatening, that Jesse was suddenly, for a moment, not sure who she was. She went straight to this boy, who was certainly bigger than she, and pierced him with devilish eyes that were promising one end, and one end only.

"Frankie is my big brother, and that's my little brother," she said, never even looking in Jesse's direction. She folded her arms and seemed to swell to twice her size. *Her voice had changed*, thought Jesse, and he felt safe, so safe. Red found the courage to walk away. Allison took her books from her brother, and they walked home as if nothing had happened.

Jesse hopped, skipped, and jumped his way home in front, behind, and all around his sister and her friends.

When he got home, he and the whole neighborhood, it seemed, had a lot of time on their hands, so they began horsing around in the way that children, at least poor ones, do: climbing trees, throwing rocks, the whole "tag, you're it" routine. Eventually they found themselves on the railroad tracks that crisscrossed many urban areas, still throwing rocks and climbing anything they could. The thrill that drew them to the tracks was "copping a train," which was a phrase someone had invented for hitching a ride on slow-moving trains. They would wait as long as it took for freight trains to come lumbering through and run along the side of it so as to grab onto the utility ladders that were anchored to the sides of each car. They would then leap to the bottom rung and ride, often miles from home.

Ever since young Jesse saw his big brother in those boots, he had wanted a pair and began soliciting his mother to buy them. She thought that Jesse was too young then, but at the start of this school year, Jesse got his fancy new boots. It was early in the school year, so Jesse's boots were still relatively new. He discovered that he did not like them as much as he thought he would. Jesse was the fastest kid in the neighborhood, but with his boots on he could not get up to full speed, but he liked wearing them to school, and it made him feel like he was somehow as significant as Frankie.

All of the children got excited as they saw the train snorting in the distance. They readied themselves for a ride on this massive iron horse. As they were getting into position, Jesse's left boot got wedged between two tracks, and while he was annoyed that he had scuffed his boots, he certainly did not think he was in any trouble. The trains were nearing the station at this point, so they were going much slower, making it fairly easy for the children to jump them.

It is a good thing because Jesse could not free himself, and he was on the same track with the oncoming train. He was stuck in such a way that he could not stand up, but still he thought he had enough time to wiggle free. Nothing worked, and the train was getting closer and blowing that wonderful whistle that now sounded like a death knell. The other children had not noticed Jesse's dilemma, and Jesse could see the inevitable. He began screaming as loudly as he could. It seemed interminable, but finally one of the children saw him and came running to help. This savior seemed so calm in the face of what would have been even his own death that it should have had a calming effect on Jesse, but it didn't. His young friend worked like a mechanic and freed Jesse only seconds before the train arrived at the spot that could have been the site of an absolutely horrific scene. By now, all of the children were watching and when Jesse was finally released, they all laughed and immediately dismissed the incident. Jesse, on the other hand, was too shaken to hop the train and watched safely from a comfortable distance as his pals enjoyed their ride.

The horror of these banalities came to Jesse when someone called him "a lucky motherfucker." And somewhere in his mind, he wondered where that boy was. That boy whose sister, less than two years his senior, had to save him from a bully. The boy who did his mother's bidding, and who had gotten the lesson his siblings had missed: "Jesse, be nice." Where had he gone? And it bothered him that he could not remember the boy who had saved his life.

"Jesse, you're up. Jesse, what the fuck are you doing, man? We got a tournament going on here."

Chapter 33

The End Begins

It was completely unceremonious. Jimmy had quite enough of Jesse. The moment came when it was impossible to deny Jesse's heterosexuality and that there was no chance that he could comply with Jimmy's wishes. Jesse loved Jimmy, loved him dearly, but he simply was not, nor could he find a way to be, gay or be intimate with a man. No matter how diligent or dedicated he was to Jimmy's needs as an artist, as an intellectual celebrity, or as a friend, Jimmy wanted something else, something more. The relationship lasted three years: three unrequited, turbulent years, from Jimmy's point of view.

Jesse knew that he had at least been honest about who he was from the beginning. Jimmy, on the other hand, one guesses, was accustomed to having his way with young pretty boys and really thought that it would simply be a matter of time before his seductive manipulations would have their usual effect. Jesse was nonplussed but impervious. As comfortable as he was in the company of homosexuals, there was nothing sexual about his comfort. "If I ever found a man sexy, I would sleep with him," he would say. This was

considered sardonic and, in some ways, insulting to Jimmy and his
friends.

"You're hiding something," Jimmy would say.

"You are not seeing something," Jesse would respond.

These exchanges rarely got any deeper than that. Sexual
disparities aside, it is difficult to have ones desires disregarded, and
this frustration finally came crashing down . . .

It turned out that Allison got her way. She had wanted to have
Jimmy at her home for an evening of entertainment, and Jesse
had convinced him to do so. His going to Detroit was not just for
Allison's sake—Jimmy had many friends in the area who he wanted
to see.

Allison was a fine party planner. She gathered her army of
helpers and worked Steven like a plow horse in making preparations.
She put together a guest list, and among the invitees were gifted, if
not famous entertainers. She knew many educated people who could
pass as intellectuals, and she had enough pretty people, gay and
straight, for a perfectly comfortable mix. Of course, her siblings were
there. Allison was a wonderful cook; having learned this high trade
from both parents, it could be argued that she was as accomplished
as either of them. She could have had the affair catered, but it was
important to her to do it herself.

There were poems read, songs sung, and a layer or two of
thoughtful intellection was enjoyed, a brilliant evening by any way of
reckoning.

Jimmy was from a large family too, and he knew something
about family approval. He even brought along his beloved mother,
and she rightly was treated like a queen during the whole evening.

It could be said that the tables were turned. As Jesse had understood that he would have been dismissed had Jimmy's family not approved of him, Jimmy needed to know that his intentions with Jesse would not be thwarted by narrow-minded family members. In the absence of parents, Jimmy followed protocol and approached Franklin as the patriarch.

"I'm in love with your brother," he virtually blurted. Frankie was not disturbed by the comment or the abrupt style with which it had been delivered.

"Does he love you back?" said Frankie.

"I think so, but you will have to give me some time for a more precise answer."

He and Frankie chuckled warmly and appropriately. Others, both family and friends, had heard this exchange, and most decided that Jesse was "turned." He was gay, and this was all the proof they needed. Even Frankie decided that his soft kid brother had found himself, and while he was not bothered by this, or even surprised, he found himself sharing in the playful, albeit tasteless gossip that followed. Jesse found no way to care. No one said anything to him, but the murmuring was palpable. Jesse just smiled.

The fine night wound down with warm goodbyes and polite promises. Allison's closest friends stayed to bask in the afterglow. Jimmy and his mother were driven to a local hotel, but at one in the morning, it was essentially midday for Jimmy. He was dutifully patient with his mother, but once she was comfortably ensconced in her room, Jimmy's itinerary continued. He had several stops to make during the night, but he would only make one more. If Jimmy stopped someplace, he would have a scotch on the rocks, or several, depending on how long he sat. He had a few at Allison's, but under the watchful eyes of his mother. Jesse could relate to that and felt real envy, with his mother gone. Now with the sun on the other side of the world and racing this way, Jimmy was in his prime time and was headed to a place where he could drink more freely.

The next stop was at the home of a magnificent woman named Ameda Jones. She was on the periphery of the civil rights movement all around the country. She may have been on the fringe of the movement as far as the media was concerned, but she was well known to many Black entertainers, and civil rights activists. She lived in the heart of Detroit, and like Jesse was nostalgically rooted there.

She was older than Jimmy. Apparently, back in the day, she was mother, cook, advisor, and voice of reason for many of the activists and stars. She was a sassy woman with a friendliness that was at once winning and disarming.

When she opened the door, Jimmy fell into her arms, and she held him tightly. Jesse had never heard him mention this woman, but it was obvious that she was someone special in Jimmy's world. She wore a flowing colorful dress with African or island suggestions about it. She was bedecked with large and small jewelry, and somehow none of it managed to be gaudy. Her house was much the same. There seemed to be too much in it. Eclectic, yes, but more miscellany, with old and new, antique and contemporary all about; it was almost as if this collection had been thrown into the house and somehow landed acceptably. Her spirit and style matched this place.

Once inside the crowded vestibule, Ameda kissed or seemed to kiss every inch of Jimmy's face, finishing flush on his mouth. She stayed closed lipped on his mouth so long that he was a bit embarrassed. When she released him, he gleamed, his exotic face creasing with joy. She looked up at Jesse, and her eyes opened wide, and she said, "Oh my Jimmy, I had heard he was beautiful, but my goodness. Come here, boy." She grabbed Jesse, holding him to her bosom much like his mother's friends and sisters used to. Jesse went immediately to one of those memories and felt good.

Her house, appearing so large on the outside, was wall to wall with people, and they swarmed Jimmy. He had had a good time at Allison's, but now he was in his element. Here he could talk "thirty-year talk." It was spirited, pensive, and tearful, full with laughter and painful reflections. Jesse knew there would be no other stop tonight.

In this group of sycophants and friends, there was a stunning creature heartily engaged in conversation with one of the many handsome and well-dressed men in the house. This fellow's back was to Jesse, and when he saw this woman, saw her seeing him, Jesse knew it was going to be an interesting night. Her eyes darted from this man to Jesse, who was making his way across the room, enduring the many introductions as he went. At one point, the man turned to see who or what was distracting her, but his eyes did not meet Jesse's.

The guests where having fun, with laughter, food and drink in endless supply. Jesse, a light eater, had not eaten at his sister's house, and Jimmy was less the consumer of food than even Jesse. Ameda insisted on feeding him, which was a complete waste of time and food. Jesse did manage to eat something, but he found it on the plate of the young beauty with whom he had locked eyes and intentions.

She had on her plate an assortment of goodies and finger food, including desserts. In the small space that she had staked out as her own, she held her plate in front of her so as not to drop it or impale anyone with a skewer. Everyone was happily contorting themselves to negotiate the tight confines, and they lost sight of each other moment by moment.

Suddenly, it seemed, Jesse was standing in her space, and Jimmy was nowhere to be found, seated somewhere in the congested room and surrounded. The gentleman she had been talking to was lost somewhere in the crowd.

"That was fun," he began, but was distracted by her equally stunning body. The dress was essentially wearing her, black, fitted, with the braids of her hair, seemingly just done, prancing along her shoulders. If she was wearing makeup, it only showed on her fingernails and lips, as she was made . . . up, if you will, by a blessing of nature.

Jesse tried to see this woman in total, but there was no way to do so in a room so crowded. He looked at her hungrily and commenced a double entendre. "I'll have a taste, if you please." He was licking his lips and staring at her mouth and face while reaching for some morsel on her plate. He lifted a strawberry, kissing and sucking it as if it were her mouth.

"A taste only," she said, with her eyes and mouth responding to his fruitful kiss.

"Well, I prefer the banquet, but there is no table to spread out on."

She touched her lips with her tongue salaciously as she said, "Come with me." Carrying the plate above her head like a waitress with one hand, she had Jesse's hand in the other. They pressed and squeezed through the crowd until they reached a corner in the hallway leading to the bathroom. She reached for the door, but it was locked and occupied, and several of the people in the hall were waiting to get in.

There was a steady hum of conversation, such that you could engage in conversation, but if you shut up, you could pick up snippets of banter all around you. She found a place to put her plate, and they stood talking nearly flesh to flesh. Jesse was burning to have her, and she for him. They kissed as in foreplay, gently touching their lips together, while whispering introductions. "What is your name?" Between moans, she said, "Billie, call me Billie. What's yours?" Biting her ear, Jesse, speaking ever so softly, murmured, "Jesse . . . are you with someone?"

"Yes, I'm with you, all night." Turning her lips to his, she said, "Your lips are so soft, kiss me again." Jesse complied, but this time he placed his tongue on her lips and slightly opened her mouth with his, tasting her tongue.

"Are you?" He was kissing her neck.

"Am I what?"

"Are you with someone?"

"Yes, I'm with Jimmy."

"Does that mean you're gay?" Her hands had found his penis, throbbing wildly.

"No, I just work for him, but I can't leave him here." These ordinary words were said in the most sensational tone, with heavy breathing and feeling.

She noticed and was apparently waiting for the bathroom door to open, and when no one rushed in, she did, pulling Jesse before the curious eyes of those standing near. Once in the room, she locked the door, and they proceeded to do the very thing their eyes had agreed upon when they first met across the crowded room.

Within seconds of placing his aching appendage inside her, an angry knock came at the door.

"Oh my god," she said, "you feel so good. Don't go far." There he was, in yet another bathroom, surrounded again by the public, and about to be exposed again.

They hurriedly made themselves presentable, opened the door, and there stood Jimmy glaring viciously at the two of them.

Jesse did not feel much of anything, having seen Jimmy throw tantrums in New York with an aging publisher and in Jackson, Mississippi, with a terrified schoolteacher. In both cases, Jesse had been equally indiscreet.

Billie was at once contrite and defiant. She apologized in perfect French, which was a perfect surprise to everyone. Jesse understood that much of the language, but the rest was lost in the mayhem and the fluent ramblings of the beautiful Francophile. Jimmy though went into an utter rage in the same language, and an ugly scene erupted. The yelling was belligerent and face to face. This was made all the worst because Billie was somehow related to the hostess. Luckily no one lowered the music and no one else spoke French, but there was no mistaking the tenor.

Ameda worked her way to the uproar, registering a look of astonishment and despair, with embarrassment only just beneath the surface.

This tumult lasted . . . well, too long, until finally Ameda overcame her surprise and disgust and forcibly removed Billie into a private room.

Jimmy stood glassy eyed before Jesse, saying nothing, having run out of words. Indeed he had had enough. For Jesse to prefer women was one thing, but to subject him, repeatedly, to this kind of unnecessary shame was more than he wanted to suffer. He felt again betrayed. He had altered his affairs to meet Jesse's family, and it was fully known to him the uses to which his social presence could be put and the advantages that could accrue. And this was his reward. He was finished with Jesse, and now it was only a matter of completing the current schedule and Jesse would be out of his life, permanently and unceremoniously.

Somehow this regrettable scene made its way into Jesse's head soon after a call had come in, now three years hence. Jesse could not remember who called him or how he came to know, but Jimmy was dead. Taken by the rigors of life, by his own life, many would say. "Fuck them," Jesse would say. Jimmy was beautiful, he was lovely, and he wept at his loss, the world's loss, and the memory of his inability to please him, to be his lover. Jesse had disappointed him; he had chipped a piece, pieces from an already broken heart.

Jesse was at the beginning of the end of his life. Drugs had come to him and taken hold, and he remained mired in impenetrable grief. He had not seen or talked to Jimmy in the ensuing three years of alienation. Still he had to be there at his interment. He missed Jimmy consistently; thought often and warmly of him. Jesse had squandered the drug money but still had enough to get on the shuttle and make his way to Saint John the Divine with all of its gothic indifference. He donned his favorite suit jacket and tie and went sadly to Boston's Logan International Airport. Seeing nothing and noticing no one, he boarded the shuttle. It seemed barely to leave the ground or stay in the air for more than twenty minutes. On the plane, Jesse was again aware of the great indifference. His friend, the profound friend of the people, was gone, and there was no evidence of his passing on their faces - no trumpets, no announcements. He thought of that insidious corridor in the hospital in Detroit, where his mother was destroyed, and how here too, as there, no one noticed. A sadness enveloped him, made all the more immense by the brutal memory of that apathetic corridor.

When the plane touched down in this city of tombstones, the place Jimmy loved, in the country he loved, which also had betrayed him, Jesse thought of how unfinished the place was, so full and yet unfinished. Nor was Jimmy finished. Done but not finished. He got into a cab, going silently the whole distance, arriving late, but with time enough to see the hordes of well-wishers and what stars there were. *They do not love him as I do*, he thought. He was wrong, of course, and had these thoughts as a self-deception, explaining to himself what he was doing here. He was not welcome, not like the others. They had not betrayed him.

They gave speeches and found points of laughter. The drums beat loudly, a tribute that Jimmy would have appreciated. The music, the rhythms of his people taking him home, a tribute to a star who never saw his own light. Jesse had seen crowds gather like this before, many times, to be in the presence of the noble wizard. Crowds like this one, wanting to get close, wanting to drink from his bottomless cup of wisdom. Still he thought, *Now you come. Where were you when he needed you?*

When the drums quieted and the tributes ended, Jesse found himself sitting alone by a stone wall, weeping abundantly in self-pity and regret. The limousines had assembled at the curb. Family, friends, publishers, and Jesse thought he saw Justin, the agent who had hired him to accompany Jimmy around the world. The family limousine was perched directly in front of the walkway of the grand cathedral, and Jimmy's favorite brother David was sitting at the curbside window. He saw Jesse and lowered the window. Their faces equally wet, Jesse kneeled, saying breathlessly, "I'm so sorry, I'm so sorry." His brother said nothing, but his eyes gave Jesse too much to think about. *"You hurt my brother." "Why did you forsake him?" "What are you doing here?" "You are not welcome here."* Jesse imposed these speculations on himself, and his grief was deepened. He watched the procession depart while trying to find his legs.

By eight o'clock Jesse was back at the Barrel, sharing his sadness with the disinterested throng. He ordered a beer and a shot, snorted a line of cocaine, and headed to the dart court, where he began to finish his own life.

CHAPTER 34

The Brotherhood

Jesse had been coming to the bar for over a year. He had no real job now, or rather, he sold drugs full time. He was a regular now and had developed a circle of his own. It was a disparate coterie of people who did not particularly like each other, but they had him and his drugs in common-that and a bottomless despair that drove them to the bar.

People now came directly to him, bypassing Harry and Sal. Word had gotten out about the best bar in which to buy quality cocaine, and people, new people, began showing up. People who did not know Harry "the Beast" O'Connell and who had not passed his muster. Some were accountants, lawyers, even police officers, and students from Harvard.

For about a month or so, members of a biker gang had been coming regularly on weekends to buy Jesse's product. They had no interest in games and generally would not stay very long. They would saunter in, unsmiling, wearing full-length leather coats or leather vests with chains oddly draped about themselves and gang insignia stitched in place, looking as intimidating as they hoped to be. Among them, they would purchase four or five grams, have a few drinks, and be gone.

Occasionally they would have women with them, and one of these women spoke and moved very much like a boy. She wore boyish clothes: a leather jacket, jeans, heavy boots, and a helmet that resembled something the Gestapo would wear, under which she wore, as did several of the men, a bandana. This woman, whose name was Hillary, and her boyfriend, whose name I cannot remember, became regulars. They honored the local leadership and went to Harry for approval or recognition. They liked darts and the persona Harry, one guesses, had developed at the bar. The woman, who everyone began calling "Hills" was particularly drawn to Jesse, in a way reminiscent of the men, baring stories and confessions of the most private kind, while standing proudly strong in spite of horrific childhood memories. All but a few confessants were this way, proud to have survived, and none considered themselves dysfunctional. Indeed they did function, creating what was for Jesse the strange, debilitating culture that was the Boston area.

Jingles, with whom Jesse had developed something akin to real friendship, seemed bothered by this attention and the fact that she seemed unable to fraternize with anyone else. Her boyfriend watched these sessions from a distance without complaint. At a point, it became evident that he was not in control, and she, unlike the other women in the club, would routinely have her way. She even asked Jesse if he would show her boyfriend how to dress. When Jesse removed the corporate uniform from his mien and began wearing casual "bar clothes," the old habits of color coordinating and sizing stayed with him, and this trait was occasionally mentioned by both the men and the women.

After only a few weeks, to the surprise of everyone in the bar, Hills showed up in a dress and high-heeled "girly" shoes. Her hair, which was cut short, was neatly coiffed and she was carrying a purse. Her boyfriend was nowhere to be found. Jesse had the habit of hugging people, the men and the women. He had done this with her and her boyfriend, who, while allowing it, was visibly uncomfortable being warmly hugged by a man. Jesse was as stunned as any one by this new look and said so.

"You look marvelous," he said, nicely imitating a character made famous by Billy Crystal. "You remind me of someone. Let me see . . . Have you been here before, or did we meet at some corporate event last year?"

She smiled and walked into Jesse's arms for her usual hug and placed her now-visible classic European body against his. For the first time Jesse could feel her womanliness, soft and fragrant. It felt as if she was wearing nothing beneath her colorful outfit. Soft in a way Jesse had never recognized before through the denim and leather. She lingered in his arms, before stepping back and pirouetting to allow him to see her feminine side. A great smile was on her face, and the onlookers oohed and aahed at the sight of it. Then she returned to Jesse, clasping his face within both her hands and kissed him scandalously, as if no one was watching.

The regulars gasped, cajoled, and playfully teased them both. But underneath this good humor there was a real discomfort. However welcome Jesse was in the bar, this was one of the great taboos: black-white sexual race mixing, and in public, no less. Jesse could feel this. When she stopped kissing him, she held him tightly around his waist, smiling brightly.

"Wow," he said, "what did I do to deserve that?"

"My treat. I mean, your treat. I want you, and I don't care what they think."

"Okay, but what does your boyfriend think?"

"I don't know, and I don't care. We broke up last week."

Jingles was among the onlookers, and later that night approached Jesse and said, "So she wants to fuck you. She's just a nasty biker bitch. Putting on a dress don't change that. Are you going to fuck her?" Jingles had a look of pure disappointment in his eyes. Something more than that actually—he was on the edge of anger.

"Look, man, I don't know what's going on. You know as much about this as I do." Jesse was telling the truth. There was nothing in his previous contact that would have allowed him to anticipate this sexually aggressive behavior.

"I'm telling you right now, she is nothing but trouble."

That night, Jingles discovered that Jesse was a card player. He and a friend were playing a game called cribbage, which Jesse had only heard about. He had never played or even seen it played, but he liked the idea of learning it. The game's weakness is that only two people can play it. This led people to begin talking about other card games, and when the dust settled, it appeared as if everyone played poker and whist. Soon, playing cards became as popular as darts, and they became the games of choice after hours.

After hours was becoming a scourge, at least at home for Jesse and Ramona. It was almost every night. The money that Jesse continued to bring home was not enough. There was more than enough money, but this was not the stuff on which a relationship could thrive, not for a couple like them. It should be said that Ramona's interest in money was no greater than Jesse's, and she had begun to complain about his absences and the poor company he was keeping. When she and Jesse first met, one of the things that brought them together was a mutual interest in art. She was a fine sculptor, poet, and painter. Jesse was an actor, or so he had said, and he promised himself that he would write and draw again. That was to be their life together, bohemians, setting the world of art aflame with their new vision and style. Jesse had gone to New York to try out for *A Soldier's Play*. He had even found an apartment there; things forsaken, a life forsaken for what had become a life of simple debauchery.

She found herself showing up at the bar, only once or twice, asking Jesse to come home and inquiring about how he could stand such "uninspiring company." "They are a bunch of hillbillies," she would say. She was as right as she was wrong, but it did not matter to Jesse. He needed their despair as much as they needed his . . . counseling. Ramona coped indifferently with her troubles. Of course this is unfair to say, but it appeared that way to Jesse. She found a way to accept what was, which should have been a lesson for him, but Jesse wanted, he needed to be unhappy; he needed the rage to buttress his retribution. These were his only weapons, as he had not forgotten his nemesis, the missing god, who only he knew where to find.

Ramona was in relentless pursuit of intellectual combat. Any discussion, it seemed to Jesse, was about winning it, not about understanding. This style was off-putting to Jesse, as Ramona would become edgy, condescending, and unnecessarily provocative. Still there was something about her that he loved, something that drew him to her, constantly, as when seeing her shashay across the auditorium in Boston in that striking blue dress. It may have been that image and nothing more. She was gritty, far more so than her high-society friends knew. She would get high with Jesse, mostly just socially, but from time to time, she would want a buzz almost as an aperitif. She believed or wanted Jesse to believe that her friends—doctors, teachers, curators, and such—would be opposed to her or anyone getting high. Jesse scoffed at this, saying, "You don't know these motherfuckers like you think you do." He went so far as to make a sexually based bet with her that at one of their upcoming elitist social events, most of them would be getting high with him, as opposed to sitting around the dining room table engaging in some scholarly discussion. Of course she lost the bet but appeared delighted at the loss.

She and he enjoyed cocaine, but, like all other confectionaries, they could take it or leave it. Most drug users were addicts, spending their days distracted by the urge and their nights satisfying it. Jesse distorted his mind with marijuana and alcohol, which simply enhanced the disarray living there since the loss of his mother. The use of cocaine was only social for Jesse, or marketing, allowing him to show and sell his product.

This was soon to change, as Jackie, the young boundary-less Russian, had shown Jingles how to cook the potion. Jingles would show Jesse, and soon his enjoyment became an addiction to the utterly demonic crack cocaine.

Card playing aside, the dart league and its tournaments were still the main event at the bar. The team at the Barrel was good enough to have gone undefeated with only a few contests left in the season. Every other week, the team had to travel to another bar, but this week was a "home game." The dart court was always a very active place, but on game night from seven to ten, only the team players were allowed on the court. Actually there was one board dedicated to the patrons, but it was little used on these occasions. Harry would always give a pep talk, like all good coaches, and put a roster together, team play, individual play, and so on. Opposing teams always showed up thirty minutes early for practice and acclimating themselves to the new environs. This was always an interesting moment, sizing each other up, and discovering top guns.

On this night, to the utter surprise of everyone, eight black males came strolling confidently into the Cork 'n' Barrel. The muttering started at the door. Their blackness was enough to create an excitement that could go either way, but they were also large, big men. This had the effect of stimulating the testosterone in the room. It is the nature of men, one supposes, to rile up, confront, defend, and protect their own. The interesting dilemma here was obvious. Whatever attitudes or opinions the locals had of black men, it had been decidedly, if not permanently, altered by the presence of Jesse Brightmeyer.

These men where just like the patrons of the Barrel, dodging something, leaving some stress behind, diverting their lives moment to moment in pursuit of playful distractions and intoxicants. But that testosterone, cracking in the air as it was, gave the people a heightened level of expectation.

As for the black team, they were just as amazed to see Jesse playing for an all-white team.

"Damn, brotha, whatchu doin' here?" This language was an affect, designed to show camaraderie, as this fellow, the captain, had a fine grasp of English.

"Where the hell did you brothas come from? I didn't even know brothas played darts. I damn sure didn't think there was a team," said Jesse, truly surprised.

"They call me Smitty. What's your name?"

"Jesse. Are you the captain?"

"Yep."

"Well, let me introduce you to our captain."

All eyes were watching, and Jesse without hesitation went to protocol. The tension here was of course silly, but Jesse knew the dynamics of it and, without any noticeable effort, circumvented any possible racial discord.

"This here is Harry. We call him the Beast. He's our captain."

"What's up, my man? Team full of brothas, huh. Well, that's a first. Look, in few minutes and for few hours, you guys are going to be the enemy. We are real serious about our darts here. But before that, what are you guys drinking? We like to get the opposition a round on the house before battle."

They laughed the laugh of gladiators, and the two captains introduced their teams. The chatter was kept to a minimum as the drinks were ordered and practice began in earnest.

The match was not close, but the games were, and the team from Boston brought a spirit of fun with them, not just cutthroat competition. The sprit they brought with them was intended, in a way, to mask the fact that they had just learned the game. This was their first season, and, more than anything, they were simply testing the water to see if they could actually compete with the "white boys." Jesse learned that several weeks later.

When the contest ended, Smitty asked Jesse to defect. He, in fact, tried to embarrass Jesse with the race bait.

"You should be playing with your people. We could've beat these guys if you were playing with us."

Somehow the fact that Jesse was comfortable here and that he had what appeared to be real friendship here escaped Smitty's perception. To him, and it would likely have been equally true had the roles been reversed, a black guy playing for an all-white team in an all-white bar was a kind of betrayal. It bothered him to see Jesse slapping hands with his mates and seeing the white girls hugging and fawning over him. And as Jesse later discovered, he envied it.

"Why don't you come on down to our place, meet the fellas? We got some fine sistas hangin' out with us."

"And for the head? What you got for the head?"

"Oh, we got the hookup," said Smitty, and he wrote down a phone number, the address of the bar, and even the dates and times he would likely be there.

"That's cool," said Jesse, "I might drop in on you guys, check out your hospitality, but I play here, with my boys."

None of this was lost on Harry, and he was bothered by what he deemed bad behavior. It wasn't the race thing—that and all of its dynamics were beside the point. It was a breach of conduct to recruit on the competitor's turf, and however quietly it was done, Harry himself had seen it. This had the potential to undo Jesse's earlier diplomacy.

After the opposition left, Harry approached Jesse and said, "That was fucked up." When Harry was upset, he became a close talker, right up in your face.

"I respect the way you handled it, but that kind of shit can't happen. You come into my house and try to steal my people. Fuck that black shit. We're brothers, right?"

"Yeah, I thought it was tacky, but you know, I'm not taking it too seriously. I know something about loyalty, and we," said Jesse, extending his hand in a shoulder-high handshake, "are brothers."

At this, Harry picked up one of his shiny steel-tip darts and plunged it into his forefinger, producing a droplet of blood. He reached for Jesse's hand, which he provided willingly, and repeated the act. Jesse winced within but showed no evidence of the pain without. They touched their fingers together . . . like children making a bond. This was an endearing moment for Jesse, and it took him home, far from here to that village, the paradise he remembered in the dreamy confines of Twenty-Third and Butternut . . .

"Jesse, ah think we is best friends, don't chu?"

Only ten years old, Cletus Hornsucker spoke with the most distinct Southern accent. He had been born in Detroit or, like Jesse, had been there since infancy, but he lived with parents and a family that had only been north for less than a decade. His family was from somewhere in Appalachia and, as they were relentlessly friendly, Frankie had made friends with his older brothers and sisters. Jesse and Cletus met incidentally when Jesse was just following his big brother. He and Cletus had been "chunkin'" rocks, climbing trees, chasing squirrels, shooting marbles, and running footraces from the moment they met.

When Jesse met him, he was noticeably intrigued by the fact that Cletus wore no shoes, and he wore clothes that Jesse had never seen on a human before. He was wearing a pair of raggedy overalls that were over nothing at all except his bare skin. Only one shoulder strap had anything to do as the buttonless bib it was supposed to carry looped over like a broken wing. He appeared to Jesse to be dirty . . . from head to toe and all of the time, and Jesse envied this in the way a small boy might. Madelyn insisted on her children being clean, always. Her children were not allowed to go to bed until they had had a bath. Their clothes, even in play, had to be ironed. Cletus also had brown teeth, at least the ones that remained. None of this was disturbing or off-putting for young Jesse, just interesting.

Their playfulness with each other was immediate and seamless. So when Cletus wanted to be, or assumed that he and Jesse were best friends, he was comfortable with it; he welcomed it. It wasn't long before Jesse and Cletus were puncturing each other's thumbs and pressing them together in the age-old bond of brotherhood.

Cletus took an empty bottle and skillfully broke it over the edge of a random stone. I say skillfully because he wanted a shard that would be spear-like in its shape. He achieved it with the very first strike.

Children have values, but they are primarily inherited or learned from parents and family. Jesse was steeped in good behavior born of strict parenting by a father he feared and a mother he adored. Cletus was from a family twice the size of Jesse's, and his parents were, how shall I put this . . . different from Jesse's. Jesse had been taught by his mother to honor all living things. For Cletus, living things existed for his perverse entertainment. Jesse had become "best friends" with a deviant. Little Jesse had no idea of how to respond when the depraved Cletus said, "Come on, Jesse, let's catch some rats."

"Catch some rats? How do you catch a rat?"

"Yeh got to find 'em firs, and ah knows jes where to look."

Cletus lived at one end of the block and Jesse at the other, and between them there was a family that appeared to be, but was not related to the Hornsuckers. These people worked on cars and had erected a medieval-looking contraption for hoisting motors, transmissions, and such. Their yard resembled a trash heap, and, on the alley side, was surrounded by high fencing that kept the unsightliness from public view. It was rumored that they were hiding much more. Whatever else they had, they valued it highly, and it was guarded by an Alaskan husky, a huge unruly beast, known to the children as "Devil." No one had ever been in this yard, and to Jesse's relief, Cletus' plan did not include entering it. Instead he climbed the fence and began terrorizing the large dog. The dog went predictably nuts, leaping heavily against the enormous sliding garage doors. Cletus then leaped down into the alley and started beating on the exterior wall with a stick. In what appeared to be no time at all, several rats scurried into the alley whereupon Cletus darted, barefooted, stepped on the tail of one of them with one foot, then quickly placed his other foot on the animal's head. He then picked the creature up by the tail while snapping it back and forth like a whip. This action seemed to cause the rodent to go unconscious. Cletus then ran to the end of the block where there was a fifty-gallon drum of scab oil from one of the machine shops in the area and waited for the rat to stir. He then dipped it into the vat of oil to simply watch it asphyxiate.

It got worse. Cletus would steal house cats and put them in a croker sack and hang them from a high wire to enjoy the ghoulish sounds they made while scratching themselves bloody, trying to get free. When Cletus decided to cook a live cat in an outdoor oven, Jesse had enough. He would see Cletus from time to time, but the "best friend" thing ended with these vile activities.

It was some fifteen years later when Jesse would again be confronted with "brother" and "race" phenomenon. The Christian brothers he first encountered when he moved to Grand Rapids were white. They took him in, as they say, and embraced him. The "society" as Jehovah's Witnesses often called themselves, had a stable of traveling elders, who on a given Sunday would be assigned to speak or preach at a congregation other than their own. When Jesse was sent from the pristine suburbs to the inner city, such as it was in Grand Rapids, the black brothers began to recruit him, so this ploy by Smitty was not new to Jesse, and he was ready for it.

Still, something inside of him wanted to see the place from which these "brothas" had come, and those "sistas" were no less intriguing.

CHAPTER 35

Pipe Dreams—The Seduction

The drugs were like the high rents of the area, wherein people would put up with each other for the sake of survival. They would also put up with each other in order to do drugs. So often, there was an assembly of people who would never, under any other circumstances, be in the same small room together.

Jesse invited a group of these to his house, Ramona's house actually, to play cards and get high. Ramona was to go out of town, and Jesse knew that if she were home, this could never happen. Ramona had again created a delightful living space. Her artwork and other interesting pieces where neatly displayed on the walls in the small two-story unit. She had managed to find many equally interesting furnishings to create a comfortable and inviting space.

When his guests began to arrive, all of them made an errant assumption, saying aloud, "So this is what drug money can buy. Damn, Jesse, this is nice," "You live here alone?" and so on. Jesse would give all the credit to Ramona, rightly pointing out that without her he would have no place to stay.

Among the invitees was a large bearded man who lived for two things: drugs and whist. His drug of choice was heroin. He would consume it any way he could, even putting it in his eyes when he could not find a vein. Unlike most drug addicts who had been withered by the drugs, he was burly and showed no conspicuous ill effects from years of drug usage. When people commented about it, he would say, "My checkbook, man, it's completely emaciated."

This man had lost, among other things, a seven-story apartment building in Manhattan, a veritable gold mine, to heroin. He was, if his story could be believed, a millionaire before being introduced to the lily-white monster. After telling his story, he said, convincingly and without equivocation, "Hell, I do it again for this shit. If God made something better than heroin, he kept it for himself."

Jesse was stunned by this, "Man, you have got to be kidding."

"Like hell I am. Heroin is the best thing in life—it is the best thing on the planet."

"Well, there ain't no heroin in the house, but I got something better," said Jackie, as she and Jingles began to set up for their alchemy. They had with them two bags of what Jesse thought was cocaine, but one of them was simply baking soda. Jesse was somewhat surprised by this, thinking that they had gathered to take advantage of his supply of drugs. Jingles, of course, had his requisite supply of weed.

There was not much room in the small kitchen where they gathered, so Jesse began moving things around so that they would have a surface on which to complete their chemistry. He did this as neatly as he could, thinking about Ramona's eventual return. Soon he had room on the counter, standing room only, but room nonetheless. He had to move the small table away from the wall to create space for four card players and to prevent people from disturbing her delicately hung pieces of art.

Jesse then opened a bag of cocaine and handed it to one of his guests, a large insatiable black male he had recently come to know, and who incidentally lived only a block or so from this house. He too was a husky fellow, but his body, and Jesse did not recognize it then, was beginning to show the consequences of abuse. He had developed a twitch, and his eyes appeared older than he. As it turned out, he was well known in the Cork 'n' Barrel but was not a popular figure, being completely self-absorbed and without a conscience. He was strangely proud of his Irish name and heritage. "Daniel McDowell," he would say, "a good Irish son." He was attempting, with this poorly received mantra, to say something about the history and the insanity of racism, but it fell always to the floor without achieving any edifying impact at all. Instead he always got strange, even hostile, looks and sometimes laughter from the white-skinned Irish.

That he was insatiable was not known to Jesse before this night. He had an irritatingly encyclopedic intelligence, spitting out facts as if he was the only person on the planet holding the information. As a high school student, he had been educated at one of the elite prep schools somewhere in New England, on a scholarship, no less. There was also a certain sophistication about him, rarely used, rarely seen in these environs, but Jesse was able to recognize it, having been raised by the effete Franklin Arthur Brightmeyer. Any similarity with his father began and ended there.

The five of them got as comfortable as they could in the neat little room. There was beer and liquor enough to go around, and it wasn't long before the whole house, and certainly the kitchen, smelled like a bar, smoke hanging in the air like fog. It was a cool time of the year as I recall, and windy; so when Jesse cracked the window to allow air in or smoke out, the wind vigorously snaked in, disturbing the fine powder, the leafy marijuana, and creating an instant chill. Jesse closed the window, deciding that he could get the smell out of the house long before Ramona returned.

They actually played cards, and these were skilled, enthusiastic players. Jackie was the cook. She liked playing cards, but nothing moved her as much as crack cocaine. She took from one of the drawers a large spoon and put a small amount of water in it. Then she placed some cocaine and about a third of that measure of baking soda into the bowl of the spoon. This concoction was placed over a flaming eye of the stove, and with a toothpick or a utensil about the size of one, she delicately stirred the mix until it congealed.

"That's fucking beautiful," she said, at which point she brought what appeared to be a small wafer about the size of a mis-shapen quarter and the thickness of a dime to the table and placed it on a saucer. "This shit ain't bad," she said, and one could hear the slightest hint of her mother tongue.

"Cooks good," she said, gleaming and ever so proud.

Among her things was a small bottle formerly committed to some over-the-counter liquid pharmaceutical, into which two holes had been burned with the hot end of a cigarette: one to accommodate a straw and the other into the opposite side of the plastic bottle to enhance air flow. The cap had been removed and replaced with tiny sheets of aluminum foil, layered, concaved, and perforated many times with a needle. This makeshift assembly was to be the screen and the finishing touch of a homemade crack pipe. Cigarettes were set ablaze for the sole purpose of farming ash as a bed for the fried crystal to nest in, before it itself would be set to burn.

Jackie, nearly prancing now with glee, loaded the clinched and perforated aluminum screen with the ash and deftly placed a small portion of the "cookie" on top of it. Jesse had never seen her quite so happy. Indeed he had rarely seen anyone appear so pleased. It was as if some colossal achievement had been successfully completed. He noticed that all of the eyes in the room were riveted on this behavior and filled with childlike anticipation.

She struck the flint on the cigarette lighter and Jesse remembered it as if it unfolded in slow motion. Placing the flame over the mound of ash, she inhaled, and the flame dove eagerly through the potion of ash and crack. She took a long swallow of smoke as the bottle filled, and the smoked swirled prettily into the small bottle, filling her lungs as well, or more precisely, her brain, with the euphoria she was seeking. She pumped her finger, rhythmically, over the air hole like a musician playing a wind instrument.

"Damn," she said, holding the bottle too long for the other anticipants in the room, "that's some good shit."

"Cookies and cream," said Daniel, reaching greedily for the pipe.

He broke off a piece of the wafer, tapped a little more ash into the small cauldron, and engaged himself as if no one else was in the room.

"Oh, yes," he said, praising the induced sensations. Then he spoke no words but leaned back in his chair, Ramona's chair, proud and satisfied. One by one, they sought and apparently found the genie in the bottle.

"Jesse, ain't you going to take a hit? Hell. Man, this is your shit we're smoking up." Jingles was offering up a treat, and he wanted his friend to share in it.

"Yeah, I think I'll try it," said Jesse, not knowing that the genie was in fact a demon, sinister and demanding. *Just being sociable*, he thought.

It seemed harmless enough. With each strike of the flint, each inhalation, the scent of vanilla would fill the air. There was no rolling of the eyes back into the head or slurring of speech. What Jesse saw and misinterpreted was a group of people smoking and drinking, and this dalliance seemed no more threatening than those time-honored rituals.

"Yeah, Jesse, get a taste. It ain't heroin, but it's pretty damn good," said Ben, the burly unscathed devotee of the art of getting high.

Jesse took a taste. Indeed it seemed to him like harmless socializing, not unlike having a beer or smoking a joint.

That soon changed. Jesse took his hit and thought nothing of it. He certainly did not take another as the others did. He snorted a few lines, drank beer and scotch, and smoked cigarettes through the night. At about four in the morning Jesse was toasted, but not so fully gone that he did not want these people out of his house; Ramona's house. Now the eyes were darting and twitching, rolling, if you will. Speech by everyone was completely incomprehensible, all but the seasoned Ben, who seemed completely fresh. Those who could get words out of their mouths had them in the wrong order, and Daniel stared mindlessly into the unknown. Luckily or unluckily, these inebriates were accustomed to making their way home, through the narrow streets of the Boston-Cambridge area, while being so completely compromised. Jesse woke up at ten o'clock in the morning to an empty, smoke-filled, and cluttered apartment.

Ramona would not be home today, which was a relief to Jesse. He would have time to clean up the house and rid it of the scent of decadence. He did that, sweeping and scrubbing until all of the evidence was gone. He found something to eat, and it dawned on him that he should have been hungry much sooner but did not relate this to a side effect of the demon drug. In fact, he did not think much about it at all. By five o'clock, he was back at the bar with pockets full of prepackaged denominations of the seedy currency ready to be swapped out for the currency of the land.

"The doctor's in the house," Sal yelled as Jesse entered the bar, and they both headed to the confines of the women's room. At this hour, only a few of the regulars were present, and the business of snorting lines seemed innocuous, somewhat like an end of the day conversation at the water cooler.

"How much do have on you? We're going to be busy tonight!" Sal talked as if there was a legitimate enterprise going on and he had to keep inventory.

The young woman that Sal had introduced to Jesse the night he first showed up with drugs was present, as she almost always was, and in the "ladies" room when Sal authoritatively opened the door.

"Enough," said Jesse, "see what you think of this batch."

"This ass wouldn't know the difference. Let me tell you what you got."

"Well, I'll be damned. Here I introduce you to the doctor, and you do me like Jeff to the left. Ain't that a bitch, Jesse? Women! That's why they need to stay home cleanin' the house and makin' babies."

"Twirl, Sal," she said, putting her middle finger into the air. They both laughed comfortably.

"Good shit as usual, Jesse. Can I get a quarter until Tuesday?"

"Sure, that all you want?"

"Yeah, I got some of my girls coming in tonight, and I owe 'em a treat. But I'll tell you, they're going to want some of this stuff, so I hope you're loaded."

The quarter gram of coke would become her commission, which was fine with Jesse. This is what the freebies were all about, a little low-level marketing.

It did seem to Jesse that they had not been in the ladies room for very long, but when they got back into the court area, it had already become a bustle of activity. Jingles was there, looking fresh and showing no ill effects of the previous night's indiscretions. Jackie too, came sprightly, glowing like a debutant after the ball.

"Now that was a hell of a party last night. I got so fucked up. I don't even remember how we got home."

She had a way about her that sometimes resembled a much-older woman. She would place her hands on her hips and assume a posture of a seasoned, worldly-wise woman.

"Jingles," she said, now sweetly, girlishly, "I'm fucking hungry. Give me ten bucks. I'm going to the Grill and get us some burgers."

"I don't want no damn burgers. Here's a twenty. Get me some shrimp, some of that slaw, and make sure you get a bunch of that sauce, that red sauce."

"Shit, since you're going, get me a burger and some fries," said Sal, reaching into his pocket for a five, searching through a mangled collection of one-dollar bills.

"I want in," came a voice that Jesse had not heard before.

"Jake, you motherfucker," Jingles nearly yelled, "where the hell have you been?"

Jake, it turned out, was a regular who had not been seen here for a while. Certainly not since Jesse's arrival. He had the appearance of a mechanized collection of wires or a stick figure formed to resemble a human being, producing angular, jerky movements about himself. Defiant hair grew in every direction on his head and in too many shades of a dusty brown. His voice, the range of it, was like his hair, rising and falling in a range that was completely unusual, but primarily it was deep—seeming too deep for such a lanky fellow.

"I'm clean, man. I had to go get cleaned up." He looked at Jesse, and in the look there was a suggestion that he had been watching the interaction for a few minutes.

"I don't remember this guy," he said, extending his hand.

"I'm Jake."

"I'm Jesse."

"Yeah, Jake, Jesse here is the new professor," Sal piped in.

"Hey, Sal, how you doin', man? You look good. What's been happening?" Jake and Sal seemed genuinely glad to see each other. They all did.

"Whatcha drinking?" said Jingles, "Let me buy you a drink."

"Bud, I'll take a Bud. Thanks."

"Hey Jingles," said Jesse, "you fly, I'll buy."

"What the fuck is this? You guys having a party at my place without me."

Harry the Beast had come in, and no one had noticed him with all of the excitement around Jake.

When Jake turned and saw Harry, a party did erupt.

"Sticks, how the hell are ya? We thought you moved out of state or got married or something."

"Hell no, I just needed a break. I got cleaned up. You know, I got a little out of control for a while."

"Well, shit, you came to the wrong place. I'm glad to see you, but hell, man, this is where you come to get fucked up." Harry was giving fair warning.

"That's why I'm here. I knew you guys would have what I'm looking for."

"Jake draws pictures," said Sal, "real fancy shit."

He was, in fact, an architect, and a pretty good one. His "fancy drawings" were of finished details of high-end residential properties. He was part of a long line of professionals Jesse was to meet who indulged in the devilment. All of them, the doctors, lawyers, and police officers would find their way into the life of drugs while maintaining a tenuous hold on respectability.

"Wait a minute," said Jackie, "you bastards are getting ready to do some lines. I want one before I go. You think you can dis me just because I'm a girl?"

"Hell no, it's because you're a pain in the ass," said Sal, and everyone laughed, even Jackie.

Anyway with Harry on-site, it being fairly early in the evening, and Jake's homecoming, they headed to the storeroom where Jesse and Harry provided some product for some snorting.

Jackie took Jesse's package and cut lines for four people. She snorted one, saying, "Damn, Jesse, that's good shit. Here, Jake, you gotta try some of this."

"What the fuck, you think I got mashed potatoes over here? This is some quality snow I got here," said Harry, defending his reputation.

"Okay," said Jackie, "if you insist." And she cheerfully snatched his straw and snorted one of the lines Harry had cut.

"Are you shittin' me? This stuff is sweet. Damn, Harry."

"Private stash, baby."

Jesse could tell that it was going to be a long, uproarious night. The party had begun, and it was not yet six o'clock. The hardcore people had not even arrived.

Jake was an eminently likeable fellow. Jesse was reminded of Cletus in that there was an immediate connection between them. He engendered no jealousy and aroused no one's competitive juices. He played the games and talked the talk, but beneath all of that, he just wanted to get high. Unlike so many others, he did not seem to be running from anything; he was just an addict. He loved cocaine, and like Jesse, he knew very little about its evil cousin, crack.

When he took his hit, there was pure joy in his expression. His eyes rolled happily, not deliriously, and he savored the high like a dieter getting her weekly allotment of ice cream.

"That's what I want," he said, "that's it." The pleasure did not compute for Jesse. He saw nothing in this drug that should elicit such joy.

Jesse thought . . . *what in his own life, what sensation could produce that kind of euphoria?* The happiness of his youth had been so complete and so pervasive, that he could not select moments to remember. Joy is what he recalled, pure and utter, in the trees, alleys and backyards of his youth. Yet the ecstasy registered on Jake's face, sent him tumbling, again . . . back to better times, back to the paradise of his memories . . .

"Wow, Auntie, these are great. For me? Really, for me?!" His mother's best friend, so much the best friend that she was "Auntie" to all of Madelyn's children, had bought Jesse a pair of Converse All Stars, the most enviable gym shoes of the day. He had wanted a pair so badly because he thought that if he had a pair of All Stars, nobody could beat him in a footrace. There was not much that was more important to the twelve-year-old. They were white with red stripes and had the all-important sole pattern that made them grip the ground unlike any other shoe.

He couldn't remember what he had done to deserve it, but when he put them on, he virtually took flight. He darted out of the house and went running, running faster than the wind, faster than the birds, the dogs, and certainly faster than all of the children.

There was in his heart that day, that moment, the kind of glow and satisfaction that he saw on Jake's face . . .

"Jesse, Jesse . . . snap the fuck out of it. Where the hell did you go? What is it with this guy? Are you with us?"

The Beast was snapping his fingers in Jesse's face like he was returning from unconsciousness.

"You want a hit or not?"

"Yeah, yeah I do," he said, returning indeed to consciousness, but not reality.

"Let's play some darts. Three bucks to get in, winner takes all," said Harry.

Jesse stayed there, in the alley, up the tree for some minutes longer, and wondered about what his boys were doing. He wept internally, thinking about how disappointed his mother would be to see him in this place, behaving this way. He saw the image of the foul god, the murderer, looming above him. *Fuck Him*, he thought. *Why did He do this to me? He brought this on Himself.*

I need to get high, he thought, as he felt the tears coming again, about to present themselves for all to see. He snorted his line and then another.

"Ahh," he said, "I need a drink. Why don't we have a second prize? I'm going to feel bad taking all of the money."

"Shit," said Harry, "you won't even get second. I got a five spot that says you don't show in the top three."

"Cool, warm it up."

The night unfolded as anticipated. Jesse and Harry sold out of cocaine, which meant the after party had to be moved, and somebody had to go get more coke. They chose to go somewhere safe because, while Jesse did not know it, many people were now cooking the stuff after hours. Crack had showed up, and people, hardened cocaine users, were not eager to let it be known that they were using it. Even in this company, "Crackheads" were presumed to be at the bottom of the depraved social structure.

Jake's place was safe and near. There, in the confines of his second-story apartment, the cooking began in earnest, and this time Jesse smoked. He decided he would learn to cook it himself, and he smoked like everyone else. Each time the bottle, the makeshift pipe, came his way, he took a hit, still claiming, as everyone was, that this was harmless—no worse than snorting. But soon he and others began showing up much later at the bar, and someone else was selling their product. Harry the Beast and other dealers found themselves leaving the bar early to obey the tyrant, the smoke-filled dictator, the dreaded pipe.

CHAPTER 36

The White Girl Phenomena

Ramona was home when Jesse got there. She was only half asleep. When she saw him, there was no way for her to not see that something was different. She was accustomed to seeing him altered by an assortment of intoxicants, but here, now, there was something else. Something she had not seen before. There was a daze on his face, a stupor through which she could see something ugly coming. She could also see remnants of the afore night's bad behavior. Apparently Jesse had missed a few things in his efforts to make the apartment presentable. Jackie had left clear evidence of the previous night's debauchery, and Jesse had missed it. She had her own little pipe and had been stealing hits in the bathroom and left it behind. Ramona, of course had never seen such a device but knew immediately what it was.

She was calm, but resolute.

"So you've turned my house into a crack house!?"

"Hey, baby, how you doin'?" Jesse was just barely able to make sentences.

"I'm doing just fine." She paused and then said, firmly, "Jesse I don't want to live like this anymore. Don't you see the danger you are in, you are putting me in?"

"Come on now, I'm just doing what I have to . . . to make the money. I got a little carried away last night, but I thought it was all right because you were not home anyway."

"Stop it Jesse. You are an addict . . . don't you see that? You are an addict and a drunk. Do you want to explain this?" She held up the small plastic pipe. You want to tell me what this is and how it got into my house?"

Jesse was busted and too witless to defend himself. He began to stammer, and Ramona decided to save him from himself.

"Jesse, I'm leaving. I can't afford this place on my own right now, so you can have it. I have acquired rights to a small studio in Boston, and I'll be moving the things I want into it. You need help, and you don't seem to want it or you don't know that you need it. I have done all I can for you. You are killing yourself. You know Patience is still in trouble, you know I need you to be supportive. She needs you, and what do you do? You hide, like a coward." She was genuinely saddened by this announcement and it showed.

"No, I was going . . ."

"Jesse, please. Don't start with the lies. I am not going to let you drag me into the sewer with you. I don't want you here, or . . . I mean, I don't want to be with you anymore. I will be gone tonight, but it will take me a week or so to get all my things out of here."

He was defenseless. He wanted to speak, to defend himself, but no words came to him, at least none that he could string into a cohesive sentence or that even he would be comfortable with.

"I am going to sleep now. I would like it if you were gone when I get up. I have someone coming to help me with the move, and I do not want to subject him to your madness."

With that, she reclined and went peacefully to sleep, or she appeared to do so.

Jesse, with his intoxicants at work on his fragile mind, sat in a chair in the corner. He stared out at whatever his eyes could see, which, as it turned out, was nothing. He could not see beyond the glaze of water that encapsulated his eyes, but no tears fell. He had no right to this woman or any woman. He had no right to live.

In his despair, he had wanted to die many times. He never contemplated suicide. He just wanted to die . . . to disappear from the face of the earth, to fall off its edge. It often felt entirely possible. Just find the edge of the world and leap. Leap into the blackness of oblivion. Reach for and find his tormentor, out there in the great darkness. Claw at his eyes, make Him feel the immensity of the pain. *Look what you've done, you bastard.*

He would find the demons, the ones He sent to torture his beloved mother, and solicit their help. Jesse knew something about demons. As a young minister among the cultish Jehovah's Witnesses, he had exorcised demons. As a child, he had watched his mother do it. He would call on them now, invite them in as allies.

It was as if he leaped indeed, off the edge, back to dark innocence and wild belief . . .

"We must pray now and call on his name. Say his name, Jehovah, call his name."

Madelyn was in the home of a woman who claimed to be possessed, and Madelyn had seen enough strange machinations in this woman's home to believe it. Jesse was perhaps ten years old at the time and was utterly impressed by what he was to see his mother do. She seemed to be everything at once. On this day, she was making her weekly visit to study the Bible with an ancient woman who had the appearance of a forsaken voodoo priestess. There was a strange darkness in her house, on a very bright and cheerful day. Candles, dozens of them, were burning in the middle of the day. The house was dirty, cluttered, and there was an odor that Jesse could not place. He could not associate it with anything. All of her belongings appeared to be as old as she, and she as dirty as them. Odd, oversized books were stacked here and there, these conditions giving the place the look of a dungeon. A spittoon was near her favorite antiquated chair, and she would erringly hurl tobacco-stained spittle at it, creating the most disgusting collection of scum on an otherwise beautiful brass piece.

"I'm tired of 'em now. They ain't doin' me no good. Done wrecked my mind. My chilren and grandchilren don't wanna see me no mo."

She was looking everywhere and at nothing. The dingy, once-colorful rag on her head was loose and dangling as menacingly as her eyes when she said, "Oh, Lord, here dey come."

With that, the front rickety screen door swung open . . . with no one there. It did this three times as if three individuals had staggered in, and then it finally slammed shut. The tattered three-cushioned couch had its pillows depressed as if someone sat on them . . . but there was no one there. Young Jesse was more amazed than frightened, but that was due to his mother's poise.

She began to pray as slippers sauntered across the room with no visible way of doing so. This astonished the young boy who did not bow his head or pray, but instead watched in amazement.

His mother was bowed and praying in earnest, in a way Jesse had never seen. She did not appear frightened, but nor did she appear to be his mother. A look of pure devotion was on her face as she held her Bible tightly and called His name. This ritual went on for what appeared to be several minutes when the cushions rose as if someone was rising from them, and the screen door opened and nearly shut three times as the invisible creatures . . . left. His mother continued to pray, and Jesse thought his mother was special indeed.

But now he would call on them, these demons to take him away. He had nowhere else to go, so he would be with them and assault the perpetrator of his pain.

He sat there, in Ramona's antique chair, dazed, for hours. He knew Ramona was right. He knew, somewhere beneath his pain, he knew he was dying, pieces of him falling away. He could not gather them up, these pieces of him now scattered over the years, over so many lives.

He was not gone when she awoke, but he appeared to be sober. He had fallen asleep in the chair and was awakened by her disappointed assault.

"Why are you still here? I have help coming, Jesse, please go away."

Another piece of him fell off. He could feel it, almost hear it crash to the floor.

"Here," he said, handing her a pocketful of money. He had not counted it, but it was certainly more than a thousand dollars. She did not count it either but placed it carelessly on the dresser.

"I'm going now. I'm sorry." He was. Sorry for everything.

Jesse brushed his teeth, threw some water on his face, and left the house. It was about four in the afternoon. He walked mindlessly up to the square, Kendall Square.

The squares in the Boston-Cambridge area are very important landmarks. Kendall Square, Central Square, and Cambridge Square make up a beaten path linking Boston and Cambridge along the heralded Massachusetts Avenue. Jake's apartment was enviably located on Mass Ave, as the locals called it. But he was not going back there. He had met, somewhere, yet another woman, who had introduced him to, or more accurately, told him about, a bar where she said, "The blacks hang out." You could get a sandwich or even a full meal and socialize "with your own kind." Erica was a beautiful black-skinned woman who wore her fine kinky hair naturally. Jesse found this attractive, not as a "black" thing, but simply as a good-looking woman. She was like so many here, on the periphery of respectability, but a willing victim of the ubiquitous white powder. She had suggested to Jesse that he should stop in as every day around five. The place would be a bustle with people getting off work and stopping in for a drink and, of course, to find something more exotic for the mind.

Jesse felt it was too early to go the Barrel, and he was hungry and was dealing now with a new layer of dejection. That he knew no one in the recommended bar meant he could be alone in the crowd, and it made the place a bit more appealing, so he decided to stop in.

He was early for the evening crowd, but there was a smattering of people, and they did not seem to be his own kind, or not what he thought she had meant by that comment. In the sparsely occupied room, there were people of several races and equally male and female. There was a very large oval-shaped bar in the middle of the room, attended by two very efficient barmaids.

The bar itself seemed a bit too splendid for its environs, nestled as it was in the tight limits of Kendall Square and serving patrons living so close to the edge. He found a place to sit, roughly in a corner of the room but near enough to the windows to see patrons coming to the door and to see, given how long he stayed, night descend over the square. There was now, for Jesse, something comforting about night falling around him. It was as if he could disappear into it, become invisible, like a mole scurrying into a hole. Jesse ordered a shot of Jack and two beers, seeking yet another way to hide. He then ordered his meal: a full red-meat American meal. He was surprised at the quality of it and the service—the young waitress having come politely from behind the bar, as it was too early for wait staff to be on the floor. He found her interesting, as her red hair bounced as she moved, almost choreographed with the movement of her head and hips. Even her freckles seem to have a role in the unintended dance. Again he wondered what the other woman had meant by the term "your own kind," as most of the few people here were not black.

In any case, he ate, forlorn, wishing to be somewhere else. Wallowing in self-pity apparently consumed a great deal of time. Soon it was indeed dark outside; the place was crowded and humming with the sound of predictably banal conversation. Jesse was revived from one of his many day-mares by Smitty, the captain of the all-black dart team that had invaded the Cork 'n' Barrel so many weeks ago.

"Hey, Jesse. Well, I'll be damned, you decided to come hang out with your people today. To what do we owe the honor?"

"What's up, Smitty?" Jesse was a little surprised that he remembered his name so readily.

"Brother, I'm glad to see you. You look like you are by yourself. Do you mind if I sit down?"

"Naw, man, have a seat. Tell me what's going on?" said Jesse, preparing to join the hum.

"Nothing and everything, but I have been wanting to talk to you, and there are some people I need you to meet," Smitty said this very excitedly.

"All right," said Jesse, "let's talk. I hope it's about one of them sistas you were talking about." He certainly did not mean that. The last thing he wanted now, or felt entitled to, was another woman.

"No, but . . . the brotha I'm going to introduce you to . . . I'm tellin' you, man, this motherfucker got it goin' on." Smitty lapsed predictably into the local tongue, the jargon of the neighborhood.

"He got the hookup and the women."

"Okay, sounds like somebody I'd like to know," said Jesse, trying to shield his indifference.

"No," said Smitty, "this is somebody you need to know."

"I should have known," came a very lilting and pretty voice in the darkening room. Smitty and Jesse looked up at once.

"Smitty, you know Jesse?"

"What's up, baby? Yeah, I know Jesse. I shouldn't be surprised that you know him. Erica and Jesse, yeah, I can see that."

"Slow down, my brotha," she said, "it ain't quite like that . . . yet." She smiled heavily at Jesse, who politely smiled back.

"Look here, I'm trying to hook him up with Cha'che. You seen him? Is he coming in here today?"

"I haven't seen him only because I have not been in here for a couple of days. He's in here every day, usually around eight." Then she excused herself, saying, "Look, guys, I have got to go, but I'll be back around eight myself. Will you still be here?"

"I don't know about Jesse, but I'll be here. I'll try to tie the brotha down until Cha'che gets here."

"Sounds like something I don't want to miss. See ya then," she said, hurrying away.

She did not want to miss Jesse meeting a guy named Cha'che. This struck Jesse as odd. It was just one person meeting another. Jesse could not see and did not ponder the import.

"So, Jesse, let me buy you a drink. I want to ask you something," said Smitty.

Jesse was not anxious to move, so this was all right with him.

"Sure, I'll have a beer."

"Man, you got it going on—the drugs, the women. That's why I want you to meet Cha'che. He's rolling too, got plenty of bitches. I want to get me one of them white girls. I mean . . . you know . . . what is it? Is it the rap, the drugs? I mean them white girls were all over you the night we met down at your place." He was nervous, as if he had to find the courage to ask these questions. There was something adolescent about the direction of this exchange.

Jesse looked at him with complete amazement. He was incredulous. Was this man for real? Jesse did not think of himself as having anything. He was aware, certainly, of the taboos of interracial coupling, but it did not cross his mind that there was this . . . desire . . . this lust . . . which was only sexual on the surface, for white women. Smitty said it as if they were a commodity of sorts. What could he do to get his hands on one or some of them? And as importantly, Jesse did not see himself as being able to broker such a thing. He was annoyed and insulted at once.

"Get you one," he said matter-of-factly.

"I can't, man. You know . . . it's like I never had one, and it's . . . you know . . . different."

"Different. How? It's just a woman. You get one like you would any other woman. Look man, there are women you can't get. That's true of everybody, but I'll be damn if it's got anything to do with what color she is. Check this place out. Now I don't see anything special about the women in here, but shit, all you want to do is fuck 'em, right? You could do that with just about any women in here."

Smitty was a nice-looking fellow. He was bright, articulate, and presentable. Jesse could not understand this conversation and frankly felt a little embarrassed about having it. Nor did he quite hear the request in the dialogue.

"Yeah, I know, but can you get me one? Introduce me . . . you know set something up?" He blurted this out and seemed relieved that he had found the courage to ask.

Jesse was beginning to feel the buzz from the alcohol. It allowed him to engage this utterly nonsensical discussion without going insane. He wanted to ask Smitty about his mother, or sisters, and how it is that women who resembled them, and in fact himself, were not appealing to him. But Smitty had not said that. It was just that he felt he was missing something; something he deemed special or important. Jesse made some inquiries.

"Why? Why is having a white woman so important to you? I gotta tell you, man, I don't understand this."

Jesse's confusion was not as genuine as it seemed. He had come from a culture where intermingling with White people was an ordinary daily event. He knew and thought that everyone should know that there was nothing special about them or any other race of people. At the same time, he remembered hearing something similar to this before.

At the age of nineteen or so, he was in the company of some older men in Detroit. It was a casual setting, in the home of one of his older friends, with the men sitting about watching television when a singer named Bobbie Gentry, famous for singing a song about someone called "Billie Jo McAllister" came on. The men began talking about how lovely she was, saying she's "fine," which was the colloquialism for beautiful in that time and in what was called the ghetto. Jesse was nonplussed by the adoration and said so. One of the men said, with absolute certainty, "Boy, there's two things you ain't never gonna see, green snow and a ugly white woman."

Back then Jesse pondered the incredible statement for some time, even shared the event with friends and family. He was certainly aware of the misgivings many blacks and white had about each other but was able to dismiss the episode as nonsense and, at that time, considered it an isolated moment in time.

Some years later, during his time with Marlena, he had the occasion of taking her as his date to a cast party after the closing of a successful play. He remembered now the envy, the animosity, and the disappointment of his cast mates, both male and female, that he had a "white woman" on his arm. What was more, he remembered how mean and insulting their comments were to him while treating Marlena like a princess.

Jesse indeed rolled between these two worlds, in and out of light and dark so seamlessly, that the insanity of and the opposition to "race mixing" could never make sense to him.

So here he was again, dealing with a by-product of the deeply rooted mythology. Smitty was caught up in the "green snow" legend.

There were so many questions Jesse had for Smitty, but he lacked the energy for the discussion.

"You must be handlin' bitches. I saw the way you was dealing with them at the bar. You must be in control . . ."

This was exasperating. Jesse had lost his wives and everything else that mattered to him, and here sat a man who could be made happy and whole by simply sleeping with a white woman. So while Jesse tuned him out, after what seemed like endless mindless prattling, he also decided to interrupt him.

"Smitty, you see those two women sitting over there?" He pointed, actually nodded, in their direction.

"Yeah, I see 'em."

"Just go talk to them like you would any other women. The trick, if there is one, is to not worry about rejection. Pick one and talk to her. Course, what I do is pick who picks me. Think about it—what difference does it make if all you want to do is have sex?"

"Right, man, you're so right. All I want to do is get busy. Hell, I'd take either one of them."

"That's right," said Jesse, "so just go over there and strike up a conversation."

"Ah, man, that's where I have problems. Don't get me wrong, I ain't no punk. It's just you know, like you say . . . the whole rejection thing. Just between you and me, I'm nervous about that."

Jesse understood this. He used to be nervous himself. But now nothing mattered enough for him to be nervous about.

"Next."

"What? Next, what the hell does that mean?"

"Look, man, you are going to be talking to someone who doesn't matter at all, right? If she says no or turns you down, you just think in your mind, 'Next,' and go to the next one."

"You guys all right? Can I get you another round?" The waitress with the freckles said this politely and with a smile. Smitty was noticeably moved by her presence.

"You see, that's what I'm talking about," he said after ordering another round in an effort to get Jesse to stay and keep talking.

"Naw, man, I don't see. The woman is just doing her job. What are you talking about?"

"Well, I'll be damned. There's Cha'che. Check him out. Brother shows up with two white bitches. One on each arm, damn."

Jesse looked up and saw near the door a man with an ear-touching grin on his face, with two Caucasian women each clinging to one of his arms. "Bitches" was an apt description. Certainly the one Jesse first noticed fit the term. She was particularly small, petite, if you will, in a sickly kind of way. All three of them were compromised by . . . well, something, but she appeared to be needing sleep and a box of donuts. It seemed as if she would fall if she released his arm. She was overly made up, and ridiculously so. If it can be imagined, she seemed to have her makeup on backward, with lipstick on her eyes and rouge on her lips. It did not help that she wore all black. Her dress seemed confused about its role, as if it had not quite decided to be a dress, a gown, or a negligee. In any case, it found no place on her body to rest, falling madly over all of her appendages. Her four-inch heels were tattered, with the patent leather rolling exhaustedly up the heel stem. A small purse with an exceedingly long strap was on her shoulder, and everything she was wearing seemed to be trying to escape her.

The other woman, who was on his left arm, provided a strong contrast to the one on his right. She appeared demure. She had a dominating crop of hair that descended to her waist. It stayed there, barely moving, appearing too heavy to do so, even when she turned her head this way or that way. It was thick, like something from the animal kingdom. She did not have the features of a slut, looking much more like a suburban housewife. She was even dressed that way, wearing modest dark pumps, a flowered dress nicely fitting her rather plump figure. She carried, and this surprised Jesse, a clutch purse, which seemed too formal for her outfit and for the bar. If she wore makeup at all, it was so tastefully done so as to not be noticed on her pale but pleasant face.

Cha'che, the man himself, was a hodgepodge. His hair was as thick as that of the woman's on his left arm, but of course it was nappy and uncombed. There were flecks of gray in it, but he appeared to be in his early thirties. He had a tie on. It fought vigorously against the multicolored nylon shirt, the knot in it, and the pattern with its many colors matched nothing. Not his green polyester suit with the white stitching about the lapel or the nearly worn out dark brown oxfords he wore. He was tubby, and his sad suit strained to maintain its position, struggling with his corpulence.

The toothy grin said something that Jesse was not sure of, but he got the impression that this pimp was giving a couple of his girls a treat. This was their reward for turning tricks and bringing him the money. They got to put on their finery and be seen with pimp daddy.

So here was Cha'che, the "Brotha who's got it goin on." To Jesse, the ensemble resembled a circus act. But hey, here were some white women that Smitty could have. Jesse felt relieved. He was just about to demonstrate to Smitty just how easy it is to pick up women when this strange trio arrived. Now he could let Cha'che handle the madness.

The stirring arrival was like watching a celebrity of sorts make his way through an adoring crowd. There was some mocking and name-calling, but that came mainly from people who simply saw the odd appearance of the entourage, not the people who knew the story or their sleazy enterprise.

It took some minutes for them to make their way to where Jesse and Smitty were sitting. The commotion gave Jesse and his mind a chance to escape, and he went, as he always did to the past, the neighborhood, the place he knew best.

His mother was there, always there in the past, doling out tender admonishments.

"No, Jesse, she is not a witch. She's just an old lady trying to make it like everyone else."

The thin waif on Cha'che's right arm brought the old lady to mind. Old lady Mammy is what the kids called her. She always wore black and carried an oversized tightly crocheted bag. It bulged, being full with all manner of witchy paraphernalia, and exciting speculations grew out of the bag, including potions, spiders, snakes, and such. There was also the black hat that resembled the Russian

Cossack brimless headgear. She had the weird habit of walking very slowly and then abruptly speeding up while menacingly, waving her black cane in the air at an invisible foe. The children found her terrifying and completely entertaining. They would sneak bravely up to her house, a stunning white house that racked ominously to one side. It was said, well, the children said, that the house was alive and that she had bewitched it. They speculated that she had dead things, even dead people under her house, in the crawl space. They would knock on the door and run for their lives, before the evil witch would come out and destroy them. The old lady never answered the door. She would come out on her own schedule, and the kids would follow her from a safe distance, saying mean things, some of them even throwing rocks at her. A great mystery grew out of the fact that no one ever saw her go anywhere. She never entered a building or a store. She would simply appear and disappear. The children loved her being, and they teased and tormented her for it, all except Jesse.

"She was a young girl once," Madelyn would say, warmly, almost as if she were a girl herself, "and you never know what people go through to make them what they are. Maybe she was a bad little girl and lost her way. So you see, Jesse, it's important to be a good boy."

Young Jesse mused and decided to be a good boy. In truth, it was just who he was. He was born with a goodness that his mother would simply hone. He wondered now, and for the first time, what his mother's childhood had been like. He had heard the stories of growing up in rural West Virginia, but now he wondered about her thoughts, her lessons, and how she became the woman she was.

"I hope you are not throwing rocks at her."

No, Jesse threw no rocks at her. He threw rocks at the miscreant god, his tormentor. And like the misguided children of his youth, his rocks missed their mark, boomeranging instead into his own broken sensibilities.

"This is the brother you been telling me about," said Cha'che to Smitty.

"Yeah," Smitty said. "Jesse, this here is Cha'che. Cha'che, this is Jesse. You brothers need to talk. Let me get you and your lady friends a drink."

Smitty was very excited, as if was working on closing a deal, and the blessing of these two "executives" was required for it to be approved.

"What's your name Sugar?" said Smitty to the thin woman. She looked at Cha'che as if to get permission to say her name. He did not object but simply looked away.

"Princess, they call me Princess," She hardly looked up while saying it. She was, of course, drunk or otherwise altered, but that did not appear to be the reason for her bowed head. She was broken. Broken by a life Jesse could only imagine. Yet she was so acclimated to whatever the pain was, that she seemed comfortable with it.

"What can I get you?"

"Whatever my man wants me to drink, huh, Daddy."

"Get what you want," said Cha'che, being gracious on their night out and someone else's dime.

"I want one of them pretty pink drinks with the flowers and shit in it."

"And how about you, baby?" he said, looking at the other woman. "What's your name?"

"Margie. And I'll have a gin and tonic." She was much more self-assured, but it wasn't clear to Jesse whether she was truly independent or had taken tacit approval from Cha'che's nonchalance with Princess.

No one introduced these women to Jesse. Princess rarely looked up or at any particular person or thing. Margie, on the other hand, had nearly fixed her gaze on Jesse, and there was that recognizable allure that he hoped would not create some unnecessary discord between the two principles.

Cha'che had not missed this attention and may even have demanded it from his girls; a kind of "see what he's made of" approach.

Jesse did not care. He was sulking about Ramona having left him. He didn't care enough about that either. He would simply go on. There was no real pain in it, except that born of indifference and the clear knowledge that he had fallen so far from his mother's wishes.

The predictable "man talk" commenced. It was at a level that might be called "players talk," because Cha'che was decidedly a man of the streets. Luckily Cha'che talked a lot, giving Jesse very little to say on a subject about which he knew so little and in which he had no interest.

Smitty flagged down the waitress, not the redhead; she remained behind the bar now that a real wait staff was on-site. He ordered the drinks for the women and was in the process of asking Cha'che what he was having when the waitress said, "Oh, I know what Cheesy wants. I'll bring his rum and Coke. You two want another round?"

Cha'che did not laugh or smile at the Cheesy comment, but Jesse and Smitty snickered a bit. When his girls smiled, he cast them a disciplinary gaze and said to the waitress, "You been thinking about my offer? You know you need to be working for me."

She was also a white woman, which seemed to be a requirement to work the streets for him.

"Dream on, Cheesy," she said, walking away.

"I'ma get that bitch. I'ma turn her out, and she gon' work for me."

Jesse could not understand the draw. What did these women see in this man? It did not register on him at the time that it was madness and sadness of the most ordinary and indescribable kind—a pain, pulsating and unreachable, that destroyed the self. It was like his own. Cha'che could not see that the cheerful waitress was not burdened by the requisite pain or that in her clear vision he was laughable.

After passing each other's muster, Cha'che had a question for Jesse.

"I share, do you share?"

"Share what?"

"Everybody shares the drugs, that ain't shit. I'm talking about the bitches. You share your bitches?"

My bitches . . . Jesse just could not wrap his mind around this. Apparently Smitty had gone too far. He had told Cha'che that Jesse was running women. He had to be, seeing how "all them white women were all over him." Plus Smitty had noticed that Jesse was the dealer in the bar, an all-white bar.

Jesse chuckled while searching for a reply. He repeated the question aloud. "Do I share my bitches? Damn, Cha'che, you go straight to the point, don't you?"

"Yeah, man. It ain't no big thang one way or the other. See, a bitch, a good bitch, to a good pimp, is like a good hammer to a carpenter. You might let your boy use yo' hammer, but not just any mothafucka get to use yo' best hammer. You know what I mean? Now you got your other hammers . . ."

He droned on and on about "handlin' bitches." This he did not to school Jesse but to inform him. He needed Jesse to know that he had his women in check. What Smitty had told him about Jesse is not fully known, but plainly he felt the need to impress Jesse with his business acuity. All of this, of course, took place with the women sitting at the table. They did not squirm or appear the least bit uncomfortable.

"Cha'che, me and Princess are going to the bathroom." Perhaps they were just bored. He nodded, giving his approval, as if they had just asked for his permission to go the ladies' room.

"So what you got for the head? I hear you the man." At least Jesse could respond to this.

"What cha need?"

"It's the hos' night out. I got to get 'em high. I'm looking for a G. You smoke. Is the shit smokeable?"

Smoking cocaine! The virus had spread, and here before Jesse was a skilled practitioner. Jesse was not to know how skilled until later that night, but there was now the need for Jesse to rise to the manful player's cause. If he had any street value with this fellow, it was now time to show it.

But Jesse was tired and depressed, and now he was also "buttered," yet another colloquialism for being mentally impaired by one intoxicant or another. With his defenses lowered and fully encapsulated by apathy, he responded. "I'm like General Motors, I got what you need."

"I told you," chimed Smitty, "I knew you brothas should meet. Y'all about to take over."

The waitress and the whores returned to the table within seconds of each other. She waited for the ladies to be seated and placed the drinks courteously before them. They seemed overly pleased at being treated like polite patrons, real people calling them ladies. Smitty paid for the drinks and tipped his "eyes desire" more than she expected.

"Thank you very much," she said, to which Cha'che responded before Smitty (nearly stammering all over himself) could get a sentence out, "You know I got you, right. You know you're mine. I got plenty more than that waiting for you."

"You can keep it, Cheesy. I'll be just fine on my own." Her dismissal of him and his proposal was complete and without irritation. She seemed so removed from his seedy intentions that there was no need for anger or insult.

As she walked away, Cha'che said to his girls, "Now don't get no ideas. Y'all know I'm going to have that bitch. You just get you something to eat and handle my business."

"I'm not hungry," said the tiny one, looking somewhat refreshed after her visit to the restroom.

"Eat, bitch, I'm not going to put up with yo' ass talking about you want to eat at midnight. Some goddamn Twinkies, you better eat something now."

"Yo," he yelled, calling the waitress back to the table before she got too far.

"Get my ladies something to eat." He mocked the use of the term "ladies" as he said it, speaking to the waitress as if she was already in his stable.

"I am not one of your girls. You need to learn how to act in public."

"You're gonna be, so you might as well start doing what I tell you."

"I'd rather eat shit," she said.

"Would you mind bringing a couple of menus for the ladies?" said Jesse with no sarcasm in the word.

"I don't mind at all," she said, "you need to take some lessons from your friend. What's your name, dear?"

"Jesse, what's yours?"

"Jannie. See, Cheesy, how easy it is to be polite?"

"Damn, Jesse, that's how you gon' play me?" He said it very playfully, as if the whole nonsensical exchange had been yet another test. He chuckled, and so did everyone else.

Princess hardly touched her food, but after they ate, Cha'che suggested that they go somewhere and get high. But he had no place to go. He clearly did not want to go to a hotel, or he didn't have the money to do so. Smitty offered his place, which was in Dorchester but very near the Boston city limit. Jesse thought getting high was a good idea, and Smitty's place would do because he did not want to be seen by anyone who knew him well. These new people were a kind of escape for him. But he was going into a dungeon, into a new depth of darkness; and for him there would be no escape.

CHAPTER 37

If She Could See Me Now

He never found the edge of the world. The planet was too large. It had a plan of its own, and it did not include Jesse Brightmeyer. His rage was madness, and his madness was rage. Fully now, out of control and falling fast, his mission to destroy the Lord of hosts was failing. Once he was able to find moments of cogency, but now discord was a constant, raining down upon him relentlessly. He was awash in despair and grief, such that his life now meant nearly nothing to him. He gave nearly no thought to the next day or the next moment. Having met the lowly and infamous Cha'che and his horde of forsaken women, he had fallen deeper into escapism than he ever imagined he could. This was not vengeance; the lashing out had stopped, replaced by habitually bad and desperate living.

However awkward Cha'che was with women, he was just that proficient with crack cocaine.

At Smitty's house, a bachelor's pad owned by a spinster with no domestic skills, Cha'che showed Jesse how to take the preparation of crack cocaine to a higher level. He used a tubular vial, such as seen in bio labs or, more readily, like those used to package high-end cigars, and cooked the nasty drug more expertly than Jesse had seen with the gang at the Barrel.

He would curl up a dollar bill lengthwise and place on it the needed ingredients. The rolled bill would allow him to insert the mixture all the way to the bottom of the glass without getting any of it on the sides.

"Got to know what you doin'," he would say.

He added a small amount of water, then held the swirling mixture over a flame while twirling the bottle dexterously so as to not break it or allow it to get too hot. The result was not a "cookie" as Jackie had produced, but a perfectly round marble of crack. This dollop of pretty, this morsel of evil, had the effect of reminding Jesse of an early recognition of lovely things, tender moments. So incongruent was the happy memory to what was unfolding here . . .

"Now, children, you have to be willing to share."

There was the spatula, the beater, and the bowl itself, all covered with the delicious remains of the cake batter. His mother was making, as she so often did, a cake from scratch, and showing her daughters the same. The ingredients were all present: eggs, flour, butter, and sugar blended to her own enviable standard. The utensils she used for the mixing had the creamy batter all over them—sweet and tasty. The children would all want to lick the tools clean. The KitchenAid stainless bowl was the mother lode, if you will, but it could not be accessed without the spatula. Sometimes only a couple of the children would be in the house, but on those occasions, when all of them were present for this wonderful treat, Madelyn would have to orchestrate the affair while giving the lessons of sharing.

Jesse had gathered so many of these daily lessons, and now, here in this room with everything about it flying hard in the face of the tender life he had known, he thought and cringed, suddenly thinking she was watching. The discordant contrast between what was happening around him and the happy memory it conjured unsettled him. He shook it off and tried to find a way to be in this moment, however ugly.

An apple may not fall very far from its tree, but the seeds and leaves often do. They are blown to sites unknown, with the seeds becoming something unpredictable. Some are crushed and contaminated, growing into something grotesque. Jesse was a crushed seed, becoming a monster, misshapen and treading on murky ground.

"Now that's a rock," Cha'che broke the silence, in Jesse's head at least. There was no real silence. The women were playing music as Smitty had allowed, and Cha'che had been talking the whole time, teaching and demonstrating. Everyone was hovering around the kitchen stove watching and anticipating the preparations, like the kids in the Brightmeyer house in Detroit longing for a taste.

Unlike the makeshift plastic pipe that Jackie manufactured, Cha'che had a glass receptacle with an artistic design, stainless-steel screens, no ash, and assorted paraphernalia for engaging this corruption.

It was odd to Jesse that this man, so tastelessly dressed and who drove an unsightly, pathetic eight-year-old Cadillac, would be so particular about these preparations. Aside from the plump whore, who herself lacked any sense of style, this glass figurine and the lovely sphere produced in the tube were the only things in Smitty's hovel that even hinted at finery.

"Princess, I'ma let you and Margie get a hit, and then I want you to take care of the fellas. You hear me?"

Cha'che took a razor blade and sliced through the delicacy as if he were preparing sushi.

"You got to let it cool if you want a good high," he said.

"Now girls, we have to let the cake cool before we put the icing on it." He heard his mother talking.

Jesse needed these thoughts of home to go away, to leave him alone. This lapse into his memories was not acceptable, not in these surroundings, and he felt as if he was visibly and deliberately shaking his head to rid himself of the memories, twitching like a spastic. He could not contaminate his sweet memories by allowing them to float in this room.

Cha'che struck the flint on the lighter and drew smoke into the pretty pipe. The smoked swirled making angel-like formations—it was beautiful. It filled the air with a scent very much like that of vanilla, and once again Jesse battled the memory of that kitchen, in that loving moment and time.

"Hum-um," said Cha'che, sucking and holding the unholy smoke in his lungs and handing the bottle to Smitty, whose apparent pleasure was indescribable.

Smitty then handed the pipe to Jesse, who deferred to his upbringing and the women, saying, "Ladies first," and handed the apparatus to Margie, who looked completely stunned. She glanced at Cha'che.

"Damn, Jesse, don't be spoilin' my bitches. Go 'head, Margie, but you better do what I told you."

She smiled at Jesse, who himself considered the irony of engaging in so disgusting a behavior while imposing a piece of polite society. He thought, *Oh my goodness, what would momma say if she could see me now?* "Oh my goodness" was an expression of hers, and goodness itself was her way. It was once his way too, but now this remnant of kindness was about all he had left.

Margie took her hit, came to Jesse, and blew her smoke into his mouth, holding the pipe aside. She then took another for herself before passing it to Princess.

When it was Jesse's turn, he imagined that this was the edge of the earth. The end of the world, and he was all right with it. He could die now, for he was dead inside anyway. He could not kill the murdering god, and he could not kill himself. But this activity was sure to do his bidding. It would take him to the edge. He would only need to jump. He saw the smoke swirling in his skull, just like it did in the bottle: the angels of smoke doing a kindness, taking him gently away.

Cha'che continued to get high while his girls complied with his orders, Marjorie, which was her real name, taking Jesse, and Princess with Smitty into different rooms.

She wanted to talk. She did what she had been told to do, and when she finished, she sat near to him. Her deportment now like that of a little girl and began to tell her story. She had very little time to do so because, while it was the whore's night out, her pimp loomed, and she knew just how far she could go before making him angry. Somehow Jesse's kindness did not imply to her that he was not a pimp, but rather that he was simply a nice one.

She decided that she wanted to work for him.

As it turned out, she was a married mother, who paid a baby-sitter to care for her children while she worked the streets at night. She confessed that it was not about the money but could not explain her attraction to this life. She was trapped, mentally and emotionally, by something she could not express. She did not know about Jesse's sadness, thinking somehow that pimps had no pain.

"I'm going to leave Cha'che. Can I work for you?"

This, of course, made no sense to Jesse. He had no experience at this and no interest, or more exactly, no energy for it. He had played the game; he had aimed at the heart of the imposter, piercing only himself. He had found the edge and was preparing to jump. She had found, or thought she had, someone to talk to. Jesse had, or so he thought, no one to talk to. Certainly now, at this moment, he was too compromised by fluids, smoke, and sadness to even contemplate such a thing.

"We'll talk later." he whispered.

CHAPTER 38

Caligula's Palace

The next day, or the next time Jesse made an appearance at the Barrel, things were quite different. Many more college kids were present. It did not seem to Jesse that he had been away for very many days, so this all took him by surprise. There was someone new behind the bar—a woman who had from time to time bought drugs from Jesse. Like Jesse himself when he first started coming into the bar, she found herself needing drugs and no one to supply them. Harry was slipping as Jesse was, and she filled the void. She was happy and proud to be the new professor. Jake, Jingles, and Jackie were not there; and the dart court did not bustle as it had with activity. It was as if all of the old guard, including Sal, had found the demon in the bottle. Or it had found them, and no one could resist it, and no one even in this company wanted it known.

"Hey, Professor, where the hell you been? What you got on you? I been getting from that bitch behind the bar. She's trying to take over. I haven't seen the Beast either. What the fuck you guys doin'?"

Sal did not just need drugs; he was lonely. Jesse had not seen Harry either.

"Where is Bruce?" Jesse was seeing so many people he had not seen before.

"They caught him with his hands in the register and fired his ass."

It was about then that Jake showed up. He did not look fresh, like he did the day Jesse met him. He had a look that Jesse now recognized, glassy eyes and an antsy longing.

Jesse still had some drugs left, but he had not made a wholesale purchase in a couple of days, and if he sold what he had, he would not be able to get high himself.

"Jesse, man, I'm I glad to see you. Where have you been?" Jesse knew why Jake was so glad to see him, and it took only a minute for Jake to say it out loud.

"Hey, look, Jesse can I get a gram till Friday? Got a little company coming over, you know, a little party."

Harry showed up just minutes later with the same look on his face. He went directly to his point. The need seemed emergent but immediate.

He ignored everyone else, saying to Jesse, "What you got, Jesse? I need a gram. I'll get it back to you tonight."

"Fellas, hold on a minute. How's a guy supposed to eat around here? Everybody needs a gram. I only got a couple of them on me. Shit, how the hell am I supposed to get high?"

"Shit," said Harry, "I got to find some coke."

"Jake, just how little is this party you got in mind? You know what I'm saying? Everybody wants to get high, why don't we just go do that. Let's get out of here and find a place to buzz. What about your place, Jake? What time does your little party get started?" Jesse was feeling for the truth.

Jake looked pleased and bothered at the same time. So did Harry. Sal was nearly crushed because he had to stay at the bar and do his job.

"You bastards. At least give me a hit before you take off."

"You guys got time. We do a little something with Sal, go get a buzz. I can re-up and get back here in time for the evening crowd," said Jesse. This "go get a buzz" had to strike Sal as odd because getting a buzz had always happened here at the bar, but he said nothing about it. Sal knew exactly what they were up to. Jesse knew that if they left, they were not coming back but wanted to give Sal some hope.

So they went back into the storeroom where both Sal and Harry had always been so comfortable. Jesse opened a half-gram package of powder and cut lines. For a moment it was like the former days, with everyone taking a hit and talking shit. But Jesse could see an underlying eagerness to be somewhere else. He felt it himself, a relentless nagging to get to the pipe.

Jesse had gone out after being introduced to Cha'che's high level of drug preparation and bought the tools. Now he had his own glass pipe, a couple of glass vials, stainless-steel screens, probes, and scrapers enough to look like a chemist. He was even anxious to show his boys his new skill.

Jesse had bought Ramona's old car, a small foreign buggy that was even less attractive than Cha'che's Cadillac, but at least Jesse was no practicing pimp. It was just transportation. Ramona, with Jesse's help, had purchased something a bit more up to date, but just as foreign.

"I'll leave my car here, since we're coming back later anyway," said Harry.

Jesse knew that was not going to happen, but he said nothing, not wanting to upset Sal.

They loaded into Jesse's car and headed only a few blocks away to Jake's apartment. This really made no sense when one considers how difficult it was to find a parking space. The net distance saved may have been one block of walking.

Jake was not the slob that Smitty was, but one could see that a new priority had come into his life. His books and drawings were not neatly stored or put away. The kitchen was also a mess, and there was evidence of the demon: scorched spoons and aluminum foil, crumpled and ash soiled.

"Let me get some of this stuff out of the way," he said, trying to hide the signs of his seduction.

Jesse began cutting more lines, and, while doing so, he could see on all of their faces what they really wanted but did not want to be the first to say. So he blurted as he was cutting, "So you guys ever smoke it?"

"What, you want me to cook some up? Sure I'll do that, if you want. I mean, I know how to cook it." Jake could barely contain himself.

"Yeah," said Harry, "I like it cooked every once in a while."

Jake headed into the kitchen and gathered the cookware, spoon, aluminum foil, baking soda, and the tell-all plastic pipe. He began collecting ashes for the filter.

He prepared a nice little cookie that gave everyone a hit. As they finished their first hit, the intercom buzzer went off and startled the three of them.

"Who the fuck is that?" said Jake.

"You said you had a date, a party or some shit," Jesse said, trying to subtly expose Jake's real intentions.

Jake did not react to the statement but rang them up, apparently without knowing who was coming. There was a cheerful climbing up the stairs to Jake's third-floor apartment and the shrill voice of Jackie chatting all the way. When she got to the door with Jingles, of course, she said gaily, "I want some." Sal had told them that the boys were together, and she figured the rest out for herself.

The Beast said, "You got any money?"

"I got twenty bucks. Jingles, you got any money?"

"What's up, fellas?" he said, "Yeah, I got a little something. I'll throw in thirty."

"Oh shit, you guys are cooking. Jesse, you like this shit, huh?"

"Yeah, but I don't like the ash." With that, he pulled out his bag of tools and said nonchalantly, "Let me cook up a batch."

He pulled out a bill of some denomination and rolled it as Cha'che had shown him. He skillfully placed the ingredients in it and then slid the contents into the glass tube. "That's why they call him 'the Professor.' The doctor is in the house," they began to chime.

When he placed the vial over the flame, twirling it expertly, they all were amazed to see another improved way of doing it, and the resulting round ball, looking much more comprehensive than the cookie, had them all wanting to try the new method, and Jackie most of all. When Jesse revealed his glass pipe, well, people started confessing about where they have been and what they have been doing. They were all junkies now, and none of them knew it, or would admit it. They were just doing drugs, like they always did. They could not acknowledge the kraken, the fiend that had come into their lives impaling them with a perverse desire and destroying them.

Jesse knew, he thought they knew. He assumed, like himself, they did not care.

At about eleven o'clock, they were out of the drug. They had been playing cribbage and talking trash while getting high. They had all taken turns learning the more efficient way of producing the maddening seed, and, in the excitement, no one pointed out that they were running out of the product. This was more likely owed to the fact that none of them had any money, and only Jesse had any product. Harry had said and believed that his contact was coming later that night as he had mentioned in the bar. As he was always the businessman, he asked if anyone had some money and did they want in when his guy showed up. No one had any money, but they all wanted in and promised to pay him later if he could front for them.

Jesse still had some product at home, but he did not want to exhaust it and did not want to be in that empty house, Ramona's house, now a lonely shell with her gone for good.

Anyway they decided to make the trip back to the Barrel to see if Harry's boy had shown up, and when they got there, Jesse would be close enough to home so that if all else failed, he could get his last stash and finish the evening with total abandon.

On the way to the car, they encountered a fellow who said he knew Jesse and needed him to do a favor.

"I met you when me and the brothas came to your bar. I didn't play or nothing, I was just moral support. I'm Joe, my name is Joe."

"Okay, Joe, I'm Jesse. What's up?"

Jesse was not all there, and he knew it. He really did not want to be seen by anybody, but this stranger was all right. There was no need for embarrassment.

"Ah, look here, could you get me some coke?" he said, reaching publicly into his pocket and handing Jesse a hundred dollars.

"I hear you got the best shit. Can you get me a gram? I'll pay you now. Can I meet you here, ah, what time you want me to meet you?"

"Yo, Joe, slow down, my brother. I won't be coming back this way again until tomorrow. I can't help you out tonight." He had already placed the money in Jesse's hand, so Jesse was making every effort to return it.

"Naw, man, you keep the money. What time tomorrow?"

"Hey, man. I appreciate the trust and all, but you . . ."

"No, no, man, you got a reputation. I know Erica, Cha'che, and that crowd. I trust you. You just tell me what time to be here in the square."

This made no sense for at least a couple of reasons. The two men did not know each other, certainly not well, and Jesse was so toasted that he may not even remember tomorrow night. He and Harry looked at each other in amazement, and Jesse said okay.

"Damn, Jesse, you think he's a cop?"

"I don't know. Hell, I didn't think about that."

"Something ain't right about this. A dude comes out of the blue, you don't even know the motherfucker, and he gives you a C-note to get him a gram. I smell a rat."

"Fuck it," said Jesse. Once again he couldn't find a way to care.

People owed Jesse money. In one case, a lot of money . . . for drugs. Jesse did not care about that either.

"About eight, I'll be here around eight o'clock," said Jesse.

When they got to the bar, Harry's guy had not arrived. He checked with his people, at least the few he could find and no one had seen his contact. They had a drink and talked with Sal, who seemed out of sorts with all the new people. There were fewer rowdy people, leaving him nearly nothing to do.

Jesse and Harry decided to leave. After all, they had some folks waiting for them, and the call of the wild thing was upon them. They went to Jesse's place, so neat and undisturbed.

Ramona's things were gone, all gone. The evidence of his children was gone, completely gone. He gathered what drugs he had left, which wasn't much, and hurried out of the sparsely furnished mausoleum and fled. That's what it felt like. In some small way it was reminiscent of being in his mother's home after her passing. It felt as if he had no right to be there.

Harry did not have any money on him, but he had his word. That was good enough for Jesse. He said he would pay for half of the slightly less than a quarter ounce Jesse had left. It was a wholesale split, given their relationship. Jesse did take the time to call his contact to order some more product, which would be delivered the following day.

When they finally made it back to Jake's place, they were all waiting like fledglings awaiting the return of a providing parent. The getting high commenced again with the foul drug making tyrannical demands.

Eventually Jesse went home. He slept the whole day until about five o'clock. He awoke to a threatening sunshine and blue sky. It was too much the reminder of the days when, as a boy, he would discover the world around him, the spiders and sparrows, caterpillars, mice, birds, and it created a longing for . . . he could not remember. The gray mass had returned. The sun shown over the area, just as it did over Detroit. Could it be the same sun? That same sky, with its occasional clouds passing used to be his friend. As he pondered his beginnings, it was the same sun that showered his mother and warmed her garden (or was it?) Were those the clouds that would come and shower her patch of earth, providing so many of his boyhood sensations? They looked ominous now, the joy, being as it was, sucked out of them. Their allegiance was to the victorious god, and Jesse no longer had any rights to it.

Again he sank, almost comfortably now, into accepting a fate of dying alone, not knowing how to free himself. He was hungry. A block away there was a Jamaican restaurant owned and operated by a young woman from the islands. There was jerk chicken and other spicy culinary delights. Usually he just ate to kill the pangs of hunger, but today, for whatever reason, he would treat himself. It was carryout only, and, as he was leaving, he ran into Daniel McDowell, the tiresome black male who appeared confused about his heritage, well, not confused, but bitter that with that good Irish name, the local Irish would not accept him. In any case, he had with him a well-muscled fellow that he introduced as his cousin, Chico. This cousin was yet another dealer, and Daniel thought it imperative that he and Jesse sit down sometime and see what they could do together.

No one could see that Jesse's indifference was fatal-that he had no interest in enterprise, legal or illegal. He was searching for the edge, and when he found it, all would be well. But with things being so different now at the Cork 'n' Barrel, other venues, other places to hide, held a certain intrigue. Jesse agreed to meet with him.

Jesse took his food home, and as he was finishing it, he heard the roar of a chopper in the parking lot behind his house. He knew his drugs had arrived. His dealer was an Italian fellow who looked too white to be one. Jesse did not know that Italians could be so fair skinned. He had met him on one of those nights at the Barrel, and he and his boys wanted to strong-arm their way into the lives of as many small-time dealers like Jesse as possible. There was no need for these tactics with Jesse because his guy, the fellow who had schooled him on the trade, was now out of business, having lost his contact to police arrest. In fact, Jesse was now occasionally supplying him, with lesser amounts, of course. So Jesse was able to posture as if he just liked these new guys, their product and the way they did business. It made for a good relationship. This time, however, Jesse discovered, and it was really a surprise to him, that he was short—two hundred and fifty dollars short. This was no big deal to the dealer, at least the amount was not a big deal. But you do not renege on drug money, and Manneo would have to do what his trade and his people called for if Jesse failed to pay.

Neither of them was worried about it. Jesse should have been. He had good credit, and he did not buy large amounts anyway, only an ounce at a time. Now, however, the drug was the thing, not the money. Jesse like the others had slipped into addiction.

Now on those occasions, when he went into the bar, he made hundreds, not thousands. The quality of his product was not the same, and he did not stay nearly as long-only long enough to get enough money to eat, buy booze, and have a little in his pocket. He forgot about his financial responsibilities, he forgot about his rent, and soon he needed help to pay it. He found the help in a most unlikely source.

He was a large unkempt fellow who was not part of Harry's inner circle, but who had become a regular at the bar, and given the collapse of the old guard, was even selling drugs there. Jesse knew him, but not well. He liked him enough, but from a distance. His name was Stanley, but people called him Crumbs because of his sloppy appearance. They cut a deal, and Stanley moved in.

On one of those incidental nights, during Jesse's fling with Hills, the woman who had stunned everyone with the metamorphosis from biker girl to dainty suburbanite, Jesse had a packed house. It was the usual misdoings of drugs, booze, and card playing. It was again a collection of people who should never have been in the same small space.

As the night wound down, most of the people left with Jesse and Hills, going to bed at about four o'clock in the morning. Jingles and Jackie had found a place to sleep upstairs in the living room, and Stanley had some woman in the kid's room, which was just behind the room where Hills and Jesse were. The kitchen was upstairs, where all of the drugging had taken place, and behind it was the living room where Jackie and Jingles had found uncomfortable furniture on which to sleep.

At some point in these wee hours of the night or morning, Jingles got hungry and decided to cook something. He was frying eggs and sausage and creating the related smells and sounds of that activity. This racket annoyed Hills at such a level that she went mad. She leapt out of bed and essentially told them to shop-to stop cooking and stop with the noise. This struck Jingles as silly and unfair, and he said so. This was not someone he liked anyway. He had told Jesse that it was a mistake to hang out with this woman, calling her a "nasty biker bitch" or something, but he had not said it in her presence. On this morning, he made the mistake of calling her a bitch to her face.

Hills's face took on the appearance of Medusa. Her eyes, already bloodshot from the night's party, became completely that from lid to lid and corner to corner. A countenance of pure evil claimed her face, and a rage ensued for which Jingles and Jackie had no way of understanding, or even believing, as it spiraled, or more precisely, sprung immediately into clinical madness. Just as immediately, an equal level of fear consumed Jackie and Jingles, for what now stood menacingly before them was beyond recognition.

She grabbed him with a strength that defied her gender and tossed him across the room, breaking many things, such things as there were, now that Ramona was gone. Jackie, who had a reputation as a feisty little imp, stood frozen and whimpered in horror, as if she saw death coming. When Jingles gathered himself, he too began to cry, which had the effect of enraging Hills even further. She began rifling through the drawers, looking for a weapon, at which point, Jingles and Jackie ran downstairs to where Jesse was sleeping. They entered without knocking, looking for refuge with the Gorgon on their heels. Well, he wasn't sleeping now as the cries were such that he too felt death or something as ugly in the house.

They, that is, Jackie and Jingles, cried out, clearly in fear of their lives. Once in the room, he placed his body against the door to prevent the now-insane Hills from entering. From the outside, she pushed and kicked on the one-hundred-year-old door, with its thin, fragile panels being held together by layers of paint, and Jackie joined him in an effort to resist the much-stronger beast on the other side of the door.

"What the fuck is going on?" Jesse screeched.

"She's crazy. The bitch is trying to kill me. She's got a knife," Jingles said this with abject terror on his face, trembling and wailing, praying, "Please, God, oh, God." But in his terror he had uttered the word again.

Just then, with Jesse about to open the door to quell the madness, a ten-inch knifepoint came through the door, splintering it brutally, and just missing Jingles's face. Hills, now absolutely lost, put her foot through the remains of the crippled old door.

Jesse screamed, "Hills, stop! Stop it! What are you doing?"

He opened the shattered door and found her standing, almost blindly, shaking and mumbling, holding the slightly bent knife at her side. She was bleeding, or there was blood on her, from exactly what or where, Jesse could not tell. The door itself was no real defense; it might as well have been a curtain as it crumbled like papier-mâché.

"He called me a bitch. I'm going to kill that motherfucker. Nobody calls me a bitch."

Hills had made her proclamation of deadly intentions with a hellish calm. Still red, with evil emblazoned on her face, but strangely calm. With equal calm, Jesse reached for the steely weapon, and she released it without resistance. He drew her to his chest and held her, tightly. The holding was empathetic, even affectionate, but as much as anything, it was intended to give Jackie and Jingles time to escape. As they fled, Hills said nothing, and slowly the red hue etched in the white of her eyes began to dissipate.

"I hate those bastards," she said and began to sob almost childishly.

Stanley had also been awakened by the commotion. He stood in the corridor, staring with amusement at the goings-on. He made no effort to assist, finding the whole incident entertaining.

Someone had called the police, and they were in the parking lot. Jesse had all of the implements of drug use in eye view, and he certainly had no time to clean it up before they came in. The call to the police had nothing to do with drugs. It more likely had to do with what was perceived as domestic violence, but Jesse knew that if they came in, he would be busted. He decided to leave. He picked up his coat, went to the front door opposite the parking lot, and walked stealthily away. He went up to the square behaving just as a citizen; dismissing the house and the madness that occurred. When he got back, some six hours later, the house looked as it did when he left it. *Except for the smell, a foulness was present so thick that it behaved like a barrier and may explain why the police had not come in,* thought Jesse. What actually happened was that Stanley had convincingly described the matter as a minor beef, and there was no need for formal intervention.

Stanley had heaved last night's meal all over the kid's room. It was everywhere: on the bedspreads, the floor, lamps, and walls, and he left it there. The turned and broken table, chairs, and dishes were strewn about, and Jesse set about cleaning up the mess. It took some time to do so, and while doing it, Jesse remembered those kinder days of working with his siblings, dusting, washing windows and dishes, singing and laughing their way through the chores with his mother looking on. He shook off the memory because it hurt. It hurt too much.

The arrangement with Stanley ended as abruptly as it started. He had not paid his share of the rent, and the landlord had decided that he had had enough. Jesse was forced to move. This was just as well. In spite of the hardship it would bring, Jesse was done, finished with the space he had shared with Ramona and the children. The place hurt him. It hurt him physically, brutal sensations like stones pelting his body and his mind. It required him to remember too much about too many of . . . his mounting failures. He made a half-hearted effort to sell what he could and gathered the remains of his life's acquisitions and devised a plan for survival. Survival. He had trouble understanding why that mattered, why anything did.

He decided to call Daniel McDowell, knowing full well that he would be willing to share space with him because of the drugs. Jesse offered to pay some meager amount, but that did not matter. The drugs were what mattered to Daniel, and he didn't know or perceive that Jesse was losing this advantage as well. Jesse did not have much to bring to Daniel's house. He had his clothes, his drug paraphernalia, his briefcase with scraps of poems, songs, and a novel he had started. But most importantly, he had Jimmy's thirteen-inch television and recorded tapes of his friend from the many stops during the speaking tour. These things he brought and stored at Daniel's house.

"Make yourself at home," Daniel said as he left, coming down the stairs as Jesse ascended them. It was on the third floor of an old house, with a gray and unsightly common stairwell completely laden with cobwebs. The steps creaked as one would expect from a centuries-old house. His space was filthy. Dirt, garbage, and mounds of debris were in every room. Jesse couldn't live like this, even in his fallen condition. So he cleaned. It took all day, but he cleaned and straightened until the place was presentable. When Daniel returned, he could not recognize the place, and he was as agitated as he was pleased. It was as if the cleaning of the place is what exposed him as a slob, leaving it filthy gave it or him a kind of invisibility.

Daniel, who considered himself a superior human being and gifted at anything he tried, had become an actor. At least he dabbled at it. This gave them something to talk about and made the first few weeks at his place tolerable for the both of them. But it wasn't long before the drugs were gone, and there was no money. They actually had no rent that they were obligated to pay, because the house that Daniel called his was, in fact, owned by his mother or grandmother, and he lived essentially rent free. But there was the issue of food and utilities. The former was in short supply, and the latter was eventually shut off.

Daniel's cousin Chico, the fellow he had introduced to Jesse at the Jamaican restaurant and who himself was a drug dealer, lived only a few houses away. He too lived in a building provided by the largess of an aging relative. It was in complete shambles. All of the utilities were jerry-rigged, and the interior did not resemble a house at all. It was more like an abandoned place which the previous owners had walked away from, leaving an indescribable assortment of things behind. It was dark and spooky. He owned dogs, pit bulls that he adored. They were large vicious animals that he fought competitively for money, but they were also the most obedient animals Jesse had ever encountered. There were three of them, and when their food was placed in the dishes, he would have them eat individually, saying quietly, even without looking at them, "Buddha, you can eat now." Whichever dog was eating at the time would leave his dish as the other animal approached. That he would have them engaging in horrifically bloody fights seemed the height of hypocrisy. If it was love, it was broken love, sick and perverse.

His house was a crack house. Jesse had been in many houses where crack was being smoked, but this was his first experience with a "crack house."

Guns and knives were all around, lost in the noisy disarray of stuff. People came at required hours with prearranged knocks to pick up drugs.

As it turns out, Chico did not like his cousin Daniel any more than anyone else did. Daniel's arrogance, even while having nothing, annoyed him as much as it annoyed everyone. He put up with him because, Jesse was to learn, Daniel had and kept in his pocket a dirty secret and would brazenly threaten to use it. It made for the most unholy of alliances.

Daniel was eventually able to talk his relatives into getting the utilities restored. When the lights came on, he thought he would celebrate with a party. This man had no friends, but he had Jesse in his house. This was enough of a lure to get people to come for a party-that and, of course, drugs and alcohol. Jesse invited Cha'che, who brought the girls. It was to be a last hurrah. The events that unfolded that night rivaled anything history reports took place in Caligula's palaces. It was debauchery at so disgusting a level that Jesse wept thinking, *How could I have come to this?* He saw his mother twisting uncomfortably in her . . . he couldn't place her. Where was she? The grave seemed too awful a place, and he could not find a way to put her near the god of his grief. She should not be in this house, even as a thought. He was ashamed of himself, and to defend himself from these images and feelings, he sought the bottles, all of them. He smoked, he drank, he wept; he smoked and drank until he wept no more. The revelry was loathsome and so far removed from the loving warmth of her that it had the effect of making him feel indecent. He felt as if he were wallowing in slime. The sensations conjured a recurring dream he had since his mother's passing. He did not dream often, or ever, it seemed, except for this one. He would see himself falling into unspeakable filth and unable to stand or get up. The dream began and ended this way, with him mired in unimaginable sewage, struggling futilely to free himself, and awakening to indescribable despair.

The night ended somehow. He could not remember people leaving, or coming, for that matter. When he resumed consciousness, he found himself lying there, on a couch, with Margie still awake and staring at him. She spoke with great sadness and pleading to be taken home, or to her car, which was somewhere in Dorchester. She needed to get home and become mother again. She looked strangely fresh, even pretty, given what she had done all night with her body and her mind. She nestled into Jesse's arms, pleading and promising to be his woman and to make him money. She wanted him to say that she had done well on this unforgettable night. It was as if she wanted him to be proud of her. Jesse, still reeling from his shame and sadness, agreed to take her where she needed to go. As he gathered himself, he noticed that the sinning he had so longed for was still under way, with Princess servicing the few men who remained. One after another, she served, and she did it tirelessly, in a way that baffled Jesse. She and this night, and all of the participants, were Jesse revealed. They were him without his pain. *But they must be suffering too,* he thought. *Why else would they have come? Why else would they be here and do these things?*

Princess was zombie-like in her participation, but she found a way to laugh. It was a false laughter, naughty and dismissive. Whatever the travail that led her to this life, a life wherein she disappeared; it was as if she had a perverse need for it. Disappearing, somewhere deep inside herself or her memories; perhaps memories she was trying to escape. Or could it be that her lifelong childhood abuses were such that this activity was common, sick, disgusting but familiar, even all she knew, as close to affection as she had ever been. She vanished of necessity to do the only things she felt capable of, worthy of, having learned it as a child.

"Did I do good?" she said.

This statement took Jesse back to a particular summer. It was in 1959. The gypsies and the Boudreaux family moved into the neighborhood. There was a particular and peculiar sameness about these two disparate groups of people. The gypsies, this group of them anyway, were degradation on foot. They carried with them an odoriferous cloud so rank that one could see it, and Jesse asked his mother about it-not just the smell, but the way they dressed, and they were thieves living on their takings. Their appearance and the language they spoke were vulgar and difficult for little Jesse to understand. Most of them resembled a heap of discolored rags as they shambled menacingly through the neighborhood. Having been taught to speak well and understanding that there were languages other than English, he was intrigued by both, but something about both alarmed him. Some danger lurked that he was unable to recognize or describe. They had animals with them, such as Jesse had never seen in the neighborhood: sheep, chickens, and mangy dogs. That they offered the sheep up for sexual perversions was not clear to Jesse, but he knew something drew the vagrants and hobos to the hovel they occupied. What he knew most clearly was that nothing about them matched what he had learned about human beings.

"Geh me a quawda," they would echo, nearly every time he encountered them. Jesse never saw the men, at least not on the streets. It was always the women or the girls, very dirty, foul females speaking an unrecognizable tongue.

Jesse thought all women smelled like or similar to his mother and her bevy of friends. It gave him an expectation that he would always encounter some manner of loveliness when he was in the presence of women. The ways of these people were completely incongruous to him. The smell and the perceived danger had him, even as a little boy on alert.

"Geh me quawda, geh me quawda. Suck you for quawda. Take child, suck you for quawda." There was a graveling rasp in the sound that matched nothing in his memory and certainly matched no sound he had ever heard emanating from a woman. These comments meant nothing to young Jesse; they did not even compute.

The Boudreaux family was similar, speaking as they did in a hillbilly patois nearly as ugly and certainly as difficult to understand as the gypsies. They were as foul smelling, but the scent was always of urine. It was as if there was no running water in their house. The house was at the end of an adjacent street at dissecting alleys. It had, as so many of the houses did at that time, that asphalt siding designed to resemble a brick pattern. The upper floor had been converted into a separate apartment and had an exterior staircase extending from the ground to the upper door. The Boudreauxes were a family of what seemed to be six children and two endlessly drunk and pitiable parents, but there were so many people coming and going that no one was ever really certain about the actual size of the household. There were two boys who were the oldest of the children. The girls ranged in age from three to eleven or twelve. The boys were not much older, but they were old enough to have been having sex with their sisters—apparently for some time. They discovered that they could when favors in the neighborhood by offering them up to the other kids in the neighborhood.

Jesse's olfactory system, to say nothing of his father, would not allow him to be close to either group, but the offensive smell did not stop many of the other boys, some even Jesse's age.

The brothers would offer up their sisters, even the three-year-old, for empty deposit bottles or anything having little or no value to anyone else.

Anyway, Jesse was close enough to both of these forsaken groups of people to have picked up the phrase "blow job." He had no idea what it meant, but it sounded like a pretty clever word to him, and so he took the verb, turned it into a noun, and began calling his sisters that.

This is how Brightmeyer got to know about the new strangers in the neighborhood, and while he did not exactly tell Jesse what the word meant, he made certain that Jesse stopped using it and that he definitely stopped referring to his sisters that way.

Were these women—Margie and Princess—just those little girls all grown up? He wondered what happen to them. For a moment, he became clear on the power of love and family.

Margie's tender girlish appeal had Jesse wondering about what she had endured in life that this behavior was acceptable to her. The way she curled up beside him was not unlike the behavior of a new bride, longing for a lifetime of affection. Even in random sex with strange indifferent men, she had a sweetness about her that said, more than anything else, "hold me, hold me close, don't let go." She was not a Boudreaux; she was not a gypsy. What she was challenged

Jesse's imagination and left him dazed. She saw in him what she saw in herself but had no other way of expressing: a profound need for affection, to be touched. Even hard, indifferent brutality was, for her, a kind of affection. In Jesse's arms, she dreamed . . . his ministerial manner was cotton candy, a treat she savored and felt she earned.

Jesse understood his ambitions; he knew why he was in the forsaken room. He accepted that he had failed, and his fate was upon him. Somehow, though, he could not find a way to understand why anyone else was here, especially the women. But only now did it vaguely occur to him that in finding these people, all of them, he had found people who suffered like him. He could not imagine that they had lost a dear mother, but they had certainly lost something, something that mattered so much that they could not go on without it. In every case, they had been so deeply hurt or disappointed by someone or something, that they too wanted to die. That's all that was happening all around him—sickness and death. He rejected these thoughts. They had not lost "her". His tears were blood, and he hemorrhaged unceasingly. Whatever they lost could not compare to his own private grief.

Somewhere in the night, the testosterone got thick in the air, and, predictably, had anyone thought about it, Daniel and Cha'che got into an altercation. However much bravado there was, it led to one threatening the other's life. They had to be separated, with Cha'che vowing to return to do what he felt was necessary, which was to "cut him up."

"He don't know who he's fucking with. He should know. I should have cut that bitch up a long time ago, but I'ma get him this time."

"Cha'che," Jesse began, trying to conciliate, "Look, man, let's do this somewhere else. There're too many witnesses here. Margie needs a ride to her car. Let's drive her to her car and talk about it. Man, we don't even know half of these people."

"I'ma cut him up man, you hear me. I'ma bleed that mothafucka."

"All right," said Jesse, "but let's get the hell out of here."

They did, driving her to her car in his. He had not slept as Jesse had. Having been up all night and getting high, he was certainly not all there, but neither was he done. He had no intentions of going to bed.

"Let's swing on by my place and smoke some stones," he said. To Jesse, or any addict, there was no defense for this. No objection could be mounted because this was the constant goal. So they went to the dreary hostel he called his house and smoked what they had between them, which was not much and never enough.

Eventually with Cha'che unable to stand, to say nothing of walk, he simply fell out, or to sleep, it was impossible to tell which, but he had found half of the sofa. Jesse fell asleep in a chair, which, if the lights were bright enough to see, he would not even have sat down on.

When Jesse awoke, he tried to awaken Cha'che—to no avail. He pointlessly said to him, "I got to go. I'll catch the bus home," and left.

During the bus ride home, it dawned on Jesse that he had to leave Daniel's house. He would approach Chico, who needed someone he could trust to help him with many things. It was not just Daniel, who only Mother Teresa could bear, but what had happened there. Indelible images were now in his head, and he knew he could not shake them while he stayed there. He had unwittingly brought his mother into this place, and he was ashamed. He had done many unsavory things in his effort to get to his tormentor, her god, but now he had gone too far. He was slapping her, not Him, and it was too much to endure.

While on the bus ride home, he took glancing looks into the eyes of other riders, wondering if they could tell how foul he was. Among them was a woman about the age his mother would be, and she was reading a *Watchtower* magazine, the monthly periodical published by the people claiming to be God's earthly representatives, and the one Jesse had peddled to thousands of people while trying to do His will. His anger at the god of his mother had not dissipated, but it had dulled over the years by the endless layers of callus that now encased his heart.

The woman saw Jesse staring. She saw the tears behind his eyes. "May I offer you a copy of the latest issue of the *Watchtower?*" she said. Jesse tried to recall the number of times he had uttered that phrase. He could hear his mother saying it. He remembered how clean he once was. He thought about the weddings he had conducted, the funerals.

"I know a lot about that," he said. "My mother was a member." He tried to never say His name. They had attached so much significance to saying His name. *I will not say His name*, he reminded himself.

"And you? What about you? I'm sure she taught you about Jehovah's blessings and promises? Have you strayed from His teachings?" She was so principled, so sweet.

"Yes, I have . . . I would have to say that is true."

"I would like to invite you to our Kingdom Hall . . ."

"I'm disfellowshipped," he said, knowing that this would end the conversation. If she was a good Christian woman, she could not fraternize with someone so unclean. "Quit touching the unclean thing, not even saying a greeting to such a man," he remembered that scriptural admonition.

She was as true as she could be.

"Oh, well, you know what you need to do. If you give me an address I'll have one of the elders pay you a visit."

"I'll be back. I am going to return. A visit won't be necessary," he said. "I'll be back," he even promised.

He did not mean it, or maybe he did. He was dying now and his sadness was bottomless. He remembered how happy he had been when he was among these blissful innocents. His only chance for survival may be this, a return to those happier days. He could do it again for her and for himself, or die. It was all he had the energy for. Dying did not appear to be such an untenable option. He was tired now, and he could not find his way home.

CHAPTER 39

The Last Chance

There was so little left, so little left for him to do. There was nothing, in fact. He remembered that he had to get the drugs for Joe, the fellow who had given him the C-note, and he owed Manneo 250 dollars. He was running out of money and time, and neither thing mattered. Yet he wanted his affairs in order.

Chad, his firstborn, was about to graduate from high school. He had to be there; somehow he had to get home. The disappointments he had heaped upon his sons were just another one of the many lead straws that were breaking him down. He had to find a way to be strong to prevent his sons and all who knew him from seeing the end on his face, from seeing death coming in his eyes. When he disappeared, falling off the edge, everything would be all right. Only then would it be as it should be. He could be dead with her, with her in that unknowable place.

The air was laden with the smells of spring, but it did not freshen or invigorate him. It used to. Now the sun falling warmly on his face and heightening those nostalgic scents seemed only to intensify his awareness of his ever-increasing despair. The songbirds and blossoms were missing, and it occurred to him that he had not seen a rainbow in all of his time here in Boston. Perhaps they would greet him, be waiting for him when he got home, back to Michigan. These allies proved to belong to Him, and that Jesse was no longer entitled to them made sense to him. Their beauty had somehow supported his perceptions of kindness, fairness, the ultimate in sharing, he thought. He had betrayed them as well. He had betrayed everything and everyone he loved, and his beloved mother most of all.

Chico had said yes to Jesse's request, but his tenure at Chico's house did not last long. Through the summer, Jesse did chores for him like a migrant worker, fixing doors, fences, and all manner of odd jobs. At night, he would be rewarded with getting a little high. He had gone from Daniel's whorehouse to Chico's crack house. Sometimes even Daniel would be there, and just as often, a string of so-called respectable citizens: doctors, lawyers, policemen, and ministers. It mattered not to Jesse; he was one of them, a once-respectable citizen, now lost and immersed in a life he no longer wanted to live.

It was, for drug dealers and addicts, the beginning of the day. He had arranged to meet Manneo to give him his money, but in order to do so, he had to sell his car. He sold it to a mechanic for the exact amount that he owed the drug dealer and felt lucky in doing so. This, of course, meant that he now had no place to live, very little cash, and no transportation.

He did have an ounce of the demon seed, which in better days he would parlay into thousands of dollars. He had a sale to make that very night to Joe, the fellow that had accosted him in the square. He would be there, keeping his word, to a stranger . . . *"honor among thieves,*" he thought. At just about eight o'clock Jesse found his way to Kendall Square. It was a very short walk from Chico's house. Joe was there, and he insisted on buying Jesse a drink, but he wanted to go to his home bar, which as it turns out, was the bar that Smitty had told Jesse about the night they met.

"You driving?" asked Jesse, "I got no wheels, and I need to be back here in an hour or so. Can you get me back?"

"No problem, Brotha. There's some people I need you to meet, but I'll get you back here by . . ."—he was looking at his watch as if it had an announcement to make—"nine-thirty. Yeah, nine-thirty, is that cool?"

"Yeah, that'll work," said Jesse.

During the walk to his car and all the way to the bar, Joe behaved as if he was in the presence of a star. He was giddy with excitement and questions about Jesse's low-brow fame, his renowned ability with women and drugs, and he, like Smitty, wanted Jesse to set him up with white women. But he was also setting Jesse up for a bet he and others at his bar had made about whether or not Jesse could have his way with a beautiful, unapproachable woman who was in weekly attendance at their social club.

"Man, nobody can get to this girl, and she's fine, man. I ain't kidding. This girl is the shit, but she won't hardly speak to nobody . . ." he rambled on endlessly.

The chatter was interminable; it chaffed, causing Jesse to wonder who these people were and how was it possible that they could not see who he was. He had no energy for this, but he was in the car and on his way. A captive of his own futility, of other people's expectations, and a mind and heart too troubled to escape. He tried to put on a face as he entered the bar.

"Well, I'll be damned. Look what the wind blew in." Smitty uttered the hackneyed phrase with a flourish that implied he was the first person to use it. It seemed so apropos. Jesse was indeed "in the wind," a wayward leaf falling, crashing with no real purpose or direction.

Smitty and Joe proudly introduced Jesse around the room to a collection of relatively happy people. There was not the look of abject sadness he had seen in so many bars. There was food here, finger food of chicken wings, shrimp, perch, and fries. The rhythm and blues playing at conversational levels was also an attractive relief from the loud and mostly unrecognizable music constantly blaring at the Barrel.

The place seemed more dimly lit than other bars he had visited, and everything was on the edge of needing some kind of repair. It appeared to have recently changed hands from its previous ownership, as the pictures on the walls and permanently etched reliefs failed to speak to the current patronage.

The bartender was an older black woman whose movements and style suggested a worldly wisdom that eliminated the possibility of motherhood or formal education. There was a sassy rhythm to her hips and hands, and all of it was more attractive than fifty years of street life should have sculpted. She managed the once-fine oak bar and the clientele that surrounded it with ease and a casual wit.

"What can I get for you Sugar?" She looked at Jesse, smiling, while resting her fleshy arms on the bar, displaying her welcoming bosom. Jesse wanted to curl up in it. There was nothing sexual about his wish. She reminded him of his mother's friends who, when he was a boy, would pick him up and hold him tightly in those soft, fragrant, and accommodating appendages.

"Get the brother whatever he wants. Macy, this is Jesse. We trying to bring the brother home. He's been hangin' out with the gray boys up in Harvard Square," said Joe, seeming too proud and too needy for Jesse's comfort.

"Is that right?" she said without judgment.

"I sit at the table that welcomes me," said Jesse.

"All right then. Well, he sho got a nice way of putting things. What you gonna have, baby?"

"I'll have a beer—any kind will do. You got Stroh's?"

"Stroh's, I haven't had nobody ask for that in a long time. You must be from Detroit."

"Yes, I am. I guess you can't get Stroh's in New England."

"Naw, darlin', how about a Bud?"

"Budweiser is cool. I'll take a Bud."

"It's on," Jesse heard someone excitedly say, and, for a moment, people were distracted, looking up at the entry door.

In walked a picture of sadness, who was as lovely as she was broken. On the surface, at first glance, this woman appeared to be completely out of place. There was about her a sophistication that was more than beauty or style; more than, other than, class-she was flawless. In the faint light, her dress, the color of which could not be readily determined, shimmered. Her hair was done in a manner reminiscent of the roaring twenties, without appearing dated. She had skin that flowed like molten chocolate and was its rich color. Her beauty was such that its initial presence created a hush in a room, no matter how many times she entered it.

She sat down at the bar to near silence, with only Macy and the jukebox knowing how to continue in her presence.

"That's her, Jesse," said Joe, salivating in awe.

Smitty threw down the challenge. "You said you could have any woman, right? Well, let's see what you can do with Rosaba. Course we just call her Rose, but she won't give up no play."

Macy prepared a gin and tonic and delivered it to the stunning Rose, who managed a half smile, meant for Macy only and perhaps what traces of humanity she had left inside her crumbling self-image. No one else was welcome or privy to this common courtesy.

"You all right Baby?" said Macy habitually, it was clear that this was to be the extent of the conversation. Macy understood this woman.

"Same ol', same ol'," she said and little else during the night.

The yammering of the patrons in his ear and all through the air was not heard by Jesse. He found himself staring at this woman, but not for her undeniable beauty. It occurred to him just how ordinary beauty was and how burdensome. He saw through that glaze and into the pained eyes. He saw again, a sorrow for which he wanted an explanation. He saw that yoke of misery and hopelessness. If he could see it, why couldn't everyone? If her pain, which was so vividly displayed, was not recognizable to these men, then the fact that his own went unnoticed finally made sense. Jesse did not want this woman, or any woman, but he was drawn to misery. He would be willing, seemed to want, to immerse himself in her trouble. He was looking for and approaching the edge; she could walk with him into that black light flickering in the distance.

"Go 'head, Jesse, you the man."

"This I got to see."

Jesse had engaged in this silliness before, but now it seemed more than silly—it seemed cruel. He knew too much about her, too much about the suffering. He surmised that her trouble was male based; that it had to do with dangerous, unrequited love; that destructive mendacity on which far too many relationships are built. This woman had wilted under its load.

"What chu gon' do, my brotha?" came the lively, frisky challenge.

"Can a brother finish his drink?" said Jesse, trying to decide if this was the right time. It wasn't, and he knew it, but he thought he had just the right measure of anguish on his face that she would not miss it. *She will see our kinship*, he thought. He was wrong.

She saw him coming, and she had heard of the maddening challenge. And worse, Jesse apparently resembled the offending male, the most recent culprit.

"Don't even try it, you pretty black mothafucka, wit them goddamn ice cream teeth. Get the hell away from me." She barely looked up. She didn't have to. She was flawed after all, scarred by the memories and not close to healing. When she did raise her head, revealing a slight and sexy overbite, she gave him a stare; a penetrating X-ray of a stare.

"I don't want to hear it. I have heard it all before, so you can carry your black ass back to wherever you came from. You hear me? I don't want to hear it!"

"All right, all right, but I was just . . ."

"You can just turn around," she said, and with that, she turned her back to him.

Jesse understood and backed away. The "fellas" were laughing, and as Jesse returned to his spot at the bar, he was embarrassed. Not by the laughter, the rejection, or by the guys, but by himself. He knew his intentions could not be discerned in this company. He knew that in this setting, this setup, there was no way for his actions to be perceived as anything but prowling.

He had not been pricked by a rose; he had been undone by his own poor judgment and in so doing, he was certain now, he would have to walk into the darkness alone.

He thought of Ramona, who had called him, more than once, a misogynist. "How else would you explain the way you treat women?" It wasn't that; he hated himself, and he thought that women, somehow being a reflection of his mother, could save him. He looked pleadingly at Macy's comforting breasts—the fount of his nourishment. *That would do*, he thought, to be held *for just a while*, and he began falling, back, down through the years . . .

"What cha'll got for the head?" A familiar voice boomed. Cha'che had arrived with enough volume and nonsense to break the spell and rescue Jesse from his debilitating nostalgia.

During the glad-handing, the guys announced to Cha'che that he had "just missed it," while laughing derisively. Rose had broken down another player; she was still "Queen Diva" and untouchable.

"Oh, y'all did the brotha wrong," said Cha'che, laughing with the throng. "See now, if I was here, I wouldn't let that shit go down, Jesse. You know, if I can't pull the girl, nobody can." He laughed a hearty laugh.

Jesse would be teased about this event whenever he saw this crowd, but apparently it was forgivable given the stalwart reputation of Rosaba. Jesse's status took a minor hit, leaving Cha'che unscathed as the leading local player. Still Jesse wondered, and convinced himself that she did too, about what could have been.

When the truth was told, Jesse learned that the episode with Rosaba was, at worst, a ruse, and at best, secondary to the real ambitions of his new associates, making the whole event all the more scandalous. Drugs were the actual motivation. They wanted to get into the business and saw Jesse as their conduit. Indeed they could not see that he was done, but he could see that they were lost, lost in the distorted seductions of the fast life, of which Jesse had had enough. They had concocted a naïve plan that included having Jesse procure the drugs, they would package them, and with Jesse's connections, they would grow the business.

He let them talk. They introduced him to their prospective runners and packers, and they wanted to take him to the place, a rented apartment where no one was to live, where all of the preparatory activity would take place. It was a place that Cha'che owned or had control of.

Jesse began thinking about how to get out of this room. He had no interest in any of this. He had in his pocket the ounce of cocaine raw and unpackaged. He wanted to get high, to escape all of the inane "let's get rich" talk.

As they spoke, Jesse thought of the improbability of all of this.

Jesse . . . a ladies' man . . . drug dealer . . . strange perceptions of his reality.

He was a defeated malcontent, undone by the indomitable power of the great Lord of the sky. "The defeat was upon him, staggering and absolute."

"Let's go see the place. We can get a little high on and talk about how all of this is going to work." Jesse wanted to get out of there, and an offer to get high was certain to work and, not that he needed it, would provide proof that this bevy lacked the necessary control to manage a drug-dealing enterprise.

Jesse never got back to the square, not that night anyway. They got high through the night, and within minutes of entering the apartment and setting up the "get high" paraphernalia, all talk of the business ended and settled into the absurd nonsense for which these gatherings are known.

In the midst of this, Jesse had thoughts of getting to his son's graduation. During the night they had consumed about half of the cocaine he had. He did not have enough money to get to Grand Rapids, but he had to be there for his son's milestone.

When Joe finally delivered Jesse to Chico's house, noonday shadows had not yet departed and were creating havens all about. The dogs announced to Chico that someone was on his property, and when he opened the door, it was obvious that something had changed. He was nervous and concerned that his little enterprise had been compromised. Someone had spoken his name to the authorities; he was now being watched and everybody, especially new people in his life, were suspects. This included Jesse. There was another fellow living in the house, a young man "from up north," was all he would say, but he was there before Jesse and was more trusted. Marijuana had been his drug of choice, which made him safe. He was not a crackhead like most of the other attendees, but it was obvious that he too was becoming seduced, so Chico put everyone out.

"Get your shit and get the fuck out," he said suspiciously and angrily.

A rat? This was inconceivable to Jesse. Yes, there were so-called professionals in regular attendance, but were they telling on themselves? It was true that Jesse had betrayed everyone he loved, but it was unwitting, it was beyond his ability to control. That he would deliberately expose the only refuge available to him should not have made any sense to Chico. But he did not know who to finger, so he shut down and made everyone leave.

Jesse asked if he could leave his things here, at least for a while, as he had no place to put them. He had to go to Michigan to attend his son's graduation, and he had nearly no money. The half-ounce of coke was his with which to barter or sell. That would give him enough money to get home and back, but his options then would be few. As obvious as this situation was, the full extent of its impact on his life did not register.

He thought again of seeing his boys, the two people left in his world that would be happy to see him. And then he wondered, who had helped them with their homework? Had he taught them enough or anything about the world at large? He was not there for the prom and other innocent rites of teenage passage. He had not gotten a gift or even a card. He knew he had not communicated with his boys as he should have. He did not know how to tell them he was dying. So fully immersed in self-pity was he that his only concern was himself. He was now morbidly consumed with self and the worries of the pitiful.

He was a failure at the thing that had mattered most to him. Suddenly, trembling, he thought, *how could he face them?* No matter, he had to go.

He struck a deal with Chico for the drugs and prepared to go to Michigan.

During the ride to Beverly's house, all manner of trepidation engulfed him. He had put on a suit so he was fully dressed, and it dawned on him that he had no time to go to her house. He was late and had to go directly to the college campus where the event was being held. He was there. He got to see his son walk the time-honored path across the stage, but Chad did not know he was there. That fact made him feel as if he was not there at all.

After the ceremony, he found his son among the crowd. Of course Beverly was there with her boyfriend and registered her disappointment with an "I told you so" kind of look on her face. Chad embraced his father with real affection and relief. Yet underneath the smile there simmered a sadness based on the fact that his graduation was not significant enough for his father to be on time. He did not yet have the courage to scold his father, and his smile and demeanor fully hid intentions that would boil over some years later.

All of his childhood friends were there and most were graduating with him. They thought of Jesse as a good father and envied Chad and Zachery. It was easy for them to do so in that they had no fathers. But Jesse's boys had to deal with the loss of him, which, in some ways, it could be argued that in every way, made it worse.

Jesse gave him some money, enough to have a good time with his friends at dinner and whatever other plans they had for the night. Zachery was invited to join them in the festivities, and after brief hugs and kisses, they were gone.

The happiness on their faces was enough for Jesse to feel some sense of relief, but now, left with only Beverly and her new boyfriend, real discomfort descended upon him. The boyfriend had been on time. He was living in Jesse's house, spending time with his boys. A house he had purchased with his mother's help, and wherein his children had been conceived in love was now being presided over by an intruder—this made him uncomfortable, more than he had ever been. There was no place for him here, and no affection. Having no transportation, he was compelled to ride with them.

The new man in Beverly's life was considerably younger than she, but he was particularly ambitious, owning big cars and several houses. He was predictably everything that Jesse was not. Among those traits was greed. He was insatiable in terms of acquiring money and completely selfish with it. Jesse was to discover how much so, later, when the conversation turned to what Jesse was doing.

Beverly, of course, was a good Christian woman living in sin, as they say. But there was no way for her to understand what had become of Jesse. His depression, his abandonment of his family was one thing, but dealing in drugs was not something she would sanction. Her friend, on the other hand, would do anything if he thought he could make an easy dollar.

Jesse had deluded himself much in the same way the "brothas" in Boston had. If he had one more chance, just a few more dollars, he might be able to make it. In this odd relationship, he found a sponsor, and he could do it without complications of his new group of sycophants. They struck a deal. Jesse would get one thousand dollars from him with which to buy another ounce of the product. He would send him a thousand dollars a month for six months. This all made sense to both of them and was considered good business.

Jesse stayed in Grand Rapids for three days, having fun with his boys and doing a good job of hiding his grief. *They will be all right*, he thought. *They will be better off without me.* He was certain now that he had nothing to offer, nothing more to give. He would be committed to the seedy business and save thousands of dollars, which he would make available to them when he was gone.

He had opted for a slow death that would come in its time. There was no plan for jumping or bullets and knives. He would do the right thing and spare his sons and his family the great sadness that was now his—only his—but he would let the drug that had claimed him take him in whatever way it would come. It was now important, more important than anything to simply join her, be where she was. He had no reason, no right to be here in her absence.

CHAPTER 40

The Collapse of the Culture

There was more sunshine in Boston than he could bear. It seemed completely incongruous to him that there should be any sunlight here at all, in this place that had so darkened his life. He began to see things morbidly now, for what he considered the last time, and he did not want those final images to be anything in Boston. But alas, this is where he was. As the plane made its final descent into Boston's Logan International Airport, over the bay, the ocean, he thought it should go down now, falling peacefully into the sea. That thought filled him with terror as he could not imagine a more horrific way to leave the planet, given his great fear of drowning, but he thought that this is what he deserved: a gruesome death, his most terrifying nightmare. This would be the delinquent God's coup de grace.

He couldn't remember what day it was. It was certainly a Lord's day, as they say in church. "A day to the Lord is a thousand years, and a thousand years but a day." He remembered that and other scriptures that his mother had shared with him, and he himself had shared with countless audiences all over southeast Michigan. He found himself mired in a thousand-year day, an interminable period he must wade through in order to be where she was. She had said, on her deathbed, "What is death to a Christian?" *Indeed, what is it?* he thought. Freedom, but freedom would have to wait.

Jesse did not feel well. He had a cold and was near dehydration, blowing his nose constantly and coughing, filling his pockets with snot-soaked tissue and rags, but he had business to attend to.

From a pay phone he called Manneo again, who dutifully brought the product, showing up as he always did on a motorcycle—black leather jacket and chaps. The pickup was made in the old bar that Chuck had introduced him to all those months ago. It was safe in that there were always so few people there and the ones that were, were old, out of touch, and always drunk. Manneo made mention of the fact the he had been a bit worried when Jesse did not have all of the money for the last purchase. "I see you're back on track," he said.

"Yeah, that last time was just a little oversight. I'm good," said Jesse hiding his sad condition.

After a drink, he went back to Chico's house with a get-high truce and some conversation in an effort to make it clear that he was no rat. This was good diplomacy, and it allowed Chico to be comfortable with letting Jesse stay a bit longer and to confess that he knew it was not Jesse who had ratted on him, but he had not wanted anyone to know what he was thinking or who he suspected.

They got high while Jesse made packages. He would not fail this time. He had made a commitment to the young capitalist now spending time with his ex-wife. His wife, that was finished business. The divorce was final; he had paid the money and endured the strange severance. The legal papers had the odd line referencing his children as, "the issue of Beverly and Jesse Brightmeyer," which had the effect of making Jesse feel distressed and yet somehow honorable. He had in fact brought into the world his beautiful boys—they were his issue. Now though he felt, painfully, like a beast on the plains of the valley leaving his young to fend for themselves. At the graduation, he saw on their faces the simple joy of adolescence. It was an image he could hold in his heart, not unlike the laminated picture he carried in his wallet of his smiling prepubescent sons.

He called Cha'che, as they had some business to do as well. Cha'che showed up around nine o'clock, driving his conspicuous yet incongruous car. It was not the bedraggled Cadillac he sometimes drove. It was an older-model sports car, not the kind of vehicle one supposes a so-called pimp would drive. The car was bright yellow with racing stripes and teenage appointments all over it. Jesse got in, and they proceeded to "check his traps" as he put it, which meant he was going to see if his whores were where they should be and doing what he had told them to do. After being satisfied that all was well, he wanted to talk about Daniel.

Cha'che was determined to "cut up" Daniel to satisfy his sense of manhood, based on some old altercation that had simply resurfaced on the night of debauchery with the whores, drugs, and insanity. Also, Jesse had told him in passing, actually while trying to calm him down, about some people who owed him money. Apparently that was part of the matter. Daniel owed him money and had kept promising to pay but never came up with it. Jesse wanted no part in the dispute but felt the need to assuage.

"How much money?" said Jesse, knowing that Cha'che did not take drug debts lightly; no drug dealers did, only Jesse, who had the temerity, or the stupidity, to consider himself something other than that.

"Three hundred," he said, "and that bitch is gon' pay me or get bled. He ain't gon' treat me like the bitch. I ain't like you, Jesse. That's why everybody like yo' ass. You let 'em get away with shit. How much them white mothafuckas owe you?"

"Around fifteen hundred," said Jesse, thinking this might put Daniel's debt in perspective.

"Oh hell naw," said Cha'che growling, "we got to get that money. Where these mothafuckas at?"

"I don't give a damn. I'll just make some more. They'll get theirs along the way."

"You got that shit right. We gon' get these bitches now, the money or some blood."

This bravado meant very little to Jesse, as he considered it just that. Getting high was always a way of getting away from any unpleasantness, so Jesse made the irresistible offer.

"Yeah, man, let's get high, 'cause right now, I feel like hurtin' somebody."

They went to his house, his parents' house actually, who were respectable professionals, vacationing in Bermuda. The basement was his retreat, and, given its dungeon-like condition: a green and dirty chamber with drug-related paraphernalia all around, it was inconceivable to Jesse that his parents did not know what he was doing here, and he said so.

"Man, my parents is old folks now. They don't never come down here."

They drank and smoked crack until about midnight, until Jesse was so transported that he approached hallucination. Though an addict, he still was easily sated, unlike most addicts who could imbibe all through the night and some would go days before finally collapsing. Cha'che was just warming up.

"I ought to kill that ho," he said.

"What, who . . . I thought you said they was handlin' their business?" Jesse was slurring his words and struggling to make clear sentences.

"I ain't talkin' 'bout my girls, am talking 'bout that punk-ass Daniel. I can't believe he playin' me like this."

Jesse said nothing to this, as he was too high for anything resembling conversation.

"Let's go. I got to pick up my bitches and get my money," said Cha'che.

This was a good idea to Jesse, as he needed some air—the basement lacked any kind of ventilation. He did not think about the fact that Cha'che was too inebriated to drive, but luckily at this hour there was not much traffic, and they made the fairly long ride from Dorchester to Cambridge without incident.

They found the girls together and working on a trick. Cha'che drove slowly by, saying in his best pimp lingo, "Handle yo' business. I'll be back."

Jesse thought that he should make a stop at the Barrel. He had packaged drugs on him, and he needed some money, but before he could make the suggestion, Cha'che announced that he wanted to go by and see Daniel.

"That's a bad idea," said Jesse, "we're fucked up, it's after midnight, you got the hos waiting for you. Let's do that some other time."

"Naw, Jesse, am just going to talk to him, that's it. I ain't gon' fuck with him tonight. I ain't even got my shit wit' me."

By "shit" he meant his knives and razors, which were his weapons of choice, but he kept guns as well. He said this with such calm that Jesse took him seriously and thought it might not be a bad idea in that he had a few things to pick up from the apartment.

The cool night air and the thought of having to deal with a crazed, testosterone-driven Cha'che had Jesse waking up a bit, beginning to return to sobriety. It was a false sense because in his condition, only bad judgments were in the offing.

When they drove up to the house, Jesse noticed that the lights were on. This was interesting and unusual because during his brief stay here, he and Daniel covered the windows in black cloth in an effort to hide their foul play from the neighbors.

"Let me go up and see if he's home," said Jesse, still thinking that he might meet need to run interference.

When he got to the top of the three-flight climb, the door was ajar, so Jesse called out for Daniel.

"Hey, Daniel, you home?" said Jesse, walking into the apartment.

"Oh, it's just you. What are you doing here? I thought you got all of your stuff."

"No, I left that bag of . . ."

"BITCH!" he heard Cha'che yell, but he had not heard him come up the stairs behind him. He was brandishing a tiny three-inch knife and reaching clumsily beyond Jesse. The blade caught Daniel's shirt, cutting it down along his torso.

Daniel let out shriek of his own, seeing the bumbling, knife-wielding Cha'che almost comically trying to cut him. He ran into the interior of his apartment, returning almost immediately with some utensil, a rolling pin, I think, that he intended to use to defend himself.

Jesse grabbed Cha'che protectively, he thought, trying to get him out of the apartment and everyone out of harm's way. But the machismo was following too fast.

"Let the motherfucker go. I got something for his ass," bellowed Daniel.

"Turn me loose, Jesse, Goddamn it. I'ma cut this pussy. What the fuck is wrong with you? Don't never get in my way when am fixin' to hurt somebody!"

The episode was nearly laughable as Daniel himself was also high. The combatants did not have the stamina, to say nothing of the stability, to harm anyone but themselves, or Jesse, who unwisely had gotten in the middle of it all.

They yelled obscenities at each other as Jesse backed Cha'che out the door. Just as quickly, they both turned on Jesse. He was a pussy to Cha'che and a traitor to Daniel, and through it all, Jesse tried to remind Cha'che that he had promised to do no harm tonight while trying to convince Daniel that he had not set him up to be stabbed.

Daniel grabbed Jesse things, which had been bagged or boxed, and hurled them down the three flights of stairs, yelling, "And don't bring your narrow black ass back here for nothing, nothing. I'm through with you."

Cha'che, upon hearing and seeing this, decided to go back up to finish the inept battle, but Jesse grabbed him again, saying, "Damn, Cha'che. What the hell are you doin'? You told me you were just going to talk, and then you start swinging like a crazed lunatic. We're too fucked up for this kind of shit. Let's get the hell out of here!"

Cha'che was breathing heavily, but oddly, there was no anger on his face.

"I almost got that bitch. I would have got him if you hadn' got in my fuckin way," he laughed. They got into the car and drove slowly away.

"I hope them hos is finished, I need to get paid. Speakin' of gettin' paid, let's go find them white boys that owe you all that money."

He said this with the same ease and conciliatory tone that he had used in convincing Jesse to go to Daniel's house. This time, however, Jesse thought, since the issue had nothing to do with Cha'che—it was his own—he did not think or anticipate that Cha'che would misbehave. It was also clear that Cha'che was not upset. This, of course, struck Jesse as peculiar. How could he so calmly decide to slash someone and in minutes act as if nothing had happened or take it so lightly? But with Jesse's mind being so distorted by the perverse chemicals, he succumbed to the folly of Cha'che's suggestions.

Jesse's cold was relentless. He was wearing a military fatigue jacket that was soiled and fitting him poorly. Jesse, without knowing it, had lost his sartorial edge and was now dressing in a manner unlike he ever had. There were days when he did not wash himself or brush his teeth or even change his clothes. The cold could very well have been owed to a growing list of unsanitary practices. Anyway, he was coughing, sneezing, and constantly loosing fluids, hacking and sneezing into a rag and tissue that he would simply stuff, wet and foul, into his oversized pockets. There was so much mucus that the coarse fabric of the military-issued coat was stained, both inside and out. There was a dirty Irish cap on his head and equally dirty work boots on his feet. Cha'che always looked a mess, so between the two of them a woebegone look of homelessness or criminality had been unintentionally achieved.

Jesse, oblivious to this dubious presentation, given the hour and knowing where the "white boys" were and that they would be up, decided to pay them a visit. Just to talk and get high. They were more like friends than enemies after all.

When they arrived Cha'che began talking as if there was a plan afoot to do harm to the people who owed the money.

"Now, Jesse, you point out the mothafuckas who owe you the money and try to get . . ." Jesse lost the sounds of his words as Cha'che reached under his seat and pulled out two handguns, one of which was a .357 magnum.

"What the hell are you talking about, Cha'che? We ain't going in here to shoot nobody. I'm going to sell a few grams, take a few hits, and we outta here."

"I know, I know, but you never know what's gon' happen. You get me around some strange white folks . . . shit, I got to have my dogs wit' me."

"Cha'che, you want to get high or not? I need you to promise me you ain't gonna start no shit . . . out here in the suburbs. Man, you must be crazy."

"I'm cool, everything is all right. I'ma just have my shit in my pocket," he said, "and here you take this little thirty-eight, you know, just in case."

"In case of what?" said Jesse incredulously.

"Well, you know . . . white folks is crazy . . ."

"Brotha, please, they ain't no crazier than anybody else," said Jesse, thinking about the absurd scene he had just witnessed.

"Just put it in your pocket. Nobody gon' see it, but if some shit jump off, you ready."

Jesse took the gun and put it in his pocket, thinking this would appease the lunatic at his side. They knocked on the door while wondering if anyone would hear them, as the music was at the oppressive levels common among young rock enthusiasts. The young man who opened the door was someone known to Jesse, but not very well. In fact, the person who owned the house and whom Jesse had come to see was not there at all. Or so he said. Still this fellow knew Jesse well enough to invite him in. There were many familiar faces in the crowd of twenty or more, and Jesse walked the rooms, greeting people in the way one does in a room filled with drug—and booze-infected souls.

There was, though, a discomfort in the air, which was likely due to their appearance and the surprise visit. Also Jesse noticed that Cha'che's huge gun could be clearly seen, and that, coupled with their blackness, no doubt caused all those who noticed them to wonder what was going on.

Jesse went to the table where the drugs were being prepared and saw a veritable panoply_of elicit pleasures. Pills, marijuana, heroin, powdered, and crack cocaine were on the table, and nearly everyone had that dazed look of people who had gone too far in pursuit of euphoria. The host, that is, the friend of the fellow Jesse had come to see, was not so high that he did not sense that something was not right. These black males, one of whom he knew, seemed to have something else on their minds. In any case, after a short time of getting high and mindless chit-chat, Jesse decided to leave, which seemed to please all attendees. It was not the best decision to pay this visit. They were not welcomed guests, and even Jesse's drugs were not required here.

On the way home, Jesse pointed out to his friend that nothing had happened and that there was no need for the pistols, taking the thirty-eight out of his pocket and placing it on the floor of the backseat.

"Yeah, but the mothafucka owe you fifteen hundred, and they got enough drugs in there to pay three times that."

As they drove through the streets, Cha'che, without speaking to it, chose to take secondary avenues, quite purposely to avoid detection by the police. His conspicuous little sports car was well known to the local five-O. It did not work. Someone had called the police. Presumably someone at the party had given them a description of the unmistakable vehicle with two "rough-looking" black males inside.

While driving down one of the side streets, Holyoke, as I remember, they were suddenly surrounded by no less than six patrol cars, all lights-a-flashing. More officers than could be readily counted darted from their vehicles with guns drawn.

"Out of the car," yelled the first officer.

"What's the problem, officer?" said Cha'che, actually speaking proper English.

"You don't ask questions here, I do, now get out of the car with your hands up, up and over your heads."

One of the vehicles was a paddy wagon, or it arrived soon after the assault began. Jesse got out of the car, sneezing and snotting all over himself. The most aggressive of the officers was dealing with Cha'che, but the uniform that approached Jesse was prosecutor, judge and jury, and he found Jesse guilty of something.

"Get your damn hands on the roof of the car and spread 'em," he said and began patting Jesse down, searching his pockets, inside, outside, top and bottom. When he placed his hands in Jesse's lower outside pockets, where incidentally the cocaine was below mounds of snot-stained rags and tissue, he jumped back saying, "Damn it!, this fuck is diseased," and cuffed him immediately. He had not found the cocaine.

"*Guns,*" someone screamed, "they've got guns." One of them had shown his flashlight into the back of the vehicle and noticed the pistol on the floor.

Well, at least they didn't find the drugs, Jesse thought, *but guns . . . we're going to jail.*

"Get these bastards cuffed and in the wagon."

Both Jesse and Cha'che, now in handcuffs, were, shall I say, less than gently placed in the back of the van, which was in effect a jail on wheels. They tethered them to horizontal rails that were anchored to the walls of the truck.

"Goddamn," said Cha'che. "The last thing I want to do is spend a mothafuckin night in jail. Hell, I got a permit for them guns, but drugs too. Shit, man, we gone."

Jesse, whispering now, said, "They didn't find the drugs. They're still in my pocket."

"What chu mean? I saw 'em search you."

"There're under a bunch of snot rags, Cop didn't want to go there."

"Jesse, you got to get them drugs in yo' ass. They gon' search you again when we get there."

"Man, I'm handcuffed just like you. How am I supposed to do that?"

"I don't know, but better find a way, or we going away for a while."

The drugs were in his right front pocket, but the only way to get there would necessitate getting both hands there in handcuffs that were too tight to begin with. Jesse began to try reaching for his front pocket, which placed a numbing pain on his wrist. It was agonizing, and he thought he might never be able to use his left hand again, as it seemed to take forever to get there. It seemed an impossible thing to do, grabbing pieces of cloth between his fingers, inching the pocket nearer to his hands. Eventually he got there, wincing to the point of tears rolling down his face. The next challenge was to get the packages, which luckily he had placed in a sandwich bag, into his trousers. This was somewhat easier, but Jesse, after all of that agony, could not see what difference it would make if he was to be searched again. But it did.

When they got to the police station, Jesse was not searched. He was held in a large, otherwise nearly empty room, for about thirty minutes. The officer who had roughed him up a bit came into the room, offering small talk, and after a moment or two wrote a phone number on a card and told Jesse to call him tomorrow. Jesse did not know what to make of this, but he was so grateful that he was not searched again that he decided he would call.

"You need to post five hundred in bail if you want to go home tonight," he said, "do you need to place a call?"

It occurred to Jesse that if he or Cha'che had had any real money on them, it would have been confiscated by this crew of cops. Everything about the episode had him thinking that these guys were crooks themselves. Jesse did not have much experience with police stations and their ways of doing things, but all of this seemed strange.

Cha'che had been released before Jesse. It turned out that his "professional" parents had been relatively high-ranking officials in the police department. His phone call had gone to one of their former associates.

Jesse used his call to reach the Cork 'n' Barrel, hoping to reach Harry, but he wasn't there. Luckily Hills was there and happy to rescue her man. She had to collect money from some of the regulars to come up with the five hundred, promising everyone that they would be paid back and reminding them of all the "nice" things Jesse had done for every one of them.

She picked him up, smiling like a proud parent. She and Jesse laughed all the way back to the bar, where he was greeted like a returning hero. He still had drugs on him, and this allowed him to pay everyone back immediately while regaling them with stories of the night's misadventures.

Harry showed up with anger and suspicion on his face. He too had been arrested, and indeed there was a rat in the camp. He was relieved to hear about Jesse's arrest, as it took him off the lists of suspects. Not that he had fingered Jesse, but his arrest made it easy for them to look elsewhere.

The culture was collapsing. Harry and Jesse were no longer the "go to" guys for drugs in the bar. Even the new barmaid would only take orders for the product but carried none with her in the bar. They all gathered after the bar closed, off-site at Harry's girlfriend's apartment. There were too many possible culprits, so they decided to wait it out. They would lay low for a while.

It the end of the night, Jesse realized he had no place to go, no place to sleep. That night, and for a few nights beyond, he found harborage at Hillary's house, but no comfort. They made their visits to the bar which used to be home . . . away from home, if you will. Now, though, things were different, and that difference was everywhere and had created a strangeness that made the place somewhat unrecognizable. It was not as if he and Hills argued, it was that Jesse could find no place to be comfortable. He thought to himself that it was this fact that undid his relationship with Ramona. Settling down—anywhere—felt like additional betrayal. Without his sons . . . with his mother gone, he felt desperately unentitled to comfort. She was gone, and they were suffering. The least he could do was to suffer too.

He managed to stay with Hills and others through the summer, sleeping usually where he found himself. Somehow it was easy for people to allow one to crash at their home during good weather, but when the skies dimmed to welcome the fall, so did hospitality.

The law enforcement community had a place for him that allowed the suffering he required. Within a few weeks of the first arrest, it happened again. A reckless desperation befell the drug fraternity, both dealers and users. Jesse had only enough drugs left to earn enough money to purchase more product. He, Stanley, and Cha'che had decided that there was a cheaper source for the cocaine, but it would not be delivered. They had to go to the source in the "projects" in or around Dorchester. They piled into Cha'che's little sports car and headed in the direction of the dealer that Jesse and Stanley would be meeting for the first time. While driving down Dorchester Avenue, Cha'che was forced to slam on his brakes as the van behind which he was driving came to a sudden halt. "Good stop," said Stanley, thinking Cha'che's reflexes had prevented an accident. But at almost the same moment, another van stopped behind them, actually touching the bumper of the sports car, an obviously rehearsed and perfectly executed maneuver.

Six officers stormed out of the vehicles, again with guns drawn, demanding that they exit the car. This time they found what little drugs Jesse and Stanley had on them. It was an eighth of an ounce between them and not packaged for sale. Only Cha'che had none, but he was the driver and therefore an accomplice, and he was the only one carrying any real money. This took place around midday, and the local residents hung out their windows to get a better view of the goings-on. Jesse was embarrassed to be in the middle of such a spectacle, but he was angry as well. Not only was he or Cha'che being fingered and followed, but now he had lost any hope of "doing it right" this time. Gone now was the potential for profit on the investment the young man had made in Grand Rapids. Jesse, unable this time to post bail, had to stay in jail for three days while waiting to be seen by a judge. There was talk of keeping him there, as he was considered a flight risk, in that he had no local ties. No home, no job, and no family here. I cannot recall what slight of tongue Jesse used to get out of this unpleasant prospect, but he did, and a trial date was set.

While in court he noticed that the prosecuting attorney was a young black woman, who reminded Jesse of his sister Rosalind. She was tall, articulate, and seemed to have putting Jesse behind bars as her highest priority. Stanley's appearance did not help. He looked on this day as Jesse did the night of his earlier arrest. Of course, Stanley always looked this way, which had earned him the nickname

"Pigpen." He was unshaven, unkempt, and had a rough, croaky way of expressing himself.

Jesse tried to distinguish himself from Stanley by using a most enunciated brand of English. He even had the audacity to approach the prosecutor in the corridor, hoping to suggest to her that she had him all wrong, that this was not what it appeared to be. She rightly resisted any conversation with him, but she heard what he had to say. Without stopping, she said, "I will not be talking with you, Mr. Brightmeyer. I encourage you to be quiet."

Anyway, he was released on "his own recognizance," but so was Stanley. They walked through the spotless hallways, and Jesse noticed the shiny inlayed terrazzo floors, the glistening glass, and stainless steel. It all seemed so foul and incongruous, this silvery place there to house and incriminate society's filthy. Out he went, with the hopelessly ecclesiastical thought whirling through his head, *It is all vanity and a striving after the wind.*

"Hey, Jess, you want to get high?"

"Hell yes," said Jesse, "but we got no drugs and no money."

"Like hell we ain't. They didn't find my real stash. I had it in my car," he said in that gravelly Bostonian vernacular.

"Well, I'll be damned," said Jesse, and they went to some forsaken place that Jesse had never been to before and commenced to doing the very thing that got them in trouble in the first place.

CHAPTER 41

In the Bosom of Christendom

A wild wind was blowing under the late July blue sky and only in one direction. His return brought about his nerve-bending release from the promise of time in jail, which should have been good news. It was, I suppose, but bad judgment had not loosened its grip on Jesse Brightmeyer. He showed up in court dressed as a business professional, carrying with him in a proper-looking file, twenty-five handwritten testimonials to his good character, his solid citizenship. This was in fact his first offense, and probation was his reward. But the capricious wind blew him past this liberty into the walled place his waywardness had built for him, and from which he could not escape.

He might have had a chance had the system locked him up in some contemplative cell. He could battle with concrete and steel, leaving behind the grief imposed by the insurmountable god. Perhaps an aloneness levied by society would have given him enough repose to find, in time, his way home. Instead he was free again and left to the many deplorable devices that had crippled him—that narrow box of pain he seemed to so desperately need, a place far more restrictive than the one the magistrate could have mercifully imposed. Prison could have spared him the trouble he was now so blindly near.

In his finery, clean and shaven, he went to the Cork 'n' Barrel. He and Stanley were surprised to find the old gang there. For his part, Stanley was not actually part of the "old gang," but he was known to them, so he was part of the celebration that ensued. Harry and Jesse told of their trials with much bravado—war stories being told around the camp fire. Bernie, the lonely intellectual, was among the listeners, but her boyfriend was in jail and would no doubt have a triumphant return of his own, albeit six months hence.

For now the booze flowed, but no one was willing to openly do lines of cocaine, as they used to in less worrisome times. When the bar closed, that close group went to Bernie's small apartment.

Even while getting high and perhaps as a result of it, Jesse allowed himself to think again of that day, now long gone, when he sat in judgment of others, deciding their fate in the small ecclesiastical enclave know as Jehovah's Witnesses. There he was prosecutor and judge, sitting on a committee of "elders," deciding the spiritual fate of some fallen brother guilty of an unholy infraction. He remembered having to "disfellowship" people for smoking cigarettes, having marijuana on them, or for some conduct that was condescendingly referred to as "unbecoming of a Christian." He lapsed into memories that would be pointless to speak to in his present company. Luckily in this group the nonsensical chatter ruled, so Jesse had his memories to himself.

Gone, completely now, were his days of innocence. He recalled the day when he would counsel the young and old about the ways of goodness in the troubled world . . . "You should live in the world and be no part of it," was an oft-used admonition. In those happy days of naiveté, he did just that. He remembered when his childhood friends would tease him for his refusal to use "cuss words," or when on those occasions he would find something of value—a dollar, a ring, or some other trinket, he would not rest until he had found the rightful owner, his mother's voice always ringing in his ear, "Jesse, be a nice boy." There had been a time when he was in demand because of his kind ways, his wholesome spirit, and a selfless willingness to help others in need. He sat now as a disgrace, a disgrace to his mother and himself, doing something that no one who knew him then would even believe him capable of.

He thought of his pretty little family, both his children and his siblings. He remembered the small manicured backyard in the old neighborhood. He could even smell the plant life and other aromas that attached him so inextricably to that long-gone place.

To his mind came the clearest vision of raking leaves with his boys and rolling playfully with them while Beverly prepared lunch or dinner. *It could even have been breakfast*, he thought, the playing and laughter had been such a constant. The image entered his mind and heart and rested so peacefully there, but in seconds, the agitation came.

Nothing here in this place allowed him to immerse himself in that lost euphoria. He sat contemplating the prospect of time in jail, prison—an inconceivable probability—when he heard Harry's voice.

"Right, Jesse?"

"Yeah, man, you are absolutely correct," said Jesse, having no idea what the question was, but it snapped him out of his dreamy remembrances.

Through the night, the natter continued until people were nodding, slurring, and generally altered by the mind-numbing consumption. Even in this condition, most found their feet and their way home.

Bernie's apartment was a tight space and very cluttered. She was an ardent reader and had magazines and books, tattered and purposely dog-eared, all over the apartment. She was the lost intellectual seeking her muse in hopeless places, each dog-ear a point of futility. The pictures on the walls were the ordinary store-bought variety, clinging drunkenly to the soiled walls. There was a galley kitchen with pots, dishes, and silverware carelessly left about, some teetering as if about to crash to the floor. Half-eaten food remained on many plates, and Jesse thought there should have been an accompanying odor, but there was none. There should have been bugs or mice, but he saw none.

He noticed, after nearly everyone was gone, that Bernie was in her bed and only half awake. He had no place to go. He had not spoken to this fact and had no plan, so this situation seemed fortuitous. Taking off his clothes, he nestled beside her, climbed aboard her, and began to kiss her for pleasure and convenience. She made no resistance as he delicately disrobed her, and she invited him into her warm dampness. In her slumbered state, she moaned as he inserted himself.

"Kiss me again, kiss me all over," she said this with a need that was equal to his. Holding, they needed holding, not sex, but it was as if the rules of holding, the rules of this necessary intimacy, demanded penetration, the moisture and the moaning. They rode each other, looking for the tenderness, searching for a place to be in the corners of each other. They found in that moment and only for that moment the comfort they sought. They lay now satisfied that there was permission to hold, to sleep, and neither had to ask for it.

When they awoke, she managed somehow in the forsaken kitchen to prepare a fine and pretty breakfast. While spreading marmalade, the needy talk began. The food, with all its tasteful trappings, was for show, but she was apparently a good cook. She would have to have been to prepare anything in the riddled kitchen. She wanted Jesse to know, in the midst of the shambles, someone to know, someone who could understand, that she was from somewhere else. She had been a woman of means and education; she had class.

She spoke of her wish to spend time with him when they first met, with pride and regret that there was no outlet in her current circle of friends for meaningful conversation. He heard about her Ivy League education and failed marriage, wherein she had the six-thousand-square-foot Mediterranean home, the five bathrooms, and the cottage by the sea. Lost things now: the musician husband gone, disappeared, and she never saw him leave or even knew he was going.

She spoke, incredulously, of want of family and laughing, happy children. Broaching the subject of his blackness, she made it known that it was of no consequence, and those "dumb asses at the bar didn't know shit from Shinola," which was the phrase used by her boyfriend on the night they met. She rolled through the dusty years like Jesse himself. Then, with indescribable sadness and depth, she said slowly, knowing as no one else did that Jesse had lost similar things. "Mr. Brightmeyer, what happened to us?"

She asked as if he were the prodigal husband returned and seeking redemption. For a moment, Jesse thought it was his turn to talk, when the tears came, a flooding torrent of despair that Jesse knew so much about. She cried the tears of the crushed while Mr. Brightmeyer held her gently, with a fierce devotion, as he himself wanted to be held. The time of tears knows no clock, but when it ended in bed, as he had carried her there, the holding was done again, intimately, lovingly, with a need as deep as history. They lay there in prodigious silence, clinging urgently to each other.

While still in his arms, with her head on his chest, she apologetically and calmly said, "You cannot stay here tonight. My boyfriend is coming back today."

This news could not be resisted. It was logistical, putting Jesse into the streets.

"All right," he said, but it wasn't. He was silent after that, for he could find no reason to share his plight with her. Rising from the bed, he went to the bathroom. Strangely he did not remember seeing it through the night. It too was tight and as dirty as the kitchen. But the necessary things were there and functional. He rinsed his mouth with the remaining corner of some generic oral wash. He found an unused, actually brand-new face cloth in her tiny linen closet and washed his face and hands. He gathered himself, his things, which were simply the clothes he came in with: the tweed sports jacket, the woolen slacks, socks, and tie and dressed in front of her. Jesse had always been fastidious about his clothes, so he should not have been surprised by how neatly they had been laid out, but he was, having no memory of doing it.

Prone on the bed, she looked up and said, "You look so . . . professional . . . what happened?" It was rhetorical and disconnected. "Will you come back . . . later, I mean, you know when we can . . . you know, do this again?"

There were a thousand ways to take and respond to these stilted questions, but Jesse only found this one: "I hope so. I do enjoy your company." With that, she managed to stand and come to him. She wrapped herself around him, cleaving desperately, saying, "Please, please come back."

Jesse bravely unwrapped himself from her meaningful grip, wanting now to get to the door. I say bravely because beyond the door was the terrifying unknown. The next meal, the next pillow, was excruciatingly dubious and distant.

He spent the remainder of the summer sleeping where he could, house to house, once or twice even at Daniel's apartment. He found a job selling cars again, but there was no magic this time. He made almost no money, but for a time he did at least have a car to drive. There was also an acting opportunity requiring him to be sullen, at which he excelled. It paid, but it was short-lived.

He bumped into Jake the architect at some point, who was now fully mired in crack use. This encounter worked for both of them in that it gave them a protected place where they could engage their debilitating consumption without judgment, and Jesse a place to sleep. He was now completely broke. Jake would take his biweekly check and buy an ounce of cocaine. They would package a quarter of it for Jesse to sell, and this would provide enough money for food, which hardly seemed necessary anymore. The rest they would cook for their deviant pleasure. Somehow they forgot about or decided that rent did not have to be paid. It was not long before Jake was evicted. The truth is, when they went to the marketplace, which is what the bar became for them—just a place to sell enough drugs to survive—they could hardly stand being away from the demanding pipe. It called to them with a tyranny that could not be opposed.

They were defenseless against it. Usually by ten o'clock they were back at his apartment, smoking the profits, the rent money. The grip of the drug was so great that as they walked to Jake's apartment, every pebble or piece of paper on the ground had the look of a rock of crack, and they would bend to pick them up as if panning for gold. Once Jesse even put his hand into a dollop of gross spittle, thinking he had hit the mother lode of crack on the street. Every activity was a diversion keeping them away from the monster that now fully controlled them. There was no longer a need for food or sex or company of any kind.

By the end of October, Jake was gone. His family had come for him, or he had found his way back to them in Vermont. He said nothing to Jesse; he just disappeared, and Jesse was without a place to be. Jake may or may not have taken his things with him, but what few belongings Jesse had at his house were lost to the landlord. No real loss to Jesse, as anything he had of value was still at Chico's place, a crack house guarded by the appearance of abandonment and three vicious pit bulls.

It was a Saturday in November now, the month of Jesse's birth. It was cold, but no snow had yet fallen, but the warming summer sun had departed, and the welcoming blue canopy had turned gray and, as a prelude to winter, was releasing a cold bitter rain. In this hostility, Jesse Brightmeyer, penniless and homeless, had to find a place to sleep. He could not. He went to the bar where he had been a pack leader. He and Harry had a regime of relative power and control. Now there was no Harry, even Sal was missing, and those regulars who saw him, avoided him, seeing quite plainly that something was wrong, that Jesse had lost everything. When the bar closed, there was no invite to the back room. Jesse walked out the door into what seemed to him, total blackness, a wet and draining blackness. He was hungry, cold, sleepy, and utterly ashamed. He began to walk, but he was going nowhere. There was nowhere to go. He felt invisible to all but the cold. It and the rain were the only things that would dare touch him. He felt as if they were seeking him out, proclaiming him the fool with torturous saturation. The rain seemed as confused as he, pelting him with wind-driven pellets one moment and the next covering him with a soft, equally cold mist, falling lightly almost like snow. After many blocks, he found a storefront doorway to take some cover and fell to his bottom, weeping with the rain. He did not sleep, of course, but he fell into a numbing slumber of mindlessness that somehow sheltered him from his senses. The walking took him like a homing pigeon, without his knowing it or planning it in the direction of Bernie's house in Somerville, one of Boston's many near suburbs. Through the night, he walked from one storefront to another, seeking a spot dryer than the last one, until at last, there in the eastern sky he saw a glimpse of the rising sun, weakly trying to defeat its wet cousin. There was no relief in the way of warmth, but there was that promise.

When the rain stopped and the sunlight rose, the clouds opposed him, darting between him and the warm savior, refusing to allow any real comfort. There was no relief.

On a Sunday morning with nearly no sun at all, he marched aimlessly on until the gleaming star found a spot between the clouds, bathing him with the most welcoming rays.

As he walked, he noticed, reflecting in the glass of the windows he passed, someone following him. It was an old crusty fellow, who in some small way was familiar, but still it made him uncomfortable to be followed. He stopped to let him pass, but the man stopped when he did, and so near to him. He paused to look at this fellow and saw, in the glass, an incomprehensible, unrecognizable reflection of himself. The man with the swollen eyes, with mucus below his nose, and the dripping wet ensemble was him, and he could not believe that his choices had so altered him, that he didn't even recognize himself. It filled him with grief and startled him like death coming. For some time he pondered what he saw in the mirrored panes of glass. Where had he gone? Where had his mother's "pretty boy" gone? He was grotesque, even to himself, now as ugly outside as within, and with this new image, he trudged on, freezing and starving. The brutality of the night had him wondering just how much of this he could take.

He had no idea what time it was, but in the distance he could hear a chorus, a familiar sound: the sound of a "joyful noise" being offered up from the bowels of Christendom to the god who hated him, who tortured him. This was a sound that he, as one of Jehovah's Witnesses, had considered the sound of heathens. It was the sound of lost sycophants who knew not of the true god. It emanated from what he had been taught to consider an evil place with no god in it. But the sound called to him, called him to come to it for survival, for salvation, for "sustenance and covering."

The great wooden doors of the old church stood away, eight vast stone steps from the sidewalk, and the music blared invitingly. He walked up the steps and opened the door, seeking whatever the reprobates would offer—something, something he hoped to save him from himself. He just wanted to be warm, seeking relief from the treacherous cold. He pushed the stately doors open.

A young man, a deacon as it turned out, was the first to see him and was immediately taken aback. The look on his face was for a moment terror, but only for a moment. Then he saw, without equivocation, a pain and sadness so deep that his apprehensions dropped immediately from his face, replaced by Samaritan duty.

"Sir, may I help you?" he said with the most humanitarian concern in his voice.

Jesse began to stammer, pitifully, "I'm so cold . . . I just wanted to be warm . . . just for a few minutes." The appeal was too genuine, and his condition too obvious to be misconstrued.

"Sure, you can do that. Are you hungry? Can I get you something to eat?"

"Yes, I'm hungry. I would appreciate that."

"I'm Charles Dannon. I'm a deacon here at the church. What is your name?"

"Je . . . Jesse, Jesse Bri . . . Brightmeyer."

"Well, it is nice to meet you Jesse . . . ?" he could barely understand through the shuddering.

"Brightmeyer."

"Yes, Mr. Brightmeyer. Come with me downstairs to the kitchen, and let's see if we can get you warmed up and a plate of food." As much as anything, he wanted to get this unsightly creature away from the innocent eyes of his flock.

"Thank you so much," said Jesse, following the young man and trying not to make eye contact with any of the other parishioners, who were eyeing the deacon as if he had lost his mind, escorting a dangerous-looking homeless person into their midst.

The morning service was ending, and the well-dressed and proper-looking congregation began to file out of the sanctuary, making their way to the kitchen as well. Their stares burned on Jesse's sensibilities deepening his shame.

Through the hunger and cold, the memory of his parents assisting hungry hobos, who knocked on doors in the old Detroit neighborhood, begging for food, came to him. He could see down through the years the ragged dress and dirty clothes of those men who came pleading to be fed. He was one of them now, and he remembered how they smelled. He wondered if he stank as they did. He had no way of knowing, as all of his senses were frozen as well. The image in the mirror was in his mind, and he could see how terrible he must look to all who saw him. But so helpless was he that he managed to endure the self-imposed humiliation, the staring, and the introductions.

The deacon first introduced him to the pastor who had been alerted that there was a suspicious stranger in the church.

"Reverend James, this is Jesse Brightmeyer. Jesse, this is Reverend James. He is the pastor here at St. Paul's."

"Good morning, Mr. Brightmeyer," said the reverend, eyeing Jesse with controlled disdain. "You seem to be having a bad time. I hope the hospitality of St. Paul's will lighten your load a bit."

"Thank you, sir," said Jesse, pausing ever so briefly before adding, "I am certainly grateful."

He pulled the deacon aside, whispering something to him. There was a brief exchange, like two lawyers plotting. The reverend then walked away, saying as he left, "You take care of yourself young man, and come back and see us as soon as you can." He was an old man, who, given his status and his subject, spoke in a grandfatherly fashion with a tinge of condescension.

Jesse was shivering from the cold and the process of thawing out. This had the effect of making him appear even more forsaken than he was, as if he had some physical ailment as well. There was no hand shaking, as it was obvious that no one wanted to touch the crusty, disease-ridden interloper.

The introductions continued until Deacon Dannon introduced Jesse to his wife and two young boys. The wife was lovely, appearing to be the embodiment of the woman with the "quiet and mild spirit," such as the scriptures had recommended. She and her children were nicely dressed, perfectly polite, and about the age of Jesse's two sons. With this introduction, the stinging image of his lost family welled up inside of him and he began to cry hysterically. Were it not for the obvious pitiful nature of the howling, it would have been frightening. His crying came from every cell of his body and was appropriate to the magnitude of his blunder, but no one here knew; they had no way of knowing about the depth of the tragedy that stood before them. His weeping was like a seizure, and those who witnessed it felt they were watching a man die before their eyes.

The young deacon, however, maintained his composure while trying to help Jesse find his. After what seemed an interminable period, the tears subsided, and Jesse, through a startling collection of moisture: tears, rain, mucus, and sweat, tried to apologize and explain.

"My sons," he whimpered, "your sons . . . are the same as my . . . I mean they remind me of . . . I lost them . . . my boys are gone . . . I'm so sad . . . I can't . . . I'm just so sad," the disjointed explanation did little to soften the scene, and the spastic crying began anew with Jesse looking more like a pile of wet rags than a human being.

"Here, Jesse, take a seat. Someone bring me a towel and some water." Turning sympathetically, he said, "You're going to be all right. Everything will work out. You just need some rest and some time to think it through."

Jesse's composure was slow to come, but when it did, he explained, certainly not with full disclosure, or what could be called clarity, that he had lost his mother, his family, and was having a great deal of difficulty coping with it. It had been eight years, but the pain would not subside. The deacon asked polite questions, but Jesse did not hear them, as he rambled, almost certainly leaving the impression that the calamity, whatever is was, had taken his family off the globe.

They prayed over him, over the meal actually, but the offering to God had only to do with saving and protecting this young man who had fallen so dramatically into their lap. Jesse ate, and as he finished, another service was about to begin. They asked him to stay for "the blessing and the liberating word of God."

Here he was, in one of the Lord's mansions, being shepherded by His flock, but the mention of the great traitor filled him with angst, not confusion. He could not find a way to be grateful to Him, this monster who had taken his dear mother. He did however manage to be courteous in his rejection of the kind and well-intentioned offer.

"Thank you," said Jesse, "but I must be going. I am too ashamed to be here. I will never forget you, but I must go."

As the congregation poured back into the sanctuary, Jesse and the young deacon waited for them to make their way back to their haven. They then proceeded to the main entry through which Jesse had come. Jesse was taken by the man's kindness and was again reminded of himself, a far different reflection than the one in the mirror, and of a time when he was the shepherd, doing the bidding of the Christian god. Again he saw, as he walked out the door, the masterful provision of the sun, but it took him to his mother and not to her god.

CHAPTER 42

Death Comes and Goes

The pavement was stained by the night's fury, with puddles receding, being soaked up by the powerful morning star. Suddenly it did not feel like winter coming. He was warm now, as the sun and a most refreshing breeze began washing away the remaining dampness, such that he thought of his mother hanging clothes on the line in the backyard of Twenty-Third and Butternut. During his hour-long respite in the church, the day had turned into something reminiscent of those pretty days of his youth. He could see the clothing swaying on the line; he could smell those days and wondered briefly what those aromas were doing here, as if they belonged to that place and that place only.

Fast-flowing streams of the tormenting water were bubbling into sewer covers, carrying the last of autumn's leaves. He remembered playing in those brooks as a child, building sailboats out of Popsicle sticks. The rain, snow, and sunshine were his friends then, and he could not recall ever having battled with them as he had through this night. No matter, he was homeless now and seeing another side of his former allies. *How fickle*, he thought, tormenting him through the night, and now bathing him so lovingly.

He followed the course of the water, flowing ever so invitingly, and in what seemed no time at all, he was standing in front of Bernie's house. He stood there for several minutes, as if surprised, before knocking on her door. She was slow to come. He was preparing to leave when she appeared breathlessly in her nightclothes.

"I knew you would come," she said, quickly leaping into and out of his arms. "You're soaking wet. What happened to you? Let me get you out of these wet clothes. Let me see, I must have something you can wear while these dry."

When she got him upstairs, she fully undressed him, leading him to her bathroom and a warm shower. Disrobing herself, she climbed in the tub with him and bathed him like a mother tenderly caring for a child. Except that the intentions, certainly the situation carried with it a sexual tension that for reasons of need, affection, and loneliness, had to be fulfilled.

Toweling him dry, she kissed all of him gently and salaciously. She took him by the hand, she brought him into her bedroom, taking his nakedness into her mouth until she had the throbbing she wanted. Placing him on her bed as if he were a doll, she had him vigorously, seeming to need this more than she needed anything. She held him tightly, nearly disallowing any movement. It was indeed, again, the holding they needed, and it appeared as if she more than he. The release was a flood of life-bearing fluids, leaving them drained, exhausted, and satisfied, if only for a moment.

Lying there, face to face, her hair shiny and black, having not yet dried from the shower, and both of them glistening from perspiration, they kissed as if preparing for another session or as if not wanting this one to end. When this afterplay ended, she nestled next to him, placed her head on his chest, sighed, and said, "What happened, Jesse? You looked so unhappy when I greeted you at the door."

This comment surprised Jesse because he could not imagine that she, or anyone, could ever have seen anything but sadness on his face. He had so little awareness of the fact that his nature, if you will, was what surfaced in the presence of others, that his grief and relentless pain were mostly shrouded by a fundamentally pleasant bearing.

Jesse had another story to tell. He did not want to tell it, or revisit the distress the retelling of the night-long trek would demand, but he thought someone should know.

Telling her about the night out in the elements put him on the verge of tears. The dam broke when he got to the part about the boys, and the young family so much like his own. Bernie was listening; she listened like a friend, a wife, and, like a good wife, she held him close while he wept like a child. In the aftermath of the sad telling, kissing and soothing him she said nothing, staying silently on his breasts.

She was a good wife, Jesse thought. *She would make a good wife.* It was the last thought he had before falling asleep. They slept through the afternoon. When he awoke, she was already sitting up and staring at him.

"You're going to need something to wear. Your clothes are not dry yet."

She began searching through drawers, mumbling as she went, "I know I've got something . . . oh, here they are," she said triumphantly, lifting a set of short male pajamas out of a drawer. They were wrinkled and worn, but they would give Jesse something to wear while his own things dried.

While Jesse was sitting up in her bed, leafing through one of her many magazines, Bernie came casually in, sucking on a crack pipe. That distinctive aroma of vanilla captured the air in the tiny apartment. She flopped onto the bed next to him while taking a deep draw from the pipe, before handing it to Jesse. He drew deeply himself and gave it back. About then they heard a key in the door, and before they could react, (not that there was anywhere to go in the small apartment) into the bedroom walked her boyfriend.

Standing before them at the foot of the bed, he stared expressionlessly at the two of them. He had to notice, but said nothing of the fact that this fellow in bed with his woman was also wearing his clothes.

Jesse was reminded of Ramona and her Scandinavian boyfriend on the night he drunkenly inserted himself into their otherwise quiet night. This fellow was not drunk as Jesse had been, but he was a bit touched by booze and glassy eyed as well. The expectation of violence was present, but it had only to do with the situation, not the behavior. He was about Jesse's height and build, with very stringy dirty blond hair. An oversized mustache gave the impression that he was of that ilk of bikers, who, from time to time, made an appearance at the Cork 'n' Barrel. There he stood, silently, with his miner's cap over his piercing eyes and his hands in his back pockets. Jesse did not move or speak and wondered which of them would break the brittle silence.

It was not clear whether he had any purpose other than to gather his things and announce the end of the relationship. He casually grabbed a battered duffel bag that was on Bernie's side of the bed.

"Don't take any of my things," said Bernie, the tone of which implied his presence was no surprise.

"You don't have a goddamn thing I want," he said, adding as he walked toward the door and tossing the keys on the bed, "and you can burn the damn shorts." He simply opened the door and mumbled, "Fucking tramp," as he left.

"Well, that was unpleasant," said Jesse.

"He's an asshole. I told the bastard to call when he was coming."

The bastard knew something Jesse was to soon discover. Bernie, like everyone else, it seemed, was fully in the grip of the fiend under glass and was in the middle of sacrificing everything to the crystal tyrant.

"Good riddance," she said taking yet another hit.

Jesse was warm and as comfortable as a homeless person could be. There was a bed, a woman, drugs, and food. What he did not know was that all of these things were in short supply. Like Jake, Bernie had paid no bills. The utilities were turned off soon, and she too would be in the streets in less than thirty days, having been evicted for nonpayment of rent.

That day came rapidly and with it, a tension rife with bitterness and accusations. Jesse was now the bastard, and the good wife had gone bad. The precarious relationship ended in the middle of the winter, and Jesse knew he could not survive even a single night in the vengeful cold of a New England winter. Bernie's mean spirit was a defense, a way of being alone with her madness.

"You have got to go. I can't take care of me, how the hell do you think I'm going to take care of you?"

It did not even dawn on Jesse that he was being taken care of, so oblivious was he to life dying all around him.

The fraternity of addicts was itself collapsing, but they all had options. They were home or near home. Jesse had no family here and was not willing to reveal his condition to anyone who loved him. There was only him and the memory of his mother now, and he would go to be where she was.

He could not fight what he saw coming. Jesse braced himself for the end, which loomed mercifully. The edge he could not find was finding him with a brutality that superseded the deep snow and howling winds. He was drowning in selfish pity. He could take his leave now, a fitting entitlement, after all he had been through. His mind bandied between the high promises of Christian tenets—"to be with her in paradise," and just how the transition would come. Where would he be? Should he call someone to announce his departure? But he had to find somewhere to live, actually somewhere to die, the living had ceased some time ago.

He called Jingles, who was also crack addicted, but had a job and an apartment that no one knew how he managed to get or keep. Jingles was happy to allow Jesse to spend a couple of weeks with him and Jackie.

"Hey, you got a television?" he asked cheerfully.

Well, Jesse did have at least that. He had Jimmy's little thirteen-inch TV. It was at Chico's place with everything else he owned. He was able to reach Chico, who was surprisingly glad to hear from him.

"Where you been, brotha?"

"Yeah, your stuff is still here . . . in the back room."

"Sure you can come by. I'll be glad to see ya."

He was so pleasant that Jesse thought he might be able to work a deal to get through the winter, but that was not it at all. He had a woman now, and he was doing all he could to make his place respectable. She wanted a real house, a real home, and she could see the potential of his place, the stately old two-story manor. She wanted to get rid of the storage, the drugs, and all of the bad company. Jesse met her once and got the feeling that what she actually wanted was a crack house of her own, where she would not have to share him or his drugs with anyone else. After meeting Jesse, she was comfortable with him leaving his things there for a while longer, but the idea of his staying there, even for a few weeks, was not an option. She was so clear about this that Jesse did not mount a request.

They sat, smoked, drank, and got high almost like polite society. But soon enough it was time for Jesse to leave. This meant going out into a beautiful night, enriched by corpulent snowflakes that had been falling all through the day and evening. They had covered the ground to a depth of more than ten inches, and Jingles's apartment was at least five miles away. Jesse could not overcome his shame enough to ask for a ride or to borrow cab fare, as he knew he had no way of paying it back.

So picking up the small television, he walked out into the treachery of an East Coast winter, the beauty of which belied its lethal possibilities. The flakes latched on to everything, sticking adhesively to street lights, ledges of the buildings, and what trees there were, and they all struggled under the ever-increasing weight.

With gloveless hands, he cradled the television, which was a kind of ticket into Jingles's apartment, as if it were an infant, and began walking. Soon he remembered that he did not know the way. He had never been there. Jingles had told him where he lived and even how to get there, but it was based on being in a vehicle. But walking—with every step the heavy wet snow tried to claim a shoe, sucking it from his wet socks and his soaking feet. Street signs could scarcely be seen through the punishing snow. Conditions were such that nearly no vehicles were on the roads, no tire-beaten paths for him to take advantage of.

It reminded him of the day when he was a young husband and father trying to provide for his family. He had taken a part-time job selling sewing machines. A prospective buyer had responded to an ad in the local paper, and Jesse had to make the trip to their home for a possible commission of forty dollars; an enormous sum in 1971. The trip took him, on a cold and wet early November evening, into rural Kalamazoo County, Michigan, which, unbeknownst to him at the time, was a Ku Klux Klan haven. He got lost in a drenched, undulating cornfield and his car stuck in the mud as deep as the snow now threatening his life. There was no snow that night, just a cold mist after a torrential rain. It was the mud, the absolute blackness of the night, which, without the moon, provided no light whatsoever, the howling dogs in the distance and the strange natural sounds that he had never heard before that unnerved him so.

He remembered, all those years ago, walking through ankle-deep mud, which, as the snow was now doing, sucked his shoes from his feet and covered him grossly in the black muck. He remembered thinking of his young wife and son (Zachery was not yet born) and how he must get home to his waiting and needy family, who had no way of knowing the trouble he was in.

Seeing a light in the distance, he made his way through the mud to that promising light, only to find himself on the porch of an avowed member of the Klan. He knocked on the door, which was answered by an understandably terrified missus whose response to his presence caused her husband to come running.

"Wha chu doin' here, boy?" The husband bellowed in a terrifying Southern twang, causing Jesse to recoil.

"I'm sorry, sir, to disturb you and your wife, but I am lost, and my car is stuck in the mud . . . in a cornfield way down the road . . ."

"You better get offen meh porch and go on back down the road," he said.

"Sir, I have only six dollars on me, but you can have it if you would just help me. If I could just make a phone call . . . ?"

"Look, I ain't helping you. Nah, you get your ass offen meh porch and get on down the road."

At this point, his wife, who could see the desperation on Jesse's face, allowed her humanity to surface and was nearly saintly in saying, "Now, Bo, you know what's gon' happen to him if you send him down the road. Cain't you just get the tractor and pull him out?"

He shut the door, and Jesse could see them discussing the situation. In a moment or two, with Jesse about to leave and take his chances with the next porch light, the door opened sharply, angrily, and the man said, "All right then. Where's yo' car?"

He took Jesse on an enormous farming vehicle of some kind to the spot where the car was stuck and pulled him out. Jesse gave him the six dollars and tried to get his address in order to send him some more money.

"I don't need your money," he said, taking the six bucks, "You just get on away from here."

Here now he felt that desperation again. Here with the darkness softened beautifully by the glistening snow and lights all around him, he felt doomed. Back then, buttressed by the love of family and the confidence of a good child of God, he did not imagine that any harm would come to him. But now, he despised the god of mud and snow, and he did not have six dollars.

He managed to walk unerringly in the right direction, and coming across a pay phone, he placed a collect call to Jingles, who gladly accepted the charges.

"Where the hell are you? I thought you would be here by now."

It turns out that Jesse was only a few blocks away. When he arrived at the door, he was completely snow covered and looked abominable. Jingles and Jackie laughed at the improbable sight before recognizing how bad off Jesse was.

He collapsed before they could get his outer clothes off of him, a job made doubly difficult by the fact that his clothes were frozen rigid. He shivered violently, with snow and icicles bullying all of his appendages. His arms were locked in the cradling position from carrying the television through the storm. He could barely talk.

Jingles and Jackie leapt into emergency mode, providing hot coffee and a sandwich. Jackie vigorously rubbed his hands that had to be only minutes away from frostbite. It took about an hour for Jesse to recover. He trembled for nearly that long, but inside of him there was to be no thawing. There he was frozen by his plight and the prospect of death. Death was coming, and he would not resist it.

There, in the friendly confines of Jingles's apartment, Jesse stayed for about two weeks. They fed him and allowed him to sleep on the floor. Jingles even made an effort at getting Jesse involved with a young woman who lived in the apartment above him, but she could see what they could not: that Jesse was the living dead. She could see that he was hapless, unkempt, and disinterested . . . in anything. She was almost insulted that Jingles would think she would stoop to be with such a man. This seemed to have the effect of opening Jingles's eyes, and soon he told Jesse that he could not stay there any longer.

He was now completely out of options. He had benefitted from the hospitality of everyone who could help him. He had exhausted them all. The fraternity of the needy had broken up, and most were incarcerated or rescued by concerned friends and family.

There was no way for him to be angry or even disappointed with his dismissal, having arrived in his mind at acceptance of his fate.

He departed from Jingles's apartment on a bitterly cold, partly cloudy morning. He walked the same walk that got him there a few short weeks ago. This time he had no television to carry, or anything else. The television had been his ticket in, and he felt the need to leave it. Jimmy's television would be in better hands than his. He felt some relief in that knowledge, but it got him to thinking about the many tapes of Jimmy's lectures that were stowed in Chico's crack house and his clothes, his few belongings. These would be left to . . . whomever, when he died. He had nothing that he had not sullied with his filthy lifestyle, nothing his children or family would want. There was nothing of value among his things. They would be trashed, as he had trashed everything, including his life.

He eventually arrived at the only refuge he knew—the bar: the Cork 'n' Barrel in Harvard Square. It was not opened—too early for the merchants of grief to be offering their product. But standing there, outside the door was a regular patron, an old crusty fellow, who, in his own forsaken way, was as entertaining as Jackie was in her precocious impishness. In their distinctly different styles, both of them were always part of the show that unfolded nightly at the bar. Jesse remembered him well, and he was glad to see Jesse.

He was in his sixties and had either never grown up or had been felled like so many by a life too full of disappointments. Gray from top to bottom, he had tobacco stains on all of his hair. His full beard and equally full head of hair and mustache gave him the anachronistic look of a mountain man. His teeth were never seen for two reasons: he did not have any, and his facial hair completely covered his mouth. Most of the time, nasal fluids would course their way down and through the unruly mane, discoloring it obscenely.

Jesse remembered sharing lines of cocaine with him, as if none of this was true. The rolled dollar bill, so often used as a straw would be soaked with mucus when he snorted, which meant he could have it, and it would allow him to afford a beer. Once Jesse had rolled a five-dollar bill in such a way and Sam, which was his name, behaved as if he had hit the lottery.

His life or his mental distortions gave him the ability to see forms, hear voices, feel spirits, but he was not able to see color. Like the proverbial hound dog, he found a way to wag his tail no matter who was present.

"He . . . he . . . hey Je . . . Jesse," he stuttered. "Wha . . . what . . . yo . . . you doing here?"

Jesse had forgotten about the stuttering because Sam spoke so seldom. He did not ask about or even seem to notice Jesse's condition. While Jesse was unrecognizable to himself, and no doubt to others, Sam felt his spirit and sensed his despair.

"Yo . . . yo . . . you hungry?" he said, as if he would make provisions for him.

"I'm starving," said Jesse.

"Me too, let's go ge . . . ge . . . get some breakfast. They got pl . . . pl . . . plenty fr . . . fr . . . free food down at the mission."

The mission and free food. Indeed Sam was making provisions.

"You can sl . . . sl . . . sleep there too," said Sam excitedly. His manner was so friendly, that it rose above reciprocity—it was goodness. He was sharing what he had without judgment, and his invitation was, for reasons of hunger and kindness, irresistible.

The mission was a mere two blocks away. When they walked in and got their place in line, Jesse was taken by the fact that he was in a soup line. He was there with the needy, the homeless, the battered and abused. He was where he belonged. There was no other place for him to be, but strangely, inexplicably, it reminded him of being at the Waldorf Astoria, only three or four years prior. The chatter, the murmuring, the need to be recognized, even the talk about who particular people in line were, who they had been, brought to mind the envy and adoration he had witnessed when certain dignitaries entered the sophisticated halls of the grand historic library, the mission of the rich.

The mission fed all comers, but the sleeping cots were numbered, and one had to beat the clock and the great many people who depended on this place for a warm place to spend the night, and neither Jesse nor Sam were good at that.

A full belly allows one to walk erect, and in the winter, it was not so obvious that basic hygiene suffered. Occasionally Jesse would bump into someone from the old gang, and there would be the impromptu get-high session where people would just fall asleep where they were. Homelessness hung over Jesse and others like an ominous cloud, but it was never spoken about. People made their way in a subculture that could be played. It was certainly known by all of the fallen that there were ways to survive. But Jesse was stuck between wanting to die and the instinct to survive. Hunger and fatigue were real sensations, and in satisfying them, he prolonged his meaningless life.

At one such gathering of the lost souls, at Chico's house, Bernie showed up. She was bubbly, conversational, and appeared overjoyed to see Jesse. She had found another place. A small nearly uninhabitable space, but it gave her somewhere to go each night and a place to call home. She had managed to keep her job as a bartender, and the proprietor had given her an apartment above his establishment. In it, there was what people in Boston called a bedroom, which was only slightly larger than the single cot it contained.

As this night wound down, she whispered to Jesse that she had some wine and some coke to share. She was taking a cab home, and he could join her.

"Like old times," she said.

Jesse remembered how she had dismissed him before, claiming she did not want to take care of him, but the thought of sleeping on a real bed, having her warmth to enjoy, and the pipe—indeed the pipe was enough.

Jesse asked Chico where some of his things were and found his briefcase and the tape recorder he had used during his travels with James Baldwin. He gathered it, his toothbrush, and a book of short stories, and said good night to all who remained. He and Bernie left like a couple.

She hailed a cab, but the driver insisted on not smoking in the car. She angrily got out, almost before Jesse could get in, and went on a rant about her unwillingness to give money to anyone who disapproved of her lifestyle. The ride, even had there been traffic, which there was not, would have taken about five minutes, so he considered it an over-reaction. It could be that she was setting up her rules and principles, however twisted, because she wanted Jesse to live with her.

When they got to her apartment, the size of which in total would not be a suitable living room in a conventional house, Jesse noticed that it was neater than her previous living space. This was due to the fact that she had not had sufficient time to make a mess of it.

They got comfortable, and they got high. She had a gallon of cheap wine, which she poured into inexpensive but fine-looking stemware. And they talked. They were far too inebriated for anything approaching intellection, but the chit-chat restored familiarity and allowed them to relax and enjoy each other before falling asleep as the sun begun to show itself through the one window in the apartment.

Upon awakening, Jesse noticed anew the tight surroundings, and so did Bernie. It was as if the place shrank overnight, and Bernie seemed unsettled by Jesse's presence. In her agitated state, she announced that she had to go to work tonight and laid out a series of rules. The door to her bedroom would be locked when she was away, and she showed him the place where, if he stayed while she was away, he would have to confine himself. He was not going to be given a key; she had learned something from her previous boyfriend's unannounced visit. There were things he could not eat and things he could not touch. There were cans of food, bars of soap, and certain lotions he was not to use. She had her values.

It was a list reminiscent of the intolerable Mademoiselle DeSusse.

Jesse said he would comply with all of her wishes. He blundered though, by eating a can of chili that she had not labeled off-limits.

"I can't believe you ate my chili. You see, this is what I'm talking about . . . men, you are all such liars."

This time he was the victim of an over-reaction which he had no place to put and no way to reasonably deal with.

He decided that he would find food of his own. Some days he would work for food at Chico's, and sometimes he would work for drugs.

On a particular day, when he could not find Chico, with only labeled food in the house, he found himself stealing to eat. He would have enough money to buy a loaf of bread but nothing else. So he stole a can of beans and a package of lunch meat. For him, stealing was a loathsome activity. When they stole cars, well, that was different—he did not need to do it. That was about vengeance. But this stealing from a small merchant, even to eat, seemed to Jesse unforgivable. *I will be gone soon*, he thought, *so what difference could it make?* He now had so many things for which he would need forgiveness; what was one more, and only a can of beans after all. But it became a routine that further depressed him.

He would leave Bernie's door unlocked, walk across the street where the aging grocer missed his not-so-sly cunning, and would take what he needed. He thought of writing five hundred times, "I will not steal," and his father's reaction to it entered his mind. "Look what you have become," he said to himself. Into his little room he went. He decided he would read a short story, get his mind off himself and his fall into corruption.

He opened the briefcase looking for the book and found in it two grams of cocaine. It was his; he could tell by the way it was packaged. He was not stealing. It was two hundred dollars' worth, and he was broke. He could go to the bar, some bar, any bar, and sell it—sell at least one of them. He chose instead to cook it up, and, for what was the first time, to smoke crack cocaine alone. With no one to hand the pipe to, he smoked himself into an empty, hellish place. In the small room with the walls so near to his face, he smoked until he could see himself, images of himself and others on the dingy wall, as if in a mirror. He smoked until he trembled and could not stand. He smoked himself to the edge. "It will be tonight," he said, convincing himself that he had found the edge at last.

Then, suddenly, he saw Zachery's face, there on the wall, and Chad's. "Daddy, don't," he heard them say.

"I must explain it to them. They have a right to know why I must go."

He was now actually talking aloud to himself. He began looking for paper and pencil to write his final note, but he could find neither. He searched deep and around the briefcase, lifting out the tape recorder when it occurred to him that he could speak his final words.

He found an outlet in the tiny room, plugged in the recorder, and began to talk. With the pipe at his side, he took another a hit to embolden himself, but in it he saw death coming. He saw, somehow again on the wall and in the smoke, an indescribable image that he decided was his tormentor. To go now would mean being with Him.

"I will not sit at his table. I will not open the door to any of his houses." He was sweating profusely, and his heart raced as if to get there, to the edge, before him.

When he began talking, it was not a goodbye. It was a plea to himself, to all that he was, to get up from there to find a way to save himself. He did not want to die. He was going to, he was sure now, but he did not want to. He did not want to risk having to face the great demon who had so utterly defeated him. Something outside of his plans was determined to keep him alive, and it baffled him. He had given up, too tired to go on, but someone else, something else was taking control and would not allow him to go, as he wished, anonymously into the next world.

He found his way up and off the bed and nervously opened the door. He donned his coat, his hat, and his boots and went out into the cold. It was a refreshing relief, given the fire brewing inside of him and on his skin. He felt danger. His nemesis had too many weapons, too many warriors.

"*I must surrender,*" he thought as he walked out into the night. "Take me now," he screamed, "why do you not take me now?"

The cold that first invigorated him now chilled him, to his core, and he went hurriedly back into the sepulcher of a house. Once there, it was clear to him that he must keep moving to avoid giving those evil spirits a chance to light on him.

He began speaking again into the recorder, walking in circles as he did so, afraid to be still.

"I must save myself," he said, repeatedly, "I must save myself," as he thought about his past and what he was supposed to have done with his life. He struggled to keep the father of the demons at bay.

"Get up," he said over and again to himself, "get up," but he could not.

Save yourself. Where did that thought come from? He was ready for his flight into the netherworld, where he would confront his tormentors face to face. This interruption was without explanation, and it left him reeling.

Then, without actually knowing it, he began to pray. He called Him, "Oh-h-h God," he said with fear and trembling, "Help me . . . help me . . . help me," he somberly begged. He prayed as he had not since his mother lay dying. It was a lapse into what he once knew; he spoke in a forgotten language. He did not want to face Him, but even more he did not want to, could not imagine, or more accurately, he could see the faces of his boys, his siblings, and he was agonizingly tormented by the thought that they would never know what happened to him. So he prayed, in his mother's tongue, for help from an enemy who he believed had forsaken him, left him to flounder for all these incomprehensible years.

A consistent side effect of the euphoria or the gloom of this addiction was an inability to sleep, but in his new confusion and the accompanying dizziness, he fell involuntarily on the bed, and in a moment or an hour, he was asleep. During his slumber, those gray, only gray, images of nothingness filled his mind's eye. He lay there waiting for the inevitable; he would awake in the other world, quaking in the presence of the insuperable god.

Chapter 43

Jesse Meets the Angel

Out the solitary window, gray skies mimicked the visions in his head, so much so that he was not certain whether he was awake or transitioned. The bitter cold outside the window seemed as appropriate a punishment as any hellish fire. Was he there yet? He was too emotionally and mentally battered to grasp where he was. Even when he staggered to his feet, he was not certain about the place he was in. Everything blurred before his glassy eyes. He fell back onto the bed, and the feel of the spread and the grimy pillow informed him that he was still here, still riveted to the chilling terra firma.

He stood again and went to see if Bernie was home. She was not; she had not come home, and he assumed she was doing what crack addicts do: taking the best offer to come along. Perhaps she had been home and left because it was about four o'clock in the afternoon when his eyes cleared enough for him to see the clock. He was wonderfully and painfully alone. He wanted no one to see his final seconds, his final hours on the planet.

Hunger was upon him, but he had no energy for stealing his last meal, and to what purpose. There was no recognizable life in him at all. The sensations of the sheets, the spread, and the pillow had dissipated; he was ghostly now, passing through things or they through him, numbed by the coming epiphany.

Pondering the improbability of being alive, he decided to go . . . no, he simply found himself out in the cold. He thought he had better go back in and put on his overcoat before discovering he had not taken it off, having simply fallen asleep in clothes he had worn for a week. He was as warm as he was going to be in clothing stiffened this time by still, coffin-like sleeping. It crossed his mind that Bernie had not come home so she would not have to see him, "take care of him."

He had missed mealtime at the mission, so falling into the familiar, he headed unavoidably to the bar. The walk happened with him seeing nothing around him. There was no awareness of the crisp air, the passersby, or the icy conditions his footfalls somehow avoided.

He opened the door to an unfamiliar place. The bar had changed dramatically, at least at this hour, and there was no one there who would even remotely care about his situation. Could it be that no one recognized him? He was like Sam now: crusty and iced over, frozen nasty fluids on his scanty facial hair. He sat for a moment at the bar.

"You all right, Jesse?" The recently hired bartender who was now the drug doctor said. She recognized him, and the tone of her voice, along with the look in her eyes made it clear that she saw the misery, the hopelessness, that had befallen the former professor and sage. That he had wilted so completely seemed to almost embarrass her.

She could not rest her eyes on him, as when trying not to stare at someone grossly disfigured.

"Can I buy you a beer or maybe a cup of coffee?" She wanted to help him, but she did not know what to do.

"Coffee . . . yeah, a cup of coffee . . . warm me up . . . it's really cold outside," he stammered.

She brought the coffee, and it occurred to Jesse that he had never known anyone to have a cup of coffee here in the Cork 'n' Barrel. He sipped the hot nectar, feeling it flow through his body as he never had. It felt as if he could see the fluid entering his entrails, disturbing them, awakening them. He finished the cup and felt an overwhelming sense of embarrassment, as if he was suddenly conspicuous and everyone, the few that were there, were staring at him. It was a sign of life that he failed to recognize. He was unstable but somehow rose to his feet, walked out the door, and went around the corner to the Grill, thinking no one would know him there; no one would have to be subjected to his penetrating ugliness.

He sat at the bar of this "greasy spoon," and a waitress nervously approached and said, "Can I get you something?" There was understandable suspicion in her voice, with this client appearing as if he had not eaten in days and there being no outward evidence that he could afford to do so today.

"A menu . . . can I see a menu?" he said without looking up.

Jesse thought this would buy some time before he would be again forced out into the biting cold. She placed before him a tattered and soiled paper, a description of the meager fare, and he tried to act as if he was reading it. But his eyes saw nothing, just the gray, the relentless gray.

He could not have been sleepy, but he began to nod as if falling asleep—a precursor to eternal slumber. In this state, snapping in and out of semi-consciousness, he noticed someone appear in the doorway of the small eatery. The person did not actually come in but stood there with his hands, shoulder height touching the door jambs, as if to hold them up. Within the frame of the door, the visual was a silhouette, only a black outline, and a form vaguely familiar to Jesse. The figure stood there just gazing at Jesse, and a warmth that he could not place or understand emanated from this personage; like a cherub in the doorway, the figure stood, causing the gray light behind him to glisten like a star.

Jesse looked again, flashing and rubbing his eyes for clarity. An angel had come for him, not the demon he was expecting. An angel in black, wearing a black full-length cashmere coat and a black knitted skullcap, had come for him.

Jesse began to tremble in anticipation of his long-awaited transition. He was as prepared as he could be, but he was not able to make sense of this improbable emissary. He was about to speak, to say something about his readiness, about his rage, his despair, his regret, when the figure approached, and Jesse saw, impossibly, a man standing before him. *I know him*, Jesse thought.

He began to tremble more violently. *I know this man!* Jesse erupted into a host of emotions at the sight of this young man. Crying, screaming, shaking with joy, relief, triumph, and embarrassment. The angel was his younger brother Ashton.

His visage was pure, loving, and without condemnation. Jesse could find no logic in this visual. What was his brother doing here? Was he his escort, was he going with him to the unknowable afterlife? He looked so real but at the same time so angelic.

He walked up to Jesse, put his arm on his brother's broken shoulders, and said very simply and calmly, "Jesse, let's go home." With that, every sense inside Jesse awakened fully, and he knew, he could see that his brother had come for him, to save him from himself, to take him home, and he burst into diluvian tears. He cried the tears of the ages. He cried for himself, for his sons; he cried for cleansing, and he was being, there is almost no other way to put it, born again.

Ashton kept a brotherly watch on his wilting older brother, saying nothing, and not being given to overt affection, tapped his brother's shoulder repeatedly. It was an angel's tapping, indeed announcing a transition to a new world: home. Jesse would be going home.

When the crying subsided, Ashton bravely faced his disfigured brother with a softness on his face that seemed to be Madelyn. He did not ridicule his stricken sibling. He watched the whimpering, holding his love for his brother in his heart tenaciously. He had found him, inexplicably, he had found him, and now he would take him home. If he was going to chastise him, it would come later. For now Ashton understood the pain, the fall, and he made nothing of his part in the redemption. He had been sent by powers of love: powers greater than hatred, greater than sorrow, greater than corruption. It was the greatest power of all.

Jesse, trying to find words with which to respond to his brother's loving invitation, said, "I'm hungry, Ashton. I'm so hungry."

"I'll get you something to eat," he said, and he called the waitress, who, upon seeing this love overflowing, showed relief on her face and a certain newfound cheerfulness. She seemed proud to be witnessing the wrenching reunion.

"What can I get for you?" she offered.

"Whatever he wants," said Ashton.

Jesse ordered something; something to quail the gnawing pain, and Ashton got some food as well. While waiting for the food, Jesse began to find his senses. He suddenly, almost miraculously, found his posture and something resembling sanity.

"How did you find me?" he queried his brother. He genuinely wanted to know. He had so deliberately sequestered himself, so thoroughly hidden his ugliness and his lethal plans from everyone that he could make no sense of this savior sitting so compassionately at his side.

"Oh don't worry about that," he said, "let's just get some food in your stomach and get to the airport."

Jesse, nearly sentient now, began to think about his things: pictures of his sons, the Baldwin tapes from the speaking tour, his expensive suits, notes for poems, short stories, and even a novel he would write someday. He could not leave those things behind. But they were scattered, he explained, all around the three communities of Boston, Cambridge, and Somerville.

"All right, we'll get your things."

Ashton, having no doubt that he would find his brother, had bought the ticket for the flight home, and he was determined that they would be on the plane at eight o'clock the next morning, some twelve hours from now.

"I should say goodbye to some people. It's just around the corner . . . at the bar I told you about."

"Yeah, I know. I was there earlier, someone told me I would find you here."

"Really, you were there?"

"The woman at the bar told me you were probably here."

They finished their meal, and Jesse was renewed. He was, for these precious moments happy and grateful, suddenly grateful to be alive.

When he entered the bar with his brother, he could see relief on the faces of all his old friends, and now many of them were there, and they came up to the two brothers, expressing their happiness that Ashton was there. They knew, all of them did, that Jesse was in trouble, but none of them knew what to do. Ashton was a hero to them as well, and they appeared happy in the knowledge that Jesse was being rescued. They bought, as the only tribute they knew, drinks for the both of them, telling stories of Jesse's time and role in the bar, and there was laughter, redemptive laughter, and the happy-sad knowing that many of them needed rescuing as well.

Jesse said his goodbyes and asked those present to say goodbye to those who weren't.

Ashton asked if a cab could be called. This was an important call, given the difficulty of two black males getting a cab to pick them up, especially after dark.

They went first to Bernie's, where Jesse had only a few belongings. Jingles' place was the penultimate stop, before going finally to Chico's crack house where the bulk of Jesse's things were.

When they got there, a full crack-smoking session was under way. Jesse saw them afresh. Daniel was there, apparently having used his secret knowledge to obligate his cousin Chico to allow him into the caldron. The woman Chico had chosen, presumably to help him right his sinking ship was not present, as he had discovered her real intentions.

The room so dark, so ominous, was peopled indeed by the fallen, and Jesse did not see himself as one of them. Not this time; he had his angel at his side, and he was risen.

To the extent that civil greetings could be had in this company, they were. Jesse proudly introduced his brother to the collection of miscreants, including an off-duty policeman and a fellow Jesse barely knew but had seen before, who claimed to be a priest. Spanning the room Jesse noticed the guns: Uzis, .357s, and an assortment of rifles. Sitting obediently among them were the three pit bulls—vicious fighters, trained to attack on command.

"Give Jesse a hit," said Chico.

"No thanks," said Jesse, feeling prideful at saying no to the scourge for the first time in two years. His brother was his armor, he was his savior, and even if he wanted to "take a hit," he couldn't, not in the presence of his redeemer. "I'm done with that," he said.

In this company, the banter was always fixed in self-deception, with the woeful participants trying to behave as if they were something other than drug addicts. They would discuss the politics, sports, and more than anything, their respective achievements in their day lives. It was braggadocio for which Ashton had no patience. In his youth, and he was certainly not old now, being in his mid-thirties, Ashton was, in terms of street credits, a powerful and dangerous man. His brother Jesse, on the other hand, was not. Ashton knew his brother to be a gentle spirit, and seeing him in this company caused a stirring in his soul that suggested to him that these people claiming to be successes and bragging about their exploits were responsible for his brother's demise. Daniel was, of course, the most boisterous and, as always, the most irritating.

Ashton listened to and endured the chest thumping for as long as he could, until his anger got the best of him. These people were the culprits, they were the reason his brother, his mother's most innocent child, had been dragged into wantonness. They had corrupted him. They had stained his family and dragged his hapless brother into depravity. Ashton was there without his weapons: no chains or guns of his own. He had instead the power of her memory and a voice humming in the darkness, and nothing, certainly nothing here could stand against it.

In the middle of Daniel's mindless bloviating, Ashton turned to him, saying, with a belligerence and rage Jesse had seen many times before in the streets and alleys of Detroit, "Motherfucker, shut the fuck up. You ain't shit, and you know it. You just a punk-ass bitch trying to impress somebody. Don't look like to me nobody is impressed wit' yo' ass."

Daniel tried to defend himself with additional nonsense, to which Ashton said, "Motherfucker, I told you to shut up. Look here, man, you can talk all you want", he said dismissively, "but ain't nobody paying you no mind." He deliberately turned his chair so that his back was to Daniel, and he said to one of the others in the room. "So what's on your mind? I know somebody must be doing some thinkin' in here, 'cause this motherfucka ain't got shit to say."

The dynamics in the room, which may or may not have been fully assessed by Ashton, were such that something dramatic or even violent could have erupted.

Ashton did not know there was an off-duty police officer or a priest in the forsaken hideout. He saw a band of corrupt, weak-minded men, who, in his prime, would have worked for him, doing precisely what he demanded of them.

When the dogs snarled, sensing the elevated tension in the dark room, Ashton glared at them saying, "shush," with such authority that they quieted as if Chico had given the command. This amazed Chico because his dogs were trained to respond only to him. It amazed everyone, and Jesse, expecting Ashton to do the harm for which he was known, was grateful. No one reached for the guns, and no one objected to his dismissal and humiliation of Daniel.

The conversation turned to what Ashton was doing for his brother. These hardened people saw in Ashton exactly what the patrons at the bar had seen. They saw, with full knowing and envy, that Ashton had brought love into the room, a room that, for the first time, was feeling the greatest power of them all. This softened Ashton and humbled him. He would never, under any circumstances, talk about himself, so this discussion about his deeds and the chorus of praise unsettled him. He was doing what the voice, the one whispering to him in the darkness, had demanded. Some voice had come to him in the twilight, in the darkness, repeatedly imploring, "Go, bring your brother home."

Jesse had gathered all he could carry, which was everything he owned. Ashton helped him load it up, putting all his things near the door. Everyone shared heartfelt goodbyes, except Daniel, who had not recovered from his spanking.

A cab was called again, and when it sounded its horn, Jesse heard a bugle, the sound of rescue. Chico rose and in his stupor walked Ashton and Jesse to the car. Once loaded, he looked Jesse in the eyes, with something like tears in his own, and said, "Man, I'm happy for you. I'm going to miss you, but I'm really happy for you. Ashton, take care of your brother, he's a good man."

Ashton paused for the briefest moment before offering this sage advice, "I will, but, man, find something else to do with your life. This is America. You got options."

They arrived at Boston's international airport three hours before departure. During the wait, Jesse tried to explain to his brother what happened, how he had fallen so far. Ashton tried to listen, but in truth he did not care. He knew the wild streets, and he knew his brother was not suited for them.

"That's all behind you now," he said.

Jesse sat in silence on the plane that seemed to take forever to get to Detroit. When it landed and they collected his misshapen bundles from the luggage carousel, his uncle was waiting for them in a vehicle as badly bruised as Cha'che's decrepit old Cadillac. It was beautiful.

His uncle, who was that by virtue of being married to Madelyn's sister, hugged him tightly, saying, "Boy, I ought to beat the shit out of you."

All the way home, he talked about the beauty and loveliness of Jesse's mother and how hurt, how disappointed she would be. Jesse listened without comment, thinking through it all how much he missed her.

He took him to Allison's house. The snow-christened trees greeted him, seeming to bow in doing so. They were not the vengeful boughs of Boston. Her house was spotless and fine. Aromas danced in the air like memories, bringing his mother's ways and style into view. Jesse thought of those days when Frankie would come home from college or the army, and his mother would insist on making everything perfect for his return. The smells of the place were that of his mother's house, the very ones that had tortured him so bitterly the night of her passing and all those years since. His entire family had gathered to welcome him home, and on their faces he could see her, in a way he could no longer see her on his own. They spoke only sparingly of his gaunt look, his weight loss, as he had so little to lose in the first place, and not at all of his travail.

She had given them, bestowed upon them, the love for which she was known, and Jesse felt, for the first time in the fifteen years of her passing, the love he had been seeking. It was here, and it had always been. The grief and the pain almost immediately lifted from his body and spirit as his personal demons were exorcised by the only power great enough to do so. From that unknowable place, she spoke, somehow, to her children, extolling them to take care of one another, and in this room, on this night, they believed they would be with her in paradise.

Ashton sat quietly with a look of knowing he had done what his parents would have done, and his siblings were as proud of him as they would have been. Frankie, who, like Jesse, was given to overt displays of affection, held his brother fiercely with a look of penetrating relief, saying, "Welcome home, boy. Now it's time for you to fly right."

Allison smiled, holding him to her bosom and kissing him ever so tenderly on his damaged face as tears welled in her eyes. "You're home," she said. "We didn't know, we just didn't know how bad it was, but you are home now. I'm so happy you are home." For a moment, she took on the appearance of his mother, and, fighting back the tears, she said, "You must be hungry, let's eat."

Someone handed Jesse the phone, and on the other end was Rosalind. She was still serving the Lord and reminded him of

Jehovah's forgiving ways and that he should "return to the Father" and everything would be all right.

Steve, his brother-in-law, wore an expression of happy remembrance as he opened the basement door, releasing the Great Dane, with whom Jesse had spent so many sad hours, walking the streets at night, and he came galloping up the stairs and greeted Jesse with yelps of recognition and gladness, lifting his 170 pounds and his huge paws onto Jesse's shoulders. They rolled on the floor like children.

Allison had prepared a spread of salad, hot soup, and a pan of homemade hot rolls and all the trimmings, a fine tribute to Madelyn's lessons. There was warmth and smiles, joking as they chatted about the "good ol' days," and Jesse's mind went to Twenty-Third and Butternut. He could see his mother there, hear the pots rattling, with sounds of laughter filling the house. The rolls were a kind of trademark of Madelyn's. Twice a week she would bake them with renowned satisfaction, and Allison had duplicated the delight, enough for the memories to sparkle like the sun-christened home of his youth. It was a symbol of the former days, and with his siblings all around him . . . *she* was in the room.

He heard her voice, lilting and warm saying, "Jesse, be nice." He could be that now, having survived a fifteen-year gauntlet of madness. In this setting of familial contentment, he thought about the miracle of his survival and how only two days ago he had wanted to die and was so precariously close to it.

Somehow he had lived; his brother had come for him. His mother, from the place her loving god had assigned her, had sent him. In his heart he could find no way to credit her god with his salvation, but then he remembered he had prayed, "Help me . . . help

446

me," he beseeched her god only one day before Ashton arrived. He went instead to her apron and the full dispensation of her milk; his mother's milk still flowing through the bodies of her children in every conceivable metaphorical way.

He recalled all those mornings when she insisted on a healthy breakfast of oatmeal, fruit, and toast. The daily hugs, kisses, and admonitions to "do unto others as you would have them do unto you." The patience she exhibited when Jesse and everyone else had given up on Ashton, and now Ashton, the one least likely to be alive all these years later, was the one chosen to deliver him from the evils he himself had perpetrated throughout his youth, as if fashioned for this improbable rescue.

He remembered while having this bountiful meal how she and his father had convinced their children of their love of chicken necks and backs so that their offspring would get the best of what there was. The endless sacrifices made—now bearing fruit in the redemption of the lost prodigal son. It flowed through their minds and hearts and made the kind of death Jesse had envisioned impossible. Madelyn would say it was the work of her loving god, but for Jesse, he could see it now, it was her and the bottomless well of love she had poured into her children. But then, what is a Mother's milk if not the hand of God.

The End

EPILOGUE

It has been twenty-five years since the end of the saga called *Mother's Milk*. I am older now and wiser too. Having lost more than fifteen years of my life, years I cannot have back or relive, I openly discuss my past mistakes for those who may benefit and for my own personal cleansing. In the telling of my story, there was much anguish; I was reduced to tears many times while revisiting one painful memory after another. I have often been asked by those who have read the drafts to explain what life lessons were learned, messages to be shared, and how the many characters mentioned in the novel have fared down through the years. A question I heard repeatedly was, "Why did you take your mother's death so hard when people die every day?" A fair question, I suppose, but that is the essence of the story. Had I been able to simply accept her death in "normal" or conventional terms, I would not have this story to tell.

Every reader will measure this story against their own lives. After all, we see what we see through our own stained gauze. As for me, I am haunted as I remember the many faces of the countless characters "Jesse" encountered as he walked down that dark path. Their faces force me to reflect on the many lives that are shattered by a single fragile moment in time, a moment that begins a process, a transformation, and for some even a pattern of total self-destruction. We all have them. Some will become better in their moment, some not. Perhaps that moment is propelled by a horrific event brought on by an abusive lover or parent, the shame and guilt of a rape, the molestation of an innocent child. Or perhaps, it is propelled by an ordinary life event, such as a divorce, a breach of trust, an unrequited love, or simply the unexplainable, or untimely death of a loved one.

In the aftermath of such events, the madness that ensues may be so traumatic, that some never recover. They become the homeless cart pushers that clutter the streets of every major city or the Jeffrey Dahmers, John Gacys, and Ted Bundys of the world. They appear normal, as I did. I am taken, especially in retrospect, by my ability to function . . . "normally" while dealing with the controlling demons that attacked my life.

We see only the remnants of those lives that are damaged beyond repair. They become the insane, the molesters, or the predators of an unsuspecting society. That it happened to me, with all the support I had, begins to explain the suffering and bad behavior we see so consistently around us: in the schools and cities of America where mother's love is nearly an anachronism, where the family structure has essentially collapsed. Yes, for all of us, there is a moment . . . a moment of unforgiving, a moment unexplained, unaccepted, unacknowledged, unloved, unexpected, unresolved-forbidden but in its wake, people are altered and lives forever changed. This change, in most cases, ramifies through generations, creating much of the despair that has wracked our cities and neighborhoods. I had such a moment that nearly took my life.

I think of the many thousands of places that house these "rejects" of society: the bars and dope dens, the hospitals, missions, shelters, and yes, . . . even the hallowed sanctuaries throughout the world. These are the many people who have simply lost their way. I think of the missed opportunities and the sadness wrought by them, but, most of all, I have chosen to think like young Jesse, the boy described in the book, who could see the good in everything, and the world becomes full of promise. I think of the power of love and healing. It is the latter thoughts which have inspired this book. Love surpasses all things, and we each hold the power to love someone today.

I remain stunned by my fall. It is inconceivable to me that I took to a lifestyle that defied everything I have ever been taught by loving parents. I wondered during the writing of this book whether or not the madness that engulfed me actually found its way to the pages. I perceived her loss as more than death, it was a betrayal. I had lovingly and faithfully served her Christian god, as did she. I was overwhelmed by anger. I felt cheated; my kids would never know her the way I had or experience her love. It devastated me. Along the way, there were many moments when I truly, simply wanted to die, finding no reason to stay here without her. It is said by people who know me now, "I can't believe that's you described in the book." I understand that. He is dead; that Jesse is dead. The boy she raised has returned, and with him the honor she instilled. You see, everything I ever knew of beauty, kindness, and goodness, came from her. All that is good in me, came from her. I had to learn that the anger that held me hostage for so many years had no real place in my life, and now I have returned to integrity. I always respected the provisions made by her and my father, but I lost sight of it all while peering through the misery.

That she was exceptional to me and all of her children surprises no one. Most children feel this way about their mother. My response to the loss of her bewilders everyone. However, I want the reader to know that while I have learned something about pain, sorrow, redemption, and recovery, I know this most of all: there is no power greater than love, and a mother's love most of all.

It has been nearly three decades since I last saw any of the people from New England described in the book. I often wonder if any of them would even recognize themselves, given my descriptions. I wonder if they made it, if they are productive members of society now. I have left that entire period behind me. It feels as if it occurred to someone else.

The "story" is not told chronologically. It is rather a kind of literary collage, which in some way mimics the disorder in the lead character's life. For good or bad, I was one of those fathers who wanted his children to know him completely. What I had not anticipated was the brutal disruption that would surprisingly and devastatingly come, as they continue to struggle with the loss of their dad for fifteen critical years of their development. Now, they too have their stories.

Initially I was writing to explain to my sons what happened to their father (I actually began writing in 1977 when, of course, there was no real story, certainly not this one to tell.) They, for right reasons, have no interest in reading about the dark and crippling period described in the previously written material. As one of them put it, "Dad, we were there." Indeed they were. My sons are men now, in their early forties. Both are artists and reside in Brooklyn, New York. They have declared their forgiveness, but the memories are still there and the pain runs deep. My absence created a void in their lives not unlike my own: a void that may never be filled, although I will spend the rest of my life trying. They are fathers themselves, giving me and their mother five lovely granddaughters. I love them all very much.

Beverly, the mother of my sons, continues to live in Grand Rapids, Michigan, in the same house we once shared. She manages to treat me cordially when our children and grandchildren gather occasionally. She is a proud grandmother. Her family is her priority; for this . . . I am grateful.

Ramona remains an artist, living in the great northwest, and we have friendly talk from time to time. She's a blogger, and her daughter is healthy and well. Neither Beverly nor Ramona ever married again. I don't know if either of them would want to relive these private moments of their lives by reading this novel. I am so sorry for the pain I caused each of them.

This is also true of my siblings, all of whom are faring as well as could be expected on this wayward planet. Frankie, Rosalind, Allison, Ashton, and I remain a rather closely knitted family and gather often. We gather mostly at the invitation and at the home of Ashton. He makes certain of that. I see him transformed from the street life to a loving father, grandfather, uncle, brother, and friend. There is no doubt, he, like all of my siblings, was transformed in some way by our mother's death. Ironically, Ashton's moment seemed to have mended him more than it shattered him. His courage to come for me, bring me home to the love and support of my family saved my life. I cannot find words to fully express my gratitude and appreciation.

Frankie, Rosalind, Allison, and Ashton have all retired from their respective jobs. I envy that. I have some catching up to do. For the most part, they manage to live good productive lives, and I see in them bits of mother's strength, wisdom, kindness, and her compassion. I live in Detroit, Michigan, my beloved city, and am self-employed, working as a private home inspector and bringing to this work, and all things, the respect and decency instilled in me by my parents and the village I was raised in.

James Baldwin, as is known, died in 1987. We spoke only once after the end of a relationship that could never be. I feel the need to mention that I am the "Skip" he wrote about in the poem he entitled, "Song for Skip." The poem can be found in his collection of lyrics called *Jimmy's Blues*. That I may have inspired this great mind in some small way gives me great pleasure. I will always love and appreciate him for his courage and the insightful literary genius he shared with me and the world. He was as kind a man as he was profound, and I have missed him, truly.

I have come to terms with the "godship." I blamed Him for taking her. There is no one who could have prayed harder than I did, to which a good friend once replied, "perhaps she did." My relationship with this "all knowing" and yet unknowable entity likely defies all conventions, but suffice it to say, we are on good terms. I waken each morning to the wonder of this magnificent planet, and I more often than not find "Him" in a loved one's touch, a decaying tree that replenishes life here on earth . . . endlessly, the smile of a dear friend, the miracle of my progeny, and the precious memory of my mom. Yes, we are on good terms.

Finally, there is Mother, . . . my beloved mother. Perhaps more than anything I needed to write of her great love; that magnificent gift she bestowed upon me, and the small part of the world she touched. I write as a way of expressing my deepest and most sincere apology to her for ever having lost sight of her teachings. I now realize that although she may not be physically present in my life, our bond, that connection, her energy . . . her "milk" continues to flow through me—everyday—never having left me for one second! She was ever-present; her love always haunting me, protecting me, guiding me home—home to the place she left behind; a place where a mother's milk flows in abundance; back to her love, and to the bosom of her family.

Mother is buried in a local cemetery in the Detroit area. I do not know exactly where and have no desire to know; I still cannot go there. I believe she is buried in the one place she could be—planet Earth. Yet, and this baffles me, if I am near the place where I believe she actually lies, I am overwhelmed with anguish and grief, such that I become uncontrollably somber and tearful. Here and still, after all these years, there is conflict. I cannot explain this more than I have in the book. I am sixty-five years old, but I see her in my mind's eye as she looked 45, even 55 years ago, and I am a boy, tugging at her apron, basking in the love she shared, wanting to be near her—a boy, who misses her at a level . . . well . . . that I simply cannot describe.

Jesse Brightmeyer

Author's Biography

Dwight Stackhouse, affectionately known as "Skip" to friends and family, is a writer who has recently completed his first novel. His artistic vision involves people and embraces diversity in all aspects of life. "Writing enhances the evolution of my thoughts," says Stackhouse, "but it is only the penultimate destination. If it does not get to the people, and 'disturb' them, then it can be said that I have not succeeded. My pen will have missed its mark."

He has performed on stage, as an actor, in Detroit, Grand Rapids, Boston, New York, and France. The reviews of his stage work were described with encouraging superlatives like "genius," "gifted," and "hidden treasure."

In 1979, while performing in James Baldwin's play *The Amen Corner*, he was introduced to the famous author, who saw much promise in this, then young, artist. Finding common ground in their shared philosophies on human rights, family history, religious backgrounds, and creative inspirations, they became friends. He is the subject of one of Mr. Baldwin's poems, "Song for Skip," published in his collection of lyrics called *Jimmy's Blues*. "There is no way to deny the guiding influence of the great James Baldwin," Mr. Stackhouse says, "or his model for the telling of insightful truths. Jimmy would often say to 'tell it like it is.'" Although Mr. Stackhouse no longer has a passion for the stage, he has shown a similar aplomb with the pen.

All of Skip's writings come from a fundamental philosophy: "we can be better than we are." The initial effort with this novel was to explain to himself and his sons what happened, he says. "They had a right to know. How did our house of love come crashing down? How could I possibly have left the principles which were so deeply embedded in me by loving parents to become the monster I was for nearly fifteen years? How could I have left my sons, my family?" These questions constitute the inspiration for this novel. "It became a 'man in the mirror' experience, which now, given the image provided by that tyrannical mirror, will last the rest of my life. Luckily, I was able to see both men and know without equivocation, the difference." It is his hope that the readers of this novel will "find for themselves more productive ways to cope with grief, support one another, and that simply knowing one is not alone, as I believed I was, may be enough to facilitate that goal."

A writer of poetry, plays, songs, short stories, and essays for many years, and having shared his work with many readers, Stackhouse was repeatedly told the work was of such quality that he should pursue publication. This novel is his first effort at doing so. At sixty-five years of age, he considers himself arriving "late in the game," but is committed to getting more literary products to the public. He has also submitted much of his work for consideration of awards, fellowships, and literary recognition. His newest project involves a registration of romantic poetry called *Forever My Heart . . . Desires*, (due out in late 2013) a collection described as "profoundly beautiful," "deeply moving," and "brilliant" in the ways of love.

"Honesty is key to real artistic development," he says. "It is what separates real art from simple talent, from dilettantes and pure commercialism." It is in this way that the writing of this book launches his future work.

—Dwight Gerard Stackhouse

Edwards Brothers Malloy
Oxnard, CA USA
August 15, 2013